THE BLOODPRINT

THE

BLOODPRINT

Book One of the Khorasan Archives

AUSMA ZEHANAT KHAN

HARPER
Voyager

HarperCollins
PUBLISHERS
Since 1817

Harper*Voyager* an imprint of
HarperCollins*Publishers* Ltd
1 London Bridge Street
London SE1 9GF

www.harpercollins.co.uk

First published by HarperCollins*Publishers* 2017
1

Copyright © Ausma Zehanat Khan 2017

Ausma Zehanat Khan asserts the moral right to
be identified as the author of this work

A catalogue record for this book is available from the British Library

HB ISBN: 978-0-00-817157-5
TPB ISBN: 978-0-00-817158-2

Printed and bound in the UK by CPI Group (UK) Ltd, Croydon CR0 4YY

MIX
Paper from
responsible sources
FSC™ C007454

FSC
www.fsc.org

This book is produced from independently certified FSC™ paper
to ensure responsible forest management.

For more information visit: www.harpercollins.co.uk/green

For Ayesha, Irfan, and Kashif

with so much love it's inconceivable . . .

(and that *does* mean what we think it means).

Siblings, best friends, and accomplices

in miracles, shenanigans, and crimes.

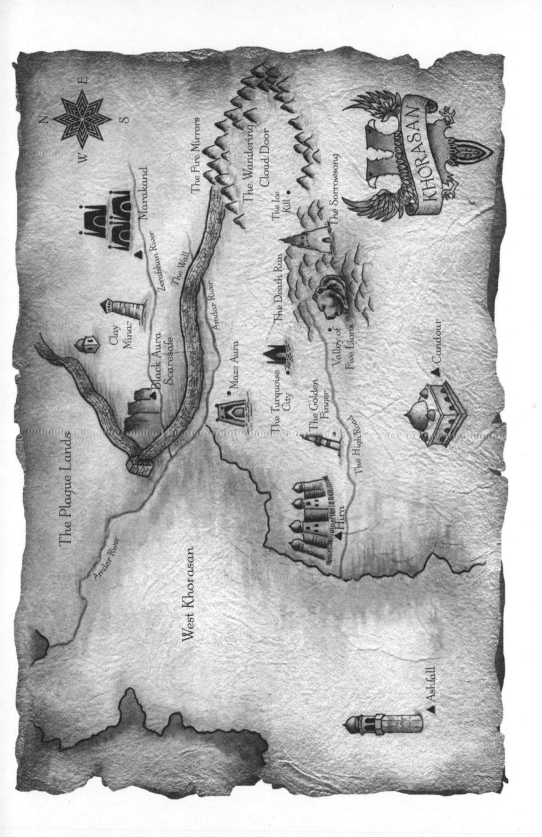

1

SEVEN. EIGHT. SIX.

Arian traced the numbers in the sand. She was crouched behind
a dusty ridge, surveying the land ahead. The wide, flat plains extended in every direction, broken in places by sparse shrubs, the
faintest traces of greenery and life. She passed her field glasses to
the coal-skinned woman perched to her right.

"Do you see it?"

"Yes. Four Talisman. Two at the front, two at the back. And a
boy who takes the tally."

"Yes." Arian's voice was thoughtful. "They beat him nearly as
much as they beat the women."

The other woman stretched to her full height. She summoned
the horses with a low whistle.

"It doesn't seem to have taught him any kindness. His whip is
as swift and furious as theirs. What is your judgment, Arian?"

Arian was the older of the two women, also the more seasoned.
She carried the senior rank. Companion. First Oralist.

"We do what we always do with slave-chains—we break them.
Get ready to ride, Sinnia."

Through the eerie quiet and the dust, the khamsa mares approached. Both women mounted, cloaks thrown back, arms bared to reveal the gold circlets they wore.

Arian spurred her black horse to the left, her green cloak stirring in the wind. She nodded to the slavers below. "Let's not give them warning. Let's fly."

They descended down the ridge, the khamsa sure-footed, hungry for speed. The thunder of their hooves was swallowed by the sand, little whorls of dust rising into the sun.

Soon they were spotted by guards at the rear of the slave-chain. The guards turned, braced themselves in a synchronized movement, bringing up their swords. Sinnia let loose two arrows, aiming for the neck.

The guards fell. A startled cry rose from the long line of women, robed in the sorrowful blue of dusk, their pale eyes tasting light for the first time that day. The women were chained together in pairs, and now Arian and Sinnia parted at the rear to outpace the column on either side. The tally-taking boy with the whip sprang into Arian's path, his crop glancing off the flanks of the black horse.

"Take him," Sinnia shouted, but Arian left the boy. The man at the head of the slave-chain was a more formidable target. Clearly battle-tested, he had gained the saddle of his war horse at the first sound of unrest. He used his shield, parrying the thrust of Arian's quick, silver daggers. He was too big for her to match in direct combat so she feinted beneath the outthrust of his sword to slice through the girth on the flanks of his horse. When the saddle slipped, the horse stumbled under its rider's weight. The slave handler went down, his foot caught in the stirrup as the horse bolted. Sinnia's arrow took him in the distance.

That left one, apart from the boy.

The man was on his knees before Sinnia. She lashed the man's hands behind his back with a thick fold of softened leather. Then she spooled out the strips of leather and staked them in the hard, cold ground. The boy rallied to his master, brandishing the only weapon at his disposal, but a flick of Arian's wrist sent his crop into the dust. She held up a hand to motion him to stillness, and as she did, the sun glinted off the gold circlet on her upper arm. A murmur of astonishment whispered through the slave-chain at the sight of it.

The boy, scrawny and dirty in his tattered rags, fell back from his master, his blue eyes bright in a wind-reddened face.

With slow, considered movements, Arian slipped to the ground while Sinnia unhooked the ring of keys from the belt tied at the slave master's waist. One by one, she unlocked the iron rings that had bound the long row of women to the slave-chain and each other. As Sinnia moved up and down the ranks of the women, she saw scarred wrists, broken fingers, bruised arms, and shadowed, weary faces emptied of expectation.

She touched each woman with a soft word and a kind gesture, and as she passed down the line, she ripped the dust-blue netting from each face, freeing the women's skin and eyes to the brush of wind and sun. Muted cries followed in her wake.

"*This is the legend,*" the women whispered back and forth. "*It cannot be real.*"

Arian pushed back her hood, her dark hair falling loose about her shoulders. The familiar gasp of surprise followed her action as she came to stand before the slave master.

He turned his bearded, sunburned face up to hers, his eyes narrowed against the sight of skin and hair uncovered, the gold circlets closed about Arian's upper arms with leather ties, in the manner of the Companions of Hira.

She had done this many times before, but Arian still took a breath to fortify her courage before she spoke.

"Do you know who I am, slave master?"

He seemed stunned by the sight of her, straight-backed with confidence, unfettered. He struggled to speak.

"How have I offended, Companion? Why did you kill my men?"

He spoke the Common Tongue with the guttural accent of his native dialect.

"Why have you chained these women?" she asked by way of answer. "Where were you taking them?"

The man looked angry. Arian felt the tension of the boy who stood poised behind her, his mouth agape at the sight of Arian's hair. She felt a twinge of empathy. The boy was unloved, abandoned, enslaved. He would be used until broken, then discarded, no fate for a child to face. Pursuing the slave-chains was Arian's means of disrupting that fate.

The man on his knees studied her. "Do you not know the laws of this country? These women have no guardians, no homes. They pollute the public square with their hands held out for alms."

"Because you killed their men and their children," Arian concluded.

The slave master tried to struggle to his feet. With a gesture she sketched with her hand, Arian sent him to his knees again.

"Instead of feeding them, you enslaved them, and you take them elsewhere, far from their homes, for some deadlier purpose. What purpose, slave master? I wish to know it."

The man's face darkened. As with all the men she had dealt with before this one, Arian could read his anger in the rigidity of his limbs, just as she could feel his urge to strike and strike hard.

Arian pitied him his anger.

"I do not answer to you, Companion. I serve the Immolan."

Arian rubbed her forehead, then turned to her friend. "Have you finished, Sinnia?"

"I have."

The blue-robed women gathered in little clusters behind Sinnia.

"What do you want to do with this one?" Sinnia prodded the boy.

Arian's eyes found the boy, read something in his face, then glanced at the women.

"I do not think this man will prove to be any different than the others." She motioned to the pack horses that accompanied the slave-chain. "My sisters, take what you wish from these horses, and flee from here as quickly as you can. Find your families, but do not head east. These men have taken the eastern road and everything that lies beyond it."

The women scattered at her words, the slave master watching the dismantling of his supplies with impotent rage.

"Haramzadah!" He shouted the filthy epithet at the boy. "Is this how you serve me? I should flay you alive!"

The threat touched something inside Arian.

"You think I would let you?" she asked, her voice cool. "Do you think I would leave you alive to visit any more pain on this boy? Sinnia."

Before the boy could speak, his master's blood was on the sand, startling a bewildered sob from the boy's throat. Gently, Arian touched the boy's shoulder, forgetting for a moment that he would flinch. Fluid leaked from his eyes and nose. He rubbed it aside with his dirty hands.

"He kept you, so you were grateful," she told him. "But this was not kindness to you. When you had served your short life of labor, he would have killed you in the street." She motioned at the women who'd fled in all directions. "Nor was that kindness, to wreak violence upon the helpless. Take your freedom," she told him. "Find what happiness you can with it."

He stared back at her. Perhaps he had heard of the Companions, heard of their magic, and waited to see if she would use it against him. But there had been no call to use the Claim, no point in trying to persuade the guards or the boy with the magic she'd been blessed with, no sense in reworking their understanding of the Tradition. It was lost now, all of it. When the lands of the Far Range had been devastated by war, all of it had been lost. The most that she and Sinnia could hope for was this continued disruption of the slave-chains.

She had killed many men in this effort.

And did not regret it.

But she would leave the boy with blue eyes. The boy had raised his crop and his voice, he'd shown no more mercy than he'd been shown, and if left to himself, he would resort to cruelty again. Yet she could sense the innocence of the boy, the bewilderment of his blind obedience, his hunger for something else.

Arian hungered for it, too. Because unlike the boy, she had felt it once. Not now. Not in the lands she had once roamed freely, where cruelty and violence were all there was.

We live in the age of secrets and fear.

We live in the Age of Ignorance.

She searched for one item in the slave master's pack, her hands careful and thorough. The boy did not leave. He watched her helplessly, sobs shaking his slight frame, until her search uncovered the Talisman flag, the only flag flown in these lands.

Sketched on the field of the flag was a book, opened to two facing pages.

It was far from a symbol of literacy.

The book's blank pages were marked with blood.

And the Talisman fist had set its message on fire.

Arian suited symbol to action. She burned the flag, planting it in the ground beside the body of the slave master. She felt no contempt for the dead, but the pity she afforded them was of a lesser shade than her feeling for their victims.

The boy had stopped crying, yet remained. As she and Sinnia drew their cloaks close around their naked arms, he raised a dirty fist at them.

"You'll know blood and loss before this day ends."

"Boy," she said softly. "There is more to life than blood and loss. May you find peace in their stead."

He wouldn't, she knew. Who in these lost lands of Khorasan knew peace anymore? Who knew safety or truth, or the innermost kindling of joy?

These were the days of the Talisman fist.

The fist that crushed everything to dust.

2

ARIAN LOOKED UP AT THE SOUND OF A CRY ON THE WIND. SINNIA RAISED her left arm, clothed at the wrist in a gauntlet. In a moment, a falcon had descended to alight on Sinnia's wrist.

Sinnia read the message gripped in its talons with a grim look. She spoke the name Arian had anticipated at the falcon's first cry, a name Arian never heard without a sense of foreboding.

"Ilea. The High Companion has summoned us to Hira."

Arian's heart misgave her. Ilea's Summons meant censure and disparagement. Rarely had the Council offered her encouragement.

She did not want to go.

She could not disobey.

She scanned the dull hills of the surrounding countryside. The blue-robed women were specks in the distance, fleeing from the ruins that were Arian's destination.

Sinnia slowed her mare. "Do you not intend to heed the Summons?"

"I came here for the Cloak. I will not leave without it."

"We will not have as easy a time of it inside the walls of Candour," Sinnia cautioned. "The slave-chains in the city are guarded by whole companies. They will be heavily armed. Swords, maces, fire lances."

But Arian knew that none of these could stand against the power of the Claim, the power that sustained her campaign against the Talisman. Sinnia had been at Arian's side for months now. She was a trusted friend who obeyed Arian's orders with diligence and resolution, if not without question. And Arian had learned to welcome her questions. They spoke of a mind unconstrained by fear. Yet, it wasn't the exchange of equals. Sinnia knew nothing of the forbidden knowledge Arian carried inside her head because knowledge, like love, was a weapon. It was too dangerous a burden to share. If that made her seem remote in lieu of a greater closeness, it was something Arian could accept.

"The Talisman have taken Candour," Sinnia continued. "Is that not a fight best abandoned?"

"I will not surrender the women of Candour. We will move on to Hira once we have the Cloak."

"What of its guardians? The Ancient Dead?"

"None that I know of survive. No, the Sacred Cloak is under Talisman guard, nothing more. And they dare not touch it or bring it to light. They fear its power even as they use it to strengthen their legitimacy."

"Then how can you hope to retrieve it from their stronghold?"

"The Blue Shrine isn't a Talisman stronghold. It will yield its secrets to us."

Sinnia was unconvinced. Sinnia was at best a minor Oralist, with scant knowledge of the Claim or its powers. She had been selected as Arian's adjutant by Ilea, the highest member of their Order. She could not know the things known to Ilea and Arian, the deeper traditions buried beneath the High Tongue, the sacred language known only to the Oralists, nor the magic and power of its rites.

Arian couldn't reassure her friend, much as she wished to. She could only show her.

She nudged her horse, Safanad, the steadiest mare of the khamsa, on a straight course to the ruined city's gates.

"Keep your arms covered but your head bare," she reminded Sinnia.

There was no idle decoration about either woman. That they were mounted would be cause enough for disturbance—women didn't ride in Talisman territory. They covered their heads, their faces, their bodies. Their voices were silenced, oftimes by a Talisman dagger, while others who survived were shackled and sent away. And though Arian had been raiding the trains for months, the destination of the slave-chains was still unknown to her. She hoped coming here would bring her closer to the truth.

A crowd had gathered about the old gates. These gates had possessed other names once, names rich in beauty. Gate of the Pomegranate. Gate of the Apricot. Gate of the Poppies. Now they were in disrepair, ravaged like the city by centuries of war. The Talisman were the last in a long line of despoilers, the victims the same in every era:

Women.

Children.

Joy.

She brushed the thought of the boy aside—the chin that trembled, the blue eyes that had questioned her actions. The spies of the Talisman would reach their masters quickly, and if the boy chose not to seize his freedom, he would soon find a new master, whose fist would bludgeon just as well, whose crop would rise over his shoulders a thousand times a day. He would drink when his master had finished drinking and would be fed from the remnants of his master's plate.

If at all.

In the Age of Ignorance, the Talisman held a monopoly on food supplies. The rest of Khorasan was gripped by a famine created by the Talisman, rugged and fierce warriors whose code determined who would live, who would die, who would eat, who would starve, while the banner of their bloodlust flew before their hordes, each orchard, each fig tree guarded by the sword of a petty and joyless tyrant.

Sinnia was tense beside her as they rode down the main thoroughfare of the ancient capital, so long ago festooned with fruit trees. Everything about the city was brown or gray—the streets, the worn shopfronts, the derelict houses, each flying a Talisman flag. A crowd composed of wild-eyed boys and belligerent young men followed the course of their horses.

As the road climbed to meet the horizon, the blue dome of the shrine spread a marbled glow across the lower half of the sky. More men gathered, their faces shadowed beneath their turbans.

Sinnia's dark skin was glowing with beads of sweat. The young Oralist was afraid, a thought that awakened Arian's compassion. She was so bent on her own purposes that she seldom stopped to consider the cost to Sinnia.

"You need not fear. The Oralists have never traveled a land without friends."

But Sinnia was pointing to the burned-out shell of a building behind the shrine.

"They've destroyed it," she said. "The Library of Candour."

That was only the first of our losses.

Arian didn't say as much aloud. Sinnia had come to her in recent months. In the decade that had passed before, Arian had traveled with great difficulty through towns and villages that had fallen to the Talisman, while further west, the Empty Quarter had been seized by the Rising Nineteen. Sinnia didn't know that from the mountains to the east, there was nothing other than silence. Sinnia came from the lands of the Negus in the south, well beyond the Empty Quarter.

She had been summoned from those lands by the High Companion herself, to be presented to Arian as an ally of consequence. Impulsive, sardonic, brave beyond measure, she possessed the kind of strength that was as beautiful to Arian as it was indispensable in the country held by the Talisman.

The destruction of the Library of Candour had been the first act of the Talisman, the white flag raised as a desolation above its storied arches. The bloodstained page on the Talisman flag spoke to a limitless capacity for ignorance. A thing to be pitied, a loss to be grieved. Something of that feeling was in Arian's voice when she turned in her saddle to face the mob. She pronounced a phrase in the High Tongue.

They wouldn't know its meaning, nor even how to form the words themselves, but the Claim held an abiding power, deep in the bones of the people of Khorasan. The men fell back from the khamsa, their faces reflecting a mixture of awe and terror.

Yes, Arian thought. *These words have been the terror of an age.*

She halted the progress of her mare before a tavern with a broken door.

"What are we doing here?" Sinnia whispered fiercely. "The Talisman have forbidden all means of intoxication."

Arian pointed a slender finger upward. The Talisman flag was nailed above the door.

"Except for the members of their command, who do as they please. We're not here to drink, though. I have a friend here. He will help us gain access to the Cloak."

A disquieting sense of hope beat against her thoughts, the lie fluttering in her chest.

She wouldn't describe the man she was searching for as a friend.

He was a beautiful, dark mystery.

And his absence from her life was a ceaseless bereavement.

Sinnia slipped into the squalid room behind Arian. Inside, a handful of men were gathered at a table, drinking from hammered metal cups. Their heads turned at the sight of two unveiled women, the tallest man in their midst rising to his feet at once. He was dressed in the loose-fitting garb of the Talisman, a thick wool pagri settled on his skull, his pointed beard reaching to just above his chest. A sharp array of knives hung from the belt at his waist. His shrewd eyes were set deep in a narrow, tapered face.

Before he could speak, Arian grasped Sinnia's hand and led her to the bar, disarranging her cloak as she passed. The gold circlets on the women's arms shone in the firelight. The man's companions whispered together until the man with the pagri slammed down his fist on the table. Watching the women, he came no closer.

At the bar, the man who tended the needs of the Talisman didn't look up. He passed a grimy cloth over a grimier surface, darkened by soot and ash. Sinnia braced her arms on the bar and waited.

"You shouldn't be here," the man with the cloth said. "What do you want?"

He was dressed in clean riding clothes. His head was bare, his dark hair loose around his skull, his beard shorn close to his jaw. In every swipe of the cloth over the bar there was anger and intimidation.

Arian drew a nervous breath before speaking. "I've come for the Cloak."

"Have you, indeed?" A silver flash of the man's eyes moved from Arian to Sinnia to the hostile group of Talisman gathered at the table. A rumble of noise from the street battered the tavern's door. "Veil yourselves, you fools, and get out of here before you cost me the little custom I have."

"They won't touch us," Arian said with more certainty than she felt. Her heart was thrumming inside her, the words dry in her mouth. The man at the bar was still here, whole and unharmed. Until this moment, she hadn't known what that would mean to her.

"Things have changed since you were last here." He looked at Sinnia, who gasped. The man's eyes were a bright, glancing silver in a face so strikingly beautiful, the squalor of his surroundings couldn't diminish it. "Tell your friend she's risking your life by bringing you in here."

Sinnia grinned in response. "She risks my life every moment of every day. She said you were a friend. I was hoping the odds might have changed."

A cold smile settled on the man's lips.

"For your sake, I'm sorry they haven't. The color of your skin won't protect you here. They take every kind of woman for the slave-chains."

It was a new thought for Sinnia. She had seen no black-skinned women in Khorasan, and she had freed none.

Arian intervened.

"Tell me how to get the key to the box that contains the Cloak, then we'll go. I won't ask for more of your help than this."

He turned his back to them both.

"The man at the table is the Immolan. He became the ruler of

Candour after the Talisman proclaimed the Assimilate. He also runs their prisons. If you don't leave now, you'll end up in one of them."

The words were meant to frighten Arian, to send her and Sinnia from Candour without the Cloak because, by any consideration, the pursuit of the Cloak was a reckoning waiting for the dead. Particularly when the Talisman's proclamation had been forcibly memorized by every citizen of Khorasan, young and old, rich and poor, male and female.

There is no one but the One. And so the One commands.

The proclamation of the law known as the Assimilate burned every corner of the earth the Talisman had reached. Those who differed in thought or practice met a swift, unmerciful fate. Save for the Companions of Hira, well able to defend themselves. "How do I get the key? There must be a way, Daniyar."

Behind them, the Immolan had reached a decision. He and his men made for the door.

"Do you still ride the khamsa?" the man named Daniyar asked, swinging back around.

Arian nodded. There had been a time when she, like Sinnia, had been vulnerable to beauty, astonished by its existence in the midst of ever-present darkness, the lost time, before the rise of the Talisman. Now she could look at Daniyar, read the rage that colored his every gesture, and want no more from him than the information that would see her through this day.

His warmth is not for me, she told herself. *I no longer wish for it.*

But when he looked at her, she could only think of him. It was an effort to remember the Shrine of the Sacred Cloak. And it was more difficult than she had expected to force her thoughts back to her mission.

No woman had ever beheld the Cloak or touched its soft folds. Arian would be the first, and in that action, she would break everything the Talisman had wrought in a war-ravaged decade. The Assimilate would fall, the slave trade would die, and the Talisman's prisons would burn to the ground.

If Daniyar would help her now.

He faced her squarely, without compassion.

"If you're planning to go to your death, don't look to me for rescue."

The words hurt as they were meant to. But there would be another time to think on why. She touched her hand to one of the circlets, a reaction to his indifference.

"Your tahweez won't work on me," he said coldly.

"I wasn't going to—"

"The key is held by the Akhundzada," he interrupted.

"I thought none of that line survived."

The noise in the street had doubled and redoubled. It was more than the shouts of the mob. It was the sound of glass breaking, the rumble of wheelbarrows in the street, the hungry lick of flame. Smoke seeped in through gaps in the tavern door.

Daniyar reached down behind the bar for his sword, its blade formed from black steel, its short handle undecorated. Arian recognized it as a salawar, common to these parts. It wasn't the sword she knew from the past, the sword with a history and legend of its own. She also knew in his hand, *any* weapon would be deadly.

"I've given you what you want, now go. Call the khamsa, leave from the back."

"Where do I find the descendant of the Ancient Dead?"

A fiery bottle smashed through the tavern's window. Daniyar glanced at Arian. She felt the heat rise in her limbs.

"He allied himself with the Talisman as a means of self-protection. He's the Immolan's right-hand man." He threw down the planks he'd gathered to shore up the window and door. "This place is lost now." His anger was evident as he turned back to Arian. "Tell me what you want with the Cloak."

Arian's reply was swift.

"The Talisman have made it the symbol of their authority. If I can reclaim it for Hira, perhaps the people will begin to doubt the Talisman's legitimacy."

The crowd was pressing against the door. Daniyar led them through a series of cramped passageways, each riddled with tiny sinkholes that stank of rot and filth. As they passed through a crowded storeroom with a ceiling that sloped to the ground, he grabbed two rounds of bread from the shelves. At the tavern's blackened exit, he handed them to Sinnia.

With sympathy he said, "For the road." But his words to Arian were filled with contempt. "No one submits to the Talisman out of choice. The Cloak will make no difference. If you won't think of your own life, you should trouble to think of your friend's."

He didn't wait for them. He kicked the door open and disappeared down a mud alley, the sword belted at his waist.

"You think of me, too," Sinnia called after him, but her jest didn't lighten Arian's spirits.

He despises me. He thought I would use the Claim against him. But I could never raise my voice against him.

As they took their own path and remounted the khamsa, the tavern exploded into flame. The fire roared on, rapacious in its greed.

"What else in this city is left to burn?" she muttered to Sinnia.

She had her answer, as the alleyway curved between rows of houses that shrunk away from the noise and flame. The Immolan was sending her a message. On the doorstep of the once-renowned

Library of Candour, a mob of men had gathered the last few remnants of the library's manuscripts. The Immolan was poised on a platform above the smoldering layers of Khorasan's history, beauty burned to ash at his command. The written word had long been banned under the Assimilate.

There is no one but the One. And so the One commands.

The Immolan's scaffold was suspended over the blaze by four cables. Behind the swaying platform, two tall and slender men dressed in Talisman garb waited to receive the Immolan onto the dais that had once been the entrance into the Library of Candour.

An age without candor, without hope.

She stared at the other two men. Which one was the Akhundzada?

"Sinnia."

Sinnia's bow was at the ready, her steel-tipped arrows launched. She aimed for the cables at the front, catching them at the juncture. The wooden platform tilted amid sounds of chaos. A flicker of blue behind the rubble of the library danced for a moment in Arian's vision. The Shrine of the Sacred Cloak, isolated on a dreary plain, shimmering like a jewel.

The Immolan lost his balance as the platform tipped forward. With a cry of fury, he fell onto the burning mound. Behind him, Arian caught a fleeting gesture before the Talisman guard checked himself. The green-eyed man to the left had raised his hand to tip the platform. His hennaed beard was unmistakable.

"That one," she called to Sinnia. "He won't stay there. His last duty is to the Cloak."

3

A WOMAN WITH GOLD HAIR COILED IN A LOOSE ROPE SAT BEFORE A twelve-sided table with a ceramic decoration as its tabletop. The outer ring of the ceramic was a turquoise frieze. The inner ring was patterned around a lapis lazuli medallion in the center of a stark white background. Marquetry inlays paneled the table's twelve sides.

A manuscript was placed in the dim light of a candle, its parchment so delicate that the pattern on the table could be seen through the page like a tracery. The woman's head was bent over the parchment, her eyes reading the ancient script.

"You would see better with a lantern," a voice drawled in her ear.

The woman looked up, a pair of exquisite amber-gold eyes lancing over the intruder. He tangled his hands in her coil of hair, his fingers brushing her throat.

"What are you doing here, Rukh?"

The woman's voice was neither cordial nor unwelcoming. She was a woman who weighed her words, choosing each one with care. The man's dark eyes glimmered in response. He read the manuscript over the woman's shoulder.

"You are late convening the Council, Ilea. If I am to wait for the First Oralist at Hira, I require something to occupy my time. What wisdom do you seek in the scriptorium?"

The High Companion rose from her seat. Rukh's presence was a disturbance she couldn't afford, but the Prince of West Khorasan was a man she couldn't ignore—nor did she necessarily want to. She entwined her hands with his, shielding his view of the manuscript with her body.

"You won't distract me," he said mildly. "I came for what you promised me. I won't leave Hira without it."

"I've told you. The Companions of Hira will have to be heard on the matter. You will need to speak before the Council."

She didn't trouble to plead or sound forlorn. Rukh knew the full extent of her authority, he wouldn't be deceived by a pretense of helplessness. He was the one man Ilea counted as an equal. He preferred her in full command of her powers.

Their black and gold heads drew close, the language between them effortless and familiar. After a time, the man named Rukh pulled away.

"What of the First Oralist?" he asked. "Does she come?"

It took Ilea a fraction of a second longer to recover her composure, her lips faintly swollen, her gold eyes languid.

"She comes with your treasure—you needn't fear. What she makes of you will be another matter."

"You sound as though you fear her."

Ilea glanced back at the manuscript on the ornamental table.

"The First Oralist is not as easy to manipulate as the others. She works her own agenda at the Council. She has the confidence to do so."

"But she brings you the Cloak." Rukh grasped Ilea's chin, searching the gold eyes. "Do not think to make a fool of me."

Ilea shrugged off his touch with a hint of anger.

"You've never known me to forswear my word. You will have the good wishes of the Council, as I promised."

"That is *not* what I came for. It is not a trifle I trade with you."

Ilea said nothing, assessing the power in the Prince of Khorasan's face. He was a man used to the dominion of an empire, but he had no dominion at Hira. Men like Rukh would come and go. The Council would rule to a time without end.

"Just as I warn you not to trifle with me . . . or the First Oralist. She is not what you think her. She follows her conscience more than she heeds any counsel of mine."

"You have ways of bringing the Companions to heel. You can't afford to have the First Oralist defy you before the Council. There are rumblings of discontent at Hira."

"And there are Talisman at your gates in Ashfall," she snapped back. "Do not question my influence, you will witness it for yourself. Worry about the First Oralist. Her actions are unpredictable."

"But you scout her course ahead nonetheless."

He would have gleaned as much from the manuscript on the table. Like Arian, Rukh was a piece to be played in a greater game. No matter his attraction for her, she trusted him not at all.

"She will not refuse the Audacy," Ilea said. "If I send her, she will go. She believes she can change our fortunes in this war—I have only to offer hope of the same."

"A fool's hope," Rukh observed. "You say she is not easily deceived."

Ilea's eyes skittered over Rukh's face, stopping at the symbol at his throat.

The black rook carved of onyx and silver was the symbol of an empire that swept from Hira to the west, as far as the Sea of the Transcasp. She couldn't afford that empire as an enemy, when there were enemies gathered on other fronts.

"She thinks she's been fighting a war, but she doesn't know the war has yet to begin. She believes the Cloak will delegitimize the Talisman, bringing the One-Eyed Preacher to heel. She knows nothing of the deeper forces at play."

"But you do."

"Yes, I do." Ilea's eyes sparked at Rukh. "And your knowledge is greater still, so you will honor your word and make the trade. Then we will see."

"What will we see, High Companion?"

Ilea's smile was bitter, even as she linked her arms around his neck.

"Whose fortunes will be the ones to prevail."

When Rukh left the scriptorium, Ilea found herself considering his words. If Rukh had heard the rumors at Hira, it meant her grip on the Council was weakening. It was why she'd made changes at Hira—changes in the guard, changes in the rituals—changes in her plans for the First Oralist.

She was playing a dangerous game, sending Arian down this road, setting her in the Prince of Khorasan's path. She knew she couldn't control him, and she didn't know if she still commanded the First Oralist.

But she knew more about the Sacred Cloak than either of the others. It was more than a holy relic, more than a stamp of authority. In the right hands, the Cloak would be a weapon of war. It would hold off the Talisman offensive, giving her the time she needed.

Arian, Sinnia, Rukh—each had a part to play in her design.

"I am coming for you, Preacher."

She sketched a complex incantation with her hand.

The silence of the scriptorium closed round her again.

4

ARIAN AND SINNIA TOOK THE ROAD OVER THE PLAIN, THE HOOVES OF the khamsa pounding against the tracks. The Shrine of the Sacred Cloak was built on a slight incline. At one time, it had been reached through a complex of buildings, each dedicated to a worthier purpose. Now the shrine's gilded archways had fallen into disrepair, just as the mirrored tiles and green marble that had decorated its exterior had long since been looted by the Talisman's militias.

What was left of such beauty was a single turquoise dome presiding over half-fallen arches. The khamsa cantered into the interior of the courtyard, and there the Companions left them. As fabled as they were, the mares could not enter a holy space.

The attention of the mob was still on the rescue of their leader from the flames, but Arian was well aware that whatever time was granted to them would be brief. The shouts of the mob were close by. The rising smoke had singed the shrine's pillars.

They reached the silver doors without incident. Here Arian took a moment to contemplate the beauty of what she beheld. The Talisman had removed the faience above and around the arch that framed the doors, erasing the written word wherever possible.

But they could not erase the flourishes on the doors themselves without breaching the shrine's security.

Beyond these doors, beneath the turquoise dome, was a relic that appeared insignificant at first glance: a dusty, ancient garment. Yet it was something that few deemed themselves worthy to gaze upon. Its power lay in its history. For any man who laid claim to the mantle of the Cloak, laid claim to the inheritance of the One. And the legend of the Cloak favored only men. No woman had breached the Shrine before this day.

Overwhelmed by a sense of history, Arian paused to kiss the inscription. Beside her, there were tears in Sinnia's eyes.

When she murmured the coda known only to the Oralists, the doors gave way.

Deep in its secluded interior, a window set at a great height allowed shafts of sunlight to pierce the gloom. Here the room's beauty was intact. The lower half of the great walls were paneled in the green marble of Helm. A cool spray of lapis lazuli tiles lined the upper gallery, their floral motifs entwined in a forest of blues and greens. Upon a plain marble stand in the center of the room, a simple wooden box reposed.

Behind the stand, the Immolan's guard stood waiting.

There were tears in the eyes that echoed the color of the marble. The hand that held his sword was trembling.

"You cannot be here," he whispered through shaking lips, the tears seeping into his beard. "This is a sacred place. You *must* not be here."

Now Arian and Sinnia raised their hoods over their hair, until all they revealed of themselves were their faces.

"I come from Hira as an enemy of the Talisman."

The Talisman guard shook his head from side to side.

"You must leave," he begged them. "I do not wish to harm you."

In a gesture of the deepest respect, Arian brought her arms together before her chest. She bowed as she did so.

"Akhundzada. Your work here is done. You have been the Cloak's guardian for many long years, bearing this burden alone. It is no longer yours to bear."

The sword wavered in the man's hand.

"How do you know me?" he whispered. "How can you release me?"

"Your people are known to the Sahabah. You have upheld the law, you have not transgressed it. You shall know neither fear nor grief."

The words were a formula Arian knew the man would recognize.

His sword clanged down to the marble floor. He sank to his knees.

"How—"

Arian waited no longer. "I need the key."

Without further hesitation, the last descendant of the guardians of the Cloak took the small silver key from the lace he had tied around his neck. As he pressed it into Arian's hand, it still held the warmth of his skin.

With a ragged breath, Arian fitted the key into the lock.

The catch gave way with a groaning sound. Arian pried the wooden lid loose with her fingers. She beheld for the first time what no one else had seen in centuries, not even the Akhundzada. The soft brown folds of the Cloak.

It smelled of honey.

These centuries later, the scent of honey still clings to its folds.

The dark cloth was coarse and heavy, yet in Arian's fingers it felt like silk.

Nothing in the years of Talisman rule had broken her, but at this moment Arian wept. And Sinnia and the Akhundzada wept with her.

A sharp object struck her shoulder with force. The box fell from her hands, its contents spilling forth. With a cry of horror, the Akhundzada leapt forward, just catching the Cloak before it tumbled to the ground. The sound of his dismay filled the small chamber.

Arian spun around, the reflexes of her body readying themselves for combat, even as her mind shied away from the thought of bloodshed in this place.

A boy confronted her.

The blue-eyed boy from the morning's slave-chain.

His face wet, he howled like a wolf as he leapt at Arian, his scarred hands empty of weapons as he sprang. Before he could reach her, a flick of the whip Sinnia carried at her waist coiled around his ankles, bringing him down. He landed on his elbows with jarring force.

"This time shall I kill him?" Sinnia asked.

"No! Blood cannot be spilled inside the shrine!"

The Akhundzada spoke in a tortured voice. He rose to his feet with infinite care, the Cloak cradled in his arms, a look of disbelief on his battle-scarred features. He spoke to the boy.

"This is the Sacred Cloak. Have you lost your wits? You cannot kill in its presence."

Arian watched the boy's face. And when awareness came, she saw the nature of his tears transform from rage into awe, and from awe to the wonder of ignorance. He reached out a dirty hand toward the Cloak. With a shout of consternation, the Akhundzada kicked his hand away.

"I accept the Sahabah as witnesses from Hira, but you are a filthy mongrel."

The boy's hand fell, his chest heaving with silent sobs. In a surreptitious gesture, he tried to rub it clean against his tattered tunic, his head lowered in shame.

Arian knelt before the boy. She loosed the laces on the waterskin she carried to pour water over his unresisting hands. His head came up in surprise when she took his hands within her own and dried them with her cloak. She used the same damp corner of her cloak to wipe the dirt and humiliation from his face. Her hands gentle, she raised him to his feet, feeling the deep trembling of his bones beneath her touch.

This boy had never been touched except in anger, and certainly not by a woman.

She turned to the Akhundzada, and in that moment, everything she kept disguised as a hunter on the trail of Talisman slave-chains appeared in the dignity of her carriage, and in the clarity of her eyes. Her cloak fell away from her arms. The radiance of her circlets illuminated the chamber.

She took the Sacred Cloak from the Akhundzada's hands, and despite the guardian's gasp of protest, pressed its folds to the boy's scarred brow.

"We are none of us impure before the One."

And to the boy she said, "You are not filthy. You are not a mongrel. You are not of the Talisman; you are not unworthy."

She slipped the Sacred Cloak over the boy's shaking frame.

"This Cloak belongs to the orphans of this world. It exists for their protection."

It was too much. The boy couldn't bear kindness when he had never known any. He returned the cloak to the Akhundzada with hands that shook with fright. Then he worked his ankles free from the grip of Sinnia's whip. He fled backward from the small chamber, his face white beneath its windburn.

"You may place it in the box."

There was too much to teach here, Arian realized. It was the work of decades, not moments.

Arian bowed to the guardian again. The box, at least, would make the journey to Hira.

"Companion," the man murmured. "The Talisman are at the outer gates, let me hide the box."

"Would that I could, Akhundzada, but the time for secrets is over. Your life may be spared, however, if you return to the Immolan's side. Go now with haste."

"They've come for us," Sinnia said grimly.

"We'll make our stand at the top of the hill."

Arian worried not for herself but for Sinnia. This was the first time she had exposed her friend to such danger. For a fleeting moment, she considered whether she had been reckless in her pursuit of the Cloak. She opened her mouth to apologize, but Sinnia spoke first.

"I wish you wouldn't worry about me." Her voice caught in her throat. "What you dare, what you attempt—the least I can do is stand fast by your side." A corner of her mouth tipped up. "And perfect the aim of my arrows."

Arian squeezed Sinnia's hand.

The mob followed at the heels of the Immolan. No longer subdued by the presence of messengers from Hira, the Immolan rode at the head of a column of fighters, his face and beard blackened by smoke. Though the mob around him called for blood, his face betrayed no emotion save for a certain brittle calculation.

They met at the top of the overlook, the pillaged grasslands of Candour spread vast and wide below them.

"What do you want, Companion? What do you seek in the lands of the Talisman?"

She had underestimated the Immolan. The leader of the Talisman spoke in the accents of an educated man. His book-burning purges could not be attributed to a veneration of ignorance.

Arian passed the box that held the Sacred Cloak to Sinnia. This gave her the freedom to uncover her hair, and to bare the insignia of the Companions—the two gold tahweez tied to her upper arms.

"By the last reckoning of the Council at Hira, Candour does not belong to the Talisman. It belongs to the people of Candour. To all the free people of Khorasan."

The Immolan smiled. It was not a smile to encourage a feeling of safety.

Arian grasped that he was comfortable. He believed he had nothing to fear from the power of the Claim. As little as he knew of it, perhaps he disbelieved it entirely.

"You are a woman, but I permitted you to speak in public. I permitted you to wander at will through the streets of Candour as a mark of respect to the Council, but you possess no authority in this city. I suggest you and your lackey retreat to Hira, while you still may be sure of a welcome. After you have given me the box."

She met his gaze calmly, motioning to Sinnia for the box. With smooth, practiced movements, she withdrew the cloak from its resting place and held it up to the bracing light of day. The cries of the mob dwindled into silence.

And then the sky was riven.

To a murmur of hushed awe, Arian slipped the Cloak over her own shoulders.

It was a challenge to everything the Talisman had taught the mob. That women were dirty, despoiled, defiling everything they touched. That they were to be kept locked up, chained away from sunlight and gardens and fresh air, serving the men of Khorasan in whatever way the Immolan deemed fit.

There is no one but the Talisman. And so the Talisman command.

Arian understood the mob for what it was. A hungry and war-ravaged people, destitute in knowledge, impoverished by ignorance, victims of the Talisman as much as the slave caravans herded to the north, stealing away the women who had lost the protection of their families.

Years of Talisman warfare had hardened these people. When she looked into their faces, trying to read something other than ugliness, Arian wondered if it had destroyed them.

Then she heard the whispers.

"She is bound by the tahweez."

"She wears the Sacred Cloak."

"It must be the legend."

She raised her voice without effort.

"The Talisman have no authority over you. If the Immolan were your legitimate representative, he would be wearing the Sacred Cloak, not I."

Her pale eyes searched their faces, Sinnia tense at her side. She had drawn none of her weapons, but the moment couldn't last.

"What is their talisman?" she challenged them. "A blood-stained page? Whose blood? What page? Do you know even so little as this? They have robbed you of your history, your memories. Now you have burned to ash the final traces of your heritage. Are they right to keep you in darkness? Do you prefer the Age of Ignorance?"

A restless murmur passed through the crowd. Arian's faultless vision caught sight of the boy at the edge of it. She wished him well away from the violence about to ensue, but it was too late to see to his safety now. She pressed on.

"Do you prefer a life of cruelty and coldness to the warmth and companionship of your women? What right do the Talisman have to enslave those whom you love?"

"They take only the women who do not obey the law," a man shouted. "The women no one wants, the widows and the orphaned."

Arian straightened her back in the saddle. This was almost the moment. The reverence for the Cloak was transforming into something else. Anger, wretched and cold.

"The widowed and orphaned are your most sacred charge," she said gravely. "If they are cast off, is it not because the Talisman have killed their protectors?"

Had Daniyar been right? Did the people of Candour follow the Talisman because they had no other choice? Or had they adopted the Talisman doctrines as law because they found comfort in the Talisman's narrowness of vision?

"You have the right to knowledge," Arian told them. "You have the right to all of your traditions. You have the right to the history of your forebears."

The mob was wavering on the edge now. Arian had donned the Sacred Cloak without setting herself aflame. She wore the golden circlets they had venerated since the dawn of their settlement in these valleys, circlets inscribed with the written word. And if she was a Companion of the Order at Hira, that meant she was also an Oralist. There was no rank more honored among the people of Khorasan.

"The written word is corrupt," another man called out from the back of a Talisman war horse. "It sows corruption in the land; it leads us astray. We have cleansed the earth of it."

"You have burned the libraries of the south," Arian answered wearily. "And condemned yourselves to darkness. That is all you've done."

She took a long, controlled breath. Holding up both her palms to the sky, she brought forth the power of the magic. This was the gift of the Oralist, these golden tones that rose and fell in perfectly measured rhythms, this lost language of the Claim, recognized by all upon utterance, known by only a few.

"If all the trees on earth were made into pens, and the ocean supplied the ink, augmented by seven more oceans, still the words of the One would not run out."

The men on the war horses covered their ears with a synchronous cry. The group of followers at their heels stayed motionless, held by the power of the words, the magic of the incantation. They swayed at its rhythm, staring up at Arian as if they'd never seen a woman.

And they hadn't. Not a woman with her long hair loose and free, her face unveiled, her bare arms gilded with sacred inscriptions.

The Immolan leaned forward in his saddle to grab Arian by the throat, choking off the sound of her words.

"Harlot," he rasped at her. "You will give me the Cloak, then I will find a use for you."

An arrow whistled through the air catching the man at his jugular vein. As a bright stream of blood erupted from his neck, pandemonium set in among the Talisman riders. The spell of the Claim shattered against the sight of blood.

"Ride!" a man's voice shouted from the rear. It was Daniyar. "Ride like the khamsin wind!"

He'd said he wouldn't help her, yet here he was at the moment of utmost need.

He'd killed a widely feared leader of the Talisman just for putting a hand to her throat. A swell of joy, quickly tamped down, surged in her veins.

He had come for her.

Would he come with *her?*

As she and Sinnia spurred the khamsa forward, she spared a thought for the boy.

With Sinnia's aid, she had freed many of Khorasan's women from the slave-chains. She had convinced the last descendant of a long line of guardians to part with the Sacred Cloak on the basis of no more than the circlets bound about her arms.

And she had won a sign of loyalty from the man who had yielded her nothing in her long war against the Talisman, the man who had buried the memory of their days among the manuscripts of Candour, turning his talents to the needs of the Talisman leadership.

She had loved him, cursed him, and forgotten him.

He had sent her to find the treasure under the blue dome on her own, consigning her to a death unmourned. But he'd saved her from the Immolan in the end.

It isn't as I feared, then. I haven't destroyed all there was between us.

With everything she had gained, she was riding from Candour victorious.

But the memory of the Akhundzada's tears, and her last sight of the boy abandoned to the vagaries of a Talisman mob, reminded her—if she had forgotten—that her victories came at a price. When she turned to look back from a greater distance, expecting Daniyar to be riding at her heels, Sinnia echoed her thoughts.

"No," the Companion from the Negus said. "The beautiful one did not follow."

A price she had now paid twice.

5

"WHY DOES HE LEAVE YOU ALONE AND FORSAKEN ON THIS ROAD?" SIN-nia asked, some time later. "I do not mistake his desertion for dis-interest."

Arian glanced over at Sinnia, who had fastened the box that held the Sacred Cloak to her back with a set of ropes, not daring to uncover it or wear it, an honor she seemed to believe was re-served for the First Oralist.

"He does what he thinks is right. I regret that doesn't mean he trusts me."

"How could he not trust you? Doesn't he know who you are? You said he was a friend."

The words held an undercurrent of outrage. To Sinnia, Arian epitomized all that was best about the Council of Hira. Through the months they had ridden together, Arian had been strong, firm, determined—and unfailingly kind. That anyone who knew her could doubt her was something Sinnia took as a personal affront.

"Not all friendships are like ours."

And her history with Daniyar was too painful for Arian to share.

He won't come for me again, I do not wish it.

He's put away the things that made him who he is—the book, the silver sword.

She tried to focus on the journey ahead. Their escape from Candour was a temporary reprieve. The road to Hira was plagued by hazards. Talisman patrols lurked in the hills. No one dared traverse the open road. It was how the Talisman maintained control of the south, shutting up the villages, choking off the transmission of knowledge through the trade routes.

Silence and isolation were the legacy of the wars of the Far Range, the countryside despoiled and dangerous, outsiders viewed with suspicion and distrust. Women caught in the open were sold to slave-chains. Men were conscripted to the Talisman cause.

And so the vast, wild country of Khorasan had shrunk into these pockets of ignorance and fear.

Most often, Arian and Sinnia had found themselves alone. And when they'd encountered Talisman, Arian had put all of her training to use.

Daniyar's training, she thought. And once more, her mind couldn't escape him.

She thought of the first time he'd tested her, the memory warm in her mind. She hadn't been able to lift the sword he'd placed in her hands.

He asked her to step back but as soon as she did, the sword crashed to the ground. His smile was softly indulgent.

"I forget that you have but half my strength."

Arian struggled to raise the sword. His smile broadened when it crashed down again.

"Half the strength but twice the heart," he amended, striding to the armory to find a blade better suited to her ability.

He stood behind her, showing her how to hold the blade, how

to lunge and block, how to parry a blow. The firmness of him against her back, the feel of his arm alongside hers stole her concentration. It took all of her willpower to focus on the lesson at hand.

When he raised his sword before her, she forgot to bring up her own.

"If you stand there so still, I think the enemy will be most obliged." The smile lingered in his voice.

Color rushed into her face.

"You will think me a most inapt pupil, my lord, but I cannot recall your instruction."

"No matter," he answered. "We have time."

He moved behind her again, positioning her arm, teaching her how to strike and parry. She moved better, fitting her body to his, learning the rhythm of his steps.

"Much better," he said. His praise was all the incentive she needed to improve.

This time when he came round, she was ready.

Back and forth they pressed, sparks striking as swords crossed, then fell away.

He circled her and she mimicked the movement, the shield arm up to block, the sword arm waiting for an opening. He quickened his pace.

She matched it.

Over and under her blade dashed, a little slower each time, blocking the advance. She was giving ground, falling back to a corner. She lunged for his shield arm, reversing their positions.

"Very good," he commended her. She realized he hadn't even quickened his breath, while she was all but spent. His sword came down and she blocked him, then quicker than her eye could follow, he fell back and lunged again. This time she was too slow to pivot. His sword struck her hard on the shoulder. Her own sword clanged to the floor.

"Truce," she said, reaching for her blade, surprised to find herself caught in Daniyar's arms, his hands searching for the wound.

"Forgive me, that was clumsy of me. I should have seen you were losing ground. Did I cause you injury?"

How blind he is, she thought. *There is only the injury to my senses whenever he touches me.*

His hand was massaging her shoulder and though nothing had ever felt so good to Arian, she stepped back from him, a smile sketched on her lips.

She was a Companion of Hira. She could never forget that, no matter the attractions of her partner.

"How else am I to learn, my lord? I shall doubtless fall many times before I prove myself worthy of your guidance."

His hand stroked over the soft strands of her hair. Then thinking better of their intimacy, he moved away.

"A gallant spirit is all that I can ask. Shall we try again?"

"I am at your service, my lord."

She didn't sleep that night for thinking on the warmth in his eyes.

"As long as I haven't winged you, Arian."

It was the first time Daniyar had spoken her name instead of using her title.

A rian?"

Sinnia's gentle voice called Arian back to herself.

"Drink," she said. She passed Arian her waterskin, her fingers warm and steady. She wanted to reassure Arian, repay some of the kindness her friend had so often shown her. To hunt and ride and kill, day after day, month after month—Sinnia couldn't guess at the toll it had taken. If the beautiful one had joined them, things might have changed for the better.

Sinnia shrugged off the thought.

She had long since accepted that the Companions of Hira relied only upon each other.

She was eager to return to Hira, to applaud as Arian's great achievement was celebrated by the Council.

The Sacred Cloak was a gift and a blessing unlike any other.

It would change the future, as it honored the past.

But she stole a look over her shoulder, in case the beautiful one had followed after all.

6

NORTH OF THE EMPTY QUARTER, IN A HILLSIDE COVERED WITH BRO-
ken stone, was a small cave known as Hira. Destroyed during the
wars of the Far Range, it had lent its name to the new gathering
place of the Council of Hira, buried deep within the well-guarded
walls of a brick fortress on a hilltop. Before the wars of the Far
Range, the Citadel had stood at the center of an extensive trade
route, serving alternately as a royal palace, a treasury, a military
garrison, and a prison.

Now it was the stronghold of the Council of Hira, the sanctuary of the Companions.

As Arian and Sinnia rode up the ramp that crossed the moat,
they faced a series of rounded towers that marked off the Citadel's perimeter. Patrolling the battlements of the fortress were the
sentries of the Citadel Guard, charged with the protection of the
Citadel and the safety of the Council.

Lately there had been rumors, questions of loyalty. Reasons to
wonder about changes to the Citadel Guard, and the hidden objectives of the High Companion.

Perhaps the Citadel was no longer the place of safety it had been. Arian was finding it difficult to think of Hira as home since Ilea's ascension to the rank of High Companion.

In a city whose beauties of construction had been directed by the far-seeing vision of a royal matriarch, the Citadel was the one building that offered nothing beyond its mud-baked strength. As they passed beneath its archway, Arian read the motif that was still the Citadel's motto, sketched out in disintegrating tilework.

NEVER TO BE ALTERED BY THE ENCIRCLING TREMORS OF TIME.

An idle boast, in a time when vanity was ill-afforded. And yet there was some truth in it, as well: there would be food, comfort, warmth, and stables for the khamsa.

They were led to the stables by an escort of young recruits to the Citadel Guard. In their leather armor, with their weapons a secondary consideration, the guards' clean-shaven faces and hopeful eyes were a welcome sight to Arian.

She was treated with deference, but when Sinnia dismounted, the young men stared. Arian patted down Safanad with a smile.

"A Companion from the country of the Negus," she said. "The first in Khorasan."

With her close-cropped hair and ebony skin, Sinnia was of a race unknown to the Citadel Guard. They were schooled in stories of the hijra, but to see a woman of the Negus was to see myth spring to life in their midst.

A young man in green leather armor stammered, "We've seen none like the Companion on the slave routes."

Sinnia flashed her dazzling smile at the guard.

"The women of my country do not submit to slavery, though skin like mine is prized beyond lajward."

She used the Khorasan word for lapis lazuli and it struck home, the guards nodding to each other in wonder.

Sinnia did not add what the slave master had screamed aloud before her dagger had found his heart.

Kill the black.

She had heard some variation of the same during each of their raids, but similar prejudice had been directed at the pale-skinned boy whose eyes were set in epicanthic folds.

What the Talisman hated was difference.

As the Companions relinquished their horses to the care of the guards, the khamsa whinnied with pleasure, rejoining the other mares. Quickly, they found the white mare with the delicate head who had mothered them all. Like the wind, she was called Khamsin, and her name came to them from the legend of a horse born of thunder.

Khamsin would bear only the High Companion of each new age.

Arian looked on fondly as Safanad fell in with her kin, grooms brushing her down and checking her hooves.

"The Council is convened," the young recruit instructed them. "The High Companion awaits you. You are wanted at the All Ways."

She shook her head. The Summons reflected the age-old power struggle between Arian and Ilea.

"I thought to rest and bathe first. Sinnia also."

She caught the quick look that passed between the guards. She raised an eyebrow at his hesitation.

After a moment, the first recruit said, "As you wish, Companion."

Arian considered. If the guards were to be punished for Arian's delay, better that she be swift to attend the Council.

Ilea doesn't believe in the innocence of messengers.

"We will refresh ourselves quickly and come," she decided. "What is your name?"

"Azmaray."

"Azmaray," she repeated. The name of a lion. Would this guard be lionhearted in her defence? "Is it a full gathering of the Companions?"

Another look passed between the guards.

"Most of the Affluent are present, but not all."

Something was wrong.

Is this not my home? Why do I anticipate anything other than welcome?

They passed through the courtyard under armed guard, Azmaray at their head. On other occasions, Arian's progression through this loveliest of Hira's courtyards had been slow and tranquil, her palm brushing each date tree as she passed, her senses caught by blooms of jasmine and honeysuckle vines, and that rarest fragrance, the roses of the coming spring.

Now she was hurried along by guards who offered to take their packs, an offer both women declined. Sinnia was adept at reading her body language. The stiffness of Arian's limbs spoke of danger, so Sinnia's hand curled about her whip.

Arian paused before the door to her chamber, prepared to say farewell to her escort. But then Azmaray stepped forward to unlock the door from keys he held at his waist.

"Wait." She stopped his movement with a gesture of her wrist. "Since when does a member of the Citadel Guard hold the keys to the chambers of a Companion?"

Azmaray appeared startled.

"It has always been so. We have just completed our training as the Guard's newest inductees."

Another deliberate gesture of her wrist, and Azmaray yielded his ring of keys to Arian, his face agape in astonishment.

"It has *never* been so. The High Companion ordered this?" And when he didn't speak, she prodded him. "Ilea?"

Azmaray gasped at the sense of pressure against his skull.

"Yes. It was the mistress."

"And who else joins the Council of Hira tonight? Other than the Companions?"

The guard frowned in concentration.

"I wouldn't know. I hold the lowest position among the Guard."

"Indeed."

Six men had accompanied them to Arian's quarters. Young, fresh-faced, frightened. A third gesture of Arian's wrist released Azmaray from her hold.

"We need no further escort. Tell your mistress we shall join her presently."

He nodded, backing away. Regaining something of his confidence, he stepped smartly to the right, calling his men to fall in behind him.

In the solitude of Arian's chambers, Sinnia spoke first.

"What has happened?"

"No man may enter these chambers. Ilea may well be the High Companion, but she possesses no real control over the sisterhood— the rank of Companion is a vocation, not a command. Tell me, Sinnia. Where does your loyalty lie?"

Sinnia shook her head. "You ask me this, after all these months together? Always with you, sahabiya."

"I ask because it was Ilea who appointed you as my companion."

"She chose well," said Sinnia with her wide sardonic smile.

Arian pressed her hand. "I do not disagree. I simply wonder

what game the High Companion plays. She sees some other purpose in you."

"Yet you answer her Summons, as I did."

"Until now, Ilea and I have not been at cross-purposes. Things have changed in the months I've been away."

"Yet everyone here knew you, as they didn't know me."

"I was brought here as a child. And though Hira has been my protection all these years, I have only known this time of darkness. It's why I went after the Cloak, instead of remaining at the Citadel. I don't know if retrieving the Cloak will change anything, I can only pray that it will."

"As your friend warned us. The beautiful one." She quirked an eyebrow at Arian.

"I knew whom you meant." She wouldn't say to Sinnia how bleak the empty horizon behind them had seemed. For how could Sinnia understand any of the sensitive transactions that had passed between Arian and Daniyar?

"Come, let us prepare. And, Sinnia. If you are loyal to me, say nothing of the Cloak until I speak of it."

"As you command, sahabiya."

"And keep your weapons well hidden."

7

ARIAN LED THE WAY TO THE UPPER CITADEL. SHE AND SINNIA CROSSED the hammam with its playful fountains, passing by the exquisitely inlaid tile of the Citadel's blue tower, to climb the second flight of stairs that led to the Council Chamber.

For their own reasons, the Companions flew no flag. It was a relief to Arian not to behold the bloodstained page that symbolized the Talisman's authority for the first time in long months. Here in the stronghold of the Citadel, the written word was a thing to be cherished. A superb collection of manuscripts was guarded in a dungeon beneath the Lower Citadel. A place that had once held Khorasan's most dangerous prisoners now preserved its imperiled treasury.

Arian and Sinnia had donned the white silk dress of the Companions. Their hair uncovered and fragrant, their bare arms aglow with the circlets that distinguished them from all other women of Khorasan, they found their sisters in the lantern light of the Council Chamber.

A quick glance at the White Throne in the center of the chamber revealed the absence of the High Companion. An imposing black chair, its lacquered back fanning out like the tail of a peacock, had been placed beside the High Companion's throne, both closed off from the rising tiers of the circular chamber by a square of murmuring fountains.

This was the All Ways. Its waters rose and fell in an impenetrable design.

Motifs in emerald and indigo ran the length of the chamber, a red spray of roses at the head of each of four raised tiers. The fountains of the All Ways were tiled in a cascade of blues that mirrored the play of the water. Each alcove in the patterned walls held a lantern worked in silver, descending from a golden stanchion.

A verse was inscribed above the White Throne.

THERE IS NO ONE BUT THE ONE. AND SO THE ONE COMMANDS.

A dictum Arian preferred to the false bravado of the Citadel's motto: *Never to be altered by the encircling tremors of time.*

Because things *were* changing even as she and Sinnia took their places among the Companions, exchanging the embraces of women who could never be sure they would meet in friendship and faith again.

The dozen or so women who filled the chamber were of nearly every race, every color, every background. They had come from lands beyond the Empty Quarter, and from all the lands of Khorasan. Many of their race names were lost to the tidal sweep of history, but their customs and dialects remained.

Each woman in the chamber was an Oralist gifted with some part of the lost language of the Claim, each holding a piece of an ancient, mystical puzzle, a language the Companions hoped to reclaim, to redeem the Age of Ignorance.

Each in her own way worked toward this end. Some were scholars, some were teachers, others were agriculturists or astrono-mers. Several were soldiers. Arian was the only linguist. Each was a thread in Hira's overarching design.

Arian made her count as she glanced around the tiers of the chamber: Dijah, the Trader. Ash, who held the influential rank of Jurist. Psalm, the General. Half-Seen, the Collector. Ware, Zeb, Saw, Moon, Rain, and Mask. Mask on their Council was a healer.

And at the center of their Council stood the High Companion, who had joined them without troubling to announce herself. She had no need to. She was a rarity at their Council—neither from the lands of Khorasan, nor from the frozen lands above the Transcasp—as a woman of the Far Range, her presence commanded attention.

She had stepped into Hira out of legend—her bloodline a secret, her knowledge of their Tradition preternatural. For the weight of history she carried, Ilea was small and slender, her stature no indication of her power. Her delicate features were set beneath a crown of gold hair, arranged in a coronet with a single long braid. She wore the circlets of the Companions, along with a golden diadem—a sapphire at its center blazed from her forehead. As she took her seat upon the White Throne, her blue silk dress swirled about her ankles.

Her gold eyes made her own count of the Companions, coming to rest upon Arian.

"There is no one but the One. And so the One commands."

The Companions echoed the words back to her in the ritual submission.

Arian mouthed the words, as well, but she felt the same strange resistance that had pressed against her thoughts the last time she had participated in the rites of the shahadah.

Something was wrong. Something she'd known as a linguist and now forgotten.

Ilea's glance caught hers, as if she guessed the reason for Arian's discomfort.

The women fell silent. In a synchronized gesture, the Companions raised their hands, the dim light of the lanterns reflecting off their circlets, then swept their palms down over their faces. The ritual complete, Ilea directed the Companions to take their seats. Her voice possessed the same crystal-edged clarity as her eyes.

Ilea had become High Companion because she alone of the women of the Council had mastered the art of combining voice and language. What she knew of the Claim from memory, she could manipulate with her voice—swaying the Council to her vision for Khorasan's future. Psalm, disciplined in tactics, was the only other Companion who could resist Ilea's control. And now she watched Ilea from her seat in the chamber, her blue-gray eyes wary and observant.

Arian wondered at that wariness—did Psalm know who else had been admitted to the Citadel? A second chair had never been permitted beside the throne of the High Companion. And yet it seemed familiar.

A throne to comprise the heavens and the earth.

Arian pushed the memory away. Her mother's teachings intruded on the rites of the Council more and more of late. In her mind's eye, she could see the woman who had trained both Arian and her sister in the Claim, with a transparency that pierced her with sadness. Her mother should have been at this Council. Along with Arian's sister. Instead, the Council had become a battleground between the two highest ranking Companions of their Order.

"I call the Council to order. Do the Companions submit?"

The women answered Ilea with one voice.

"We submit."

"Then peace be with you, my sisters." With a small, concise gesture, Ilea nodded at Arian. "First Oralist, your return is most welcome."

A murmur of support ran around the room.

Arian bent her head. "Exalted."

"And yet I must question you also."

Arian felt the shift. Every Companion was now looking at her, except for Sinnia, whose attention was held by Ilea.

"As you wish."

"You were late to the Summons. I trust you will have reasons, other than your relentless engagement with the Talisman."

"As the Exalted knows, the Talisman's power grows stronger, not weaker. To disengage is to cede all the lands south of Hira. The lands to the east have already been lost."

"It is not your place to determine where the battle should be joined."

"You would not say so if you had seen the slave-chains. They traverse Khorasan from end to end."

Arian saw approval in several of the Companions' faces. Psalm. Ware. Half-Seen, the Collector. Women who came from lands that were free. Yet she had challenged Ilea in front of the entire Council, and she knew the High Companion would not suffer that to stand.

As if to prove this true, Ilea rose from her throne, her gold eyes narrowed to slits.

"To what end, First Oralist? Where do the Talisman take the women of Khorasan? What information do you bring us?"

Shame and regret welled up in Arian's throat at the High Companion's words. It was a trick Ilea had mastered in her role as the Golden Mage. A technique of interrogation keyed to the weakness of each Companion. Arian readily admitted she had failed in her pursuit of the One-Eyed Preacher—freeing the women of the slave-chains had been her first priority. But none of the Talisman slave handlers she had captured had yielded an answer to the Preacher's whereabouts as none could be made to fear death. And Arian could not inflict pain. She could only make these small incursions into the Talisman's ever-replenishing numbers.

Ilea spoke for her.

"You do not know. You've spent years tracking the caravans without learning anything of value. You've gained little from your disobedience to the wishes of the Council. It would seem you have killed for nothing."

Whoever takes a life strikes against all of humanity. Whoever saves a life, saves us all.

Arian bit back her anger. What she had done wasn't worthless, but it was an argument she'd had many times with Ilea, though never with the full Council assembled. She willed herself to speak calmly, ignoring Ilea's rebuke.

"We fight the same battle, Exalted. And though you doubt me, I have brought with me something other than death. Something that may raise our hopes."

"Ah, yes." Ilea pointed to the wooden box Sinnia had placed beside her seat. "Show it to us, Companion."

Her use of Arian's lesser title was deliberate, a careful insult intended to disparage Arian before her sisters. Arian shrugged it off. And knew she was right to do so when she held up the Sacred Cloak, so that all the Companions might see it.

A thrum of excitement whispered through the Council.

And then a man's voice spoke.

"Your faith in your Oralist was not misplaced, Exalted. She brings you a fine prize indeed."

A gasp of dismay echoed through the chamber.

The Council was barred to men.

But their discomposure was momentary. They searched for the man who had spoken. When he stepped into the light, the Companions held still. No woman took up her veil to guard against his intrusion.

This was the Council's chamber—it was their ground to hold.

The Jurist made her way down to the waters of the All Ways.

"High Companion! You violate the law. Remove this stranger at once!"

An angry chorus echoed the demand.

The intruder waited, his black gaze lancing over the chamber. He extended a hand to his throne, curling his fingers around its arm.

And at last, Arian recognized the Black Throne, its lacquered back embossed with the pieces of a shahtaranj board, a single piece set in mother-of-pearl poised for the killing strike of shahmat. It was the black rook known as the castle.

The symbol of Ashfall, the capital of the west. The city of the Prince of West Khorasan.

And the man whose arrogance had breached their Council none other than the Black Khan himself.

8

"WHY HAVE YOU PERMITTED THIS, ILEA?"

"Shall I, Exalted?" The Black Khan moved as close to Arian as the All Ways would allow. The hand he held out was not to touch her, but to take possession of the Cloak.

The water danced between them in lovely and complex configurations.

"You did not tell me the First Oralist was such a beautiful creature." His voice was sleek with insinuation.

The Council erupted in outrage. They may have been prepared to wait for the High Companion's introduction of the stranger, but the stranger's presumption was an insult to them all.

Arian held up her hand for silence. Though Ilea held the senior rank, it was Arian who commanded the Council's respect.

Now she turned to meet the Black Khan's gaze.

For the past ten months, she'd seen nothing but famine and horror. If there had been a note of beauty, it had been at the Shrine of the Sacred Cloak . . . or in the flash of silver eyes.

But the Black Khan had come to Hira out of time. He was tall, clean-limbed, and graceful. His patrician face was framed by waves of hair that fell past his raised velvet collar. The jet-black eyes that glinted at Arian presided over a hawk-like nose and thin, sensual lips. He was dressed as if he'd arrived from his court, in an opulent tunic that fell to his knees. Its silver belt was inscribed with his titles. He wore no crown, but at his throat was an elaborate silver collar that supported the weight of numerous strings of pearls. Set at its center was his emblem, an onyx rook mounted on silver.

Arian read cruelty in the thin line of his lips. His eyes sparked with amusement; she guessed it was at her expense. Her gaze searched out Ash, who stood rooted before the All Ways. Ash nodded at her to continue, and Arian drew a sharp breath.

"I demand to know why a man has been permitted attendance in the Council. The Jurist will tell you there are no dispensations—not even for the Prince of Khorasan."

A ripple of surprise met Arian's disclosure.

Ilea negated Arian's authority by speaking to Ash directly.

"As High Companion, I have the right to contravene the rules of Council. You know this to be true, Jurist."

Ash glanced quickly at Arian, before saying, "Yes—should the Council's need be paramount. I cannot recall a single instance of such necessity, so you must make your case, High Companion."

Ilea's response was brusque.

"War is upon the Citadel. The Black Khan comes to our aid."

For a moment, Ash didn't respond. Then she gathered her composure and spoke to Ilea's revelation. "We have protocols for that, as well."

"Hear me out," Ilea said, without retreating an inch. "I do not usurp the Tradition. We are at the place of utmost vulnerability, our lands facing the same threat—a common strategy is necessary at this time."

And when did you decide that? Arian wondered. *Are the stratagems of the sisterhood now determined in the western capital?*

The chamber grew still. Arian listened carefully as Ilea relayed her news. She spoke of a fresh insurgency, of the One-Eyed Preacher's recall of his militias, and of his new deployments. This, at least, was news to her—she hadn't realized how far to the west the Talisman's reach had extended. If the Talisman were to advance from both the western front and the south, the Citadel's position would be perilous. It would need the best defence the Companions of Hira could mount, with the aid of the most skilled commanders of their Guard. She shot an apprehensive glance at Psalm, who nodded at her grimly.

But Arian wasn't convinced they had come to a moment when they would seek beyond their sisterhood for aid, willing to trust the Black Khan as an ally.

Ash was listening, as well—when Ilea concluded her presentation, she ruled in the High Companion's favor, though not before expressing her misgivings.

"What we permit in dangerous times must be held as exceptional. The traditions of Hira are sacrosanct—they must never be profaned again."

As she returned to her seat, the Black Khan inclined his head.

You need me, his bold look said. *And you will come to know it, soon.*

The legitimacy of her actions strengthened by the ruling, Ilea dismissed Arian to her seat.

"Replace the Cloak, Arian. The Black Khan and I have much to impart."

Straight-backed, Arian did as bidden, but not before she heard the Black Khan murmur, "Your name is Arian? Whose history have you claimed, I wonder."

She answered coolly, "None but my own."

And then Ilea was speaking, in the ritual incantations of the shura, recounting the history of Hira.

"The words of the Claim have been sown in these lands for centuries. The wars of the Far Range destroyed the ancient capitals, but they did not eradicate all traces of the Claim. Inscriptions on ruins and tombstones still exist. Suhufs have been found in caves, the treasure of those who protect them. They hold the line against the One-Eyed Preacher, who would reserve the Claim's power to himself. His Immolans burn scripture wherever they find it, all but assuring his ascendancy."

As Arian feared from watching Sinnia's rapt face, the High Companion was giving them more than a history lesson. She was using her voice to match her words to the fears and hopes of the Companions. She was reading each one of the women as she spoke, but finding Arian impervious to her probing.

Arian felt the hooded gaze of the Black Khan upon her—she kept hold of Sinnia's hand. It was all she could do to protect her friend during Ilea's recitation. The Black Khan appeared to have no need of such protection. Ilea freshened her voice.

"His Talisman hordes set Khorasan aflame—we are the last to stand against them. But we are not winning this battle." She paused, turning her attention to Arian. "Tell me, Arian, have you learned anything of the Preacher that would be of assistance to this Council?"

Arian stared back at Ilea, impassive.

"He remains as elusive as the Claim."

"You were assigned to uncover his identity. That was your only task."

"Trust that I did not forget that task. But what of the slavechains?" Arian challenged. "Was I to abandon the women of Khorasan to their fate?"

"You were to complete your Audacy," Ilea snapped. Like a jagged blade, her sudden use of the Claim slashed at Arian's composure, taking her by surprise. Ilea's powers had grown.

"Thanks to your disobedience, the Preacher remains a mystery. We know his mission, but nothing of his origins. His philosophy holds sway over Khorasan, variants of it have spread to the Empty Quarter and to the lands of the Negus. We hear nothing from the mountains, unless you can tell us otherwise?"

Arian held herself still, tamping down her anger. "No."

"No. So what do we have? Ten months in the south lost, with even less to show for the decade before that, the decade you spent in Talisman country."

"The Talisman have no country." Arian bit out each word. "These are the lands of *our* people. And I would not count that decade lost, Exalted. Every manuscript in Hira's care is one I rescued from the flames and delivered to you personally."

"Yet none, not a single one, contains so much as a couplet of the Claim."

"You know the manuscript of the Claim was a missing treasure long before the Talisman surge. None of the Companions have ever gazed upon a verse. Neither has anyone else."

"I have," the Black Khan inserted smoothly. "That is why I have come."

He crossed one leg over the other, the immaculate surface of his riding boots gleaming in the play of lamplight over water.

There was an instant of dumbfounded silence. Then a murmur of disbelief rose from the assembly. The Companions' words were lost in the clamor of voices demanding to be heard. Ilea's hand went up sharply, and the chamber fell silent again. She challenged Arian, directly.

"Do you see now? Do you see that you are not the one to forward the purposes of Hira? I know what the Talisman are. We have no better strength against them than a written proof of the Claim."

Every woman in the chamber knew Ilea's words for the truth.

The Talisman's chief weapon against the people was its rigid understanding of the Claim. With none to dispute him, and no proof offered as refutation, the One-Eyed Preacher had spread his philosophy unchallenged from the city of Candour to the threshold of the Ice Kill. North, south, east, and west, his joyless rhetoric had taken root. His law had superseded the law of Khorasan, Khorasan's parliament disbanded, its leaders and scholars scattered or killed. The Talisman flag had been raised over the ruins of Khorasan, and the Houses of Wisdom, which could have explicated the emblem on the flag, had been fed to the fire, along with their inhabitants.

The Talisman Assimilate was a codification of the One-Eyed Preacher's teachings, a doctrine none could dispute.

Unless the Companions of Hira had something more credible to offer in its place.

No hand had dared strike at Hira yet, but the Companions' power was weakening, and soon the protection the Citadel afforded the Council of Hira would erode.

The killing of the Immolan at Arian's behest would accelerate it.

Even her presence unfettered and free in the streets of Candour had been in violation of the unwritten law, the Assimilate recited from Talisman pulpits, no more than a series of strictures:

No woman could leave her home, unless in the presence of her husband or guardian.
No woman could practice any trade, study at any House of Wisdom, or give or receive the care of the healers.

No woman could speak in public, even if suitably accompanied.
An unaccompanied woman would be sold to a slave-chain
    without delay.
An uncovered one would be beaten first.

The Talisman's penalties for violations of the law were of a severity unmatched in Khorasan's history. Any act of joy, great or small, earned its commensurate punishment.

In the Talisman's new ordering of the world, even birds were not permitted to fly.

And Arian and Sinnia had appeared in the streets of Candour, astride the exquisite khamsa, with their arms bare and their heads uncovered, and taken the Sacred Cloak.

The taking of it had been a bold gesture, breathtakingly defiant and proud. At its heart, Arian had hoped it would be the one act sufficient to undermine the Talisman's authority. But proof of the Claim was the only thing that could deter the Talisman, the written word writ large over the face of Khorasan.

Had the Black Khan truly seen a written proof? And had he come here to share it with the Council?

Arian found herself shaken by his pronouncement—she could only stare at him. His hawk-like face was closed; she found she couldn't read him. Perhaps he had learned to shield himself through his close association with Ilea.

He came to his feet, his movements measured and elegant.

Arian rose to meet him.

"Does the Black Khan bring this treasure to the Council?"

"You will address him as Excellency," Ilea reprimanded her.

He waved a dismissive hand at the High Companion, a gesture that echoed Arian's disdain.

"You may call me Rukh and dispense with titles, just as I will call you Arian. And no, I have not come to offer you treasure."

"Then why *have* you come?"

A gasp of anger sounded through the chamber, as the Black Khan's hand stretched through the waters of the All Ways to grasp hold of Arian's arm.

His touch was warm, insinuating. She flinched from it, taking a step back.

And saw at once that this was what he'd intended, causing her to lose ground on the very ground that was hers to defend.

His action shamed her. And it made her angry. She hardened her voice, raising a hand to her tahweez.

"Do not presume to touch me. Unless you wish a taste of my power."

The Black Khan smiled, his dark gaze unwavering. He touched his own hand to the rook at his throat. He spoke low enough that only Arian could hear, the words intimate, seductive.

"That is *not* the part of you I wish to taste."

Fury erupted in Arian's mind. She pressed her tahweez into her arm, the incantation searing her throat. White-hot sound blasted the Black Khan back to his throne, nearly lifting him off his feet. Angered in turn, he raised his hand—whether to strike her or to call his own power forth, she wasn't given the chance to discover.

Ilea struck her hands together with a short, sharp bark of the Claim.

The words froze them in place.

Ilea waited until she had gathered their attention—only then did she loosen her grip.

When she addressed the Black Khan, her words had a meaning Arian couldn't interpret.

"Do *not* presume to touch the First Oralist," she echoed grimly, holding his gaze with her own. "In this chamber or at any other time. Unless you wish *all* your purposes undone."

He studied Ilea for long moments. And then he dipped his head.

"Your pardon, High Companion. I did not mean to offend."

Ilea rounded on Arian, her voice sharp-edged and dismissive.

"How dare you resort to violence in this chamber?" She flicked a glance over Arian's shoulder. "Stand down, Sinnia. The Black Khan is not your enemy."

Arian turned to see Sinnia on her feet, her bow strung before her, her arrow poised to strike. Sinnia answered without her usual humor.

"Any enemy of the First Oralist is my enemy. Just as you taught me, Exalted."

Ilea flicked a hand at Sinnia—the arrow she had nocked twanged harmlessly to the ground.

"No one is to bring weapons before the Council, I'll deal with your trespass later."

The Companions muttered to one another. This was more upheaval than Hira had known in decades.

And it wasn't over.

The Black Khan recalled their attention to himself.

"You quarrel over a verse, whereas I have seen the whole. A manuscript entire. A manuscript of the Claim."

No—Arian didn't believe it was possible.

The weight of history pressed against her thoughts. The teachings of her mother, the sacrifice of her family to protect the last remnants of the sacred Tradition, the sacred teaching.

The words of the Claim expanded inside her mind. They sang to her. They demanded the truth of her.

"Show us," she whispered, a little dizzy.

It was the Black Khan's turn to retreat. Something of her emotion had sparked at him, a brief, infinitesimal hope.

"The manuscript was recaptured. It has long since left my lands."

"Then how can we know it was the Claim? How could the Claim have survived?"

"Will you ridicule those who believe?" the Black Khan quoted softly.

Raising his voice, he addressed the chamber.

"Did you think the Talisman's emblem was merely a legend?"

His dark gaze found Sinnia, who slowly worked out the meaning of his words.

"Do you speak of the bloodstained page?" she asked.

"Yes," he said, at once. "Known to you as the Bloodprint." He looked around, his smile widening at the Companions' bewilderment. His next words shattered the world.

"It was the Bloodprint I held."

9

CRIES SOUNDED IN THE CHAMBER. SILK WHISPERED AGAINST STONE, THE
Companions' words rushing over each other. Ilea called them to order.
She rose from her throne, taking the hand the Black Khan extended.
Arian marked out those who objected. Psalm. Ware. And Ash.

Ilea came forward a few paces, raising an imperious hand.

"You will give me the Cloak now, First Oralist."

And this time, Arian couldn't resist the High Companion's
power. Her movements stiff, she yielded possession of the box.

Now the High Companion did a thing unprecedented in the
Council's history.

She removed the Cloak from the box and placed it on the Black
Khan's shoulders.

He raised his head, wings of dark hair casting shadows over his
cheekbones. His tone became formal.

"I swear to the Council of Hira by the power of the Sacred
Cloak and all it represents, the Bloodprint was placed in my
hands. I know it to be real."

His words were greeted with silence.

The Cloak did not permit blasphemy.

And wearing it, the Black Khan was different. His mantle of

arrogance had vanished. Their eyes met, and Arian understood he was telling them the truth.

A decade gone, every possible risk ventured against the hostility of the Talisman, the loss of everything that had given meaning to her life, the look she couldn't forget in silver eyes—a look of the profoundest betrayal, *and now this.*

At last, a reason to hope.

Overcome by revelation, she stumbled forward. The Black Khan moved swiftly to aid her. Catching herself at once, Arian retreated behind the All Ways.

He held up his hands in a gesture of surrender.

"I meant only to offer my assistance."

"I do not require it," she said with dignity. And then after a moment, "Thank you for your courtesy."

He bent his head, his lips quirking as she avoided the use of his name.

Frowning at the exchange, Ilea addressed the chamber.

"The Companions are sworn to the secrets of the Council, at any time. You are not to speak of the Bloodprint, even to each other. A task will be assigned to each of you, and you will each fulfill your duty, is that clear?"

A rumble of protest sounded. Justifications were demanded, accusations flung. A sibilant whisper chased up the tiers of the chamber.

"Blasphemy," several of the Companions cried.

The Claim thundered over the assembly. Ilea stared up at the Companions, confronting them one by one. Sinnia covered her ears.

"*Which of the One's favors will you deny?* You, Mask. Answer me!"

Mask muttered through her teeth. "None, High Companion. I dare deny none."

"And you, Ash?"

The Jurist couldn't look away from the High Companion. Breathless, the Companions observed their silent duel.

Whatever her internal struggle may have been, Ash was next to submit.

"Yes, submit," Ilea mocked. She turned to the rest of the chamber. *"Soon the One will settle your affairs."* She used the Claim as an ominous threat. "And do you submit, as well?"

The women of the Council looked to Arian.

"*I* am the High Companion, look to *me*! Do you dare defy me?"

And when the Companions still hesitated, Arian moved to intercede.

"This was a moment of wonder for us. The Sacred Cloak should have raised our hopes." She searched the faces of her sisters. "I wore it for a moment in Candour."

Mask's eyes filled with tears. "Did you truly, Arian?"

Arian's smile was tremulous. She had wanted this moment for her sisters. Ilea had stripped it away.

"Truly," she said.

Furious at being usurped, Ilea rounded on Psalm.

"General," she demanded. "Will you uphold the rules of Council?"

Psalm's reply was calm. "I note your fidelity to those rules." Her gaze swept over the Black Khan. Then she nodded at Arian. "I defer to the First Oralist. As she decides, so will I."

Ilea's fists clenched in the folds of her dress. The First Oralist had been away from Hira for months. But her influence had lessened not at all. With little effort, she had humiliated Ilea before the Council and before a valuable ally. But Ilea contained herself. She couldn't take Arian on before the Council; she would have to choose her moment.

She raised an eyebrow at Arian and waited.

Arian faced the assembly of Companions.

"Let us not shame ourselves in the presence of the Cloak. If the Black Khan wears it, his words must be true." She touched her tahweez. "If you cannot trust him, I accept that. But you know to trust me, my sisters." And then with a hint of prescience, she added, "If this is to be my Audacy, I will search for the Bloodprint to the end."

The rites of the Audacy had never been witnessed by an outsider. The chamber was quiet, the Council dismissed, and Arian was alone with Ilea and the Black Khan. His presence was an invasion of her privacy, but set against Ilea's bold-faced enmity, she counted it as nothing.

At an intricate gesture of Ilea's hands, the All Ways soared to new heights, trapping Arian within their waters. The All Ways formed a blue square, its thin spires of water resembling a cell.

Ilea and Arian had never been close, but Ilea's recitation of the Audacy's rites was marked by a freezing contempt.

"You have been bold before the Council, but the Audacy still demands your ritual submission. Do you accept this task?"

If the Bloodprint was real . . .

She gave the only answer she could.

"I do, Exalted."

"Then you will undertake a journey—a journey you've already guessed at. You will seek out the Bloodprint, wherever it may lead you. You alone have knowledge of its language. You alone can confirm its identity. And you will bring it to Hira."

"Shall I undertake this Audacy alone?"

"Are you not capable? Despite your promise to the Council?"

"I am not your enemy, Ilea."

Ilea shrugged the words aside, refusing to acknowledge the Council's revolt.

"I can spare Sinnia."

Arian knew she meant it as a punishment for Sinnia, so she tested Ilea's resolve.

"Psalm would be of greater use on an Audacy such as this."

"That is not for you to decide." Ilea's voice was harsh. "The Black Khan has also offered his assistance."

She motioned to Rukh. He tipped his elegant head to one side, studying the woman before him. Arian faced him squarely. He was the reason for the Council's insurrection: it was time he answered for it instead of Arian.

"How did you come across the Bloodprint?"

His thin lips sketched a smile.

"A spy from the northland brought it to Ashfall."

The seat of the Black Khan with its dissolute court.

"Do you understand what I'm telling you?"

Arian focused on his words.

"The Bloodprint came to you from the northland." Her voice faltered. "Do you mean to say *all* of the legend is true? It comes from Task End, the Stone City behind the Wall? There's no way behind the Wall, we've known this for centuries. We don't even know—" She broke off. She had just remembered the rest of the Bloodprint's legend. Her lips became numb.

"What of the Bloodless?" she whispered. A confederacy of scholars had guarded the Bloodprint through the ages, handing down a legacy of commentaries on the Claim. They were called the Bloodless, ascetics who renounced the pleasures of earthly life.

No one had ever seen the Bloodless. No one had witnessed their arcane rituals. If the Bloodprint was ever under threat in Task End, they were said to spirit it away to their safehold.

"You said the Bloodprint was brought to you by your spy," Arian said. "How could he have breached the sanctuary of the Bloodless?"

Even an Oralist of the highest repute would have little chance of discovering that safehold. And if she did, she would still have to face down the Bloodprint's guardians.

How could a spy of the northland have been worthy of such knowledge? How would he have discovered the safehold?

The Black Khan's response was curt.

"I did not send rabble after the Bloodprint. The man who discovered it had certain skills."

"Then where is he now?"

For the first time, he hesitated. His eyes flicked away from hers, and she knew he had considered withholding the truth before he decided against it.

"He was . . . confronted . . . by the Bloodless. Then he disappeared."

Arian took in the words. And took another breath.

Very quietly, she said, "How can you expect that I would fare any better?"

A hint of sympathy warmed his eyes.

"You will not be seeking the Bloodprint on your own. My men will find you in Marakand."

"Is that where the Bloodprint rests? Is that where its safehold is?"

His black gaze dwelt on her face, reading more than she knew, appreciating the use he could make of her. This time his answer was firm.

"No. They will take you to Black Aura Scaresafe."

Arian recoiled from the words. At her obvious anguish, the waters of the All Ways receded, leaving a pall of dread in their wake.

Black Aura was a place of untold horror—it was ruled by a tyrant whose infamy was eclipsed only by his savagery. He was known as the Authoritan, and Black Aura was his capital.

When she flinched at the name, the Black Khan murmured, "Come, I hadn't heard you were faint of heart."

"Yet you wouldn't choose to make the journey in my stead."

He laughed at that, his laughter beguiling.

She took a moment to examine his words. She could almost fathom an Audacy that would take her to Task End—the thought of an Audacy to Black Aura paralyzed her with fear.

"After the wars of the Far Range, the Bloodprint was preserved at a Task End scriptorium," he explained. "It was the Authoritan who ordered its transport to Black Aura—as he would have done when it was recaptured."

"Then why do I go to Marakand?"

"I have men in Marakand who will guide you further."

"But Marakand lies behind the Wall. How am I to breach it?"

And now she turned back to Ilea, wondering. What did the High Companion seek here? If she could discard the power of the Sacred Cloak so lightly, yielding it to a man she scarcely knew and could not trust, what would she do with the Bloodprint? How would she use its power if she was at odds with the Council?

Did the Bloodprint represent deliverance or deception?

There were only four among them who would be able to read it, even if by some fortuitous working of fate, Arian was able to find it. Herself, Half-Seen, Ash, and Ilea.

And why would the Black Khan help them? Solely for the sake of the Sacred Cloak?

She raised her eyes to his face.

"You do not seek the Bloodprint for yourself, Excellency? You were the one who thought to—intercept it."

Thief, her eyes called him. And liar, as well.

"Rukh," he reminded her.

She pretended to soften. "Rukh, then. You said you have proof of the Bloodprint. Are you able to read the Claim? Is it true you were schooled in the High Tongue?"

A glimmer of amusement in his eyes suggested he fully understood the things she hadn't expressed, her private dismissal of his character.

"I'm not as fluent as the Companions of Hira." He made a small bow to Ilea. "But neither am I ignorant."

No, Arian thought. He wouldn't be. And he'd evaded the more important question. She returned to it.

"You do not expect to retain the Bloodprint, if I am able to retrieve it?"

"If you are able to retrieve it, all of Khorasan will be at your feet."

"That is not why I pursue it."

It was important to her that she convince him of this, though she couldn't have said why.

His eyes narrowed, as if he'd grown tired of her.

"A Companion who does not seek power, perhaps because she wields it so wholly." There was a caustic note in his voice. "The Bloodprint doesn't matter to me. I have taken the Cloak as payment, it will serve me well enough."

His words challenged her to deny him.

Arian didn't think twice.

"It isn't a prize to be bartered." She turned to Ilea, prepared to risk the High Companion's wrath. "And the Cloak isn't yours to cede. It belongs at Hira. We are its rightful guardians."

An indefinable expression crossed Ilea's face.

"It was the price I paid for the Black Khan's counsel. A counsel we desperately need." There was a bitter edge to her voice. "You've been away too long, in pursuit of your misguided quest. I've had other priorities at Hira." She made an impatient gesture with her hand. "Either accept your Audacy, or refuse it. I will not countenance further debate."

Why not? And then realization struck Arian. For all of her discouragement of Arian's efforts with the slave-chains, Ilea had *expected* Arian to bring the Cloak to Hira. How else could she have known to make her bargain with Rukh?

She had *known* Arian would seek it. And she had meant to trade it away.

She was swamped by a feeling of grief. How had she and Ilea come to this point?

"Why do you look so betrayed? You chose to pursue the Cloak for your own ends. I understood it would serve a larger purpose."

"What purpose?" Arian whispered.

"The defence of Hira. The defence your actions made necessary."

"My actions?" Arian echoed the words without understanding their meaning.

Ilea's response was cruel. She had found a way to strike back.

"Yes, *your* actions. Your unceasing war against the slave-chains has put the Citadel at risk. The One-Eyed Preacher brings his war to Hira. And when he comes, the Citadel *will* fall."

Arian blanched at the words. Was the High Companion right? Had she brought destruction to the Citadel? When everything she treasured was at Hira?

"No," she said, grief in her voice. "That cannot be true."

The Black Khan murmured something to Ilea, and the waters of the All Ways resumed their careful dance. Ilea crossed her arms, pressing both hands to her circlets. She waited impatiently for Arian to mimic the gesture.

"This is not an Audacy to undertake only as it suits you. Our very survival is at stake—the lives of the Companions, the sanctity of the scriptorium, the Citadel itself. Will you accept this Audacy? Or does your courage forsake you at the outset of the war?"

This isn't the outset.

I've been waging this war for a decade.

At too great a cost, she now realized. But Arian accepted the Audacy's rites. The time for dissent had passed. She had no choice but to seek out the Bloodprint.

Or face the end of the world.

10

ARIAN WAS TIRED TO HER BONES. SHE STOOD BEFORE HER WRITING DESK in the lowest chamber of the Citadel, a section of Hira's scriptorium reserved for her personal reflection. A manuscript lay open on the table, and though she knew she should savor the time she'd been given to read, she wished for the peace of a dreamless sleep, where the thoughts that occupied her mind were comforting thoughts of her mother. Her kind face, soft with the joy of knowing herself beloved, wise and patient with age and experience, radiant with the essence of the Claim.

Arian's mother had taught Arian everything she knew of the spirit that breathed beneath the forbidden language, the reason she believed in the Claim at all.

And though she was no further forward in her quest, the Claim had kept Arian safe.

Mother, she thought. *I do not know how to summon my courage. Ilea was right to judge me. I carry the weight of a ruinous future, even as I fail to understand the past.*

She'd spent months riding across a desolate landscape, risking the life of a friend she loved in what she told herself was the pursuit of a higher calling, but which she knew in her bones was something else.

I am lost, Mother. Lost without you all.

And no matter how I search, I cannot find my sister.

She was tormented by thoughts of Lania, taken from Arian too soon. She remembered her sister's face, the luxury of her beauty, her youthful self-assurance. The gentle forbearance as Arian had followed her from room to room of their home, through their private scriptorium.

Like Arian herself, Lania had loved to read, she had been a student of the Claim under the tutelage of their parents. But when Arian had recited the Claim in her turn, Lania's eyes had lit with a spark of admiration and something more, something Arian had never been able to quantify.

As the Claim surged to life in Arian's throat, Arian's mother would look to their father with quiet pride, visitors would call at the scriptorium to meet the children of the conservators who were scholars of the Claim. They would listen to Arian's recitation with astonishment, wonderment in the glances they exchanged with her parents, while Lania stood by, her beauty eliciting another kind of wonder, as she studied, listened, observed her younger sister.

Arian learned a new word, a word she heard frequently in the presence of her parents' friends—*linguist*.

"This is the one," they would say. "This is the one you must send."

And Lania would smile and press her hand when Arian protested she would never leave their parents' home, or the comfort and love of her brother and sister's companionship. She couldn't imagine a scriptorium greater than their own, or a deeper warmth than she felt from the friends of her parents, who came to study the manuscripts and to share their own knowledge. Kind-eyed men and women who spoke with dignity, their fingers tracing over fragile parchments, yet all of them falling quiet when Arian recited verses of the Claim.

She learned it was a kind of magic she possessed, a magic that won her the loyalty of a new circle of friends.

She hadn't known then that her enemies would soon outstrip her friends in number, her parents and brother lost, her sister stolen from her.

But where? Where had they taken Lania? What use had the Talisman found for her?

And as always, when she came to this question, she refused to think beyond the present moment, the present task. She couldn't bear to imagine the truth, Lania broken and used.

One day, there would be a reckoning of her loss. Her injuries were personal, deep-rooted—they required the justice of an accounting; the breaking of the slave-chains was the merest restitution. Slave handlers, Talisman, book-burning Immolans—Arian had felled them all, taking the measure of her enemies. Waiting for the day she would stand before the Preacher, her circlets ablaze on her arms.

But even that was not enough. She owed more to herself, to Sinnia, whose loyalty was an unlooked-for gift, friendship in a time when few would dare to be counted as friends.

She thought of the man who had trespassed their Council.

When the reckoning came, would he prevail as enemy or friend?

"What brings such sadness to your eyes?"

Arian whirled around. As if she had conjured him from her thoughts, the Black Khan stood at the door to the scriptorium, still attired in the Sacred Cloak. He had loosened the silver collar at his throat, and had a look of rakish dishevelment.

"You shouldn't be here."

There should have been guards on the other side of the door. She suspected Rukh had persuaded them away.

He nodded at the manuscript unfurled upon her table.

"My gift to you. I brought it with me from Ashfall. I thought a linguist of your caliber would find something to admire in it. Tell me, what did you think?"

Arian brushed a hand over her forehead.

"I haven't read it yet."

"No," he agreed. "You were lost in your thoughts. Are you worried about your Audacy? Or do you worry over what happened at the Council?"

Her generous mouth tightened. The Audacy of a Companion was a thing closely guarded, shared only with those the Companions relied on. And she would never speak of the Council's deliberations before an outsider.

"We are not on such terms that I would confide my thoughts."

He raised a winged brow at her.

"What offends you most, First Oralist? My transgression of the Council, or my trespass upon your privacy?"

His dark eyes glittered in the glow of the candles. Arian's retort was swift.

"That you set your hands on the Sacred Cloak, when you had no authority to do so."

He moved closer, the folds of the Cloak rustling in the silence of the scriptorium. When he was at her side, he dropped his voice.

"Where would you have me set them, then?"

Their eyes met, his dark gaze intimate and searching. He was standing so close that his lips were a whisper's breath from hers. She had only to raise her chin and her mouth would be brushing his. She lowered her head instead, murmuring the words in the vicinity of his collarbone.

"Your overtures are unwelcome. Just as they were at the Council."

"Are they, First Oralist?" He touched a finger to the pulse at her throat. "And yet, you are not indifferent."

He raised a hand to her hair in a sudden gesture. Arian ducked at the unexpected movement. Surprised, he let his hand drop.

"You have no need to fear me," he said.

She shook her head at what her actions had betrayed.

"I thought you meant to strike me. It seemed you would at the Council."

He frowned at the explanation.

"I am many things, First Oralist, but never—for my sins—an abuser of women." He hesitated. "Do you rank me among the Talisman? Have my actions earned such a judgment?"

She heard the regret in his voice and relented.

"I do not know you, Prince of Khorasan."

A hint of devilry lit his eyes. "We could rectify that without difficulty."

He was making it clear that he wanted her. And if her heart had not been encumbered, she might have found herself attracted to him in turn. But there was Daniyar to consider. There would always be Daniyar.

The Black Khan seemed to read her thoughts.

"Is it the Cloak that comes between us? Or is it someone else?"

Arian parried the question.

"The High Companion seemed to compel your interest at the Council."

A wicked smile shaped his lips.

"Do you find our congress disturbing?"

"I question your true motives."

"She's a beautiful woman, as are you."

Arian's response was dry. "And is it beauty that brings you to the Citadel? Or is it the Sacred Cloak?"

Unable to help herself, she touched a hand to the Cloak, tracing its folds with her fingers. She inhaled the scent of honey and closed her eyes. The messenger of the One—the man whose Cloak this was—had loved the taste of honey.

And in that moment it was too much—the loss, the sorrow, the endless conflict with Ilea, the wonder of the Cloak—and tears sprang to her eyes. How much this Cloak would have meant to Daniyar. But Daniyar had chosen not to follow her. He'd sworn never to cross Hira's threshold.

The Black Khan mistook her tears.

"Do you find me so contemptible that it pains you to see me wear the Cloak?"

Arian shook her head. How could she possibly answer?

" The Cloak is a sacred trust. I didn't risk its purchase for you."

His rejoinder was soft. "You said you wore the Cloak in Candour. Do you see yourself as the bearer of that trust?"

Arian looked up at him, the tears magnified in her eyes.

"In what way do you find me unworthy? Other than that I'm a woman?"

The words were not a lamentation. They demanded an accounting—from the Black Khan, from every Talisman slave master whose slave-chains she had disrupted, from all the men of Khorasan—from the One-Eyed Preacher himself.

He seemed to understand the nature of her demand. His face became thoughtful. He reached down for her hands, covering them with his own. It was an intimacy she had encouraged by raising her hand to the Cloak.

The warmth of his touch seared her skin.

"These delicate hands are deceptive. How much blood have they shed?"

Her face became pinched.

"Enough," she said. "Too much, I fear."

He took pity on her, admitting, "Neither are mine unsullied."

She found herself looking at his hands, powerful and elegant. And then she glanced up again, her breathing harsh in her chest. His smile had a sensual edge to it. His black eyes were bewitching—she felt drugged by his allure. And she wondered at the nature of his power—or whether he used his power at all, and she was merely susceptible to his appeal.

He jerked her close. She stopped him, her fingers catching in the pearls that looped below his collar.

"Complete your Audacy," he said. "Then come to my court at Ashfall. Your presence could only enhance it."

"I'm not an ornament to be displayed at your court." She gathered up her pride. "I am First Oralist of Hira. If war is coming, my place will be here."

His dark voice taunted her. "I assure you, your uses would not be merely ornamental."

They stared at each other in silence, the minutes ticking away. Now he touched her hair again, and this time Arian let him. The same hand trailed down her neck to her arm, coming to rest upon her circlet. She shivered against his touch.

He turned her earlier words back on her, tracing the script on her circlet.

"I've had the barest taste of your power. It would serve me well at Ashfall."

And then Arian understood his seduction for what it was.

She disentangled herself from him, the spell between them broken.

He let her go, a smile curling about his lips.

"You think to use me," she said. "But a Companion of Hira is not for any man's use." She clutched a fold of the Sacred Cloak. "I will not add to your ill-gotten gains."

His smile became knife edged. He unlatched the Cloak from his collar and laid it across her desk.

"It was an honorable exchange, Arian, though you choose to deny it. If you thought the Cloak would serve you, imagine the power of the Bloodprint. Imagine what it would be like to read it."

He spoke her name with an unforced intimacy, using language that had lost its meaning.

To read, to write, to behold a manuscript. To feel as much as see the weight of the written word again. To have language as proof, a vocabulary of love and deliverance.

He offered Arian her dreams, her long-forgotten hopes.

And she wished she could trust his words.

"Do you truly cede the Bloodprint to Hira?"

"No." And when her face fell, he held up his signet ring and kissed it. "But I do cede it you."

Was the gesture meant as a promise? Did he pledge his word on his ring?

"Come to my court," he said again. "You would find its gardens tranquil. There is no sight in Khorasan as beautiful." He dipped his regal head. "Unless I am looking at you."

A painful color burned Arian's face. What had she allowed him to believe? She didn't want this—she *couldn't* want it. She needed to turn him away. To turn him against her, if necessary.

"I have been to the court at Ashfall," she said. "As an emissary of the Council."

"No," he denied. "I wouldn't have forgotten."

"You were not Prince of Khorasan then. It was your brother's court."

The words made the Black Khan withdraw, just as she had intended. A look of hauteur settled on his features. Years ago, he'd been imprisoned at the court's Qaysarieh Portal for conspiring against the throne. A conspiracy he'd seen to fruition. Few dared speak of it now.

"I was the legitimate heir," he said flatly. "I have always been Prince of Khorasan."

He reached behind his neck and snapped his collar back into place. The gesture was meant to remind her of who he was.

"You think me unworthy, un*trust*worthy—but what do you know of Ashfall? You know nothing of what I've faced, you know nothing of what faces me now. You may have dismantled slave-chains, but I defend a nation."

His rigid rebuff made Arian ashamed.

"My lord—"

He held up a hand.

"Don't apologize—you wouldn't mean it." He nodded at her desk. "The manuscript I gave you as a gift—it's a history of the Oralists." His anger abated slightly. "A history of your family. It's why I risked its safety on the road."

He gathered up the Cloak and left the scriptorium without looking back.

Both relieved and regretful, Arian let him go.

11

Psalm met them at the stables. A gray-haired woman in her fifties with a no-nonsense manner about her, she separated Arian from Sinnia, taking her aside into one of the stalls of the khamsa.

"What road do you take?" And before Arian could respond, she said, "Do not take the road to the north. We've sent emissaries to the Wall before this. None have returned." Her face grim, she added, "I would not wager they were captured by the Authoritan."

Aghast, Arian asked her, "What are you saying? The trouble was here at Hira?"

Psalm waited for a patrol of the Citadel Guard to pass by the stables before answering.

"You've been away too long. There are deceptions here you know little of."

"There are always deceptions with Ilea, but why would she send emissaries of Hira into a trap? What end could that serve, when we ourselves are vulnerable?"

Psalm's response was sharp.

"Have you encountered any members of the Guard that you trust since your arrival at Hira? Any of the senior captains?"

Arian frowned. "None."

Psalm nodded. "*They* are the ones she sends to the north. The Citadel Guard is made up of new recruits."

"What do you suspect, Psalm? What's happening at Hira?"

The older woman paused, looking beyond Arian's shoulder to where Sinnia had the horses saddled for departure.

"The scriptorium still has its dedicated guard. *Our* friends. But everything else is changing. We no longer retain control over our private chambers. Ilea says this is for our protection, but where does she find her new recruits?"

Arian shook her head. Psalm was right. She'd been away from the Citadel too long.

And now I'm being sent away once more . . .

"She claims some of the new guards have deserted from the Talisman."

"But you don't believe her."

Psalm shrugged. "It's the others who concern me more."

"What others?"

"The ones who came from Ashfall. The ones who accompanied the Black Khan . . . but did not leave with him."

"This wasn't his first visit to the Citadel?"

A wry smile twisted Psalm's mouth.

"It's the first time he addressed the Council, but whatever interest he demonstrated in you, his assignations with Ilea have been frequent and private. He was *expecting* you to deliver the Cloak."

"They're working together," Arian said, her suspicions confirmed.

"They're planning something for the Bloodprint, as well." Psalm motioned at Sinnia. "Don't tell Sinnia you know this. Ilea sends her with you for a reason. Arian—" For a moment, the Citadel's brilliant tactician seemed lost for words. "If you do find the Bloodprint, you must think carefully before you bring it to Hira. I cannot say what Ilea intends for it."

Arian drew a shaky breath.

"If the Talisman advance on Hira, the Bloodprint is our only hope. Surely, *that* is Ilea's intent."

"Perhaps."

"Has she instructed you to prepare the Citadel's defence?"

Psalm looked weary.

"Yes. But she chooses allies I do not trust. These new recruits, for example."

Arian had similar misgivings about the motives of the Black Khan. Another worry occurred to her.

"Then are the manuscripts in the scriptorium safe?"

Across the courtyard from the stables, Arian caught sight of a silver-white shadow that moved between the palm trees, something stealthy in the movement.

Psalm jerked her chin at the hidden figure.

"Ash will make sure of it. She's with us on this."

But Arian didn't know what *this* was. The betrayal of Hira? A plot of the Black Khan's contrivance, or the genuine plan to defend the Citadel of Hira from the Talisman assault?

"What of the Citadel?"

"Leave that to me," Psalm said. "I won't allow us to be caught by surprise."

Arian tried to find that reassuring. She thought of Ash hiding in the shadows and pressed Psalm's sturdy arm—the arm that had always defended the Citadel.

"Don't let anything happen to Ash," she said. "If we can't trust Ilea, we have no one else as rooted in the Claim. If I do find the Bloodprint, Hira will need her."

A cold smile settled on Psalm's lips, her eyes sharp and canny within the hood she raised over her gray hair.

"They'll have to go through me to get to Ash."

She rested her hand over Arian's.

"Do you think the Black Khan lied? Does the Bloodprint exist?"

For the briefest moment, Arian detected a trace of wonder in the eyes of the battle-hardened tactician, the Citadel's foremost General.

Her reply was soft.

"My mother always told me it did."

Psalm cleared her throat.

"Then we can still change the future. Take the eastern road, but watch your back."

There were rumors that the wars of the Far Range had laid waste to a wide swath of territory that fell between the borders of Khorasan and North Khorasan. Whatever plague had devastated those lands, the Wall had been built to prevent a second encroachment. The men who guarded its battlements were a combat-hardened force known as the Ahdath, warriors of the north. They had never given quarter, nor did their master permit them to surrender.

The eastern road through Hazarajat would take them to the mountains, through passes that would be snowbound for another three months. It scaled impossible heights to reach the fertile valley that bounded the Authoritan's territory on the eastern part of its border. Once they struck north into the Authoritan's lands, Arian and Sinnia would trek west to Marakand, a city north of the Wall, in the hope that some small part of the Black Khan's tale was true. And that a defence of Hira was possible.

As they rode down the ramparts of the Citadel, across the moat that provided its first defence, Arian didn't look back. The countryside ahead would be a mixture of snow-covered plains and dark, rutted tracks, steep brown defiles interspersed with infrequent traces of pasture. They would find peasant farmers and their livestock, as well as stray dogs from a stock known as mastiffs, partly wild, partly hungry for human companionship. All the while, the air would be bright and cold, the sunlight harsh. But the people of Hazarajat would be friendly, she reminded herself.

And that would be something to set against the miseries of the past year, and the greater losses that had preceded it.

Arian's pale eyes tracked the flight of a falcon across the thin, white line of a sky too impoverished even for clouds.

So Ilea watches over us. Or just watches us.

Psalm's warning echoed through her thoughts.

"You don't like her, do you?" Sinnia asked, at her side.

They had left the Citadel behind them in the distance. Ahead on the road, there was silence and muddied snow, and a thin green line that wound ahead. The river. Flowing down to Hira from the east, filled with dirt and debris, well above its seasonal levels. The winter had been long, the snowmelt abundant. The road would continue to climb until they reached the Ice Kill. When they could climb no higher, she would send the khamsa back to Hira.

"My relationship with the High Companion has never been easy," Arian said. "We may want the same things, but we see the world in different ways."

"She is young to serve as High Companion, but I've never doubted her wisdom."

"Nor I. I doubt only her motives."

Sinnia urged her mount forward over a patch of tricky ground, where stones had loosened under the hard crunch of snow.

"Do you? Are you sure it was Ilea's motives that preoccupied you during the Council?"

Arian glanced at her friend.

"Speak your mind. I'm not likely to guess what you're hinting at."

"She is young and much too beautiful. She is also something of an exotic, seeing as we have never seen a woman of the Far Range before, nor had reason to believe that any person from beyond the Boundary might have the smallest knowledge of the Claim, let alone rise to become the High Companion. Before Ilea, you were the senior member of the Council, and the most respected. You must have noticed how the Black Khan treated her."

A sly note crept into Sinnia's voice. Arian frowned, shading her eyes against the attenuated light of the sun. A short distance ahead, a shallow line of blue wedged itself against the horizon.

"The Black Khan is nothing to me."

Sinnia laughed aloud. "Isn't he? He is not so beautiful as your friend from the tavern, but certainly there is a majesty to him, a sleekness. When you stepped forward to the All Ways, he was no longer thinking of Ilea. He touched you."

"To stop me from falling."

"The way it looked to me, he would have taken any excuse at all to touch you."

Something twisted inside Arian. Rukh's image rose in her mind, the dark hair, the hooded gaze, the insinuating voice.

"You said yourself he was dangerous."

Sinnia reached over and squeezed Arian's shoulder, her gold circlet catching the light as she moved. Her glance said she was well aware the Black Khan had overstepped his bounds, but she teased Arian, anyway.

"Dangerous men are the only ones worth knowing. Witness your beautiful friend."

"Never mind any of that, Sinnia. What dances against the wind, up ahead? There, do you see it?"

The blue line Arian had mistaken for the lower edge of the horizon shifted against the wind. It was heading toward them, accompanied by a sound unmistakable in its harshness. The repetitive fall of the lash.

A slave-chain. Not more than an hour distant from the Citadel.

These were the lands of the Council of Hira. Arian knew the eastern towns had been taken, but that was in the south of the country. Not here, not in the territory that stretched from Hira to the roof of the world.

Ilea had been telling her the truth.

"Ride!" she urged Sinnia. "They'll see us long before we can reach them. We must use the Claim before they can disarm us."

Sinnia caught at her horse. "Arian! We cannot risk the Audacy. We can take the High Road by the river to circumvent the slavers."

She flinched from Arian's incredulous glare.

"I am not leaving the women of a slave-chain to its misery. Follow me, as you choose."

Safanad streaked ahead like the wind for which she was named. Sinnia followed without a second thought.

Where you ride, I ride, she had once said.

And that summed up her entire history with Arian. Sinnia might disagree, but she would never turn away from the woman she admired with her whole heart, the woman she considered her sister.

As she rode, she could see that Arian had forecast the danger correctly.

The Talisman guards were waiting for them. Half a dozen armed men barricaded themselves behind the women whose chains were now staked to the ground beneath the snow. Sinnia's arrows were useless. She could not strike without risking the lives of the women. The strategy was designed to engage them in close combat, where they thought the Companions would be helpless.

Arian rode ahead at a furious pace, standing in her stirrups, her dark hair streaking behind her like a banner of war. Her sword was braced in her right hand, and as she descended upon the slave-chain, the women let out a terrified wailing. They hadn't heard of the mystic rider freeing women from slavery across the length and breadth of Khorasan. Arian didn't wait to use her sword. As she reached the slave caravan, the Claim took shape in her mouth.

A terrible pronouncement issued from her throat, language leaping like flame over the huddled mass of women, a wall of sound that battered the soldiers of the Talisman, sundering their shields.

Two of the men fell dead at the sound. A third and fourth scrambled into the distance, their booted feet struggling for purchase on the snow. These two fell to Sinnia's calculated aim, their human shields no longer preventing the use of her bow. The remaining two stood their ground.

They were tall and well built, their beards close-cropped, swords in one hand, short daggers in the other, and their strategy was to unseat the woman who descended upon them like a cataclysm.

Safanad danced away from a knife thrust at her foreleg, a gesture that enraged Arian further. Words ignited like sparks from her tongue.

"When the sun is wrapped up in darkness, when the stars fall dispersing, when the mountains are erased and the oceans are aflame, then will you know everything you have wrought."

One of the men staggered to his knees, his hands covering his ears. Sinnia leapt from her horse to engage the other. Her wickedly curved scimitar balanced to her strength, she dodged the frantic thrusts of the man's sword, her blade slicing through his sternum. He fell to the ground without another word.

Sinnia rode to the front of the caravan. She leapt down from her horse to unstake the iron shafts that secured the slave-chain. As she touched the ground, an arrow whistled through the air.

It caught her in the shoulder.

"Sinnia!"

Arian wheeled about. The surviving Talisman guard bounced to his feet. Instead of using his sword, he flung a loose length of cloth around Arian's throat and tightened it. She fell to her knees before him. His broad fist struck a blow that wrenched her head to the right. Moving fast, he gagged her first, then secured her wrists and ankles.

"Boy!" he shouted up the bend in the road. "Bring the irons!"

Another guard and an undernourished boy descended on the caravan from their hiding place in the brush that covered the bend in the road, and Arian realized the men had staged an ambush.

Pinned to the ground by an arrow, Sinnia lay defenceless. All she could do was watch.

The head guard joined the caravan, distinguished by an aigrette on his turban. He kicked at Sinnia with his boot, moving past her to Arian.

His whip struck, but Sinnia was not the target. It was the boy at his heels with leather cuffs on his wrists.

"Hazara," the man spat at him. "Kill the black."

He tossed a dagger to the boy, whose blue eyes were set in folds in a face marked with bloody welts. The boy's nose was running; he wiped it with the back of his hand, the dagger gripped precariously in the other.

Sinnia recognized him at once. It was the boy they had spared from the slave-chain in Candour.

Stumbling toward her, he reached down with the dagger.

Sinnia brushed his feint aside with her unpinned arm, feeling the painful sting of blood against her palm. She steeled herself to meet the next blow. Instead, the boy reached out a tentative hand to her cloak.

The commander of the Talisman guard strode toward him, flicking his lash against the boy's face.

"Worthless Hazara, I'll do it myself."

The boy pointed to the gold circlets bound on Sinnia's arms.

The Commandhan slowed.

"Is that gold? Bring those to me, then kill her."

He flicked the boy with his whip again, jolting him out of his thrall. The boy he had called by the race name Hazara was careful not to touch Sinnia's arm. He moved the circlet sideways so its leather tie was invisible to the Talisman commander. Then he yanked at it. As expected, the circlet didn't shift.

The Commandhan lashed him again. Hardened to it, the boy yanked at the bracelet a second time.

"Use the dagger I gave you."

"It's not wide enough," the boy said, in his own dialect.

"Then use my sword, you useless piece of filth."

He thrust it into the boy's hands.

It was the opening the boy had been waiting for. He belted the dagger at his waist, gripped the Commandhan's sword in his palm, whirled about in a sudden, quick motion, and swiped the sword across the Commandhan's throat.

Taken by surprise, the man jerked forward onto the snow, falling dead.

Sinnia called a command to her horse. The boy leapt into the khamsa's saddle, the horse uneasy beneath his attempts at control. With a bloodcurdling cry, he launched himself at the guard who stood over Arian. Swinging sideways from the saddle, he drove the sword into the man's arm.

The Talisman guard staggered back but didn't fall, wrenching the boy from the saddle, beating him down from the horse.

The boy lay still in the snow.

"Don't touch him!" Sinnia screamed. Arian watched, helpless. *Use the Claim,* her eyes pleaded with the younger Companion. Sinnia tried. Her voice was weak as it left her throat.

"I warn you about the blazing Fire. None burn there except the wretched."

It wasn't powerful enough to stop the man, but his movements were sluggish as he kicked the boy over with his boot. He raised his sword for the killing stroke.

The boy opened his blue eyes and waited.

When the Talisman guard leaned down, the Commandhan's dagger in the boy's hand darted its way to his neck. Rolling over in the snow, the boy evaded the man's body as it fell. For a moment, he lay still, his breathing harsh. Then he struggled to his knees and cut Arian free, trembling as he loosened the gag from her mouth.

"Hazara," Sinnia called. "Help me."

The boy flew back to her side. Bracing his knee on Sinnia's back, he yanked the arrow from her shoulder.

Blood flowed from the wound. Sinnia staggered to her feet.

Arian called out to the women.

"Are there healers among you? Can any of you aid my friend? Here." She gave the boy the loose cloth she had freed from her neck. "Hold this against the wound, it will staunch the blood."

A little dazed, the boy took the cloth from Arian's hands. Arian moved to free the women, using the Commandhan's keys to unfasten their shackles. As Sinnia had done with the last caravan, she ripped the netting from the women's faces as she raced down the length of the chain.

"Please. We are Companions of Hira. We need a healer."

She knew the women would be frightened. Revealing themselves as practitioners of the healing arts earned the death penalty from the Talisman.

"Please," she said again, reading one face after another. "I will allow no harm to come to you."

She heard the familiar gasps of wonder. Her circlets glinted in the harsh light off the snow.

"Whoever does an atom's weight of good will see it."

A murmur of amazement whispered through the caravan.

An older woman with fine lines around her eyes and mouth raised her hand. She came forward, her body moving as if still weighted by the chains. She stared at Arian rapt, her mouth agape, her eyes uncomprehending at the sight of the golden circlets.

"Companion," she breathed. "Can it be true? Have you been sent to deliver us?"

"If you continue down this road, you will soon be at Hira. But first, will you help my friend? *Can* you help her?"

The woman's sense of dignity and purpose reasserted itself.

"My tools were taken by our captors. They tied them to one of the pack horses. If the boy will help me?"

The boy wasted no time. He searched through the packs for the healer's belongings. He ran to Sinnia's side, eager to be of help.

Worry in every syllable, Arian addressed the women of the caravan.

"The Talisman have twelve pack horses here. If you leave behind their supplies, riding two to each horse, you will be at the

Citadel well before noonrise. Tell the Council of Hira that you have been sent to them for sanctuary by the First Oralist."

A second wave of shock quivered through the caravan.

"The Claim is merciful!"

"The First Oralist walks among us."

"The Talisman will fall."

"There is hope for Khorasan."

"Our time has come."

Arian wished she could share their hope.

12

She could promise these women nothing. Except that Ilea would not turn them away. Even if the High Companion sought to move against Arian, her retaliation would not take this form. Not with the entire Council assembled at Hira. Not with the Black Khan in residence.

Ilea would wish to appear bountiful. She would set her stratagems aside to demonstrate this, though doing so would be another device that served her purpose. It was not upon Ilea's kindness that Arian relied. Zeb and Mask were at the Citadel. In their lands, they were protectors of the innocent. They would defend the women of the caravan with their lives. Ilea would be able to do no less.

Arian waited as the healer bound up Sinnia's shoulder.

"Will my friend be able to travel?"

It was as close as she could come to voicing her deep sense of loss at having to part with Sinnia.

The healer nodded. Her name was Ghotai.

"Do you travel the eastern road?" she asked Arian.

"Yes. We thought to take shelter in Hazarajat, the Hazara's lands."

Ghotai shook her head. "We came by that road. The Hazara's lands are forfeit to the Talisman. Their reach has extended north, well beyond Candour. It would be madness to take that road. No one ventures outside their villages without a Talisman escort."

More proof that Arian had been in the south too long.

If the Talisman had taken Hazarajat, how long could the Citadel hope to hold out?

"There is no other way."

Ghotai hesitated. At her feet, the Talisman commander's blood snaked a path through the snow. The sight of it seemed to hearten the healer.

"I served as a healer in Hazara lands for years. The Talisman do not deem them worthy of enslavement. Instead, their people have been massacred, their villages burned. If you are heading east, there is only one place of safety, and only one road by which to reach it. You must take the High Road."

Arian frowned. "I don't understand. The High Road *is* our path to the east."

"I do not mean the pass through the mountains. You may not have lived in this country, so perhaps you do not know its names. The High Road is a name given also to the river. Perhaps you know it as the Tejen. If you take the river, it is said you will find refuge under the Turquoise Mountain, in Firuzkoh."

"The frozen city? You speak of a place out of legend or myth. No one has set foot there in living memory."

Ghotai touched a hand to one of Arian's circlets.

"I swear it by the tahweez. Firuzkoh exists, and the river will take you there. You will find it at the junction where two rivers meet."

"Then why have the Talisman not taken it? If, as you say, they've taken the lands to the east?"

"They haven't been able to find it. To enter the wrong pass is to be lost forever. But at the meeting place of two rivers, Firuzkoh will reveal itself to you. If I knew more, I would tell you more, Companion. But we are a cloistered people now, trapped by the Talisman, sealed inside our history."

Arian did not doubt her sincerity. The woman's lined face and tired eyes spoke of the horrors she had witnessed.

"Do you know where the caravan was heading?"

The healer shook her head. "They spoke to us only to beat us. The road was difficult and dry, with little in terms of provision. All I could tell is that we were headed north."

The Wall was to the north.

But even the Talisman would not dare the Wall.

Or the Plague Lands held off by the Wall.

So where were they going? Arian found she had no answers.

"May peace be with you, my sister."

"And with you, Companion. May you find safe passage into the mountains, if you dare to travel at all."

Arian and Sinnia thanked her.

The Companions helped the women of the caravan onto the horses, apportioning the caravan's food and water among them, then called the khamsa back to their sides.

Throughout this exercise, the boy with blue eyes stood by, quiet under the care of the healer, watchful as Arian spoke in conference with Sinnia.

"You saved my life, Hazara," Sinnia said. "I shall not forget it."

"That isn't his name—it's his tribe. Do you have a name of your own?" Arian asked the boy in his own tongue.

He hung his head without answering, the lash mark on his cheeks less vivid under the salve applied by the healer.

"How did you come to be on this road, recaptured by the Talisman? So close to the Citadel?"

Again, the boy did not speak.

"Were you following us?" Arian's voice was gentle. "You said you would serve me blood and loss. Instead, you saved our lives. What kindness can I offer you in turn?"

The boy's head swung up.

"I want to go with you."

Had Arian been on any Audacy but this one, she would have granted the boy's wish. She could have read his hunger for the most meagre affection from as far a distance as Candour.

"I am headed to a dangerous place. I would not risk your life there—it is precious to me."

The boy blinked at the words, wiping his runny nose in a now-familiar gesture. She could see he didn't believe her.

"Will you leave the horses and take the High Road?" he asked without expression.

She saw no harm in telling him the truth.

He kicked at a bloodstained patch of snow with his foot. Instead of boots, he was wearing a pair of threadbare shoes whose stitching had given way.

"The river flows west," he said with a scowl. He pointed at Sinnia. "She is injured, she won't be able to help. Hazara will help you fight the current."

He was telling the truth. And Arian had not stopped to question Ghotai about the river.

"Have you been to the Turquoise Mountain? Do you know how to find the lost city?"

He shook his head. If he had ever been there, the boy had no memory of it.

"If you truly wish to come with us, first you must tell me your name."

With a start of surprise, she saw that the boy was crying. He knuckled his eyes, ashamed, his face flooding with color.

And then Arian realized. The boy had no name. He had never been given a name. Born into slavery, all he'd ever known was the word *Hazara* used as an epithet, a mark of damnation.

She slid from her horse, to stand before the boy until he looked at her.

"I told you that your life is precious to me and I meant it. I would not willingly put you in harm's way, but would you risk yourself at my side? A Companion's journey is not an easy one."

Nothing about this boy's life had been easy.

He nodded, looking from her to Sinnia and back.

"Then you must have a name of your own. You have been loyal to me, so I would give you a noble name. I shall call you Wafa, my loyal friend, if you accept. The choice must be yours."

The boy's bright blue eyes stared through her, his breath ragged in his chest. Two tears slipped from his eyes, leaving tracks on his dusty face.

Arian wiped them away.

A sob escaped the boy's throat.

"Wafa," he said, when he could speak. "I am Wafa and I will be loyal."

13

THE CRAFT THEY FOUND BY THE WATER DIDN'T APPEAR STURDY ENOUGH to combat the roll and pitch of the river that risked overruning its banks. Left moored by a peasant farmer, its flat, wide interior was used to transport livestock from one bank to the other. Cakes of ice had built up around the boat, preventing it from crashing onto the banks.

As there was no other choice, Arian and Wafa loaded the boat with their supplies while Sinnia watched, her arm still throbbing from the Talisman arrow. Before they had left the caravan, Arian had made Wafa exchange his clothes and shoes for new ones from the Talisman's pack horses. Dressed in warm layers, the boy seemed prepared for the chill wind over the river.

When they were settled on the boat, Arian paused to bid the mares of the khamsa farewell.

Safanad nuzzled her palm in acknowledgment.

Arian helped Sinnia into their watercraft, then she and Wafa took up the paddles at the stern of the boat.

"I still think it would have been safer with the horses," Sinnia grumbled.

The boy shook his head but didn't speak.

"Well? Say something if you know anything."

His blue eyes wide, he paddled harder.

"Talisman don't like the water."

As the boat tossed its way against the current, Arian pondered how the boy knew this. The river was narrow and deep, a dense green-brown crowded at its edges with the hard crust of snow, stones and debris bobbing into their path, brought down by snowmelt from the mud-packed hills. A brown-and-green country rose against a wasted sky, the harshness of the landscape also its sole beauty. The cry of a falcon sounded above them. As they made their way east, there were no people or livestock to be glimpsed.

The sun rose to its apex, warming them as they paddled. Arian shrugged off her cloak. Light from her circlets bounced off the hills to cast bright patterns on the water. She applied herself to the task of piloting the boat.

They paddled for several days, with few opportunities for rest.

As the days progressed, Sinnia lay back in the boat, exhausted by pain. Arian and the boy did not speak, nor did the boy complain about the task. Now and again, he would glance at Sinnia's dark face and arms, but if she glanced up, he would wheel back around to the river, embarrassed to be caught staring at her.

The hills on either side became steeper as the river climbed alongside them. And then suddenly they were in the midst of rushing water.

The craft surged from side to side, jarring their bones as it rose before plunging back to the depths. The boat crested and fell a dozen times or more, cracking with each new thrust.

"Hold on!" Arian called to Sinnia. "I think I see a break ahead."

Wavelets of foam began to form on the water. Propelled upward, the boat flew into the air, casting its passengers aloft. Arian and Wafa used the paddles to steady themselves against the pitch, benefiting more from luck than skill.

Each time the boat landed in the river, icy water sprayed its passengers.

By the time the boat rolled ahead into a tranquil pool of green, they were soaked, their teeth chattering. The pool mellowed, joined by a second stream. At the place where the rivers met, a mud-brick tower rose from the headwaters, casting a shadow over the boat.

Wafa steered their craft to the shallow waters at its base. With rope in hand, he leapt to the shore.

"Shorn Rock," he said happily. "This is Shorn Rock."

When you reach the hills known as Shorn Rock, you will find the guardian of the lost city, known as the Golden Finger. Read it well. It will show you the path through the hills.

These were stories of legend, stories her mother had recited to Arian as a child, some of the earliest memories she possessed. The same stories gave rise to the mythology of the Rising Nineteen. Despite the snow and the etiolated sun, there was warmth in the air.

The Golden Finger, the tower of the faithful, the minaret beyond the river.

I might have found this sooner, had I not spent a decade in the Talisman south.

Arian turned back to the boat, helping Sinnia from it before busying herself with supplies. But the tower drew her gaze again. It tilted off its vertical axis, resting upon an octagonal stone base, the tower crafted of ornamented stucco over baked brick. Less than halfway up its burgeoning column, a glazed band of blue ceramics gleamed above the still waters. At the top of the tower, a dull brass lantern could be glimpsed between a company of arches.

The tower was ancient, small flowers turning up their faces in the soft wind at its base. A few sheltered trees flourished in its wake, their leaves rising like a fan and spreading wide.

The tower was structured like a starscope, its four columns tucked inside each other in stages, the widest stage at the base, the narrowest at the top.

Arian pointed to the uppermost band.

The tower was inscribed with the written word in a place safe from the Talisman's reach.

The Companions of Hira read the inscription.

THERE IS NO ONE BUT THE ONE. AND SO THE ONE COMMANDS.

A crumbling calligraphy pronounced other words, names, titles, and ages swallowed by the march of time, but it was the writing beneath the commandment that touched a chord of memory for Arian. A woman's name was written there—the name of the Adhraa—a name that resonated through history, inherent to the Claim, even as the Talisman worked to scrub all other traces of the woman away.

If the name survived on this tower, it meant the lost city was safe.

Arian read the words that told the woman's story, cheered by the small rebellion.

SHE WITHDREW FROM HER FAMILY TO A PLACE IN THE EAST,
KEEPING HERSELF IN SECLUSION.

Much of the writing was chipped away. Lower down, at the base of the tower, a formidable warning faced north.

HOW MANY GENERATIONS WERE DESTROYED BEFORE YOURS?
DO YOU SEE AUGHT OF THEM OR HEAR OF THEM NOW?

Arian sensed the power of the verse. The ground at her feet trembled beneath the eroding force of the rivers. The verse was a bewildering discovery like the Bloodprint itself, a gift to soften a perilous journey, a thing foreordained.

But Arian hadn't known she would take the river. Or that its course would lead her to this place.

She read the band again, memorized the verse.

The last of the light was leaving the sky, the wind rising. It would be difficult to find passage through the hills in the dark. They needed shelter.

"Look," Sinnia said, reading her thoughts. "The tower has two balconies. And look at the lantern at the top. There must be a way in, if someone hung that lantern there."

Arian nodded and took up her pack while Wafa hoisted Sinnia's and his own.

A wooden door was bolted against intruders. Before Arian could stop him, the boy threw his shoulder against it. It didn't move.

"Let me," said Sinnia. She murmured the inward incantation. The door gave way to muffled layers of darkness. They entered cautiously, Arian reading the musty passage as they moved.

The tower smelled of damp and peat, and something else, like candles burned in a ceremony of obeisance. A meagre light filtered through the windows. Ahead, a pair of staircases spiraled up to the balconies.

"This is far enough," Arian said. "We'll be warmer down here."

Camped against the wall, they set out their bedding and built a small fire, the smoke escaping through cracks in the door.

Warm and well-fed, the boy seemed content. Arian prepared a tonic for Sinnia to drink, adding a measure of turmeric and ginger to ease the pain from Sinnia's wound before she changed the dressing.

Wafa stared spellbound at Sinnia's bare shoulder.

"He may be older than we think," Sinnia teased. "He knows how to appreciate a woman."

Wafa flushed. He took another piece of bread, hunching over the fire.

"I'm not sure why we brought him," Sinnia said. "He doesn't keep his hands clean."

"Do not shame him," Arian rebuked her. "He carried your load, he did your share of work. Without him we wouldn't have gained the safety of the river. It was his strength that overcame the High Road."

Sinnia was unabashed. "This country has strange names. In my land, the westward river is called the Tarius. Others know it as Arius."

Arian nodded, resting her back against the minaret's curved wall. "The people of the Aryaward, the southernmost lands, know it as the Horaya. They say the ancient people named it for one of their gods. The people of the Plague Lands called it the Tejen."

Mention of the Plague Lands rattled Sinnia.

"To cross those lands would be to choose death for ourselves."

Dismayed at the thought, Wafa looked from one woman to the other.

"Do not worry, Sinnia. The healer says there is a safe pass through the hills. Come the morning, we will search for it."

"She also said the Turquoise City would rise around it," Sinnia pointed out. "I don't believe in folk tales."

"Don't you? 'She withdrew from her family to a place in the

east,'" Arian quoted. "Some would call the Claim a folk tale, no more than legend—with no proof it existed as the sacred teaching of a people."

Sinnia's dark eyes sparked in the firelight.

"You make a false comparison, Arian. The Claim is like race memory to us. We know who and what we are. When we hear the Claim, we know it for the truth."

"Perhaps." Unwilling to concede, but too weary to argue, Arian turned to Wafa. "Are you still hungry? We have plenty of stores and will hunt as we travel. Look. I brought something special from Hira."

She opened her hand. A yellow-and-pink fruit sat in the middle of her palm.

"Take it," she encouraged Wafa. "Its sweetness will surprise you."

The boy reached for it. His ability to make deft, quick movements without encountering touch was a means of protecting himself. Now his teeth sank into the soft flesh of the apricot, his delight at its taste and texture obvious. He ate with care perhaps because he didn't expect such generosity again.

Arian spoke to Sinnia in a quiet voice.

"How deeply the Talisman have wounded so many."

"The boy is clever. You share the bloodline of Talisman tribes, but he doesn't fear you. He can distinguish between a friend and an enemy. It's the reason he's still alive."

Watching Wafa, Arian wondered what the boy's life had been like before he'd been captured by the slavers. Had he ever had occasion to play, kicking a ball with friends or chasing a kite through the streets?

She didn't think so. He'd known the exigence of killing—he'd killed for her once already. She had no wish to place the same choice before him again, though she knew the quest for the Blood-print would claim something from each of them in time.

And that time would come swiftly. Each moment of delay would cost them.

Wafa watched her across the fire. She smiled at him and, almost as if guilty, he shut his eyes tight, slowly opening them to look at her once more. Arian let him pretend he wasn't watching her and settled in to sleep, puzzling over the verses embellished on the tower, wondering what the morning would bring, and where the Talisman militias were gathered now. How long would it be before they moved against Hira?

Just before her eyes closed, she thought of Daniyar.

14

THE MORNING WAS BITTERLY COLD. SNOW FELL IN THICK, WHITE FLAKES that gilded the eaves of the tower. As Sinnia and Wafa fussed over breakfast, Arian climbed the stairs to the second balcony, seeking a glimpse of the hidden city. The staircase wound about a central pillar, narrow and cramped, sprouting landings at intervals lit up by lunettes. In contrast to the ornamentation of the exterior, the interior walls were a dim yellow brick.

From a tiny window, Arian could make out the ice-covered merging of the rivers, the tower shaking with a subterranean rumble. The plains of Khorasan stretched into the distance, the rugged hills rising in the west, their flanks polished by a diamond-bright snowfall. The path on one side of the river wound upward into blackness. Similar passes, alike in peril, rose from the opposite bank.

If the path to Firuzkoh could be found here, the minaret did nothing to mark it out.

Each conqueror who'd ascended these stairs in hopes of victory must have felt the same disappointment. A quick glance around showed there was no map to the lost city here, no signpost to Firuzkoh. The Golden Finger held its secrets close.

Arian climbed higher to reach the lantern, the narrowness of the staircase pressing against her shoulders, creating a sense of suffocation. It was a relief to reach the pinnacle, the slenderest stage of the starscope, a platform framed by arches, open to the elements. Suspended above the middle of the platform, the lantern hung from an iron rod welded to the tower, its glass surface blank and unvarnished. Arian peered at the lantern in vain. She'd hoped to be guided by further inscriptions.

Even an encrypted inscription.

The thought made Arian smile.

Despite her great reverence for it, much of the Claim was cryptic, unknowable.

As she looked around the ethereal arches, she found the lantern a clumsy thing, immitigable by light. Her hand scraped the bottom of the lantern, the farthest she could reach. She paused. There were grooves in the base of the lantern. It took her several attempts to launch her body close enough to examine the grooves. Disappointed, she realized the grooves formed a handhold designed to lower the lantern, perhaps to protect it from intemperate weather, or to refill it with oil. But the handhold didn't help. The lantern refused to budge, its chain welded to the rod by years of neglect.

After several attempts at shifting the handhold, the brick around the brace began to crumble. The platform shook under Arian's feet. She swiveled round, her hands releasing the handhold. She caught herself on the edge of the staircase, her toes slipping, her fingers catching at the brick. For a moment she was looking straight up, blinded by the light that arrowed down the staircase.

"Arian!" Sinnia called. "Have you hurt yourself?"

Arian didn't answer.

When her eyes refocused, she was able to see to the top of the tower.

A line of script ran around the inside like a ring.
She read it to herself.

HALLOWED IS THE ONE WHO HAS SET UP IN THE SKIES GREAT
CONSTELLATIONS, AND PLACED AMONG THEM A RADIANT LAMP
AND A LIGHT-GIVING MOON.

She looked back at the lantern and in that moment understood.

"I think I know how the Golden Finger will help us. The lantern hangs there for a reason, the verse from the Claim is the clue to its purpose."

Sinnia was right—the Claim was as much part of them as race memory, buried beneath layers of consciousness, secretly held in their cells.

The lantern was the lamp described in the verse.

The moon would make it radiant.

And through the lantern, a path would be struck through the hills, the safe passage into the lost city under the Turquoise Mountain. All they required was moonlight. But she chafed at the passing of time, conscious of Hira's vulnerability at her back.

So she made Sinnia rest while she circled the tower to study its graces. In this remote, inaccessible place, choked off by mountains, there was quiet except for the cries of sparrowhawks and harriers. She found it a soothing accompaniment to her study, this object of beauty molded from mud and clay. The stage of the starscope, closest to the base, was also the most decorated, the decoration divided into vertical panels, bands of inscription forming the borders of the panels. She read to her heart's delight, marveling at the words, daring to trace them over with her fingers. This was the story of a woman, each word intact, the nineteenth chapter glorious and whole.

SHE WITHDREW FROM HER FAMILY TO A PLACE IN THE EAST.

Alone and untouched, except for the presence of a guardian.
Why this story? This *woman?*

The tower had been built long before the wars of the Far Range, and though it cast a long shadow on the river, this story of the most venerated woman of the Claim, in lands under siege by the Talisman, was remarkable to Arian.

She could stand and read the verses forever, the unadorned script more meaningful than any manuscript she'd held in her hands at Hira. The beauty was in the story.

Far out of Arian's reach, the turquoise tiles gleamed in the wintry sun. When she stalked away from the tower some distance, she could read a list of names and titles: the emperor of this valley, the architect who'd built the tower. Here the script was ornamented, magnified, terminating in a dense set of scrolls, a single palmette captured at the center of each.

Its geometric patterns were of surpassing loveliness, stars, flowers, medallions, leaves, palmettes. She returned to the tower, tracing the script again.

A hand moved beside hers, fumbling over the brick.

"What is this?" Wafa asked.

Arian had missed his approach. She smiled down at him, noting that he had cleaned his hands.

"This is writing, Wafa. This is what the Talisman burn. The words pose a danger to the Talisman." His eyes darted about the valley. He didn't understand.

"It's why the Talisman destroy these inscriptions," Arian said. "You see how we are speaking to each other using words? If we wanted to remember what we'd said, or what we thought about anything, this is what we would do. We would make symbols to take the place of our words, we would etch them into stone or paper."

"Paper? Like on the white flag?"

The boy must not have seen a manuscript before.

"The symbol on the Talisman flag is the Bloodprint," Arian told him. "The Bloodprint is a collection of words written down on parchment, sacred words we call the Claim. Have you heard of it?"

He nodded, his blue eyes wary. "The words that killed Talisman? I heard you use them." He touched his fingers to the inscriptions. "Is this—writing—what you used to kill them?" And at her nod, "Then isn't it dangerous to us?"

Arian sighed. How could she explain to a child of Jahiliya— the Age of Ignorance?

"Do you not think that if we wanted to teach each other something of what we knew, what we'd learned through decades of struggle, it would be more dangerous still to take our words away? To steal your words is to silence you, yes, Wafa? Do you wish to be silenced?"

The boy struggled to understand. He picked at the crumbling stucco with a finger. Arian stilled the movement by covering his hand with her own. He held his breath, looking down at their hands.

At last he raised his head, his blue eyes suspiciously bright.

"I want to speak," he said. "I do not want Talisman to stop me."

Arian smiled.

"I don't want them to stop me, either. We are alike in this, you see. As are all the people of the Claim who wish to be heard, who wish to share their knowledge with the world."

She read the verses inscribed in the panels again, testing her memory of them.

"These aren't words that kill," she said to Wafa. "These are verses that gave birth to hope."

It was difficult to wait for nightfall and moonrise so Arian scouted the surround, considered the different passes on the north bank of the river, some with broken ridges, others whose snowbound heights soared and dipped like the humps of dromedaries. There were a dozen different choices she could make, and from those choices ripples would spread, leading them astray, leading them away from the Bloodprint. Any mistake would cost her time necessary to Hira's survival.

The verses on the tower, the verses she had learned from her mother, renewed her determination to find the priceless book. As Wafa stoked the small fire, camped beside Sinnia in the twilight, she thought of Lania.

Though Lania was older by a decade, she had never minded that Arian was the one gifted with the Claim. Arian was the one they spoke of at Hira, the Council endlessly patient, waiting for Arian to join their ranks. Arian was the one the friends of their parents had come to hear recite the Claim. Perhaps their brother had minded it more, withdrawing when visitors came to the house.

But Lania had stayed, listening, encouraging, her hands weaving braids in Arian's hair.

"You will be First Oralist," she would say. "Your name will be spoken in every corner of Khorasan."

Arian had been an anxious child, unwilling to accept a thing predetermined.

"Then I will be alone, without any of you. I don't want to leave, I belong here."

Lania had faced her young sister, her words weighted with warning.

"The Claim is given to few as a charge, fewer still as a gift. You may choose to refuse your gifts, but you will never be safe from them. Hira will be your new home, in time. But you won't be alone, I promise."

She had kissed the top of Arian's head.

"You will be under my care at Hira. That's what they prepare me for—to act in your service."

The words had confused Arian. "But you're older than me."

Lania had laughed.

"I'm your sister, Arian. I'll always be there to protect you."

How much I wish I could have done the same for you.

It's time," Sinnia said, waking Arian from her reverie, giving Arian a moment to gain her bearings.

"You'll watch from outside? In case we can't see the path from above?"

Sinnia nodded. Arian and Wafa rose and climbed one side of the staircase.

The sky was cloudless and clear, stars winking over the mountains to the east, the air spiky with cold. Arian shivered. It was the perfect night for sighting a path, if the light of the moon was meant to strike the lantern. She and Wafa waited in silence. The moon moved over the horizon, a half-formed disc, its light unsullied, breaking against the spine of the mountains.

She could see Sinnia marching away from the tower, a speck of movement on the ground below. Moonlight splayed over the platform through the glass. Arian stood on her toes to follow the angle of the light. Wafa waited for direction.

There was nothing.

The lantern glass shone dully above the stage.

Arian moved around the circle, testing the different angles. Wafa explored the view from the arches. From the ground, Sinnia called up, "There's nothing. No revelation of any kind."

Arian tilted her head back, struggling to make out the ring of inscription.

A RADIANT LAMP AND A LIGHT-GIVING MOON.

Perhaps the lamp referred to the sun instead of the moon. But then what purpose would the lantern serve?

"Let's wait through the night. There must be something we're not seeing."

It was a reasonable plan, and they set themselves to it, hoping to find the way from the valley. The moonlight bounced against Wafa's eyes, silvering them, making them flash for a moment like antique coins.

Arian pushed down a surge of longing.

Why had she sought out Daniyar?

Why had the Silver Mage come to her rescue only to ride away?

Her questions remained unanswered.

The sound of Wafa's chattering teeth distracted her.

"Go down. Fetch Sinnia from outside, too. I'll call you if I see anything."

The boy scowled, shifting himself closer to Arian's warmth, stopping shy of touching her. Arian gathered him close.

"I won't leave you," he said. "Wafa is loyal."

Arian smiled, pressing a kiss to his curls.

"Loyal in this case does not mean shivering to death at the top of this tower. Go down, stay warm. I will need your help in the morning."

She held him for a few minutes more, then nudged him down the staircase.

She waited out the night alone, but the path did not appear.

At sunrise, she was awake, hoping the sun would illuminate what the moon had failed to reveal. Her bones were brittle with cold, her joints stiff. She stretched her limbs, shaking a coating of frost from her hair.

Wafa appeared at the top of the stairs, a metal cup in his hands. She drank the sweet tea he'd brought her, gazing out across the landscape. She spied a set of small ruins climbing the hill just north of the tower, a sight elusive in moonlight.

"Watch the lantern," she told Wafa. "I'm going down to explore."

Sinnia was asleep. Arian let herself out into daylight. The ruins were a short distance from the tower, crumbling blocks of stone, half-smashed, half-drowned by the river, forming a shape and a pattern.

Arian paused beside a shelf of limestone marked with runes.

A sister-script to the language of the Claim, known to the Council of Hira as the Everword. The people of the Everword were people of the Claim. Arian had read their histories at Hira's scriptorium. She was shaken to discover this proof of their existence in the shade of this lost minaret.

She read the markings on the stone.

It was a headstone listing the names of those who had passed in a long distant time, before the wars of the Far Range. The outcropping was a cemetery.

She pocketed one of the smaller stones, trying to understand the place of the tower in geography and history. An Everword cemetery to the north of the tower, and the story of the woman in seclusion inscribed upon the tower itself. How should she interpret the verse at the top of the Golden Finger? She looked up. Wafa was watching her from the platform, a tiny, dark figure poised at the edge of the starscope.

Neither moonlight nor sunlight had given them an answer.

She took the stone to show Sinnia.

"We can't afford to spend another night here," Sinnia said. "The Talisman will be tracking us." She flexed her arm, testing her strength. "It's healing, Arian. Don't linger on my account."

"I share your urgency, but which path would you choose?"

"Something, anything."

"We could stray into a crevasse."

"Shall I scout the path ahead?"

"No," Arian said. "You need to recover your strength. And we must discuss the writing on the tower, there is something here—something prearranged."

Sinnia's lush mouth formed an O.

"What do you mean, prearranged? Do you speak of a thing fated?"

Arian hesitated. "Wafa can scout, if he wishes. Let us work out the meaning of this tower. The verses, the graveyard—they have a purpose. But the key to the mystery is missing."

"Another night is the most we should risk, Arian. Then we must decide."

Arian's answer was diplomatic. She felt the pressure of the Black Khan's intercession, as much as the fear of the Talisman advance. Slave handlers, whipmasters, the lackeys of the ignorant—could they truly bring down the Citadel? But she was reminded that

Daniyar had chosen to live in Candour, keeping the Immolan under surveillance.

She pressed a hand to her forehead.

There were too many questions.

And hidden in this tower, an answer.

15

WHEN SINNIA HAD RESTED ANOTHER NIGHT, THEY CLIMBED TO THE TOP of the tower together. The valley spread below them, the hard-scrabble ground interrupted by the rush of water. The mountains rose on all sides in scarred and jagged lines. A whistle sounded from Sinnia's throat.

"Those mountains will be the death of us."

Arian feared many things on the journey ahead. The treacherous road was the least of her worries.

"We'll deal with that when we reach them. For now, do you see anything that might help us understand?"

At the sight of the ring-verse at the top of the tower, Sinnia had bowed her head for a moment. Now she considered the lantern.

"A poor thing, if its purpose is light." She paused. "*Is* its purpose light? Or do we read the Claim amiss?" She read the ring-verse again, frowning. Clouds were gathering over the mountains to the east. "We should call Wafa back before the storm breaks over his head."

"He's more adept at survival than either of us—but Sinnia, what do you mean? How do we read it amiss?"

The woman of the Negus flashed her bright smile at Arian. She pointed to the verse.

"This lantern hangs here, a useless thing. Neither sun nor moon is married to its purpose, neither gives it light." She chewed her lower lip. "But if the lantern is the lamp, as it must be, perhaps the light it sheds is metaphorical, not literal—the light of truth."

"Do you think the verse is the key to Firuzkoh?"

"I think it's the key to the *lantern*." She looked up at the rod above their heads. "They must have been tall, these gatekeepers, to hang it so high."

Arian followed her friend's gaze.

"No, I don't think so. There's a grip at the base of the lantern, but it's locked in place. I couldn't move it."

"Climb on my shoulders. It will give you more leverage."

"It's too much for your arm. And I fear the platform is unstable. Perhaps with Wafa, I could try."

"There's no time for that," Sinnia said briskly. "Here. Stand beneath the lantern, I'll climb up."

Lithe as a gazelle, she vaulted atop Arian's shoulders, reaching for the lantern. Her fingers scratched at the base.

"Light-giving moon, indeed," she muttered.

Arian shifted beneath the other woman's weight, grasping Sinnia's ankles.

"Do you have it?"

"Hold on, I can feel it."

Sinnia fitted her fingers around the grip, tugging with one hand, then both.

The lantern wobbled. The rod shifted in its grooves, scattering dust over their heads. Arian stumbled.

"Steady," Sinnia warned. The handhold didn't budge but everything else on the platform began to shake.

"You'll bring the tower down," Arian gasped, trying to keep her balance.

"I've almost got it. Just—one more moment."

Sinnia yanked at the grip with all her strength. Her feet slipped on Arian's shoulders. Arian staggered forward, falling to her knees, leaving Sinnia suspended midair.

The lantern grip gave way with a groan. Sinnia fell, pulling the chain with her. The rod skidded down its grooves, skimming Sinnia's head. She toppled back on her heels, the lantern swinging over the platform. Brick began to crumble around the arches. The platform shuddered, skewing wildly to one side.

Sinnia grabbed at Arian, dragging her to the staircase.

"Run!" she shouted.

"Wait! Look at it! Look at the lantern!"

"We don't have time!"

"It might be the only chance we get!" Arian scrambled to her feet. Twice she tried to grab at the lantern, twice she missed. Sinnia slid down the first few stairs. Arian caught her by the shoulders, throwing her body flat, holding Sinnia in place.

When they both stopped moving, the platform shuddered once more, then went still.

Sinnia opened one eye, her head and shoulders coated with powdered brick. She inched her way back onto the platform, where Arian knelt under the lantern, her face and hair covered in dust.

The grip that Sinnia had freed from the base of the lamp wasn't an iron bar.

Instead, the handhold had come apart in two halves, each formed like a fan small enough to fit a woman's hand.

Wordlessly, the Companions stared at each other.

They were looking at two palmettes.

She had clarity now, the knowledge singing inside her veins. She'd forgotten her mother's words.

"When you reach the hills known as Shorn Rock, you will find the guardian of the lost city, the Golden Finger. Read it well. It will show you the path into the hills."

Read it well.

The words had a literal meaning, as did the ring-verse that capped the Golden Finger.

Grabbing Sinnia's hand, Arian flew down the stairs, dust streaming from her hair. She dragged Sinnia outside through flakes of falling snow.

"Read," she insisted.

Sinnia took her time, working her way around the panels, stopping when she came to the trees planted in the shelter of the tower. A colony of date palms spread their wavy fronds up and over the river.

She read the words on the panels facing east.

"*Grieve not. The One has provided a rivulet beneath you. Shake the trunk of the palm tree toward you: it will drop fresh, ripe dates upon you. Eat then and drink, and let your eyes be gladdened.*"

"This is the story of the people of East Wind, the sacred story," Sinnia said. "It is renowned in the lands of the Negus." She took a deep breath. "It's the story of the Adhraa—the woman who was chosen."

They stared at each other, deeply moved by this demonstration of esteem for the Adhraa.

"Why?" Sinnia breathed. "Why did the people who built this tower honor a woman of the East Wind, whom my people call the Esayin?"

Arian took Sinnia's hand and squeezed it.

"I've been thinking of this. A graveyard for the Everword, a tower for the Esayin—the Claim throughout it all. These were people who built bridges between worlds. People of tolerance, unlike the Talisman who tolerate no one. If they found this tower, they would bring it down."

The realization planted a small seed of hope inside Arian. There were things that had escaped the Talisman's blind destruction, things powerful enough to endure. Was it possible to return to a world such as the Esayin had known?

Sinnia paced the ground. "Do the palm trees help us? Does the verse of the Adhraa?"

Arian scrutinized the tower.

"Not by themselves. But look at the bands of turquoise. What do you see?"

Sinnia's voice was dry. "Yet another male glorifying himself for posterity."

Arian smiled at that, shaking her head. "I mean besides the names and the titles. What else?"

Sinnia circled the tower again, appraising the scrolls that illustrated the words. A pair of palmettes nestled inside the decoration, one at each end.

"Whoever was responsible for the beautification of this tower introduced the palm as a motif. That can't be a coincidence."

Arian thought of her mother's instruction.

Read it well.

What if there was more to read on this tower than the verses of the Adhraa? What if the palms were meant to tell them more?

The storm was gathering, blanking out the sun. On the north bank of the river, Wafa staggered through a snowdrift to reach them.

"Bring me parchment and charcoal," Arian said to Sinnia. "And hurry." Sinnia hastened to obey. She and Wafa reached Arian's side at the same time.

"Warm yourself," she said to the boy. "Go inside, light the fire."

He shook his head. "We don't have time," he said. "Something watches from the mountains." He went on before they could question him. "I didn't see it, I could feel it."

Arian believed him.

"Read the tower," she said to Sinnia. "Show me the places on the tower where you see a palmette."

"Where do I begin?" Sinnia asked.

"At the palm trees. We'll move right to left, as the Claim is written."

She took the parchment in hand, making dark notations with the charcoal. "Don't miss any," she cautioned.

The wind began to howl, slipping inside their clothes. The women moved quickly, one calling out, the other marking the parchment, Wafa trailing in their wake, a second pair of eyes for Sinnia. They came full circle to the palm trees.

Arian and Sinnia peered down at the parchment, Wafa wedging himself between them.

A jagged sequence of dots marched across the page.

"What is it?" Sinnia asked. "A map?"

Moving right to left, her hand sweeping up the parchment, Arian traced a series of lines between the dots.

"It's a landscape," she said. "Do you see it?"

But she couldn't wait for the others to reach her conclusion.

"Let me take it to the top of the tower."

Sinnia held her back. "It's not safe up there. We barely made it out last time."

"Wait for me on the stairs, then."

Arian ran lightly up the stairs, snow swirling through the lunettes, the parchment clasped in her hand, Sinnia and Wafa at her heels.

"Don't come any further."

She inched her way onto the platform, ducking under the lantern. She held up the rough sketch of the landscape, assessing the terrain through the first of six arches.

The wind whipped against the parchment, almost snatching it from her hand.

She had drawn a path from the palm trees, a path that breached the river and wound up the side of a granite ridge—but which ridge? Which of these passes led to Firuzkoh? The platform trembled under her feet, the lantern swinging to and fro. Arian gripped the wall, buffeted by the wind. The snow was falling like a dense cloud, obscuring her view of the ridgeline. She moved from one arch to the next, feeling the ground shift with each step.

"Arian!" Sinnia called. "Look east!"

SHE WITHDREW FROM HER FAMILY TO A PLACE IN THE EAST.

The palm trees were planted to the east.

She would have to climb to reach the other side. She hunkered down to the floor, crawling across the stage, the parchment tucked in her vest. Bricks began to shift as she moved.

"Come back!" Wafa called. Then to Sinnia, "Tell her to come back."

Arian looked over her shoulder.

"Get down!" she said, her heart in her mouth. "The stairs might collapse!"

Neither listened to her—just as she hadn't listened to them.

She forged ahead to the other side, scrambling to her feet.

She couldn't see; there was too much snow. She grabbed at the parchment, holding it up in vain hope. The wind snatched at it again, rising, roaring, and then with a stroke of fortune at last, clearing the clouds from the horizon.

Tipping off the eastern axis, a broken ridge took the shape of the sketch on the parchment. The sun broke through the snow.

For the briefest moment, Arian could see the path to the Turquoise City.

When the clouds shifted again, it was lost.

Wind roared through the small enclosure. The lantern broke free, rolling down the platform, off the edge of the tower. It crashed to the ground below.

Arian held her breath.

The rod stayed in place.

She scooted beneath it into Sinnia's waiting arms.

The boy's face was white. When they reached the ground again, he buried it in her shoulder.

16

THE EASTERN HORIZON BROKE INTO FRAGMENTS OF GOLD, RIVULETS OF warmth trickling through the dark.

"There's a bridge up ahead. We should cross the river for a new vantage point."

She went first, Sinnia and Wafa treading behind her on broad, wet planks slick with snow. The rope bridge swayed in the wind. Below them, the icy mouth of the river opened up in a deadly black swirl.

One by one, they reached the far bank.

As they climbed the rise, Arian looked back at the tower. The starscope had shifted but not fallen. She didn't know if it was a trick of her vision as they gained the distance, but it seemed to her that the palm motif was gilded by motes of light in such a way that it mirrored their path.

A long-forgotten scholar of the Claim had mapped the road to Firuzkoh on the flanks of the Golden Finger. The clues had been laid so that even if the Talisman should find it, they would miss the significance of the palms, because they denied the significance of the Adhraa.

Why should a woman speak? What could she have to say that mattered?

Arian's answer was not for the Talisman.

Mother of the Esayin, your words of wisdom deliver us.

They followed the steep path indicated by the tower, the air growing cold as they climbed. Soon, they began to feel the exertion in their legs and lungs. The higher they climbed, the less they saw of the sun, the heavy snowfall masking the little of the light not swallowed by the crowding mass of rugged gray cliffs.

It was a day's climb along a narrow, icy trail that slithered off into a fatal mixture of snow and rock. In the distance, the path dipped below the horizon, vanishing between granite ridges that closed in on each other. A shadow crossed the path up ahead. Arian motioned to Sinnia, who shook her head.

"Talisman?"

"I don't see anything."

But something had moved ahead of them, large and quiet. And it wasn't the shadow of Ilea's falcon, tracking their progress east.

Sinnia drew back her cape, leaving her whip hand free. Arian considered the possibility that the Talisman had found their road, and were on the hunt.

She had disrupted too many caravans to be safe. And she had taken the Sacred Cloak.

A pang smote her at the thought of the Cloak on the Black Khan's shoulders.

Was he the man to wear it? When she'd last been in the western capital, the court at Ashfall had been known not for its dispensation of justice, but for its dissoluteness.

She remembered her sense of wrongness at Hira, of something

out of place. A ritual absent of peace, a witnessing of something other than submission. And though this feeling was different, she knew she had cause to worry.

"Be on your guard," she told Wafa.

They climbed another five hundred feet without incident. And then the trail began to descend, low into a sloping valley. As it curved around the side of a cliff, Arian thought she felt something heavy and warm brush against her shoulder.

In the snow, she could see nothing. When she looked behind her, the pass they had crossed through disappeared, lost in the overlapping shadows of the hills.

Straight ahead, a cliff of sheer gray stone rose before them, banded with streaks of blue. As the trail sloped downward, the ridges on either side fell away. And as they did, an impossible sight unfurled on the snow-covered plain below.

A series of irregular blue domes crested a small city preserved in a mantle of ice.

Firuzkoh.

"By all the known and unknown verses of the Claim," Sinnia murmured. "The healer spoke the truth."

At her heels, the boy nudged Arian. She had learned to pay attention to his silent communication. His shy nod indicated the road ahead that wound to the valley floor. Here the snowfall was soft and sparse. Arian cleared snowflakes from her brow and lashes.

She witnessed a wondrous sight.

People were gathered in dozens of little groups at the end of the secret pass. Clad in the thick shawls and caps of their custom, their full faces peered out from behind folds of cloth. They were mostly dark-haired and dark-eyed. Here and there Arian caught flashes of eyes like gold and green gems and silky hair the color of sand. The fold of skin that cut off the inner angle of the eyes told her that these were the people of Hazarajat.

The boy's people.

He looked at their wind-reddened faces in awe, his wide blue gaze traveling from person to person. In the clusters gathered at the trailhead, there were dozens of faces that resembled his own, whereas the bloodline of the Talisman was tellingly absent.

"Who are you?" he asked them in his own language.

"Hazara," they chanted in the same tongue.

The boy fell quiet, made tentative by new discoveries.

There were others who looked like him and spoke his language. And they were not enslaved.

Under the mantle of ice, the people gathered in the valley had made the ancient city their home. The signs of occupation were scant. They had taken great care with the city's panoply of domes and towers, making use of a paved square at the city's center to keep their livestock. Smaller dwellings that ran along the perimeter of the city had been opened up and used for shelter. Families crowded together in narrow doorways.

And every surface carved of stucco and brick was inlaid with geometric motifs and the faintest traces of calligraphy.

Here, as in all the lands of Khorasan, Arian found the commandment stenciled beneath a small blue dome.

THERE IS NO ONE BUT THE ONE. AND SO THE ONE COMMANDS.

She said the words aloud, pitching them to the receptivity of her audience, drawing the words out to offer solace in lieu of the Talisman menace.

It must have worked.

As Arian and her companions passed through the crowd of

people to find shelter beneath the largest of the blue domes, the men and women held up cloth bags full of sweets, offering them to the newcomers.

These were sacred sweets. They reflected a desire to share the blessings they embodied in a time of famine. Ten years in the south had lessened her memory of the hospitality of the Hazara, but this she remembered. The sight of almond-eyed women in colorful shawls thronging the public square heartened her. Yes, Arian carried the bloodline of the Talisman, her graceful features and pale eyes a symbol of that line. And yet she was still welcome.

As were Sinnia and Wafa, each distinct from the other.

She searched the faces in the crowd, but could see no one who might serve as the leader of these people, the Mir of the Hazara.

"May we shelter here for the night?" she asked. "Would the Mir grant us permission?"

In lieu of an answer, a group of young men ushered them forward through doors that led to the inner sanctuary of the dome. Thick wool carpets in jewel-bright reds and blues covered the floor, a barrier against the cold. Small lanterns hung at intervals, cast their pendants of light upon a room rich in geometric motifs. Under a carved niche in the wall, a slender man with a smooth goatee waited, his head covered by a dusk-blue turban set back upon his skull.

His features were as neat and precise as his dress and manner.

He greeted them politely, his eyes flaring at the sight of Sinnia.

"May peace be with you, travelers. You are welcome at the Hallow. Have you come here fleeing the Talisman, or in hopes of observing ziyara?"

As he spoke, he invited them to join him and his followers on the carpets, and they took their seats at a respectful distance. Sweet tea and tawa bread were served to them all. Wafa sat down at Arian's heels, studying the face of the turbaned Mir with interest.

"Ziyara?" she asked when they were settled.

"There is a graveyard behind these walls where our people lie buried."

There was something this punctilious leader of the Hazara was not telling her. And she guessed the reason why when she saw his gaze travel from her face to the boy at her heels.

"Is this your servant?" he asked her.

Which meant that despite the warmth and grace his people had shown her, the Mir knew more about them than she had revealed.

"No," she said. "Wafa is not my servant. He is my companion and friend."

The boy ducked his head at the words, his face heating up. But he couldn't resist a quick peek at the Mir, to see how Arian's words were received.

It was not the reply the Mir had been expecting. He looked thoughtful, trying to connect the three travelers in his mind.

Arian tried a question of her own. "My lord, why are your people gathered here instead of in their own lands? What graveyard do you speak of?"

"If you speak of Hazarajat, it fell to the Talisman. The villages were burned, the people and livestock massacred."

A murmured prayer whistled through the ranks of his hearers. Arian caught the word *qiyamah*.

The Mir's followers understood it as a judgment or cataclysm.

She knew its deeper meaning, as rising or resurrection. But she understood the sense of what the Mir was telling them. The Talisman had visited a cataclysm upon Hazarajat.

"Did they take your women for their caravans?"

"No. The women they captured, they killed along with our children."

"So you found safety here."

The Mir smiled a pensive smile. "We were guided. To this hall in the valley that we have named the Hallow."

"How?"

And when he did not seem as if he would confide any further, Arian removed her cloak and laid it across her knees. Wafa leapt to his feet to help Sinnia do the same.

They had been speaking the Common Tongue, but now Arian used the dialect of Khorasan native to the Hazara.

"Peace be with you, Alamdar." She gave the Mir the most venerated title of his people. "We come not as your enemies, but as your helpmates in dark times from the Council of Hira."

The leader of the Hazara braced his palms on his thighs.

"That cannot be."

"Then which of the One's Blessings will you deny?"

The Mir's response was automatic.

"The stars and the trees both prostrate."

For the first time in months, a smile reached Arian's lips. How long she had traveled, through such dangers and hardships as she couldn't account for, through shattered and desolate country, her victories no more than a handful, her hopes edged by nightmare. And here in this ancient capital, where a helpless people had gathered to shield themselves against the Talisman thirst for death, she found such words, offered with sweetness and pride.

As the Mir moved to bow to her, she stopped him.

"Alamdar, I am your humble guest, no more. We seek a night's shelter and would hear the story of your people before we take the pass to the east."

"You would risk the mountains? No one has traveled those

132

passes in decades. The paths have worn away, they are no longer sound." He looked at her wistfully. "There has been no news of the north or the south. You are the first travelers from the west to have reached Firuzkoh."

"We have no choice, Alamdar. It is through the mountains we must go."

The Alamdar paused.

"Your need must be compelling if you do not fear the Talisman."

"I believed their strongholds were in the south. How far north have their forces encroached?"

"They control the passes up to the border of the Chalk Road. How much further they may have ventured into the mountains, I do not know. The people of the mountains have vanished from time."

Which meant the Hazara had forsaken their traditional pasture lands. And the Mir had confirmed what she had learned of the mountains north and east.

"And the Valley of the Awakened Prince—the valley of the statues?"

"Lost to the Talisman, as well. They leave behind empty hollows in the cliffs."

The Talisman were a people out of time. They found nothing to regard in the heritage of others. They would have blasted the statues down, holding fast to their culture of death.

"Why do you take that road?" the Mir asked. "Where does your destination lie?"

Arian hesitated. The Mir posed no danger to them that she could see. But it was possible that her Audacy might pose a danger to the Hazara. Respecting his candor, she replied in kind.

"I worry that my crossing of your path may bring you further loss. I have made an enemy of the Talisman."

"Are you not from among their people?"

Unlike the Black Khan's, his eyes were humble upon her face.

But how to answer him? That she was a descendant of Candour's most venerated clan? That her family had been the first to be targeted by the Talisman, despite their close bonds of kinship, because of her father's position as curator of a scriptorium? That her mother had been renowned throughout the provinces of Khorasan for her peerless knowledge of the Claim? That the women of her family had been Oralists long before Arian had risen to join their ranks? Or that her young brother, a scholar in training, had been murdered before her eyes?

Her father and mother had died with the words of the Claim on their lips, after hiding Arian in the secret room that served as the family scriptorium. Her sister, Lania, had been sold to a caravan, her fate still unknown.

She had never seen any of her kin again.

Ilea's predecessor had sent the Citadel Guard to reclaim the bodies of her family, and had buried them at the Citadel with honors. The Citadel Guard had taken Arian to Hira, along with her family's treasury of manuscripts. There she had been trained since childhood, the last in a gifted line of linguists, imprinted with a deeper knowledge of the Claim than even the Council suspected.

Such were her memories of the past. She shared a bloodline with the Talisman without sharing any of their beliefs.

In the end, she gave the Mir the simplest answer.

"My people have fallen far. In the country of the Talisman, the sparrow flies with one wing only. Women are held now as slaves."

The Mir nodded.

"And the boy?"

"The Talisman kept him as a slave and used him to herd the

caravans. If he was given a name or had a family of his own, he doesn't remember them."

The Hazara understood this. They had known the same loss, the same persecution, their eyes gentle on the boy's face.

"I will assume responsibility for him," the Mir offered. "These are his people."

Here was a solution Arian could not have hoped for: to find a place of safety for Wafa, among his own kind.

"My friend is injured. Sinnia is a Companion of Hira. Will you keep her also? She will be of great use to you, if the Talisman discover this valley."

It would be a boon to the Hazara, and a means of easing her conscience on two fronts. Her bold intervention with the last caravan had seen her friend suffer injury on her account. She had also put the Hazara at risk by seeking safe passage through Firuzkoh.

Sinnia listened patiently to the exchange before speaking.

"Where you ride, I ride," she reminded Arian.

The boy spoke, too, anxious not to be left behind.

"Wafa is loyal. Wafa stays with you."

He wasn't schooled enough to know to thank the Mir for his offer.

Arian hastened to smooth over the lapse.

"The Alamdar is most kind. I would be glad for Wafa to find sanctuary here, if I might leave him."

Wafa scrambled to his feet.

"No!" he shouted. "Wafa is loyal! Wafa will show you! Beat me, starve me, do as you like. I will carry the packs, I will break the snow. I will do anything you ask, just keep me with you! You said I was precious, you *know* that you said so." He started to cry. "No one ever said that to Wafa."

He collapsed in a heap, burying his face in his knees, sobbing wildly.

Several of the Hazara girls collected around him, patting him on the shoulders, offering colored cloths to wipe his face.

Her thoughts whirling, Arian knelt before him.

"Wafa," she crooned. "I promise you, you are precious. You saved me from the sword of the Talisman, just as you saved Sinnia. If I wish to leave you here, it is not because you do not matter. It is because you matter too much. The road I travel brings death. Here you have a chance at something more."

The boy stopped crying. He glared at the girls who had gathered to help him until they moved away. Resting his chin on his knees, he measured Arian with his gaze. Instead of using a dirty hand to wipe his nose, this time he used a cloth to clean his face, defying anyone to take notice of his tears.

A crack in his voice, he answered her. "I was dead anyway. You said you would take me with you, so you *must* take me."

Sinnia ran a hand through the boy's sandy hair, cuffing him lightly.

"And if you are going to take this slip of a boy, you cannot leave a Companion behind."

Arian saw that she had no choice but to capitulate.

She thanked the Mir again, and she knew from his grave nod that he understood her dilemma. Now he called for blankets and washbasins to be brought into the hall, urging them to rest for the night. The Hazara women and girls prepared a communal place to sleep where they could offer each other the warmth of their bodies.

Arian followed the Mir and his men to the door.

"I wish to warn you, Alamdar. I fear someone or something was tracking us from the Golden Finger. You should double your guard."

He stopped at the door.

"Did the city seem deserted when you first approached it?"

"Yes. Just a few of your people were gathered in the valley."

The Mir clasped his hands before him.

"In fact, they populate all of Firuzkoh. We have learned to make ourselves invisible, but I will double the guard, as you say. There is nowhere left for my people to flee."

"There is one place, if it comes to that: you must follow the road to Hira. Take the river if you can. Find refuge at the Citadel."

"Will my people be welcome there?"

Their eyes met in perfect understanding.

"Two of the Companions are Hazara. They will insist on your safe passage."

And she realized she still didn't have an answer as to how the Hazara had found the lost city, or known to take refuge there. This time, she asked the question directly.

"Come," the Mir said. "You have called me 'Alamdar,' the standard-bearer. You must know something of our powers."

"You said this was a place of ziyara."

"When the Talisman hunted us from village to village, killing everything they found in their path, we had one means of safety. A trail of alams, marking the path west from the lands of Hazarajat. The elders knew the secret of the tower that stands at the meeting place of two rivers. The finger of the minaret pointed us to safety. The martyrs left their flags along the path. They were our guides."

"And the ziyara?"

She heard the grief in the Alamdar's voice.

"A graveyard is a site of blessings. We carried our dead along with us."

17

ARIAN REMEMBERED THE LEGENDS TAUGHT TO HER BY HER MOTHER. The white flags that marked sites both sacred and blessed were invisible to the Hazara's enemies. By planting a trail of flags through their pasture lands, the Hazara had found their way to safety.

Even then a mounted guard was wise, in order to sound the warning so the people could disappear again, hiding their livestock, leaving nothing behind but their graveyard.

If they were found, there was still the refuge of Hira.

If the Citadel would open its gates, as she had promised. Ilea's recent actions had given Arian cause to doubt the High Companion's motives. But she didn't know what else to offer, or what other choice the Hazara might have.

"I would like to pay my respects at the graveyard, to recite a passage for the dead."

The Hazara gathered behind the Mir went still. The Mir brushed a hand across his face, uncertain of what he'd just heard. This woman was a Companion of Hira, which meant she was an Oralist. But she was also connected to the Talisman by blood.

"You would recite the Claim to honor Hazara?"

"Without question. Why not?"

As she looked from face to face, she saw that the Hazara had the shine of tears in their eyes. The hands the Mir had clasped together were shaking.

"The Talisman call us a people of unbelief. The One commands our death, they say."

A dart of pain shot through Arian. What could the Preacher seek by this teaching? What benefit could there be in such hatred, or in bringing so many to grief?

"We were made different nations to know one another," she recounted. "Your ways and beliefs are righteous. People of dignity must not let themselves fall sway to the Talisman."

This time she could be glad when the people called out in gratitude, "Sahabiya, sahabiya."

"Why do you risk the pass into the mountains?" the Alamdar asked again.

She met his honesty with honesty.

"Because we are headed to the northland."

The Mir's eyes sharpened.

"Beyond the Wall? To the Stone City?"

She was at a loss to answer him. He gripped her arm, the gesture urgent enough to explain the discourtesy of it.

"I fear you are seeking the Bloodprint. And if you are, there is something you must know."

A thrill of excitement brought a spark to Arian's eyes.

"Take me to your graveyard. We can discuss the matter there."

What the Alamdar shared with her was folklore—the folklore of the Hazara. A case had been built to hold the sacred pages of the Bloodprint, the strong square print of Kufa inked upon its parchment. Because of its iron binding, the case was called the Cast Iron, but it was said to be made of gold, set with emeralds and precious stones. The Bloodprint was a treasury of lost knowledge. The Cast Iron was a treasure.

It had been taken from the Stone City, its hiding place for centuries, and transported to Marakand. Where it was now, the Alamdar could not say. What he did know was that the Authoritan held it dear, not as an ancient record of the Claim, but rather for its encasement.

In the lands of the Authoritan, the Bloodprint was far less prized than the case that contained it.

And it was the secret of opening the Cast Iron the Alamdar had confided.

While the others slept in the crush of warm bodies in the Hallow, Arian remained alert, pondering what she had learned. And wondering what else Ilea had promised to the Black Khan, who'd made no mention of the Cast Iron.

The Cast Iron that couldn't be opened, obstructing access to the incalculable knowledge within.

The Black Khan had sworn to the truth of his revelations, on the Sacred Cloak itself. She couldn't accept that a prince of Khorasan would dare hold his oath so lightly—the Cloak was so deeply hallowed that blasphemy was unthinkable. It would never have occurred to Arian to doubt him. Yet the Black Khan had chosen not to mention the Cast Iron. How had he opened it? Had he seen it at all? Had the Bloodprint ever been in Ashfall?

The prayer Arian recited over the graveyard of the Hazara provided comfort only to her listeners. She was at a loss, disturbed by the things Ilea and the Black Khan had concealed from her. And now she sensed something else. Movement. A scurrying. A conspiracy of wind and silence that clawed against the small comforts of the cold.

A man she recognized as one of the Alamdar's guards came stumbling into the hall. His face was white under his box cap.

"They've found us. Wake the women. The Mir calls us to the Vanishing Point."

Arian didn't wait for details. She could hear the sound of the Talisman approach, horses snorting in the blue wind, pawing the ground. Men's voices deadened by snowfall, the ring of steel against its sheathing.

The women rose silently, prepared for this day since the moment they had made their home in the valley. They arranged themselves in rows, leading Arian, Sinnia, and Wafa to the rear entrance of the Hallow, through a door of blue tiles that blended into the wall. A group remained behind to black out the lanterns. None of the women spoke. They pressed each other's hands in communication of their strategy.

She followed them into the murky tunnel that extended beneath the city to the rise above the graveyard where she had paid her respects. The women had turned their colorful shawls inside out. Now they were masked in white.

White chadors were lent to her and Sinnia, Wafa engulfed in the cloth.

They escaped the cramped, dark tunnel for the bracing air of the winter night lit by the pinprick of stars. In a smothered silence, the people of the valley assembled upon the ridge that overlooked the graveyard. Like the women from the hall, their clothes were shrouded in white. To the eyes searching for them from the pass into the valley, they would blend into the hills.

The Mir had perfectly calculated his Vanishing Point.

The Hazara brought nothing with them, although each man, woman, and child held a white flag in one hand, wraiths standing motionless on the rise, watching Talisman troops descend in two long columns down the path into the valley, the lost city of Firuz-koh yielding its secrets at last.

"Alamdar. You must take the road to Hira. Or if you find a vessel, take the river."

The leader of the Hazara shook his head, watchful as the Talisman began to hunt through the maze of streets.

"They will find the city empty and leave. The Vanishing Point keeps us safe. The blind do not know how to search, let alone see."

Arian held her breath. The Talisman were warriors, heavyset and strong, practiced in battle. They wore black leather armor instead of traditional Talisman garb, their feet booted against the snow, their turbans wrapped around their heads.

A senior commander directed the search, quartering the empty city in a systematic sweep that should have terrified the Hazara, who waited quiet and still.

"No footprints on the snow?" Arian murmured, as a question.

"There is no one but the One," the Alamdar responded. "And so the One commands."

Arian suspected it was more than that. The Vanishing Point was well-chosen. It was a trick of sight, a line that gave its people shelter, invisible from every angle, much as Firuzkoh remained shrouded by snow until one found the path into the hills. The One had endowed the Hazara with the gifts of intelligence and forethought.

The utter stillness of the children spoke of the massacres they had witnessed in their homeland. They were schooled in the art of survival.

And then she understood how the Talisman had tracked her to Firuzkoh.

Unable to find any trace of Hazara occupancy or of the Companions, the senior commander let out a piercing whistle.

Two giant mastiffs with thick, white fur and slavering jaws leapt into the valley from behind the flanks of Talisman horses. Their long snouts picked up the trail to the Hallow, the Commandhan and his men falling in behind them.

"This way," he called. "She was here. Search each house, each building. Break down the doors if you have to."

Arian cursed under her breath. As she'd feared, she'd led the Talisman straight to the Hazara. It was a Talisman mastiff she had sensed on the pass, his white fur blending into the snow, taking his discovery back to his masters.

"You must leave now," she hissed to the Alamdar. "The mastiffs are tracking dogs. They followed me here."

"My men will fight if they must."

"Your people will die. A white flag is no match for the Talisman. They are skilled warriors, hardened by years of war."

The Alamdar looked faintly pained.

"I thought a Companion of Hira might know about my people. You said two of your sisters are Hazara."

This was not the time for a conference on the rituals of Hira or the reasons the Companions kept secrets from each other, more secrets than Arian had guessed.

"What do you speak of, Alamdar? You must lead your people to safety!"

He stood immovable, his people ranged in silent ranks behind him, their animals lower down on the rise.

"The alams of my people possess their own power."

Talisman soldiers tore through the Hallow, breaking the door, despoiling the carpets, cracking the lanterns, stampeding through the corners of the hall, smashing the faience as they searched.

They found nothing.

The mastiffs circled the building from end to end without picking up a trace of the trail through the tunnels.

The search was ending in other parts of Firuzkoh, as well, the methodical sweep having turned up no trace of the Companions or of the dwellers of the valley.

Arian felt tension seep out of the line of women and children, who had shown such resilience in the eye of the storm.

The Commandhan's men came back to him to confer. He took a step back, flicking his whip against the leather of his boots.

One of his men pointed to the flourishing script beneath the Hallow's blue dome, its height rendering it legible for miles.

Arian held her breath. It was an ancient treasure in a language most Talisman couldn't read. Perhaps the Commandhan was different. His lash struck out at the snow.

"Bring it down."

And there was nothing she could do but watch as arrows were holstered in their crossbows, declaiming a battle cry of doom.

The blue tiles broke apart, the faience cracking like delicate shells against a stony shore. Arian felt the tiny fissures of pain in her bones.

The Hazara remained stoic in the face of the Hallow's destruction.

I brought this to them, Arian thought. *And I will bring them further loss yet.*

Wafa shrunk up beside her, taking her hand in his own, clinging tight.

It was a lesson to him, to be patient and still like the Hazara when his most feared enemy was at his heels. Watching the tiles he hadn't known how to value crack away from the dome's face, he gripped Arian's palm as if feeling the sting of the arrows himself.

Sinnia's lips thinned as she watched the ancient script break apart.

"They will tire of this," she whispered to Arian. "They have done their worst, now they will leave."

The larger of the two mastiffs let out a wild howl. It made the hair on the nape of Arian's neck stand on end, fear flooding her senses.

It was a cry of discovery.

The Commandhan held up his hand. The Talisman gathered around him.

"Find the dog!"

They fanned out behind the Hallow, climbing the rise of the hills to the south.

The ranks of Talisman were no more than a hundred feet away from the Hazara motionless on the rise. In a well-choreographed gesture at a sign from the Alamdar, the Hazara raised their white flags in the air.

The terror of howling dogs and crunching boots receded.

A thick veil of soundlessness fell between the two groups, dulling the clarity of the night, leaving the Hazara as indistinguishable from the landscape as gods carved of stone.

"Commandhan!" a soldier called.

Arian struggled to hear him.

"It's a graveyard. Look at the flags and the offerings."

In that moment, panic seized Arian's heart.

She knew what the Talisman would do.

And she knew how the Alamdar would respond.

The protection of the alams would be as nothing once the Talisman undertook their desecration of the site of ziyara.

She clutched Sinnia's arm.

"Lead the women to the river. Use the flags to mask their path."

"If you wait for me."

"I'll wait for you. And if I fall here, you must continue this quest."

They pressed each other's circlets.

"I swear it."

The boy looked uncertainly from one Companion to the other.

"Go with her, for my sake," Arian begged him. "Come back to me when your duty is done." Bravely, the boy nodded.

The Talisman rode into the graveyard, swords smashing at gravestones as they surged forward. Sinnia disappeared down the rise with the women, dragging Wafa by the hand.

With a cry of despair, the Alamdar hurled his flag down into the graveyard, where it hit the ground with the ring of steel on steel.

Arian covered her ears.

What power did these alams have? What secrets did the Hazara keep?

There was no more time to wonder. The Hazara flags rained down into the graveyard, the shroud of secrecy lost. With a roar of discovery, the Talisman turned their horses toward the Vanishing Point. The battle was joined.

Arian overtook a rider on the foothill. She cut him from his saddle, leaping into his place. She wheeled into the midst of the battle, Hazara at the heels of her horse, the verse she had memorized welling up from her throat as a battle cry.

"How many generations were destroyed before yours? And where are they now?"

Some of the Talisman fell back, the Hazara in pursuit.

"Will you stand while the innocent fall? Will you raise your swords to bring down calamity? No. You, too, will reap the corruption you have sown in the land."

Harsh, blazing, biting, stinging, the words leapt like fire from her throat, turning the frozen city into a fortress of burning cold.

And still Talisman leapt into the fray, the blood of the Hazara crimson against the white clothing they had donned as a shield.

They wore no armor. Very few carried weaponry. And they were cut down in droves, as Talisman horses wheeled and plunged over broken gravestones and bones.

"To me, Hazara!"

The Alamdar took a stand at the top of the rise, rallying his men to his cry.

Arian ducked between riders, avoiding the blows of swords and lances, fighting her way up the rise. The Alamdar was surrounded by his men as they were cut down, the Talisman losing one soldier for every group of Hazara that fell, a terrible arithmetic to contemplate.

Arian's path up the rise was littered with bodies, but Sinnia was well away. Arian could find no trace of the path the women had taken, and she took some comfort from that.

She called out verse after verse of the Claim, her voice shuddering against the night, the stars rolling back into the distance.

It slowed the Talisman advance, but could not stop it.

"Leave her to me," the Commandhan shouted. "Kill the Hazara. Kill the Mir."

And before she could summon a verse deeper in power and majesty, an arrow sang out from the darkness and planted itself in the Alamdar's chest. With jerky movements, he tumbled face-first, burying the arrow deeper. His turban came loose from his head, rolling down the rise. A Talisman soldier scooped it up on the end of his lance. He promenaded it through the graveyard, laughing.

"The One is Great!" he shouted into the night.

"The One is Great!" Talisman echoed.

"The One is Great," Arian said softly, reclaiming the words for herself.

For long minutes, there was nothing but the sound of steel burying itself in blood and bone, the white spike of dawn beginning to crack the night, while Arian fought back, hoping to spare a single Hazara life.

The mob of soldiers pressing her grew thicker.

A rope circled the air in front of her before catching around her waist. With a tug, she was yanked from thc Talisman horse to the ground. She landed on her knees.

She reached for her sword to free herself too late. The Commandhan's sword was at her throat.

Beyond them, the killing continued.

"Do not speak," the Commandhan cautioned her. "Or I will cut your tongue from your mouth. And what price your precious Recitation then, First Oralist?"

The Commandhan knew who she was. He'd tracked her for a predetermined purpose.

She watched him warily, shutting the Alamdar's death from her thoughts. There were still people she could save.

"As you wish," she said, raising her arms in a gesture of surrender. At his nod, she rose to face him.

"I am Commandhan Hask. I've tracked you for many months across the path of our caravans."

Hask, Arian thought. *Summit of the mountain*. It was a strong tribal name, but not from a tribe she belonged to.

Instead of speaking, she placed a hand over her throat and lightly massaged her larynx. The Hazara would hear her. With their leader fallen, she used the Claim to urge those few who could gather their alams to flee along the path the women had taken.

Commandhan Hask remained oblivious to the dwindling cries of battle, confident of his victory. Tall, strong-shouldered, with green eyes set in a weathered, watchful face, he kept his attention on Arian.

"Have you?" she replied, playing to his sense of importance. "I wouldn't have thought the efforts of one woman would so preoccupy a leader of the Talisman."

"I told you not to speak," he said sharply. He flicked his crop at her as a warning, stopping short of making contact, his vanity pricked. "You've heard of me, then."

This time she waited for his permission. When he gave it, she schooled her voice into bland tones of reassurance.

"You are one of the Shin War. Your tribal name is legendary in Candour, as are your exploits. They say you are the Preacher's most feared Commandhan."

She'd read his tribal affiliation from his body language and from the green crest at his throat. The rest was invention. An intelligent adversary would recognize her flattery for what it was. A lesser man might be tricked by a more subtle use of the Claim.

He touched a gloved hand to his crest, a stroke of black against a field of green.

"I don't see what there is in me to interest a Commandhan such as yourself. Unless it is the Preacher who commands you."

Her voice pulled his attention to her, shutting out the sounds of Talisman frustration as Hazara dispersed at the Vanishing Point. Her tone conveyed her own lack of importance as well as admiration for Hask's role as a confidant of the Preacher.

The riding crop wavered in Hask's hand.

"I told the Preacher you were of no consequence. For every caravan you disrupted, we sent four more to the north. But the Preacher has his reasons."

Arian's heart plunged.

Four caravans sent north for every one displaced. It was a hopeless record of her efforts.

"What lies to the north, Commandhan? Why do you traffick your women there?"

She made her tone confiding, even as she read suspicion in Hask's eyes. She had very little time to learn anything from the Commandhan before his men gathered to his side again. In the near distance, she could hear the hooves of a rider approaching. She held her gaze steady on Hask's face. The slightest shift in expression could tell her something she didn't know.

This time the crop struck at her waist.

"I'm not here to answer your questions. If I had my way, you'd be sent north, as well. It's the Preacher who sees a different use for you."

She shuddered, but not from his words. It was only with an effort that Arian kept herself from reacting to the sight of the Alamdar's body being stabbed by Talisman swords.

Don't let them take his head, she prayed. *Let this man of peace go to his grave in peace.*

She pressed on.

"But north for what purpose? Surely, a captain of the Shin War is entrusted with the One-Eyed Preacher's secrets."

She saw at once that she had erred. She'd revealed too much of her desperation to learn the Preacher's deeper intentions. Hask raised his whip arm to strike.

The stroke never fell.

In one clean gesture, the rider who approached severed the Commandhan's arm. Hask gaped at the darkness in shock. The rider swung around on his black horse. This time a blade found the Commandhan's throat.

A strong arm wrapped about Arian's waist, seizing her from the ground. The rider grasped a series of white flags as the stallion pivoted sharply. Throwing down the flags at his rear, the rider urged his horse up the pass that led out of the valley of Firuzkoh.

Rider and Companion vanished into the night, leaving Hask to bleed away his life into the snow.

"Wait!" Arian called to her would-be savior. "I cannot leave the Alamdar's body as sport for the Talisman."

The rider spurred his mount onward, ignoring her.

"You should know in this country the dead receive few honors."

The rider was dressed as a Talisman soldier, in riding clothes that doubled as leather armor. At his throat he wore the same crest as the Talisman commander. A black stroke on a field of green, a symbol of the power of annihilation.

The Shin War symbol.

But the man who'd rescued Arian had never been a follower of the traditions of the Shin War.

As the light began to break and the rider turned his head, she caught a flash of silver eyes.

Daniyar . . .

18

THE SILVER MAGE WAS A GUISE DANIYAR KEPT SECRET FROM THE SHIN War, his strongest affiliation of identity. From the grim set of his shoulders, she could see that his attack against his own tribe was painful to him. He had rescued her from Hask, an act that had brought him no joy.

"Why did you come after me? And where do you take me now?"

They were leaving the sounds of the battlefield behind them. No one had given chase.

Daniyar left her first question unanswered, the curve of his mouth bitter.

"Where do you think? To the river. Your companions will meet you there."

So he'd found Sinnia. She didn't have to ask to know that he'd seen the Hazara to safety. The Silver Mage had always stood by the helpless.

Arian tightened her grip around his waist, feeling the muscles of his torso shift under her hands. She thought for a moment of pulling back his hood to rest her cheek against his neck. But given his hostility, he would view it as a trespass.

"Please stop. I've just come from Hira—I cannot follow the Hazara to the Citadel."

Daniyar didn't slow his pace at her request. Once she had needed no more than a glance to urge him. This antagonism was new.

Cries at the discovery of Hask ricocheted up the ridge. Arian and Daniyar dropped down the other side, lost to the sight of the valley. But it wouldn't take the dogs long to track them again.

"The mastiffs," she tried again. "They'll find our trail. The flags you planted behind us won't hold them for long."

"Then use the Claim for something other than killing."

She went still in the saddle behind him, stunned by the harshness of the words. She had *never* used the Claim to kill, she had used it on behalf of the innocent. If Daniyar read her actions in that light, they had grown more distant than she'd realized.

"Can you still recite? Or did Hask cause you injury?"

Now Daniyar looked back at her, his face bleak. His quick assessment should have revealed nothing, but the Claim served him in other ways than it served the Companions, gifting him with the ability to read truth in the words and gestures of others—he was an Authenticate. His gift had won him the highest possible rank among the Talisman, an unparalleled honor.

Daniyar had refused it.

"I'm fine," Arian muttered.

She hadn't been this close to him in years. She could see the droplets of mist that matted the web of his lashes, leaving a fine sheen along his cheekbones. She felt the blood rush to her temples. His eyes slid over her skin like softly falling rain.

"Don't read me."

"There's a lash mark over your ribs."

"It's nothing. Here."

She drew a shaky breath, using the Claim to distract herself from the force of his attraction.

"I call to witness all that you see, all that you cannot see."

In the valley they'd left behind, snow began to swirl from the ground even as it fell from the sky, first in mist-like trails, then as an impenetrable veil. It muffled the cries of the Talisman, descending like a shroud upon the graveyard. In moments, the lifeless body of the Alamdar was hidden away from the Talisman's boots, cloaked by the purity of snow.

"Would that you had never been shown your record, or known your account! Would that this death of yours had been the end of you. Of no avail to you is all that you have ever possessed."

The snow firmed itself along the pass that led from the valley, forming a second ridge, first knee-high, then waist-high, then shoulder-height. It froze as it fell, swaddling the valley in silence.

The pass to Firuzkoh was lost. It would be closed off until someone with greater ability, or deeper knowledge of the Claim, broke through its veil of secrecy and snow.

Daniyar reined in the black stallion at the head of the next pass, turning the horse to give them their first clear view of Firuzkoh since they had fled.

Its blue domes and softly rounded towers were mantled in white. The graveyard had resettled behind the walls of the Hallow, as if no one had passed through the city in centuries. Men and beasts spoke and moved and argued, but no sound reached the riders on the ridge.

The city was icebound again.

Arian slid from the horse to the ground, gathering herself.

Daniyar watched her, his face tense.

"You were slow to use the Claim. You could have saved the Hazara."

Arian swallowed. The Silver Mage threw back his hood. His dark hair fell in waves to the collar that bore the Shin War crest. His eyes pierced her, absent of understanding.

"You think nothing then, of affording people the dignity of their traditions. The Hazara were safe on the rise. It was the desecration of their gravesite they could not tolerate. They gave up their safety to protect it."

His lip curled. "I'm not surprised the First Oralist defends her shortsighted actions and herself in such terms."

His words were angry, bitter, meant to hurt.

"Do I need to defend myself to you?" she asked bravely. "Are we no longer allies, as we once were?"

With a savage gesture, Daniyar leapt down from his horse. He gripped her chin with his fingers, his gaze as penetrating as the white gleam of steel. Heat radiated between them. She found herself trapped in the rhythms of the past.

"There is so much in your words to offend me, I find I scarcely know you at all. Tell me, when have I ever moved against you? When have I ever harmed so much as a hair on your uncovered head? I saved you from your recklessness in Candour." He scowled at the memory. "And I followed you down this road, knowing you were destined for discovery."

A terrible pain burned through Arian's heart. She could feel herself fraying inside. His fingers were bruising her, their grip implacable. She looked for some hint of gentleness in the silver depths of his eyes, in the hard curve of his mouth. There was none to be found.

She expected Daniyar's hostility.

It didn't make it easier to bear.

"You should have taken the river further east. The High Road would have carried you through Hazarajat. You would have avoided this place, and the Talisman on your trail."

Angry at himself, he let her go.

Shaken, she found herself craving even the contact that hurt her. She flattened her voice to hide her sense of turmoil.

"I was sent on this Audacy by Ilea. Now I think I may have been meant to come here to discover the things Ilea keeps hidden."

The wind polished the traces of tears on her cheeks, turning her face into a mask.

"You are right to accuse me, I did bring death to the Hazara."

"That isn't what troubles you. You've killed before, you'll do it again."

The words cut through her, incursions against her self-possession.

He was reading her, scorching a trail wherever his eyes touched.

"Don't," she said again. "I'll tell you what you wish to know. I sent the women and children of the Hazara to the Citadel. But I cannot be sure Ilea will receive them."

"Mask will help. And Half-Seen."

He named the two Companions drawn from the ranks of the Hazara, relenting at her worry. This time the hand that touched her was gentle.

"Do you have some reason to doubt the High Companion?"

Arian drew in a breath. Should she tell him? Or should she hold back the truth for a moment when it would serve her better?

He dropped his hand at once, reading the deception before she could decide on it.

"You haven't changed," he said in disgust. "You still work everything according to your own schemes."

He reached for the waterskin on his horse, untwisting its tie with animal force, drinking without offering a drop to Arian.

She closed her eyes in shame.

When was the last time she had committed herself to another person without calculation? When had she last shared even a part of her struggle with another soul? Daniyar had been unequivocal about his ultimatum: *Stay in Candour with me or find your way alone.*

She had ridden alone for ten years.

She wasn't an Augur. She couldn't anticipate how the future would unfold. She didn't know if the Bloodprint was anything other than myth or if she would ever find it. Nor did she know if the secret the Alamdar had confided would serve the purposes of Hira. She couldn't be sure those purposes were still her own.

If Ilea was in collusion with the Black Khan—and Psalm was convinced that the Citadel was at risk, both from within and without—who was left that she could she trust?

Her shoulders sagged.

For the first time in months, she felt young and alone and afraid.

She had lost Daniyar once through her practiced deceptions. Yet he'd followed her regardless, heartbreak and promise in his hands.

Before she could convince herself otherwise, she reached for him, words tumbling forth without further thought.

"I fear that Ilea may not be acting in the interests of the Council. She devises Audacies for each Companion alone and in secret. None of us know the workings of the others."

Daniyar waited, unresponsive to her touch.

If he mattered to Arian, she would have to say more. She wasn't used to providing an account of her actions. She had used her rank as Companion of Hira to shield herself from intimacy. Now, as she struggled to find words Daniyar would accept, she realized the price she had paid was too high.

You can be a Companion of Hira or you can be a woman who loves me. You cannot be both.

Did he know how his silver eyes burned her? Would he ever offer his love again?

A little lost, Arian said, "Sinnia thinks me jealous of Ilea—that I seek to become High Companion in her place. It isn't true. I've had work that needed doing, work that Ilea neither dissuaded nor encouraged. I've been hunting Talisman since I left you in Candour."

He tried to free himself from her grasp. Arian held on fiercely.

"You'll forgive me if I don't require a reminder."

"Then read the truth of this! Ilea admitted a man to the Council of Hira when I was last there. And not just any man—Rukh, the Black Khan!"

This time Daniyar made no attempt to read Arian.

"How is that possible?"

"She made it possible. He was there to barter with her."

"For what, exactly?"

Her heart smote her. She knew very well that she'd delivered the Sacred Cloak into the Black Khan's hands. No one else could be held accountable for her disastrous choices.

What could he possibly think of her now?

"The Sacred Cloak. He takes the Cloak to Ashfall."

Daniyar fell silent, working out the reasons for the Black Khan's course of action.

"And what was the High Companion promised in exchange?"

They spoke of everything, except what was necessary between them. And they found themselves at a place of truth.

She murmured the words like a confession.

"The Bloodprint."

Now it was Daniyar's hand that gripped hers, his palm rough and firm.

Sensation shivered through her body. It was an effort to remember the rest.

"The Black Khan promised her the Bloodprint."

19

On the ramparts of the Citadel, the Citadel Guard conducted a series of exercises, the small patrol led by Azmaray, the soldier who'd served as an escort to Arian.

The Black Khan watched the patrol work through its maneuvers with a slight frown on his face, smoke curling into the indigo sky from a slender cheroot between his lips. Ilea joined him, dressed in blue silk, small blue flowers worked through her unbound hair.

He touched a hand to one of the flowers, then let it fall.

"Where are your senior commanders? Your patrols are lacking in every sense—numbers, skill, discipline."

"The business of Hira is none of the Black Khan's concern."

"If you leave your Citadel defenceless, it becomes my concern. You house one of the few remaining scriptoria. And you've just admitted a flock of refugees."

Ilea's lips tightened. "And what would you have me do? Gainsay the First Oralist, when her Companions are gathered here? Mask and Half-Seen are Hazara. If I'd sealed the gates, they would have chosen to leave with their people. I cannot afford to lose a single Companion. When the Talisman attack, I will need every one of them."

She heard herself offering explanations where none were due, heard the weakness of the words, and realized she'd underestimated Rukh's ability to sway her. She wanted to please him, a feebleness that undermined her stature as High Companion.

The Black Khan's arrogance was part of his allure, but turned against her like this, it was less pleasing. And she had not forgotten his response to Arian, his hooded eyes intent.

"Trust me to know my own purposes. The invocations of the Claim will defend the Citadel until my commanders return."

Rukh turned to her. His cheroot blew smoke in her face, but when she took a step back, he caught her by the waist and pulled her close.

"And where have you sent them, Ilea? If you wish Ashfall for an ally, you will need to be a little more forthcoming."

"An ally should know his place. Hira is not the Black Khan's fiefdom." With a dismissive gesture, she freed herself from his grip. "My falcon has returned with news of Arian—I presume that is where your true interest lies."

He crushed his cheroot beneath his boot, his cruel face alert.

"You sound jealous," he said. "My interest is pragmatic. I seek to know if your plans are well laid and are destined for fruition. Will she carry out this Audacy? Will she find her way behind the Wall?"

"Or die in the attempt." The High Companion moved away, her gaze sweeping over the plains of Khorasan. "Though it won't come to that, I hope. There's been a complication. Arian has found a helpmate."

Rukh followed her down the rampart. In the distance, the river wound ahead, a thread of green that disappeared into mud-brown ravines.

"You sent the dark one with her, though she is inexperienced and of little use."

Whatever her own motives, Ilea disliked hearing the Companions spoken of as pawns in the Black Khan's game. She took a certain satisfaction in giving him her news.

"Besides Sinnia. The First Oralist is now joined by the Silver Mage."

The words provoked an unanticipated response.

Rukh wound his hands in her hair, crushing the blue flowers. He pulled the long strands tight around her throat.

"Do not lie to me, Ilea. It doesn't become you."

Rage flared in the High Companion's eyes. Her hands flew together and apart, striking at hidden cadences of the Claim.

The Black Khan's hands were wrenched away, his palms scored and bloodied. He held them up in surrender, a smile curling the edge of his lips.

"Forgive me, High Companion," he murmured. "I did not mean to offend."

Ilea's voice was cold.

"I've indulged your presence at Hira as a courtesy. But do not set hands upon me again."

She signaled the Citadel Guard to escort her back into the depths of the Citadel.

Rukh spoke to her back.

"And should you ask me to, High Companion? Do I dare refuse you, then?"

His mocking laughter followed her on the wind.

20

DANIYAR AND ARIAN RODE ON IN SILENCE. SHE ASKED NOTHING OF THE route east, he asked nothing further of the Bloodprint. As Authenticate, he knew she was telling the truth, and for the moment that was enough.

They rode from ridge to ridge, the black stallion steady under the weight of two riders, the light breaking across the landscape in filaments of amber. The air tasted crisp, unsullied by the death the soundlessness represented. After a time, Arian picked out the striped wings of Ilea's falcon against the sky.

"Ilea tracks me."

"I know. I found your trail by following her falcon. Saqar remembers me. Look there." The falcon dipped low against the unvarying ridges. "Saqar has found us our path."

A spangle of green broke out against the snow, catching the light on its fluted rills. The High Road, contracting its passage through channels of ice.

"You will find your friends there. Though you are wrong to take the boy with you."

Arian was tired from holding herself aloof in the saddle. She let herself slump forward, forcing Daniyar to take her weight. The impact of her body would be negligible to a rider of Daniyar's skill, and she wanted the chance to savor his warmth. She placed one hand on his arm, testing its strength.

He relaxed in her embrace. She knew a stroke of pure joy at how perfectly she fit against him, suppleness to suppleness, the scent of wild mint in the dark fall of his hair.

"I couldn't abandon him. The Talisman captured him twice on my trail."

She could feel Daniyar's voice rumble through his back, sending sparks along her nerve endings.

"He chooses to go with you? When he could have remained behind with the Hazara?"

"I think he was stolen from them young and knows nothing of them. He doesn't recall if he was given a Hazara name. He has no family."

Daniyar turned his head. She caught the curve of his smile against his beard.

"So you named him, of course. What name?"

"Wafa, the loyal. Was he with Sinnia at the river?"

"He was causing no end of trouble to your friend, desperate to return to you, doubtless." His voice was wry. "It seems time has not dimmed your enchantment."

Arian stifled a smile against his back. If he could remember something other than betrayal— A flutter of hope pulsed through her chest. Greatly daring, she drew away his hood, her fingers tracing the nape of his neck. Her hand moved sideways, probing the contours where leather met skin.

"The boy should see you as one of the Talisman," he said, his voice suddenly deeper. "Why doesn't he?"

"I killed the guards who enslaved him."

If she were to confide in the Silver Mage about the Bloodprint, it would have to be before they reached the others. And perhaps it was better that he couldn't see the rise of color in her face.

"The Black Khan claims to have seen the Bloodprint. One of his men brought it to Ashfall, but his spy was intercepted and the Bloodprint disappeared. Rukh says his men will help me track it from Marakand."

"You call him Rukh?"

There was a studied quietness in Daniyar's voice. Arian's hand stilled on his shoulder.

She thought of her encounter with the Black Khan. He'd known about the Cloak, almost before she'd determined to take it.

"It *is* both his name and his symbol. He called me Arian before the Council."

The tendons in Daniyar's neck tightened.

"How typical of his insolence. Did he feel himself encouraged?"

Arian bent her forehead to his neck. He didn't pull away.

His skin was cool and firm to her touch. The faint tang of pomegranate mingled with the scent of wild mint, masculine and sweet. She wanted to press her mouth to the sensitive skin of his nape. She choked back the thought of where her longings would take her.

"You know that I wouldn't." She bit her lip, remembering the spell the Black Khan had woven in the scriptorium. "I permitted his familiarity because I needed to know why he'd come to Hira."

The black stallion lifted his head. He could smell the river now. He galloped ahead, causing her to slide against Daniyar. Daniyar held her in place with a hand on her knee. Warmth coiled through her body at the touch.

They reached the green twist of the river, the stallion snorting through his nostrils, tossing back his head. Arian patted him in thanks, dismounting swiftly to put distance between herself and Daniyar. She was beginning to lose the sense of her Audacy.

Daniyar followed suit, rubbing the stallion's flanks with agile movements that Arian watched in silence.

He freed the horse of encumbrances. The stallion picked his way down the ridge.

Arian considered two questions.

Did Daniyar intend to journey at her side? And what did he know of the mountains?

21

ARIAN LOOKED OVER THE BARGE. IT WAS LARGE ENOUGH TO ACCOMMO-
date their supplies, while sleek enough to navigate the river's narrower tributaries. Sinnia and Wafa were waiting by the craft. They
embraced each other with joy, the boy ignoring Daniyar.

It was dusk and the temperature had fallen.

She grasped Wafa's hands, warmed by the contact.

"You are safe. And you helped your people, yes?"

He pointed at Sinnia.

"She is my people. You are my people."

He made no mention of Daniyar. Arian tried not to smile.

"Well," she said lightly. "I'm glad you are here. I wouldn't wish
to face the mountains on my own."

She turned a questioning glance on Daniyar, who'd used the
time to set up a makeshift meal, a warmed-up lamb stew with
tawa bread, heated over a fire inside a ring of stones. He doled out
a portion to the boy, who took it without thanking him.

Arian shook her head.

"I see I shall have to make proper introductions. It's time I told
Sinnia who you are."

At Daniyar's nod, she withdrew a small object from the depths of his pack. It was bound in black leather, a silver inscription worked into its surface in a brilliant, discursive design. Two letters in the High Tongue formed a single word on its cover. Letters Sinnia hadn't seen except in the crumbling of minarets or the shattering of blue tile.

"You have a copy of the Claim," the younger Companion whispered. She stared at Daniyar, bewildered. "Then *why*? Why do you aid us in our quest for the Bloodprint?"

"If it was the Claim, I wouldn't risk your safety through Talisman territory." He finished his meal, setting it aside. His gaze strayed to Arian. "Tell her, if you wish."

Arian pressed the surface of the book to her forehead, then to her lips. Flames cast a muted reflection over its burnished surface, dancing points of gold over silver.

"Why do you kiss it, if it is not the Claim?" Sinnia persisted.

"Look," Arian said, turning the pages with delicate hands. "I haven't touched a book in so long. The Candour feels—as beautiful as I remember it."

"The Candour?" The name trembled on Sinnia's tongue. She edged closer to the book, the line of her mouth going slack. "The Candour is a fable, the book of the Silver Mage." Her voice faltered in disbelief. "There is no Silver Mage."

"Isn't there?" Arian asked with a smile. She was looking at Daniyar.

Slowly, Sinnia raised her head from the Candour. She took note of silver eyes, of the quiet strength in the face of the man who had just prepared and served her meal. She now discerned what she'd missed before—the hint of hidden nobility.

She flashed a horrified glance at Arian.

"My lord, forgive me," she managed. "I meant no disrespect—I didn't know."

"Companion," he said, with a courteous nod. "You showed me no incivility. And if we are to travel together, it is best to dispense with titles."

"My lord, I cannot—"

"Your friend calls me Daniyar, a name I am fond of."

"But you are the Silver Mage," she whispered, half-doubting herself. She gestured at the book, her dark eyes glistening with hope. "Tell me, what does it teach?"

"The duties of the Silver Mage. The powers that come with the guardianship of Candour."

The words meant nothing to Wafa. Oblivious, he reached for another helping of stew. Mortified, Sinnia thumped him on the back.

"What?" The boy looked up.

"Thank the Silver Mage for rescuing us. And for feeding you with his own hands."

Wafa shrugged. "I don't know what a Silver Mage is." He filled his bowl, unconcerned. Sinnia stared from Arian to Daniyar, scandalized. Arian was smiling, her head brushing Daniyar's shoulder, something else for Sinnia to ponder.

"Useless excuse for a miscreant child," she muttered under her breath. "How did a woman of the Negus get stuck with you?"

Daniyar waited to address the boy until he'd finished eating.

"You were hungry," he said. "Perhaps for a long time. Do you know how long you've been with the Talisman?"

The boy spat at the ground at Daniyar's feet. Sinnia let out a shriek.

"No," he said, wiping his mouth clean with the back of his hand. "Always, maybe. I don't remember when I was small."

If he hadn't been so undernourished, Arian would have guessed his age as fourteen or fifteen. His eyes were wide and watchful, perhaps because he didn't know how long he could expect any-one's kindness to last. Or when he would have to shift for himself again.

"Did you have a name before the Companions found you?"

"Hazara," he said. "But I like Wafa better." His face became pinched. "You can't have it," he said to Daniyar. "You can't take it back."

Daniyar studied the boy across the fire.

"I haven't come here to take anything from you." The boy's eyes stole to Arian's face. "Much less the Companion who acts as your guardian. You have nothing to fear from me."

The boy pointed to the crest at Daniyar's throat, the thrust of black against green.

Shin War, the boy mouthed, no sound leaving his throat.

Daniyar cleared up the meal without waiting for help, stowing their supplies on the barge, motioning Sinnia aside when she tried to assist. He returned to warm himself before the fire, watching the smoke trail vanish into the sky.

"The Shin War existed before Talisman came to these lands," he said finally. "We have our own history."

The boy pointed to Daniyar's crest again.

"You wear their colors, you ride with them."

Daniyar glanced at Arian. "I have my reasons for doing so. They are not just my tribe, but my family. Commandhan Hask was my cousin."

Arian stared at Daniyar over the boy's head, her heart thudding in her chest.

A hard smile edged his lips.

"I will suffer no man to touch you. Not even my own kin."

A charged moment passed before he added, "I will see you safely to Marakand, by way of the Wandering Cloud Door."

Sinnia pressed her fingers to her lips, startled by the suggestion.

"You yourself arose from myth, now you speak to us of legends. The Cloud Door, the Ice Kill, the vanishing lake known as Lop Nur, the Damson Vale." She kicked dirt over the last traces of the fire. "These are stories told to children, stories of dragonhorses and ghost cats."

Daniyar smiled at Sinnia, who caught her breath at the beauty of it.

"The Wandering Cloud Door is more than a story you were told in the lands of the Negus. It's the passage beyond the settlement at the Ice Kill." He glanced at Arian. "You know that I've been to the Damson Vale."

An arrow of pain stabbed at Arian. How often Daniyar had spoken of the beauty of the Damson Vale with its apricot orchards and vineyards. And how often she had refused to journey there by his side.

"The Ice Kill is the southernmost point of the Cloud Door. We would pass through the valley to the Fire Mirrors—the mountains in the north. The Damson Vale lies on the other side of the mountains. Then we would outflank the Wall to reach Marakand, by far the safer road."

Arian did not doubt the Silver Mage—yet her Audacy seemed much more treacherous now. Ilea had not marked this road for her. Nor had the Black Khan hinted at these obstacles.

"But a longer and more difficult climb."

"Yes. But there's more. It's a journey we cannot undertake unless we have something to trade for passage through the Cloud Door. The dwellers of the valley will forbid our trespass otherwise."

The mountains had been silent for as long as Sinnia could remember.

No one inhabited the Cloud Door—that was part of the lore she'd been taught. But when she asked the Silver Mage to reassure her that she hadn't misheard, he dipped his head in response.

Arian considered the road ahead. There was little of value they would find on this ruined road, and they carried with them nothing except their provisions. She felt a sudden chill.

The path Daniyar had described would take them past the Sorrowsong.

"You mean to suggest we trade for our passage with lajward, the blue stone found in the mountains. But you know who holds the quarries of the Sorrowsong mountain. The Talisman war is driven by lajward. You said we would gain our safety by taking the river east."

Wafa sidled closer to Arian, frightened by something in her voice.

Daniyar turned to her, regret in his eyes.

"The river ends well before the Ice Kill. We must reach the Blue Mountain on foot."

"We would be walking straight into Shin War lines."

Daniyar nodded. Arian knew the dangers as well as he did. The Shin War controlled the lajward mines to defend their network of privileges, control they had wrested from the tribe of the Zai Guild. The pass to the Sorrowsong would be heavily defended.

He could use his ties to the Talisman, and she the power of the Claim, but it would come to the same thing in the end.

A man, a child, and two women braving a Talisman redoubt.

To capture the stone of heaven.

Symbol of the Eternal Blue Sky.

22

THEY TOOK TURNS PILOTING THE BARGE, GIVING WAFA AND SINNIA A chance to rest. Sometimes the river ran deep and smooth, in other places the current raged against them, white eddies forming around the barge. During the nights, Daniyar took over, his eyesight keen in the dark, aided by his familiarity with the terrain. From time to time, they would hear the sound of ice cracking around the barge.

The High Road merged with a second river as they approached the Valley of the Awakened Prince, a river that curved and followed the bend of the land, a joining forged by the shifting of the earth in the aftermath of the wars of the Far Range. Before those wars, the river had spent its force in the plains of Hazarajat. Now it twisted to the east.

As the river wound ahead, the first crust of ice broke over the blue gleam of the Five Lakes, far out of their path to the north.

The plains of Hazarajat were empty, some of the deserted villages still smoldering, the white flags that marked the pathway to escape invisible to all save the Hazara against the snow. The river slowed past the hollows where icons of an ancient civilization had once gazed upon the valley, their faces cut away from the hills, their contemplation of history lost to time. The hills were pock-marked with scars, the signs of a calculated violence.

In place of the head of the giant statue that had occupied the embrasure, a flag was nailed to the cliff. The Talisman flag with its bloodstained page. Daniyar frowned at the sight.

"The blood on the flag is fresh." He lowered his voice so the boy couldn't hear. "Hazara blood. A warning to flee, ahead of their descent upon Hazara villages."

Something hung over this valley other than the flag. A foul wind rife with ill will.

The river picked up speed, turning north.

The air grew cooler around them, the river shallow, until their paddles were striking against rock. In the pallid light of the moon, they could see streaks of blue in the water.

"Residue from the mountain," Daniyar told them.

The source of the river was high in the mountains, the Blue Mountain dwarfed by others in the jagged chain of the Death Run.

They moved in its shadow, ever forward.

After five days on the river, their small company had passed through the deserted ruins of Hazarajat, with no sign of the Talisman presence.

"Do you know the approach to the Sorrowsong?" Arian asked Daniyar, as he found a place on the banks to moor the barge.

"We have a trek of several days on foot before we find the approach," he answered. "We'll need to replenish our supplies. Stay with the barge. Wafa and I will hunt."

Sinnia protested at once. "I am the hunter, my lord. The Companions have always fended for themselves. We need no one to provide for us—ask Arian."

She had no need to draw his attention to Arian. She did it to tease him. The Silver Mage was possessed of a single-minded intensity. As he spoke of hunting, he thought of Arian's safety.

A corner of his mouth eased up. He tossed Sinnia a sharpened spear. "Perhaps you could try your hand at fishing. There's light enough from the moon."

Sinnia was affronted. "I was raised on the shores of the Sea of Reeds. I've no need to *try my hand* at anything. You underestimate my skill, my lord."

He laughed softly. Sinnia pressed a hand to her heart, amazed at Arian's indifference to the sound. Did she not feel the power of Daniyar's attraction? How could she resist such a man?

"In that case, I'll look forward to my supper."

Their voices trailed away from the barge, Wafa casting a reluctant glance back at Arian.

"She'll be fine," the Silver Mage assured him. "Did she ever tell you of the time she shot me with an arrow?"

Sinnia joined Arian at the side of the barge, claiming a spot in the moonlight.

"Let me look," Sinnia said. "My vision at night is keener than yours."

She held the spear in her hand, high above her shoulder.

They stood side by side without speaking, watching the rush of water over stones in the riverbed.

After a time, Sinnia murmured, "You shot the Silver Mage?"

Arian grimaced. "Not on purpose, Sinnia. He was trying to teach me archery. You know it is not my best skill."

Sinnia grinned, wide and bright as the moon.

"Your talents lie with books, not arms. It's why Ilea chose me for you."

"There!" Arian's slender finger had no sooner pointed to the water than Sinnia flung the spear like an arrow. Blood spurted into the water.

"Lower me."

Arian held Sinnia by the knees. The spear had struck the shallows of the riverbed. Sinnia was able to dig up the spear, the carp still attached.

"A net would make this easier," she said, flinging her catch to the deck.

"But somewhat unsporting, oh woman raised at the Sea of Reeds."

Sinnia glared at her, until Arian started to laugh.

"What?" she asked. "You said it with such conviction, I thought you'd been fishing the reeds all the days of your life."

Sinnia laughed, too, a touch of impatience in her voice. "A man like the Silver Mage should not think of a woman as helpless." It was her turn to tease Arian. "Unless it is at the sight of him, as any woman would be. Your ability to resist him astonishes me." She raised the spear again, finding the patch of moonlight. "Enough talk," she said, giving Arian a respite. "This won't be enough for all of us. Wafa will swallow this down by himself."

She made several more attempts, turning up snow trout, silver carp, a stone loach, and a catfish. When she was satisfied with her catch, she turned her attention to gutting the fish with the dexterous movements of a boning knife.

Her skill and speed were such that Arian was reminded that indeed Ilea had chosen Sinnia as her companion for a reason. Sinnia may have been young, but she lacked nothing in confidence or ability.

Sinnia tossed a second knife to Arian.

"Are you planning to help or just watch?"

She found she was glad that Sinnia no longer treated her with the reverence of their first meeting, as if Arian was a piece of storied celadon porcelain. She took up the knife and knelt at Sinnia's side.

"It's good to see you get your hands dirty. Though if I were you, I would occupy my hands with something more rewarding."

The two women shared a smile.

"You mustn't say such things to a Companion of Hira."

Sinnia was unrepentant.

"He looks at you like a man who is starving before a feast. You never told me—what is he to you? Who is he to you?"

She flung the skeleton of the catfish over the side of the barge.

Arian's actions were slower, less sure. Sinnia motioned her away.

"Clean up," she said. "I'll finish this." She nodded at Daniyar's pack. "He carries most of the supplies." She moved on to the bones of the snow trout, sectioning the fish with steady, proficient movements. "Bring me a pan for the flesh."

She had asked the question that occupied her thoughts, but she had also given Arian the chance to deflect it if she wished.

Bent over Daniyar's pack, Arian's voice was muffled as she said, "I am not indifferent to the Silver Mage. In Candour, he was—everything. Now nothing, as he chooses."

Sinnia sat back on her heels, the pearlescent flesh of the fish spread before her. Arian passed her a pan from Daniyar's pack. Sinnia's dark eyes were shrewd.

"If that is what he chooses, why did he follow you? It's not an easy road ahead. And I see that he doesn't let you off this barge unless he is there to protect you." She snorted. "You are First Oralist, Companion of Hira—hardly in need of any man's protection."

No, Sinnia thought to herself, remembering their first meeting in the Citadel's scriptorium, *hardly in need at all.*

Arian was at work before a writing box, a Kamish pen in her hand, her parchment illuminated by a ruby glass lantern.

The scene mesmerized Sinnia—fixing in her mind a sense of awe that was never entirely dispelled by daily contact with Arian.

The ebony veneer of the box was richly inlaid with sadeli mosaics in ivory and bone. A six-point star dominated the composition, floral panels to either side, a vegetal vine flourishing at the borders. A marvel of symmetry and artistic execution, the writing box was an object of such beauty that only the woman seated before it could eclipse it.

The woman held a pen in her hand—a pen cut from reeds that grew along the Sea of the Transcasp, its pointed tip black with ink that she blotted with likka, raw silk fibers designed to soak up the excess.

She applied the pen to a sheet of vellum, a delicate script springing up beneath her hands.

She was writing.

An act Sinnia had never witnessed before.

She choked back her tears, the sound alerting Arian to her presence.

The First Oralist rose from her desk, the ruby lantern casting a blush over her skin. She wore a gown made of ab-e-rawan, the sheer muslin known as running water, a crown of rubies set on the long, dark hair dressed in a single plait. Fastened to the plait was a winding gold ornament that trailed down Arian's back. It glowed with a string of rubies, casting a red fire over her hair.

She wore no rings or bracelets. But on her arms was a pair of tahweez identical to Sinnia's.

"Forgive me, First Oralist," Sinnia gasped. "I'm not dressed for the honor of your presence." She blushed at the thought of her dusty riding clothes, her skin too dark to give the blush away.

The First Oralist's answer was kind.

"These are ceremonial robes. I'm dressed to receive an emissary from the Empty Quarter, but he is capricious and chooses to keep me waiting. I thought I would pass the time in the scriptorium, pursuing a little of my art." She looked down at her ink-stained fingers, the gesture rueful. "You are much more sensible than I am. I find the Citadel quite cold."

She rubbed her arms below the golden circlets, leaving smudges of ink on her skin.

A woman who valued the written word more than any of the ornaments of the world.

In that moment, Sinnia loved her.

In the many months that had passed since, she had never seen Arian dressed in the regalia of First Oralist again. In Hira's Council Chamber, Arian had dressed as any other Companion, the ruby crown stored away. Tonight, the smell of freshly cleaned fish strong in the air, showed just how little Arian cared for trappings.

The First Oralist sank down beside her on the barge, Daniyar's pack in her hands.

A rush of affection surged through Sinnia. The woman who had worn a crown was just as happy to have her hands in the innards of a snow trout.

"Do you need anything else?" she asked Sinnia.

"Does he carry any spices?"

Arian rooted through the pack, well aware that she had given Sinnia half-answers to her earlier questions about Daniyar, and why he was with them now.

I loved him, but he no longer loves me.
Such is the price of betrayal.

"What of you, Sinnia?" she asked. It was not a subject the Companions had broached with each other before. "Did you leave someone at the Sea of Reeds?"

Sinnia flicked aside the head and tail of the trout.

"No one. I was destined to be a Companion from birth. The Negus kept me sequestered from the men of his court." She finished with the trout, moving on to the carp. "But I'll tell you this, Arian. If a man like the Silver Mage wanted me the way Daniyar wants you—I wouldn't think twice. I would already be in his arms."

"What of Hira?" Arian asked.

Sinnia nodded at the pack. "I would find a way to be true to both."

The words echoed through Arian's thoughts. Absently, she searched Daniyar's pack. Her hands slid over something hard and smooth. Curious, she reached for it. A leather band four inches wide and two inches thick, it unfastened between her hands, its sides separating from a heavy, metal lock. It was an object she recognized, one that she loathed. A slave collar for a woman's neck.

What was Daniyar doing with a slave collar?

Sinnia's response to the collar was matter-of-fact.

"I told you he wanted to own you."

Arian stared at her, breathless.

And then she started to laugh.

23

Daniyar heard her laughter from the trail. His keen eyes searched for her in the moonlight. She was standing against the rail of the barge, her head tilted up to the moon, close and unutterably lovely.

His pulse quickening, he moved faster, hurrying Wafa along.

There was warmth and welcome in Arian's face, such as he hadn't known in the course of many hard years in Candour. Barren years, empty of Arian's laughter.

But he had stolen her laughter long before this moment.

On that last day, she waited for him in the Library of Candour, her hair caught by the wind like a curtain of silk on a clear blue morning.

The sight of her unbound hair still had the power to break him.

He buried his face in the silk of her hair, inhaling the scent of jasmine she wore so lightly. And then he took note of her attire.

"You're dressed for the road."

He dropped the arms that held her. It was an argument they'd had many times before. He was out of patience with it.

"You've decided, then. You intend to pursue the caravans, putting your life at risk."

"You know why I must go. I would never leave you otherwise."

"And what of the promises you made me?"

In that stolen time when the dictates of Hira were forgotten. He felt the tantalizing brush of her body, the warmth he had longed to claim for himself. In an instant, his anger dissolved, giving way to desire.

"If I kissed you now, you wouldn't be able to leave me."

"Daniyar—"

"Arian," he mocked her. "What would you have of me?"

He pulled her close, his eyes smoky with threat.

"This?"

He tasted her lips with his own, probing the sweetness of her mouth.

"Or this?"

His mouth slid to the side of her neck, lingering under her ear.

"Don't," she whispered. "Whatever path I take, I will always be a Companion of Hira."

"Then why are you still in my arms?"

He kissed her until she was shaking in his embrace. When he opened his eyes again, he was shattered by the sight of her submission, the soft lips seeking his own, the delicate hands tangled in the hair at his collar.

He pulled away. In scant minutes he had disarranged her hair, trapping her between his chest and the wall. His blood stirred at the sight of her captivity, but he struggled to clear his thoughts of desire.

"Give me your hand," he said gruffly. When she had placed it in his own, he slipped his gift onto her finger. He pressed his forehead to hers, his voice a raw slide of silk in his throat.

"I am not patient," he warned. "Nor am I tender." His actions belied the words, for he touched her as though she were breakable, the arms that held her careful and reverent. "I am possessive by nature, and I will not share what is mine. You will leave the Council of Hira."

The supplication in his voice contradicted his words.

Give yourself to me, it said. *I will make you forget everything else.*

"Arian?" he prompted, for still she had not spoken. "I know I deserve your silence, but will you not tell me your thoughts?"

The strain in his voice woke her from her reverie. He drew away to look into her eyes. Humbled by what he read there, he bent to kiss her hand.

"Answer me. Tell me if you will wear it."

He turned her palm over to show her the ring.

"It's priceless to me," she said. But her eyes were fixed on his face and when he challenged her, she could not tell him the color of the stone.

He was moved beyond his ability to convey.

The Silver Mage was coveted, sought after—but he had never been *loved* like this.

"Please look at it."

She looked down at the ring he had placed on her forefinger.

The ring of the Silver Mage.

A silver-white band with a stone that captured a quicksilver light, bright and glancing like Daniyar's eyes.

The stone was inscribed with a single word.

Iqra.

Read. Learn. Teach.

The oath of the Silver Mage.

She had come to the moment of decision.

"We found our way to each other," she said quickly. "My path led me to you and I—I accept you, lord."

His sudden kiss was fierce and dark.

"Daniyar," he warned.

She linked her arms around his neck.

"Daniyar," she repeated.

He watched her for a moment, desire hard and brilliant in his face.

"Then you won't deny me what is mine by right."

She bowed her head before him. He had to lean in to catch her words, scorched by the heat of her skin.

"I cannot deny you anything."

One hand tugged at her hair, needing to be sure. Her lashes lifted to reveal such helpless longing that he was the one vanquished.

"Arian," he groaned. "Don't look at me like that. I am not one of the Bloodless."

Her lashes fell again but not before he'd witnessed the constraint in her eyes.

Like a fool, he hadn't known what it meant.

At the end of the night, when he'd returned from his conference with the Shin War, Arian was gone. She had left behind his ring, a message tucked inside it.

Forgive me one day, my love. I cannot abandon Lania.

And now they had come to this.

The decade she had spent in the Talisman south had shown him what he'd refused to accept in Candour. She would take her own path, honor her own commitments. There was nothing he could do to dissuade her, nothing he could offer that was worthy of her love.

She was no ordinary woman.

She was a woman who belonged wholly to Hira—her laughter could only remind him of his loss.

With her brow quirked, Sinnia held up the pan full of fish. The Silver Mage had failed to hunt any provision.

"You've come back empty-handed, my lord."

"My hands have always been empty." A note of grief colored his voice.

The laughter died on Arian's face.

He took the slave collar from her hands.

"It's not what you think it is, Arian."

Arian's glance was quizzical. She settled on a sigh of resignation before she answered, "I think you've decided on a ruse."

24

THEY WERE CLIMBING TO DIZZYING ALTITUDES THROUGH PASSES HEAVY with snow, the warm light of morning a myth against the thinness of the air. Their breath burned in their lungs, making each step ponderous and difficult, ice freezing over in places, secret crevasses giving way, demanding a hasty reassessment of the path. The Sailing Pass had taken the lives of many who'd thought to find their way to the valley beyond its ridges.

It cared little for their purpose.

As the light broke over the mountain in waves, the river unspooled beneath them, a thrumming thread of green, softening the harsh mysteries of the world. Clouds spun away on the empty horizon, making their own small notations against the wind.

"You said the snows would melt in the spring," Sinnia gasped. "I don't see how we can climb higher. Are they mining this stone in heaven itself?"

The boy didn't speak at all, or look anywhere but at his own feet. He followed behind Daniyar, his smaller feet falling into the path laid by Daniyar's boots.

The wind was high, and there had been no recent snowfall. For an immeasurable distance ahead, they could see no footprints save their own. Far in the distance, the timid grass of the Valley of Five Lions cracked open beneath the snow, a green murmur of spring.

A glimmer of light several passes away caught Arian's eye. It was the strike of the sun against a pair of field glasses.

"The Talisman are closer than I thought."

To Sinnia, the thought of warfare along these narrow, deathly ridges was preposterous. Daniyar didn't agree.

"The patrols haven't seen us yet, or they would have sounded their Avalaunche."

"I'm from the south," Sinnia said. "I feel as though I'm breathing ice. So what, my lord, is an Avalaunche?"

Daniyar looked back briefly. "A warning horn, the first defence of the Sorrowsong. There have been skirmishes with the people of the mountains; the Avalaunche warns against encroachment."

Sinnia was skeptical. "If I lived at this altitude, a horn wouldn't frighten me away."

"It doesn't just sound the alarm, it triggers a landslide of snow. An avalanche is a suffocating force. It buries men in moments."

Arian looked up from her study of the trails that crisscrossed the peaks of the Death Run.

"Do the avalanches not block the passes to the Sorrowsong?"

"When you have lives to spend against the snow, you do not worry about outcomes."

Daniyar's words sobered the boy. Wafa had suffered many things at the hands of the Talisman, but the men of the plains had not fed him to the raw forces of nature. The very thought of the men at the Sorrowsong terrified him. If the Silver Mage's plan was forestalled, what use would the Shin War put him to?

"Why not take the low road?" Sinnia asked. "The valley looks safe enough."

Daniyar spared her a glance. "The Valley of Five Lions is a

battleground between the Shin War and the Zai Guild. In history it belonged to a different people. Though it is held by the Shin War, the Zai Guild make fresh incursions each day. We will find no safety there."

For a long while no one spoke, preserving their air to combat the steady encroachment of the altitude upon their strength. When Sinnia could travel no further, they camped inside a hollow in the ridge. Here they ate cold rations, drinking sparingly of their water.

The night and the next several days brought more of the same: close calls along the ridges, the occasional glint of light against field glasses covering the passes ahead, light-headedness, thirst, and always the rigid cold.

When it came, the snowfall was thick and furious, a glittering whirl of destruction. The sun was high in the sky, the passage ahead blind. They had passed over the valley, the thin lash of the river wending out of view in the soaring peaks of the Death Run.

Arian's breath huffed out in gasps, lingering in the swirl of snowflakes.

"We must stop. We'll fall to our death."

But there was nowhere they could take shelter. Their supplies were nearly finished. The boy had not complained, dogged in Daniyar's tracks despite the increasing difficulty of their passage through the run. He simply trudged on.

Arian caught Wafa by the waist. When Sinnia reached them, Arian motioned her close. She called out to Daniyar, lost to her sight. The glare of the snow made her temples pound. Where was he? Still forging the path ahead, unaware that his companions had gone astray? Or had he lost his way, straying from the path to a perilous fall? Her mouth went dry at the thought.

The snow muffled sound and light alike. They held hands to

warm each other. And then something brushed against Arian that she could not see, something warm and solid.

At first she thought it was a mastiff.

She waited a moment; it brushed past her again. The boy let out a choked cry.

Through the thick clouds of snow, she caught a glimpse of blue eyes.

She began to hum, a gentle working of the Claim in her throat, a sound mild enough to entice the creature closer. She blinked, trying to make out a pattern of markings against a white slate of snow. She felt a warm mouth nuzzle her arm.

The boy tried to pull away, terrified. Arian held him fast, keeping her voice even and deep. The mouth nuzzled her again.

She released her hold on the others, dropping down to kneel on her haunches.

This time the creature appeared in full, no longer disguised by the snow.

"Shan," she murmured softly, inserting the name alongside tender verses of the Claim. "How beautiful you are."

"What is it?" Sinnia asked. The boy looked on, dumbstruck.

A velvety head turned in her direction, giving her an impression of the creature's blue eyes. It nuzzled Arian's throat and face, knocking its graceful head against her shoulder. A pattern of black markings stood out against its coat.

"A ghost cat," Arian answered, running her hand over the cat's dense fur. "A name given to the snow leopard in these parts."

Arian stroked the cat under its chin, eliciting a deep rumble. She held out a hand to Wafa, encouraging him to do the same. He shrank away.

The snow leopard yawned, exposing a double row of fangs. The boy pointed to her claws.

"She won't hurt you, Wafa. She came to us for a reason."

"Why didn't we see her?" Sinnia asked.

"Ghost cats are camouflaged by snow. It makes them effective hunters."

Wafa shivered. "How do we know she's not hunting us?"

Arian rose to her feet. "She's a creature of the Claim. She is tied to its majesty. Come, she's leading us somewhere."

The cat bounded ahead a short distance. Her markings stood out against the blinding white of the snow.

"She is choosing to let us see her. She wants us to follow."

Arian took a length of rope from her pack and tied it around her waist. She linked herself to Sinnia and Wafa, doing her best to disguise her worry for Daniyar.

The ghost cat moved ahead on the ridge, sure-footed and calm, keeping her charges in view. Their steps were sluggish behind her, often miscalculating the depth of the snow, sinking waist-deep before fighting their way out again. The chatter of the boy's teeth could be heard against the mountain's vast solitude. They continued on like this for a time.

"There!" Arian pointed to a shadow on the ridge where the ghost cat had disappeared. "It's a break, perhaps a cave."

They fought their way through the snowfall. The snow leopard leapt ahead and returned, urging the small group forward. A depression in the side of the mountain led inward into darkness. The carcass of an ibex lay frozen at its entrance.

"It's her lair," Arian said. "It's where she takes shelter."

A voice sounded out of the cave's interior, familiar and welcome.

"I knew our friend would bring you to safety."

"I thought you had fallen," Arian said to Daniyar.

He helped them unloop the rope from around their waists, his touch lingering on Arian.

"Not without you. I sent Astara to you."

The ghost cat approached at the sound of her name, butting her head against the knees of the Silver Mage, purring as his hands caressed her head.

Sinnia shook the snow from her shoulders.

"Only lay such hands on me," she muttered. "You should be jealous," she said to Arian. "The ghost cat receives what you can only hope for." Sinnia grinned, oblivious to Wafa's scowl.

"We'll wait out the storm here," Daniyar said. "We can use the time to rest. We're nearly at the threshold of the Sorrowsong. There's a Talisman patrol at the entrance to the mineshaft. No doubt they're expecting us."

"Can Astara help us? Does she know of another entrance to the Sorrowsong?"

Daniyar shook his head. "The Shin War blasted the other tunnels closed. The only way in is the road they defend." He stroked the cat's head. "I'm afraid Astara will come no further with us. The Talisman hunt the ghost cats for their fur."

Wafa sidled up to the ghost cat. In the close confines of the cave, her giant paws and lustrous tail were a wonder to behold.

"She speaks to you?"

Arian answered him. "All creatures of nature can be read by the Authenticate because they are creatures of truth. They recognize each other."

Astara paced around the boy in a circle, taking swipes at his face with her tail. He fell back on his heels, bewildered and pleased.

"Astara," he said, putting out a hand to stroke her. "Nice cat."

They arranged themselves in a huddle against a wall of the cave. Once they had eaten, Astara came and settled herself beside them, lying over their bodies like a thick fur blanket. The boy rested his head against hers, a smile playing on his lips. For a while they slept, listening to the wind rage against the walls of the cave.

Hours later, when the storm had passed, the ghost cat vanished. Arian woke to find herself cradled in Daniyar's arms, the boy lying against her feet, Sinnia huddled beside him.

For a moment, she savored his heat and strength against her back, the soft brush of his breath over her skin. Then she moved away.

"You don't have to do this, Daniyar. You are one of the Shin War."

His mouth tightened at her withdrawal.

"The risk is greater for you if the ruse fails. These men haven't seen a woman in months. If I take you there as my prisoners, your rank will not protect you. It would be wise to remove your tahweez."

The words didn't frighten her.

Not when he had sworn, *"I will suffer no man to touch you."*

But what he asked of her . . .

"You know the bond with the tahweez is one that cannot be severed. The tahweez may betray us, but they will also protect us. We will use the Claim when the time is right, when you've bartered us for the lajward."

They woke the others, rehearsing the plan with haste. Daniyar passed a tally-taker's crop to Wafa. He produced slave bracelets from his pack, fitting them to the women's wrists. The leather collars were next. Like the bracelets, he left them unlocked.

"These weren't part of the ruse," he told Arian, his hand on her collarbone. "The Shin War use a dagger to the throat. The collars will protect your use of the Claim."

His lips brushed her ear. "Nearer to you than your jugular vein."

His fingers slid under the collar, finding the pulse at the base of her throat.

It hammered wildly beneath his touch.

He savored the small triumph before he let her go.

It was nearly nightfall, a treacherous time to descend. They walked single file, Daniyar at the head of their group, Wafa to the rear, the tally-taker's crop in his hand. The frugal light of the moon illuminated their progress.

A horn sounded, sharp and commanding.

Sinnia and the boy tensed, but Daniyar calmed their fears. "It's not the Avalaunche. They're asking us to identify ourselves." He called out the Shin War greeting in the language of his tribe.

A pause, then the greeting was echoed back, a note of doubt in the voice of the guard.

"I bring a message from the Immolan," Daniyar called. "And a gift."

They continued up the rise to the black mouth that broke the purity of the ridge. The pass widened so the women could walk abreast, the snow tamped down by the passage of many boots.

A hundred feet ahead Talisman guards gathered at the drift mouth of the mine. Against the paleness of the moonlight, Arian saw the telltale bands of blue that had given the Sorrowsong its name. *Sar-e-Sang* in the language of the people of the Death Run.

The Blue Mountain.

Twelve men were gathered at its entrance.

She and Sinnia kept their heads down, their posture submissive. A sideways glance showed her the crop in Wafa's hand. A sheen of sweat had broken over his face. He had known men like the guards all his life. Hardened and made cruel by the dictates of the Preacher, the Shin War a breed apart.

When they were face-to-face with the patrol, Daniyar threw back his hood to disclose the crest at his throat. His body language was easy and confident. The guards responded in kind. Arian watched them from beneath her lashes. Neither she nor Sinnia spoke.

The Shin War were tall and lean in their musculature, long-haired and bearded, but with a military precision hinted at by a sharp attention to dress. They wore black leather armor, their throats marked by the same crest worn by the Silver Mage. Each guard was armed, his face lined by years of war, his eyes sharp and clear from living at high altitudes, his bearing proud—a sign of the Shin War's distinction.

Each one of them had marked out the women and the Hazara boy, but none addressed the issue, engaged in the prolonged courtesies of greeting. They spoke to Daniyar with respect, taking him for one of their own. Daniyar gestured at the women without mentioning the lajward.

Within the depths of the mine, Arian could hear the repetitive strike of hammer against dull rock. The unmistakable tang of smoke wafted toward them. The treasure they sought lay within the mine, but at no time did the Silver Mage express an interest in its interior.

He asked after his own kinsmen. The captain of the Talisman patrol, a striking man with discerning gray eyes, glanced over Daniyar's shoulder. His eyes fell upon the crop in the boy's hand, taking the measure of the bracelets that bound Arian.

"Raise your head," he said to Arian. She obeyed the order at once.

The captain of the guard strode to Arian, flicking aside her cloak without touching her. A murmur rose from the men behind him, as they took in the sight of the woman in close-fitting clothes. Her dark hair cascaded down her back, covering her arms. To distract the captain from closer examination of her bracelets, she lifted her face into the moonlight.

A rush of excitement rippled through the patrol.

The captain was not diverted. He hadn't moved her cloak aside to examine her beauty, he was testing the bracelets at her wrists. Satisfied, he stepped back to address the Silver Mage.

"This one shall have my protection. The men can draw lots for the other." He studied Wafa, his nostrils flaring as he identified the signs of the boy's Hazara ancestry. "We shall want the boy, as well."

"As you wish. You will find him useful in the mines. The women were intended as a gift to your commander."

Wafa turned pale. He had no need to feign his terror. It was evident he thought this had been the plan of the Silver Mage all along.

The captain shrugged in disgust.

"I am Captain Turan, second in command. Sartor commands here." He waited to see if the name meant anything to Daniyar. When the Silver Mage was silent, Turan went on to add, "We will not be using the Hazara in the mines." He avoided the boy's eyes. "The Commandhan will—ask for the boy. Come, I will take you to the camp. You will tell us of Candour, and how the Shin War fare on the plains, and we will do our best to honor the Immolan's emissary."

He held himself aloof from his men as he spoke, the words sounding forced in his mouth. "There are women in our camp, should you desire their company."

The captain was telling the truth. Arian could read as much from Daniyar's expression. He nodded at Wafa, who raised the crop in a gesture of menace.

They fell in line behind the Talisman patrol. They were led away from the mine to a large encampment lower down the rise, where a small plateau jutted from the darkness. Fires roared in the center of the camp. Fed by dry furze, they were tended by men who looked less like soldiers and more like peasant farmers. Over a large campfire, a sheep was roasting. Mouse hares and partridges were tended over other fires, the fire pits fed by myricaria shrubs.

The entire camp was staked on a cold, stony ground, two large black tents to either side, without more adornment than lanterns that gave a sparse light to the darkness. Talisman soldiers were gathered about the fires in great numbers, armed and clad in leather, their pagris fitted to their heads, displaying a uniformity in dress that spoke of military discipline. A surge of anticipation rustled through their ranks at the sight of Arian and Sinnia.

Wheelbarrows full of stone were dotted about the camp. From their depths Arian discerned the blue gleam of lajward, fractured and discarded, broken bits of stone that would not serve to earn their passage through the Cloud Door.

The Talisman kept a small herd of livestock at their camp: ayali sheep that were the natural prey of ghost cats, small goat antelopes known as gorals, and several mules weighed down with supplies and thick pallets of gorse.

Most of the soldiers lounged near the fire, prodding the hungry men who labored over their supper. But a seasoned patrol maintained watch at the perimeter, horns around their necks, weapons at hand, their light eyes watchful.

"You will eat well tonight," Captain Turan told Daniyar. "I'll wager you haven't tasted mutton since you crossed into the Death Run."

He clapped the Silver Mage on the shoulder. Daniyar was back among his own people, if not his own family. There was an ease and familiarity in the way he spoke to the Shin War that had been absent in his dealings with the Immolan's men in Candour.

What lay ahead would not be easy for him.

And as difficult as these realities were, when they had stolen the lajward, Daniyar would have forfeited his place among his tribe. He would be hunted by the Shin War for his betrayal of their code.

I brought this to you, Arian thought. *But I did not want this for you.*

He didn't look Arian's way, engrossed as he was by Turan's conversation.

A whisper of voices from one of the tents claimed Arian's attention, a sound out of place in the camp at the Sorrowsong.

Sinnia pressed her hand, amazed.

The voices belonged to women.

25

Daniyar expressed his gratitude for Turan's hospitality in the civilized accents of the Shin War. Questions whirled in his mind, but to mention the women the captain had referred to would be a breach of etiquette. Nor did he think Captain Turan wished to revisit his offer.

The women couldn't be family members, or the captain wouldn't have spoken of them. A man of the Shin War never mentioned the women of another man's family. He behaved as if they didn't exist, inquiring after the health of a man's sons, wishing him the success of an honorable line.

The women would be captives. But where had they been captured from?

Arian would have the same questions. She would seek answers before Turan's men retired to their pleasures for the night. She would see the captives as her charge. Just as she kept her eye on Wafa, the blue-eyed Hazara boy, the boy whose devotion worried Daniyar.

Would Wafa understand his place in the forthcoming exchange? Would he trust Daniyar's plan?

Captain Turan escorted the Silver Mage to a small tent behind the others. When Commandhan Sartor emerged from the tent, he wasn't the man Daniyar had expected to oversee the Sorrowsong.

Sartor was neither as tall nor as fit as the men he commanded, his heavy frame softened by luxury, his eyes bleary in the mountain air, his movements sluggish.

He wore the Shin War crest, but there the similarities to his men ended.

He was drugged, Daniyar thought. Likely from the opiate that grew in the valleys of poppies to the north of the Sorrowsong mines. A sigh from the man confirmed this: his breath had a sickly sweetness.

Sartor would be a political appointee. Unwilling to leave his comforts in Candour, but commanded to do so by the more powerful members of his family, to reinforce their access to the purest lajward in Khorasan, however unjustly attained.

Daniyar hadn't missed the contrast between the well-fed warriors and the laborers who worked the mines and tended the Shin War camp.

Nor had he missed the absence of the Talisman flag, so far from the reach of the One-Eyed Preacher. The Shin War had accepted the Talisman code, quick to profit from the slave-chains, but they were Shin War first, Talisman second. In the absence of an Immolan, or of the One-Eyed Preacher himself, tribal identity was quick to reassert itself.

Daniyar exchanged the customary pleasantries with Sartor, his manner relaxed.

Sartor had lined his eyes with kohl in the manner of many of the men of his tribe, but Daniyar could read the derision of his officers. Sartor was an outsider, unschooled in the hard life of the mountains. Instead of boots or armor, he was clad in plush robes belted at his waist, and soft, velvet-lined shoes. His head was bare of a turban. The cloak he wore over his shoulders was the stunning pelt of a ghost cat.

His languid gaze drifted from Daniyar to the women who waited behind him.

Stiffly, Turan explained the gift. Sartor waved it away, his gaze sharpening as it came to dwell on the boy. He had not looked at Arian.

"Keep the women to use as you please," he drawled, ignoring Turan's grimace of distaste. "Make the boy ready and send him to me. I have duties for him." He made a slight bow to Daniyar. "You will excuse me for the night, Lord Daniyar. My duties as Commandhan of this encampment are tedious and consuming. My men will fête you well." He tore his eyes from the boy to study the Silver Mage, perhaps sensing his hidden power. "You were sent by the Immolan, you say? Does he plan to honor us with a personal visit?"

Daniyar feigned a polite smile.

"He is not so hardy as members of the Shin War. He prefers not to trek through the Death Run, and asks that I report on your progress in his stead."

"Of course." Sartor did not trouble to mask his delight. "He is Hazara?" he asked, pointing to Wafa. His tongue lingered at the corner of his lips. Daniyar nodded. "A blue-eyed Hazara," Sartor said, with a freshening of his voice. "Now that I have not seen."

Standing at his shoulder, Daniyar could sense Captain Turan's revulsion at the direction of Sartor's thoughts. But Turan would be unable to do anything for the boy. He had no choice but to accept the dictates of his Commandhan.

"The Immolan expects to hear of your progress at the mines," Daniyar said. "The quality of the stone should be much finer than the last shipment he received."

With an effort, Sartor returned his attention to the Immolan's representative.

"I didn't realize the Immolan found the previous shipment unsatisfactory. We send the best the quarries have to offer, but you know the labor force is not recruited from the Shin War. They do not share our standards of excellence." His gaze drifted to Wafa. "We must ensure the Immolan is satisfied. We would not burden him with a personal inspection. Turan."

The captain snapped to attention.

"Make sure the Immolan's representative is well-served tonight. Fête him well—show him to the pleasure tent." He bared his teeth in the travesty of a smile. "Find him a virgin, if your men haven't run amok." He bowed to Daniyar again. "Does that suit my lord Daniyar?"

Daniyar dipped his head.

"The Commandhan honors me. Yet these are not honors the Immolan may share."

Sartor's interest in the Silver Mage sharpened. Here was a man who appeared to understand him, one bound by the same trivialities required of men of state. A man who would report favorably to the Immolan, if his needs were met.

"Stay with us until you are satisfied. You may inspect the mines yourself, and when you return to Candour, we will send an example of our finest stone with you. You may choose the lajward to present to the Immolan according to your discretion."

"I am in your debt, Commandhan. You have understood my needs perfectly. But I fear I've no more than a night to spend with you, as the Immolan expects my imminent return."

Sartor's unpalatable smile spread across his face again.

A man of the Shin War would never conspire against a member of his tribe or seek to end his life with a dagger in the night. But it was satisfactory to Sartor to know that he would not suffer this stranger long, whereas the Immolan's gift would provide him with gratification for months upon end. What was even his finest piece of lajward measured against that?

He dismissed Daniyar, unaware of how closely he was watched by both men.

"Shall we feast?" Turan asked with an effort at courtesy. Something in the man's eyes bespoke his antipathy for Sartor, as clearly as if he'd declared it.

Daniyar gestured at the women and Wafa.

"If you permit me to unchain them, they may eat with us."

Women of the Shin War did not eat in the presence of men but these were slaves, and might be subject to different rules.

Turan refused. But Daniyar sensed this was because he did not wish to expose Arian and Sinnia to the eyes of his men.

Turan motioned to two of the guards.

"Take these women to join the others." He viewed Wafa with stony eyes. "And tell the women to prepare the boy."

One of Turan's adjutants snatched the crop from Wafa's hands.

"You shouldn't have been Hazara," Turan said to Wafa. "Nor should your eyes have been blue."

Wafa's eyes went wide.

"Send me to the mines," he pleaded. "My back is strong, I will work hard."

The crop in the adjutant's hands struck him across the face.

"Hazara do not speak before Shin War," the adjutant warned. "You will do as you are told. And when the Commandhan is finished with you, you will find your place in the mines."

The boy's eyes clung to Daniyar's face, alarmed. He hadn't foreseen this variant of their plan.

"I am hungry," Daniyar said, turning away to the fire. "What delays us?"

Arian, Sinnia, and the boy were led away to the tent on the far side of the fire.

Daniyar's gaze did not follow them.

"I will eat," he said. "And then you will show me the lajward."

26

A RIAN AND S INNIA WERE DEPOSITED INSIDE THE TENT BY THE ROUGH
hands of the soldiers.

"Make the boy ready for the Commandhan," one of them
barked at the women. "Sartor will call for him soon."

When they were gone, Arian's eyes sought out the women the
Talisman had captured at this outpost of the mines. They were
women of a kind who hadn't crossed her path before, women of
mixed ancestry, dressed alike in crimson frocks that covered their
billowing trousers. They wore thick leather boots on their feet.
Their ears, foreheads, and necks were decorated with strings of
silver medallions. Their fingers were dressed in rings.

Some of the women were pale-skinned, others were darker.
Their eyes were of all colors, some set in broad faces with distinct
eye folds, others with narrower bone structure and wide-set eyes.
Their hair, of varying colors, was braided in two plaits beneath
embroidered box caps. Long red veils descended from the caps.

Some of them resembled Wafa. Some resembled women of the
Transcasp, others South Khorasan. Their faces spoke of a place at
the crossroads of history, a trader's route, where different peoples
had mingled to set down roots.

Two of the women came forward and took the boy, their hands firm on his arms. They led him to a washbasin behind a partition. He cast an anxious glance at Arian.

"It's all right," she promised him. "They won't hurt you."

The interior of the tent was bare, save for a stove fed by coals. Thick wool carpets covered the floor from end to end. Drifting panels of cotton created partitions of privacy.

Arian tried the Common Tongue.

"My sisters, are you well? Have these soldiers harmed you?"

None of the women answered. But they did approach Arian and Sinnia in slow, hesitant steps, fascinated by the differences between them.

Why are they not afraid? Arian wondered. *Why have they not been beaten down?*

Sinnia tried the language of the Negus. When she spoke, a murmur of surprise went up from the women.

Arian repeated her questions in several of the tongues of Khorasan. The women seemed to recognize a word here and there, but not the full sense of her questions.

Where had these women come from? Who were they?

As if to answer her, a beautiful girl with sandy braids and golden eyes gestured beyond the flap to the camp outside.

Arian looked over her shoulder.

Was the girl pointing to the Talisman or the men they had brought to work in the mines?

The girl brought her hands and forearms together to form a peak. She pointed to the flap again. Arian lifted the flap just enough so she could see without alerting the guards.

Daniyar was with the Shin War guards at the largest campsite. A communal meal of rice and mutton was being served to the group.

But the girl wasn't pointing to the men.

She was pointing to the shadows silhouetted against the colorless light of the moon.

Arian felt a shock of recognition.

She spoke the words of a language she had thought no more than myth, a tongue that had died out after the wars of the Far Range.

The faces of the women broke apart into smiles.

They gathered around Arian and Sinnia.

The sandy-haired girl spoke.

"How do you know our language?"

It was Irb, the language of the clouds, the tongue of the mountains, found in the Wandering Cloud Door.

"Do you speak any of the languages of Khorasan?" Arian asked her.

The women conferred among themselves. A much older woman with gliding green eyes and a crooked smile introduced herself.

"I am Tochtor. Some of us know the language of the Talisman, but we keep our knowledge secret to aid in our escape."

Arian switched to the Common Tongue so that Sinnia might follow along, keeping her voice low.

"How did you come to be captured by the Talisman?"

The women seated Arian and Sinnia in the center of the tent, running their hands over the Companions' strange clothes, smiling as they showed the Companions the jewelry and decoration they had pieced to their own clothes.

"We were with the winter caravan. A storm came and separated us from our men. We strayed to the Sorrowsong in error, where we were captured by Talisman scouts."

"Have these men used you?" Arian asked.

Tochtor shook her head. Arian sensed a purposeful waiting.

"They've been on patrol for a fortnight. There was some disturbance in the passes, they were caught out in the storm. Tonight, the patrols returned."

The two women shared a bleak look.

"I'm too elderly to interest them, so I serve in other ways." She nodded at the sandy-haired girl. "A few they have said they will not touch because they intend to barter them later. But tonight they will come."

"How do you know this?"

"Their Commandhan came to our tent. He told us to make ourselves ready because his men had earned a reward."

Arian muttered a prayer under her breath. If she was to save these women from the Talisman, she and Daniyar would have to set their plan in motion sooner than anticipated.

"Would that you had not fallen in their way. The pair of you are too beautiful to remain untouched." Tochtor gestured at Sinnia. "She is unlike any of the women here—they will want her. But you—" Their eyes met and held. "Their captain will not share you. He is a better man than the rest. If you obey his will, he will keep you from the others. The boy is lost, I'm afraid. Turan cannot countermand his Commandhan's orders."

Tochtor recounted her advice in a calm, unhurried voice that left Arian silent with amazement. In two weeks, Tochtor had taken the measure of her captors, understanding them far better than they supposed. And as gentle as the women gathered about them were, there was a harshness to them, as well, a forbearance.

They may have been victimized by forces they were powerless to oppose but they were resolute about their fate.

"You haven't tried to escape?"

"There is no need. My son is coming. We simply prepare the way for him."

Tochtor fingered the silver medallions at her throat.

"Your son?"

"Zerafshan. He is Lord of the Wandering Cloud Door, Lord of the Buzkashi. He will come for us." She leaned forward, her hand on Arian's arm. "Turan is not an evil man. It was he who decided my two youngest must not be touched. If Sartor wanted them, they wouldn't have been spared, whereas Turan is harsh before his men, but does not command them to unnecessary cruelty. That is in their own savage natures."

"It is the Talisman law that has warped its people."

Tochtor nodded. "We have long since concluded that the Talisman are a blight. And the Commandhan preys upon children."

"Wafa is not the first?" Sinnia asked.

Tochtor lowered her voice. "Sartor broke the body of the last one. He threw him from the mountain."

Arian knew his cruelty wouldn't end there. "The captain's intervention will not be enough to save your youngest. There are too many soldiers and too few of you. Even should Turan resist their wishes, the Commandhan may gainsay him. We must escape now. I will see Sartor dead before I allow him to harm Wafa."

The sandy-haired girl approached them.

"How will you escape? The man who brought you here chained you."

She ran her hands over the slave bracelets.

"This is Storay," Tochtor said. "My youngest daughter."

Arian was taken by the woman's unruffled calm. For a fortnight, she had borne her captivity with grace, knowing that circumstances could change at any moment, leaving Storay vulnerable to a harrowing fate.

Arian nodded at Sinnia. Sinnia jiggled her cuffs, careful not to make a sound. The bracelets shifted until the catch found the groove and came apart. Sinnia buried the cuffs in her pack. She hastened to undo Arian's cuffs.

Before the astonished eyes of the women gathered round, Arian and Sinnia removed the packs they had kept hidden beneath their cloaks.

"Some warriors," Sinnia said. "They couldn't be bothered to search us. Wafa, come."

Arian glanced at Sinnia, freeing her daggers from the pack. She strapped them to the belt at her waist. She had given her sword to Daniyar before attempting entrance to the Sorrowsong.

"They had no reason not to trust a member of their tribe. If they had searched us, it would have insulted Daniyar. The captain wouldn't have wanted to risk that, given that Daniyar is Shin War."

"So do our traditions undo us," Sinnia murmured. She passed two of her knives to Wafa, who took them with the injured expression of a whipped cur. His wild hair was combed, his hands and face clean, his eyes lined with kohl. He found his way to Arian's side. Arian turned to Tochtor. "Can you help us? What can you tell me about the men who guard this tent?"

Tochtor quelled the whispers of her kin with a look.

"Two guard the front, two the rear. There is no path across the camp from the rear. We are on the steep side of the plateau. Behind the tent, the drop is thousands of feet deep." Her green eyes took Arian's measure. "We would do better to wait for my son and his men. How can the two of you take on so many soldiers? You will stand no chance against them."

Arian considered the same question. She had no doubt that she and Sinnia could kill the men who guarded the tent, but what of the men gathered outside?

She risked another glance through the tent flap. His meal finished, Daniyar was engaged with the captain. But there was no sign of the promised gift of lajward.

Yet now she must consider whether they still *needed* it.

If she could deliver the women of the Wandering Cloud Door safely to their lord, would she not have won his gratitude? Would he not allow her small party to cross his territory to reach the Damson Vale? Perhaps he would even aid them.

But Daniyar had been adamant about the customs of the people of the mountain. She couldn't be certain that rescue would be enough or that it would be successful.

What if her actions precipitated greater violence against the women in the tent? What if they were killed during her attempt to escape? It was possible the Lord of the Cloud Door would hold Arian responsible.

Arian looked from Wafa to Sinnia, to the faces of the women. She didn't want to use the boy as a killer, but she needed his hand at her side.

The men outside were restless. How long could the courtesies of their captain hold them back?

She considered whether the women of the Cloud Door had been spared the assault of the Talisman because Turan had sent his men on patrol. Could they hope for an ally in this captain?

Turan had claimed Arian for himself, but he hadn't touched her. He had shown no similar regard for Sinnia, offering her up to his men.

Arian's thoughts slowed. She retraced Turan's comments to Daniyar.

He hadn't offered Sinnia to his men.

He'd said his men would draw lots for her.

And what of his words to Wafa?

You should not have been Hazara. Nor should your eyes have been blue.

What were the captain's true intentions? Where did his loyalties lie?

"Tochtor. Was Captain Turan among the men who took you captive?"

The old woman thought for a moment.

"No. We were brought here by his men. Had it not been for the storm, they wouldn't have waited so long."

"What happened when you reached camp? What did Captain Turan do? Was he angry?"

"Why would he be angry?" Tochtor's tone was imperious. "With such a prize in his grasp, as the mother and sisters of the Lord of the Mountains, servants of the Eternal Blue Sky?" She traced the layered strands of crimson beads at her bosom, striking the silver jointures with her knuckles. "He was calm about our capture. He looked us over, one by one. It seemed—" She frowned in reflection.

"What?" Arian asked.

"It seemed as if he was counting us."

But to what end?

"Sartor joined him. And promised the women to his troops. He said there should be a banquet to celebrate their conquest. But in truth, he seemed to have no idea where we came from or what we were doing in the passes beyond the Sorrowsong."

"What did the captain do?"

"Annar," Tochtor called.

Another pretty girl with a moon-shaped face and inquisitive eyes stepped forward. Her heavy-lidded eyes shone like obsidian. Arian studied her, puzzled.

"Turan told his Commandhan that Storay and Annar must be

set aside as gifts to the Immolan. When the spring thaw came, he said they would be sent to a city in the south. And then he told the Commandhan the banquet would have to wait because he needed his men to patrol the western borders. He didn't say why."

"Did he speak to you at all?"

Tochtor considered this. "No. But in my hearing he told Sartor that my presence would calm the girls, preparing them for his soldiers."

"Did the captain frequent your tent?"

"No. He set a guard and he told them—" Her voice trailed off, sinking beneath the weight of revelation. "He said that if they dishonored us, their lives would be forfeit to the tribe."

Dishonored.

A curious choice of words for a man who was sworn to the Talisman.

27

It was obvious to Arian that the Talisman had sent Turan to oversee the extraction of lajward from the Sorrowsong, and that Sartor was little more than a figurehead—Turan was the man they trusted to deliver the stone.

As such, Turan ran his camp as the Talisman would have run it, yet without any evidence of the Talisman flag. He was a man of contradictions, doing what was expected within his tribal structure—subjecting the laborers to hardship and disdain, obeying the commands of a lesser man because he was more highly placed in the tribal hierarchy, delivering Wafa to the corrupt desires of his commander—yet he appeared to work a secret agenda, as well.

Who was he? Arian wondered. And what did he want?

Would he stand with or against his men?

The noise in the camp was growing louder, the men becoming unruly.

Her eye to the flap, Arian watched Turan raise Daniyar to his feet. With a stoic face, Turan gestured at the women's tent.

"The old woman will help you choose. They do not speak the Common Tongue, but that should not trouble you."

The men clustered around the campsite murmured their approval of his words.

Daniyar ignored them.

"Before I consider my own pleasure, I must see that the needs of the Immolan are met."

Turan hesitated. The Immolan's representative had surprised him. But he couldn't refuse the request.

"Perzo," he called. "Bring the Immolan's gift."

A scowling man with a heavy brow ambled away to the other tent. He reappeared a few moments later bearing a sturdy, wooden tray covered with a coarse cloth. He brought the tray to Turan, who whisked the cloth away.

Arian stifled the sound in her throat.

The tray bore three substantial pieces crafted from the stone of heaven.

The first was a puzzle box that turned green in the flickering light of the flames. It was carved from sabz, the least valuable form of lajward.

The second was a ewer with a graceful, scooped neck and a long, narrow spout. Set into its side was a dark green medallion, intricately marked. It gave the impression of solidity. Its hue was a pale blue, closer to the early sky of morning, and named asmani after it.

The third was a finely carved key, a rich indigo in color, large enough to spill over the palms of a man. Streaks of white glimmered from within its depths, like the perforation of stars against the evening sky. This was neeli, the true stone of heaven.

These were not frivolous gifts, chosen of a moment. They were something Sartor had *selected* for the Immolan.

But as a bribe . . . or something else?

"Please present these to the Immolan with gratitude for his support of the Shin War." Turan nodded at the key. "He would value the dark stone most. It is most representative of what is mined at the Sorrowsong."

Daniyar tested the weight of the key in his hands.

"The Immolan has seen other veins destroyed by careless blasting."

The men grew impatient, speaking to each other over Daniyar's words.

Arian could see that the captain was considering his next move. He held a hand up to silence his men.

"We've been careful at the Sorrowsong. We select the spot to be quarried, then kindle a fire to make the rock soft. When it has achieved the texture we call nurm, the rock is beaten with hammers. The process is long and exacting, the layers are peeled back flake by flake. Peasants are sent to seek out the stone, but skilled men *work* the stone. They pick out grooves around the lajward, using hooked bars to detach the stone from its matrix. We take the utmost care to exploit each vein to the fullest."

"How do you light fires at this altitude?"

"The flame is fed by dry furze—we send patrols into the passes for this purpose. It burns better than anything else. Even then we require vast quantities of it." There was a curious hesitation in his voice. "Does that satisfy the Immolan's representative?"

Daniyar nodded. "The Immolan will know how to value the Commandhan's generosity."

Though whether generosity could be attributed to the Commandhan, when other hands had worked the stone, and other lives been spent in pursuit of it in the quarries, was a matter for debate.

Arian knew these distinctions would be irrelevant to the Immolan.

The wind began to howl through the camp, a sinister sound

that echoed off the mountains. A lament composed more of warning than sorrow.

"The Sorrowsong," Turan explained. "It gives the mountain its name."

"I would think it would drive men mad."

At the fires behind him, the men stirred angrily.

"Will you choose now?" Turan requested, his words formal. "It would be an insult to refuse a gift under normal circumstances, but you have seen Commandhan Sartor. If you would prefer one of the women sent by the Immolan, it will cause no offence if you take none in return."

"And after I have chosen?" Daniyar kept his voice neutral, hiding his surprise. He turned to look at the women's tent. A rumble of laughter passed through the camp.

"There are private quarters, if you prefer. My men wait upon your choice."

It was a signal to Daniyar to act. Daniyar took it as such.

He strode to the women's tent, dismissing the guards at its entrance. The women inside were gathered near the back at Arian's instruction. Sinnia had dispatched the two guards who flanked the rear. Taken by surprise, they had fallen without a sound.

Daniyar's sweeping glance assessed the situation.

"Hide the girls at the back. Wafa, stand before them as a shield. The soldiers are about to descend on this tent. Arian, I will take you to the center of the camp, where I will ask Turan for use of his quarters. Take your quiver back from me, Sinnia, and empty it when I do. Take out the warriors first. That will give us time to summon the Claim."

Tochtor reached for Arian's hand.

"This is madness. You cannot save us like this. You must wait for my son."

"We no longer have the luxury of choice. I will not allow the Talisman to dishonor your daughters."

Tochtor's face hardened.

"I think you underestimate our ability to resist."

"I think you underestimate the power of the Claim. This is not a debate."

Daniyar closed the subject by taking Arian's arm. He drew her out of the tent. He sealed the flap behind him, so the men in the camp could not see. With careless strength, he led Arian to the center of the camp.

"Show me the way," he said to Turan.

For the first time, Turan looked at Arian directly, her skin pale as moonlight, her eyes that shone like cut crystal, the delicate set of her head. When she met his gaze with the force of her own, recognition flared in his eyes.

Turan knew who she was.

He studied the leather collar at her throat.

She opened her mouth to issue the Claim . . .

He made no move to stop her.

An arrow whistled through the air, followed by another. The men roared to their feet in surprise. Two guards stumbled into the women's tent. They were met by the quick flash of Sinnia's knives. The air filled with the sound of flying arrows.

A sword appeared in Daniyar's hand and in Turan's.

Neither man moved.

Bellowing with rage, the Talisman guards advanced on the tent.

Sartor appeared at the entrance of his tent, startled and confused.

"Turan!" he shouted.

The captain raised his sword.

The Claim began to swell within Arian's throat.

Before it could take shape, a new sound thundered across the plateau. The drumbeat of horses' hooves, accompanied by a cacophony of horns.

The horns were nothing like the sound of the Talisman horn that had greeted them earlier. Richer and fuller, the sound seemed to come from everywhere at once, the depths of the mountain, the sky above them, the crackling lick of the fire, the shadows of night.

The Talisman guards wheeled in confusion.

Horses thundered into the camp, bringing with them the lethal flight of arrows.

Daniyar threw Arian to the ground, covering her body with his.

With the cry of battle in his throat, Turan took up a post in front of the women's tent.

"To the tent!" he called to his men, but they were already engaged.

Leather-clad warriors on barrel chested horses cut through the Talisman ranks. The warriors turned their horses expertly in the narrow encampment, moving with precision, sparing none in their path.

Arrows thudded into the snow at Daniyar's head. Bodies fell around them, the Talisman taken by surprise, unprepared for the skill of the horsemen.

A tall man mounted on a proud stallion called out an order in a language unknown to the Talisman. His men gathered around him in formation.

Two lariats flew through the air, capturing Sartor, then Turan.

The horses surged forward, dragging the men off their feet.

Sinnia and Wafa appeared, daggers in hand, astonished by the sight that met their eyes.

"Wait!" Arian called to them, the air squeezed from her lungs by the pressure of Daniyar's body. They hesitated and were captured by the men who'd taken the camp.

Two men prodded Daniyar and Arian from the ground, forcing them to their knees. The laborers who tended the fires had fled into the mine. The remaining Talisman guards were rounded up by the horsemen and slaughtered.

Four or five men guarded their captives, ignoring their shouted threats.

The rest collected the bodies of Talisman they had dispatched, to send them over the mountains.

Sartor stuttered his displeasure at this treatment and was cuffed across the face. Turan watched the work of the horsemen in silence. Their actions were swift and methodical. When they had finished, they arranged themselves in military rows behind the captives, turning as one to wait for their leader's command.

Arian appraised the field.

The Talisman were dead. Of their ranks, only Turan and Sartor remained alive. Many of the laborers had been killed in the crossfire.

She, Wafa, and Sinnia had been spared for the moment.

And Daniyar. Grouped together with the leaders of the Shin War tribe.

A dozen men had brought four times that many to their knees, their swiftness and skill making up for their lack of numbers. They rode horses of a kind unfamiliar to Arian, with dark coats that flamed red in the firelight. The horses' legs were short, their bodies barrel-chested, their lungs powerful. Their nostrils steamed in the aftermath of battle.

Their leader's horse was of a different breed, its profile scalloped like a bowl, the legs long and lean, its bearing regal.

In the shadows of the Sorrowsong, its coat gleamed white

as snow. Planted beside the horse in the snow was a spear that rose into the night. Flowing from its head was a banner woven of horsehair.

The man who commanded the horsemen strode into their midst. Tall and heavy with muscle, he was clean shaven with pale gold hair that fell past his shoulders. His high cheekbones and icy eyes suggested an origin high in the Transcasp. It was an arresting face, if not a handsome one, backed by his powerful bearing.

He was dressed in a leather brigandine covered with small, square plates. Like his men, he wore leather greaves and gauntlets, a sword on one hip, a beautifully carved horn on the other. At his waist was a brace of knives.

What set him apart from his men was the thick, white cloak that fell from his shoulders to his heels. The coat was made of yak's fur, fastened with a leather choker. Mounted in the center of the choker was a rectangular blue stone threaded through with glimmers of white.

Arian caught her breath, astonished.

The stone was inscribed with writing.

28

THE COMMANDER OF THE HORSEMEN CAME TO A HALT BEFORE THE SHIN War leaders.

"Kill them," he said in the Common Tongue.

"Wait!" Arian cried, struggling to her feet. "Call your mother, my lord. Your women are safe, you will find them inside."

There was no rumble of protest from the horsemen that a woman had addressed their lord. Nor did the commander strike her across the face. Only Turan became alert.

The commander held up a hand to stay his men. Arian's cloak had fallen from her hair, and he studied her with bold interest.

"By the Blue Stone, you are beautiful. What misfortune brought you to this camp, I wonder."

Daniyar stirred at the man's words, but could do little else for the blade pressed to his throat.

"Yeke Khatun," the commander called out, "I have come."

Arian had little time to marvel at the resonant tones of the commander's voice. She had no sooner translated his words as *Great Empress*, when Storay flew out of the tent. She launched herself at the man, flinging her arms about his neck. His high-planed face broke out in a smile. He lifted her high in his arms.

"Storay, you are not hurt?"

"None of us are. We knew you'd come, as soon as we heard the Plaintive. They were terrified by the sound of your horn."

Tochtor proceeded from the tent in a more stately fashion than her daughter. When she reached him, her son took both of her hands in his own and kissed the palms. As one, those of his men who were still horsed dismounted. The riders sank to one knee.

"Yeke Khatun," they echoed. "May she be blessed, may she be honored."

The golden-haired man raised an eyebrow at Arian.

"You do not kneel in the presence of the Empress?"

Arian bent her head. She was mulling over the fact that Tochtor had shared her name instead of her title.

"I meant no discourtesy, my lord. I kneel only before the One who raised the Eternal Blue Sky."

The answer seemed to please him.

"Aybek!" One of the riders rose from his kneeling position to grasp Daniyar's head by the hair. He pressed his blade against the throat of the Silver Mage. "Those who took the Yeke Khatun must be punished."

The leader of the horsemen nodded. "Those who took any of our women must die."

Tochtor replied before Arian could.

"You will wait until you are asked to speak, Altan." She glared at the young rider who had spoken out of turn. Then she turned to her son. "Zerafshan, the Gold-Strewn, Aybek of your people, Lord of the Buzkashi. Do not act with haste, this man is not one of them." She moved from Daniyar to Sartor. "This man, however, is a pederast. He keeps children as catamites. Nail his body to the mines."

She spoke in the Common Tongue for Sartor's benefit, but there was little sign that Sartor was conscious of his plight.

"You have no idea what powerful forces stand behind me, woman—Shin War and Talisman both. If you dare to move against me, all your people will die."

The Aybek struck Sartor with the back of his hand.

With an air of recitation, he said, "If you had not committed the gravest of sins, the One would not have sent me like a punishment upon you."

The horsemen shouted their approval.

Zerafshan nodded at Altan. Releasing Daniyar, Altan swiped his blade against Sartor's throat. Turan flinched as Sartor's blood sprayed his cheeks. Altan grasped Turan's hair, pulling back his head to expose his neck. Another man took hold of Daniyar. Both awaited their master's command. A whimper of fear escaped Wafa's lips.

Arian addressed Tochtor in the tongue of the Cloud Door.

"May I speak, Yeke Khatun?"

Tochtor nodded. Arian turned to the Lord of the Buzkashi.

"It was the Talisman who took these women, but these men here are not Talisman."

"Oh?"

"They are Shin War."

"You speak our tongue and that intrigues me," the Lord of the Cloud Door replied. "But as far as the Buzkashi are concerned, we make no distinction between Shin War and Talisman. We know them for an enemy. None shall mourn their loss."

"Wait, please! It was not Captain Turan who captured the women of the Cloud Door. He acted as their guardian. He gave orders that Annar and Storay were not to be touched. He took none of your women for himself."

"He is a commander of men. He will be held responsible for the actions of his men."

Turan didn't speak in his own defence, perhaps because he could not follow their discussion. It was Tochtor who intervened, using the Common Tongue.

"My son, she speaks the truth. You may do as you please with him, but he did not act as our enemy."

Zerafshan prodded Turan with his boot.

"Shall I do as the women say? Shall I spare your life and take you captive?" His tone was derisive.

The Shin War captain pushed back his shoulders and raised his head.

"My loyalty is to my tribe. As I have failed to defend my men and my position, you should not take me captive."

"An answer I can respect," Zerafshan said. "Your wish will be granted." He signaled to Altan.

With a deft turn of Altan's blade, Turan's blood colored the snow.

"No!" Arian cried.

But it was too late. Turan's body slumped back a little. His head turned in her direction, the gray eyes grave. And she realized again that he knew her.

Blood seeping from his neck, he rasped, "I would like to hear the Claim. Just once before I die."

The light seemed to leave his eyes.

Arian knelt beside him, oblivious to the actions of the Buzkashi.

In a voice made tremulous by grief, she sang to him.

"From the One you came, to the One you return."

She raised her hands to his hair. He stiffened against her touch.

"There will be gardens beneath which rivers flow. Rivers of honey and wine."

Tochtor called out a series of commands. Arian's hands stroked Turan's forehead.

"You shall not know fear, neither shall you grieve."

Turan closed his eyes.

Gentle hands pushed Arian aside, preventing her from attending the captain's last breath.

At the Aybek's swift nod, two women took her place, kneeling beside the fallen captain. A thick cloth was pressed to his throat. Tochtor signaled two of the riders to carry Turan's body into the tent. The women followed behind.

"What did you say to him?" Zerafshan asked.

"You killed him for nothing." Arian's voice was choked. She was not entirely sure what she had witnessed, but she feared now for Daniyar.

"The Buzkashi have a saying. 'Kill. Don't mourn.'"

But his eyes were gentle on Arian's face.

"Your words. I would know what you said to the captain of the Shin War."

Curious, Zerafshan touched a hand to the collar at Arian's throat.

When Sartor and Turan had fallen at his side, the Silver Mage hadn't moved, accepting Arian's right to determine their course of action. He'd read the Aybek's intent toward Turan, understanding the stakes at hand. But at Zerafshan's trespass, he surged forward. The blade at his throat drew a thin line of blood.

"Do not touch her," he warned the Aybek.

"Is she yours?" Zerafshan asked, a gleam of amusement in his eyes. "She must be, as you've shed blood for her—and you will shed more."

"Aybek." Arian drew his attention back to herself. "You misinterpret these circumstances. The man you would kill is not just Shin War. He is the Silver Mage."

At that, Zerafshan's eyebrow arched. "Raise him, Zelgai."

The rider who held Daniyar by the throat urged him to his feet. He sheathed his blade, holding Daniyar by the shoulders.

Zerafshan touched the tip of his sword to the crest at Daniyar's throat. Wafa whimpered, reaching for Sinnia's hand.

"You wear their crest."

"It's the Shin War crest," Arian said desperately. "It does not represent the Talisman. Their creed is not a creed the Silver Mage upholds."

Zerafshan smiled a scornful smile.

"You let your woman speak for you?" he said to Daniyar.

"She belongs to herself," he answered.

"Yet you travel with her."

Daniyar nodded at Wafa.

"We have a chaperone."

Zerafshan laughed, a golden, boisterous sound.

"Yes, your chaperone pleases me mightily. A boy? A man? A mouse hare?"

"You would find out to your cost," Wafa said.

This time the riders laughed.

"I doubt it, but I commend your spirit."

He studied Daniyar.

"I will give you a choice. You seem to be a man of strength. If you truly are not pledged to the Talisman, you may join the ranks of my Buzkashi, or you may continue on your way. Whatever your choice, I will take this woman you say is not yours, for she is comely indeed."

Daniyar did not react. He was reading the Aybek's words, along with the movements of his body.

The designation of Silver Mage was one that Zerafshan recognized. And his threat was intended for display.

"I cannot accept either of your choices. Nor, I think, would you wish me to."

The Buzkashi roared with laughter.

With a hint of steel in his voice, Zerafshan countered, "Believe as you choose, man of the Shin War. I will take this woman, though you need not despair—I will not misuse her. She is lovely enough to take to wife."

It was clear to Arian that the Aybek was trifling with them. There was no undercurrent of threat in his words.

She canvassed the circle of warriors. She noted with surprise that very few of the Buzkashi resembled their leader. Like the women, they represented a mix of races, conjoined and commingled by time. Unlike the Talisman, the men were of a stocky build, their faces deeply tanned, their skin pigmented in shades of brown, their black hair sleek against their skulls, their goatees narrow and pointed. Their eyes were shaded by folds at the corners. Their limbs had been made powerful by the mastery of their horses.

Only the rider called Altan was similar in appearance to Zerafshan. Taller than the others, his hair and skin pale, like Zelgai, he seemed to hold a special rank, each with a small blue stone in his collar.

She wondered why the people of the Wandering Cloud Door had accepted a man so different from themselves as their leader. Only the slight fold at the corners of his ice-water eyes indicated a hint of shared origin. And his mother, the Yeke Khatun, bore a closer resemblance to his men than she did to her son.

Arian knew little of the Wandering Cloud Door. She'd heard stories from her mother and learned the language of the Cloud

Door at Hira. Knowledge would have served her in this instance. In its absence, she would have to trust to the workings of the Council.

She nudged her cloak from her shoulders, holding out her hands. The golden rings on her arms shone beneath the harsh moon of winter.

"You know what these are," Arian said to Zerafshan, her tone weary but respectful. "I am a Companion of Hira, an Oralist of the Claim."

Zerafshan's stallion reared up on its hind legs, its tension communicating itself to the horses of the Buzkashi.

She heard the word *sahabiya* slice like a blade through the snow.

"What is Hira to us?" Zerafshan bluffed. "For all we know, you show us ornaments you wear for adornment."

His note of challenge rang out across the encampment.

Arian motioned Sinnia to her side. When Sinnia discarded her cloak, the Buzkashi gasped.

"I've not seen your kind before," the Aybek said.

"Nor I yours," Sinnia rejoined. "Your hair is as golden as the sun that rises over my homeland. In my country, they would call you Russe."

The Aybek seemed surprised that the names of his people were known so far beyond the Cloud Door.

"My forebears are from lands north of the Transcasp. They were called Russe."

Arian caught Daniyar's sharp glance.

The Wandering Cloud Door was a myth to the peoples of Khorasan. But the Buzkashi knew a history shared by all. They knew of the Transcasp. Some spoke the Common Tongue. Their leader knew more of the world beyond his valley than any of them had suspected. There were other forces at play in Khorasan than legions of the Talisman.

Did Ilea know? Could she have known I would seek a path through the Cloud Door to find my way to the Bloodprint? Have the legends of our sisterhood been sown among the people of the Eternal Blue Sky? Has the path of this Audacy been prepared for me?

She didn't like the thought of being outmaneuvered by Ilea, no matter Ilea's intent. She thought again of Psalm's warning about changes at the Council of Hira. And she wondered if she could trust this bear of a man not to harm them, when with little thought, he'd spent the blood of the man who'd died at her feet.

With a nod at Daniyar, Arian loosened the collar at her throat, taking Sinnia's hand in her own. Even if Sinnia didn't know the verses, her presence would lend clarity to the Claim.

"Are you not aware that the One sends down water from the skies, whereby fruits are brought forth of many hues, just as in the mountains there are streaks of white and red of various shades as well as others raven black?"

Arian's voice rang out like a bell, the notes hanging like pendants on the air.

"Just as there are in men and in crawling beasts, and in cattle, too, many hues."

The syllables flowed out, one into the other, a gliding cascade of sweet and plangent notes. She shaped them with the magic, made them over so that every man listening felt the threat of tears in his throat, felt the hot shame of it behind his eyelids.

It was meant as a lesson to them all.

"Of all the One's servants, only such as are endowed with innate knowledge stand truly in awe of the One. For they alone understand that truly the One is almighty and much forgiving."

It was enough. The last notes filled the air with a sense of hope and loss, and mutual discovery. They were different from each other, unknown to each other, but it did not make them enemies.

Arian let the words fade. She had triumphed over the Aybek, but did not want him dishonored before his people. She spoke quickly in his language.

"My lord Zerafshan, we need your protection through these lands. We risked the pass to the Sorrowsong, so that we might find the way to your valley. We hoped your people would aid us. When we found your women taken by the Talisman, we knew it for a sign."

She gestured at Daniyar.

"The Silver Mage is an Authenticate. He will confirm the truth of my words."

The Aybek was not a fool. He had witnessed the power of her words upon his men. They gazed at the First Oralist with awe. Altan clung to Zelgai's side

The Buzkashi bowed their heads, whispering the word *sa-habiya* to each other.

Zerafshan withdrew the tip of his sword from Daniyar's neck. He sheathed it without taking his eyes from Arian. He chose the Common Tongue for his apology.

"We didn't know the legend was real. Forgive me, sahabiya."

"My name is Arian, and this is Sinnia. You would honor us by taking our names."

"The honor is mine, sahabiya. I took you for a woman of the Talisman, instead of what you are."

Daniyar answered him.

"A Companion of Hira, *First* Oralist of the Claim."

The whispers in the camp redoubled.

"First Oralist."

"The First Oralist comes from Hira to save us."

"Our prayers are heard."

"We are blessed to stand before her."

The Aybek nodded, his eyes canny.

"Very few know our valley exists. The passes to the Cloud Door are closed most of the year. Your reasons for coming must have been urgent. Have you come to teach us?"

Arian bit her lip, an act the Aybek followed with close attention. Daniyar shifted closer to her, and Zerafshan threw back his head and laughed, his voice booming through the mountains. He slapped the Silver Mage on the shoulder.

"She may belong to herself, but you would have her belong to you. Has she refused you?"

There was a twist in Daniyar's voice when he replied. "She refuses me still."

The other man slapped his shoulder again, a broad smile on his face.

"You are not Lord of the Buzkashi, perhaps your enticements are fewer. I offer her the honor of reigning in my valley. Storay, share with the Companion the first of my wedding gifts."

At the Aybek's command, the girl approached Arian. Not as she had first done, with curiosity and warmth. Now Storay's attentions were hushed and respectful, a shift that reflected the stature of the Companions.

"Come to the tent," Storay said. "If you would see the Shin War captain."

Arian's eyes sought out Zerafshan's face. He shrugged.

"The man of the Shin War was valued by you. I give his life to you as a gift."

"How can you gift me his life?" Arian protested in disbelief. "You killed him before my eyes."

Though the Buzkashi shouted their laughter, the Aybek troubled himself to explain.

"A feint, nothing more. My men know a thousand means of killing. This was the slow death, permitting intercession."

Arian stared at him, unconvinced. His smile hardened at the edges.

"Come, First Oralist. Just as Hira holds its secrets close, so do the warriors of the Cloud Door. We do not share our stratagems of war."

And Arian asked herself what the Aybek knew of Hira. And why he spoke of war. Again, her thoughts returned to Psalm's warning. What had happened at Hira in her absence? Had Ilea prepared this ground for her in the Cloud Door to see Arian successful in her Audacy, or did the Aybek of the Cloud Door know of the workings of Hira for other reasons?

"Go," the Aybek said gently. "See him for yourself."

Arian caught the words he seemed to mutter to himself.

"And perhaps then you will tell me why he matters."

29

IF THEY HAD THOUGHT THE TREK TO THE SORROWSONG TREACHEROUS, it was a trifle compared to the journey from the encampment. First, the Aybek had asked her what she wished him to do with the captives, the laborers who hadn't fallen or fled.

"Let them go," Arian said. "They did not seek this life, nor will they trouble you."

"Very well, but they will perform a service for me first. My men require a share of bounty."

He sent the men into the mines with instructions to return laden with the stone they had carved from the mountains. Once this task was accomplished, he set the laborers loose.

Sartor's corpse received no such mercy. The orders of the Yeke Khatun were carried out, his body nailed to the drift mouth as a warning to whoever captured the Sorrowsong next.

"They will think it the work of the Zai Guild. The Zai Guild will call it a Shin War rebellion among the ranks," Zerafshan said.

Arian caught the slight flare of Daniyar's eyes. He knew what the Aybek did not—rebellion among the Shin War was unthinkable. No member of the tribe would betray another.

"And what would you have me do with your captain? This fine soldier who concerns himself with the fate of women?"

Arian had visited Turan in the tent. The cut on his throat was not as treacherous as it had seemed, but he lay unconscious and she would not leave him to an uncertain fate at the Sorrowsong. Turan would not thank her for it, but she could see no other solution than to take him with them. Even then, jostled on a horse along passes bound by snow, where death or harm could come in an instant, Turan might not survive.

Arian wasn't sure that any of them would.

"May we take him with us? I will tend him myself."

"Would you ride with him, Arian? Perhaps a man without his senses is no threat to you."

She was startled by the use of her name, the sound of it in Zerafshan's mouth. She imagined the Claim in the rich tones of his voice. How evocative and meaningful it would be. And then she understood the sense of his words.

Like the Black Khan, the Lord of the Buzkashi had his own attractions, an undeniable charm. But she was chaste, as a Companion of Hira was required to be. She could not think of men.

And even if she didn't deceive herself and did so, she would think of the man she had loved in Candour, the man who risked himself for her without the slightest promise in return.

Her thoughts turned to Turan. There was a connection between them, one she couldn't explain. If they survived the trek to the Cloud Door, she would have to seek the answers.

She worried also that she had nothing to barter with the Lord of the Cloud Door. The Buzkashi had effected a rescue without her aid. The Aybek had taken the lajward he wanted from the mines. What could they barter in exchange for passage to the

Damson Vale? She didn't know whether to take his attentions seriously. Nor could she barter herself.

The Buzkashi had brought horses in their train, and these they loaned out to Arian's company. The women of the Cloud Door rode with their men. Zerafshan offered a seat on his horse to Arian.

"It would not be meet," she said to him, flustered by his affectionate smile. "A Companion of Hira may not ride with a man."

She watched Daniyar mount his horse with an effortless grace and thought, *unless that man is the Silver Mage.*

But she was heartened by the knowledge that the Buzkashi suffered women to ride, nay, expected them to, as the Yeke Khatun rode alone beside her son. Everywhere she had seen scenes of tender reunion between the Buzkashi and their women.

It gave her reason to hope.

I would ride with this golden lion," Sinnia muttered to Wafa. "But does he look at me? Does any man when Arian is present?"

Instead, she and the boy shared one of the barrel-chested horses. The boy ducked his head at her words, for his eyes tracked Arian on her mount.

The Aybek scooped up his sister from the ground to settle her on his horse instead of Arian, his stallion quiet beneath his hands. Sinnia spurred her horse forward, closing the distance between herself and Zerafshan, leaving Arian to follow the Silver Mage.

"Your stallion is not like the others, Aybek. How does he survive in the mountains?"

Zerafshan reached out a hand to the bridle of Sinnia's horse, bringing her closer yet.

"Aiyaruk was bred from a long line of mountain dwellers known as the jorgo. Their lungs have adapted to these altitudes.

The jorgo run fast and wild through our valley. My men ride a breed we call kuluk. They are known for their stamina." His eyes traced Sinnia's dark skin, fascinated by it. "They came down from our legends as dragonhorses."

"Dragonhorses," Sinnia echoed, the name familiar to her. "With flame-red coats."

"Their talents would surprise you," the Aybek said.

Wafa squeezed her waist, a smile breaking out on his face.

"Ghost cats and dragonhorses," he said.

"You know of the ghost cats?" Zerafshan asked them.

"When we were lost in the storm, a ghost cat led us to safety. She was drawn to Arian."

Zerafshan looked over to where Daniyar and Arian rode in close congress, Turan's body saddled on a kuluk horse between them.

"The Companion is most compelling."

Sinnia sighed and reminded Zerafshan of Arian's status. "Do not spend your thoughts on her, Aybek. She is duty-bound, she will take no man as consort."

"What of the Silver Mage? He has marked her for himself, I can tell."

"That changes nothing. And if he can't win her after laying down his life, there isn't much hope for a man from the clouds, even one such as you." She grinned at him, nudging their horses together. "You stand a better chance with a woman of the Negus—a fearsome woman like me."

The Aybek laughed, pleased with her daring, but Sinnia was not certain she had meant it as a jest.

"There will be a need to barter," he agreed. "If you truly require passage through the Cloud Door. I'm sure the First Oralist has thought of an offering."

His eyes returned to Arian, leaving Sinnia with the sense of a missed opportunity. But she had been as bold as she dared because this man of the mountains was something new.

Fierce and golden, his confidence was dazzling.

She didn't like the mountains.

The man was something else.

30

THEY ARRIVED AT THE ICE KILL, A DESCENT TO THE VALLEY FLOOR THAT took them through the night and the following day. The Aybek rode ahead with his men, keeping his own counsel. They were beyond the reach of the Shin War who quarried the Sorrowsong or the Zai Guild who fought them for control of the mines, yet the Buzkashi remained alert to the possibility of ambush.

The valley when they reached it was snowbound, its lake frozen over, with patches of brown that marked a well-used trail, and flashes of green beneath the snow. Pasture land broke through in places. To the north of the valley, an organized camp huddled below the rise. Several herds of sheep and goats were corralled inside a paddock, its circular walls built of stones taken from the foothills. Atop the walls, large cakes of animal dung were collected for use as fuel.

On the open plains, yak covered with heavy blankets grazed the first shoots of grass on the treeless plateau. Beyond them was a series of colorful yurts near the lake. Poles supported felt-covered walls, reinforced with bright red fabric. Their roofs rose like miniature domes, bobbing like tufts of cotton in the wind. Wooden doors imported from lower altitudes held the improvised dwellings together. Outside each home, a lamp was burning in a bowl.

"This is our geshlaq," Zerafshan said, riding ahead. "You will be welcome here."

Cries of greeting rose from the yurts. The Aybek's people spilled forth from their homes, dressed in traditional clothing, the women in layers of colorful dresses, the men in tunics and caps made of lambswool.

In very quick order, men came to unload the supplies the Buzkashi carried, pasturing the horses. An ululating cry went up in the valley as the villagers reunited with their kin. When the Yeke Khatun dismounted, the village girls hastened to receive her.

One of the yurts was much larger than the others, large enough to house several families. Throughout their ride from the Sorrowsong, Altan had carried the horsehair banner. Now he thrust it into the ground at the door of this yurt. Then he disappeared into its interior with Storay and Tochtor.

Zerafshan had informed them that Altan and Zelgai were both his brothers, though only the former resembled Zerafshan. "Altan, as the youngest, is Otchigen, Prince of the Hearth, so he will see you settled. Once you have rested, we will convene a khuriltai."

But Arian could not settle when she was still so far from seeing her Audacy through, when the Talisman could strike Hira at any moment. She looked to the east where a thick veil of clouds descended over the mountains. A sense of urgency hammered at her thoughts. How much time did the Citadel have?

The road to the Damson Vale lay beyond the Cloud Door.

And it appeared the Cloud Door was sealed.

Inside Zerafshan's yurt, they were treated as honored guests. They were seated on a thick wool carpet patterned in red and gold. The fire from an iron stove warmed the center of the yurt, burning yak dung that gave off an odor of surprising sweetness. A kettle of tea was on the boil. It was served with yak milk and salt, a concoction that made Wafa grimace.

Storay hurried to serve them. A large platter was laid with cuts of lamb, alongside a hard cheese served with rounds of flatbread. On a separate platter, a thick mutton stew flavored with tiny, wild onions was presented with more bread, and endless cups of tea.

Arian wanted to collapse upon the pile of furs and fall upon the food. It was the first time she had felt warm in weeks.

But she needed to wash. And there was still Turan to think of.

"I must tend him," she said to Daniyar. "The ride through the mountains weakened him."

"You must eat first."

"I fear the captain's health will brook no delay. I must use the Claim."

"Then I will go. I know more of healing than you."

He didn't wait for Zerafshan or Arian to agree. He gathered his pack, asking to be taken to the yurt that housed Turan.

Zerafshan faced Arian across the warmth of the stove, his mother in the seat of honor beside him, his sister leaning against him.

"You are even more beautiful in the firelight of my ger," he said quietly. "You must think of my home as your own."

He nodded at one of the girls of his family. She brought forth a basin for Arian to wash her hands. Without being told, she brushed a damp cloth across Arian's face. Arian thanked her with a smile, arresting the Aybek's attention.

"By the spirit banner of my people, the Companion is beautiful. I would see you dressed in our finery, adorned with the stone of heaven. But what could match your eyes? Or the mystery of your smile?"

Arian bowed her head at his praise. Beside her, Sinnia shifted in her place. Jealousy was a new emotion to her. She wasn't happy to feel it over this horseman of the Cloud Door.

"The Lord of the Buzkashi honors me with his notice," Arian answered with care. "But has the lord no wife? These are your sisters, I believe."

The girls were a distinct mix. Some resembled Tochtor, others Storay and Zerafshan.

If the Yeke Khatun held the place of honor at Zerafshan's right hand, it meant none of the women in the yurt was his wife.

His mother answered for him.

"Many of our women do not survive childbirth. My son's wife and heir died this past winter."

If the Aybek was without sons, it would explain at least a part of his interest.

"From the One we came, to the One we return," Arian murmured, banking the power of the Claim. The words escaped her as a reassurance.

"From the One we came, to the One we return," the women echoed, their voices hushed in wonder.

Zerafshan added nothing more. They finished their meal in silence.

When Daniyar rejoined them, his portion was heated for him, tea placed at his elbow.

Altan brought forth a horsehead fiddle called a morin khuur. He ran his bow across its strings. Storay relaxed into her brother's shoulder, her gaze darting from Arian to Daniyar. She seemed as taken with him as Zerafshan was with Arian.

When the meal was cleared away, Arian waited for Zerafshan to speak. He took his time, thinking over his words.

"You seek passage through the Cloud Door. Why?"

"It's a matter of some discretion. Who would you have share in this knowledge?"

Zerafshan dismissed all the women save his mother. Altan put down his bow. He and Zelgai placed themselves beside their brother.

"You may speak freely, then I will decide what to share with my council."

It was a fair offer. Arian took it as such.

"The Companions of Hira are each tasked with an Audacy. It is a sacred charge, and one that must be fulfilled once we have committed to its undertaking. My Audacy takes me to the Damson Vale."

Tochtor eyed her shrewdly.

"You seek to avoid the Wall. The Damson Vale is your means of doing so. Otherwise, you would take the passage north of the Ice Kill and you'd have no need to enter the Cloud Door. The Damson Vale is not your destination."

Zerafshan sat back on his heels, alert to any deception. "So what is it you seek beyond the Vale that you would risk the road west? Those lands are held by the Authoritan. The Talisman may smother joy, but the Authoritan smothers life."

"This was not your first encounter with the Talisman, then." She knew the answer, but she was prodding him for information about the slave-chains.

"The Talisman have ransacked the Sorrowsong for decades. They've laid waste to the valleys of the surround. They are at constant war with the peoples of Khorasan. We know they disdain the written word, we have seen the smoke from the burning of libraries. We have witnessed the journeys of their slave-chains."

There it was.

Arian had the answer to her question.

"And may I ask, my lord, what you have done about all you've witnessed?"

She tried to keep the anger from her voice. She could see that life was different in the Ice Kill, where the Buzkashi had built their winter camp. The men and women mingled easily. There was love and laughter between them, each with an assigned share of the tasks necessary to survival on the plateau.

They had climbed so high it seemed to Arian the stars were well within their grasp. The winter camp of the Buzkashi was at peace because the remoteness of the Ice Kill separated them from the rest of Khorasan. If the stories were true, the Buzkashi would climb higher still, packing up their yurts to pass through the Cloud Door, to graze their livestock in the spectacular valley that lay between the Fire Mirrors to the north, and the Death Run to the south.

The Talisman hadn't guessed that in the valleys of the Death Run, an army superior to their own had been raised, capable of defeating them. And of rescuing women from the slave-chains. Why the Aybek had not acted to this end already, Arian couldn't guess.

If she'd had men like the Buzkashi at her command . . .

Zerafshan took note of Arian's anger with interest.

"The Talisman live by their code, we live by ours." He held up a hand, spreading his fingers wide. "Just as the One has given different fingers to the hand, so are men given different ways. If the Talisman encroach upon our borders, we will face them on the field." He closed his hand into a fist. "When they took the Yeke Khatun, we dealt them a killing blow."

"And what of the rest of the women of Khorasan? Do you know where they've been taken, or what purpose the slave-chains serve?"

Zerafshan grimaced. "They are not my charge. We are bound

to follow the laws of our ancestors. We do not mimic the ways of others."

Daniyar murmured to Arian, "There's more. He hasn't told us all."

"The Authenticate reads you for the truth," Tochtor told her son. "He will not accept less."

Zerafshan fixed Arian with his ice-water eyes.

"If I hold something in reserve, I'm not the only one to do so."

A wave of fatigue swept over Arian. The air was thin, the days were long, the ride hard. Each new day that passed without bringing her closer to the Bloodprint put those who chose to help her further at risk. Sinnia. Wafa. The Hazara who'd fled to Hira. And most of all, Daniyar.

All this for an Audacy sanctioned by Ilea and the Black Khan, neither of whom she could be sure she trusted.

What had she to lose by giving the Lord of the Buzkashi more of the truth?

"I seek the capital of the Authoritan. The Wall cannot be breached, so I must approach from the Damson Vale."

Zerafshan let out an oath. He glared at Daniyar.

"And you sanction this? You would send her as a lamb to the Authoritan's slaughter?"

Daniyar's response was cold. "I told you. She belongs to herself. As she will not forswear her Audacy, I choose to stand at her side."

"And these?" The Aybek nodded at Sinnia and Wafa. "This slip of a girl? This boy who remains mute, terrified of everything that crosses his path? These are the companions of choice with whom she will brave the Authoritan? Little do you understand his rule. Better to perish in the passes of the Fire Mirrors than to stray westward, north of the Wall."

"You underestimate them," Daniyar rejoined. "The First Oralist isn't defenceless. Alone, she liberated many caravans. These months past, this slip of a girl has been Arian's right hand, whereas Wafa has defended the Oralist's life many times over, with no thought to his own."

An expression of stunned gratitude crossed the boy's face as he listened.

"Please," Arian interrupted. "My companions are who they are, and I would not ask for others. What matters is simply this: will you take us through the Cloud Door? Will you serve as our escort? Yeke Khatun, will you not speak for me?"

The old woman reached out to take Arian's hand.

"You are schooled in much wisdom, First Oralist. And the Council of Hira is honored in our lands. But do you not know where the slave-chains are headed?"

"Do you?" Arian whispered, gripping Tochtor's hands. A stroke of premonition stabbed through her thoughts.

Had the men of Khorasan become servants of the Authoritan, the tyrant of the north? How did this aid the Preacher or fit with the Talisman creed?

"The women of the slave-chains are sold beyond the Wall."

Premonition shrank into warning, insistent and throbbing inside her skull.

"For what dark villainy?"

Zerafshan answered her.

"We have intelligence of the north. The young women are taken to the palace to serve the warriors who guard the Wall. A second group is sent to the cotton fields, to be worked until their bodies are broken. Their fate is better than that of the women in the third group."

"Then what can you tell us of the third?" Sinnia dared to ask.

But Zerafshan's attention was captured by the signs of Arian's anguish.

"Tell me," Arian said to him. "What could be worse?"

His answer was blunt.

"The third group is sent to the Plague Lands. No one ever returns."

31

Daniyar took Arian outside, wrapping his arm around her shoulders. For ten years, Arian had labored to learn this secret. And now that she knew it, she couldn't think of the Bloodprint.

Inside the tent, the mood was just as somber. "You shouldn't scowl like that, Aybek," Sinnia said to Zerafshan. "I told you that Arian is duty-bound. She thinks only of the journey beyond the Wall, nothing you say will impede her."

"The Cloud Door is sealed. The pass to the Damson Vale is closed."

"Is there another way? If we cannot enter the Cloud Door?"

She caught the glance that passed from mother to son.

"What would you barter in aid of an answer?" he asked.

"I have nothing to barter except myself," Sinnia said, wishing Zerafshan's attention would fix on her for a moment. She had never spoken like this to a man. But his gaze was held by the woman in Daniyar's arms.

So she called to the Silver Mage, who brought Arian back inside the yurt. She waved her arm at the Aybek.

"The Aybek will not risk the Fire Mirrors, he says. Just as he says the Cloud Door is sealed. But there must be another way, a safer passage than the Cloud Door." Sinnia feigned a lightness she didn't feel. The Lord of the Buzkashi stood transfixed by Arian. "Will you not share your secret with us? Will you not show Arian a safer course, for she is determined to go."

Zerafshan ignored Sinnia, speaking to Daniyar.

"You have the advantage over me. You can read the truth of my words, whereas I must guess at your motives. I have given you the truth of the slave-chains. What do you seek beyond the Wall?"

This time Daniyar didn't wait for Arian to decide. There was more, much more, he needed to learn.

"It will seem as legend to you, much as the Cloud Door was to us. What I share with you must not pass beyond those of us gathered here. Your khuriltai must not learn of it."

He waited. Zerafshan nodded his assent.

"We seek the Bloodprint."

Tochtor gasped. "You risk your lives for a myth," she said.

"Mother, they do not." Zerafshan patted Tochtor's knee, calm in the face of revelation. His glance traveled from Daniyar to Arian. "You didn't ask me what the Talisman purchase at the price of the women they sell."

"Because I already know. Riches, treasure—it is all they care for now."

Zerafshan shook his head.

"Indeed, you are mistaken. Jewels may satisfy the Talisman, but they are not what the One-Eyed Preacher seeks."

His eyebrow quirked when he saw that he held them in thrall.

"The Preacher buys the Verse of the Throne. The Authoritan delivers it. A letter at a time."

32

ARIAN'S SLEEP THAT NIGHT WAS POOR. THEY WERE HOUSED IN THE AY-bek's ger, women to one side, men to the other. The fire was stoked throughout the night, either by Altan or one of his sisters. She was warm and well-fed, but her thoughts were not easy.

A throne to comprise the heavens and the earth.

The phrase was the only part of the Verse of the Throne known to the Companions of Hira, or so it was held. A verse of profound majesty and depth with cataclysmic power. In the hands of the unrighteous, the Verse would cover the world with doom.

If the Authoritan was peddling the Verse of the Throne, it could only be from one source.

The Bloodprint.

The Black Khan had told them the truth.

The Bloodprint was real.

The Authoritan had found a use for it, though why he hadn't kept his knowledge to himself, Arian couldn't guess. Another cause for worry.

They woke to a morning without snowfall. The sun bathed the valley with light. Tea was aboil on the stove, two of Zerafshan's sisters busy with the preparation of breakfast. Apart from them, the ger was empty.

"Where is the Aybek?" Daniyar asked Storay.

Storay stirred a savory concoction in a pot on the iron stove.

"The khuriltai is meeting," she explained, with a shy glance in his direction. "My brother divides the khubi among his men's families before he hears the law. When the khuriltai disbands, there will be festivities to honor the Companions of Hira."

"We should attend," Daniyar told Arian. "Perhaps you can sway the Aybek."

The bitter words struck at Arian. Before she could answer him, Altan entered the ger.

"The dakhu is recovered. He wishes to speak with you."

Dakhu was the local word for a person of objectionable character. Turan was likely the first of the Talisman to have reached the valley at the threshold of the Cloud Door. None of the Buzkashi would trust him. Nor did Arian know what fate she could leave him to. Here in this valley, he would be an enemy of the Buzkashi. Sent back to Candour, he would warn the Talisman hierarchy of Daniyar's betrayal.

Taking him to the Wall was also impossible. They could not afford a prisoner, and the captain was too dangerous to accompany them unfettered.

They were running out of options for Turan.

Daniyar grabbed his pack, directing the others to stay and breakfast.

"We must leave today. With or without the Aybek's help."

"I'm coming with you," Arian said. "I need to speak to the captain."

"This is the first opportunity I've had to speak to him alone."

It wasn't a question of trust. Two men of the Shin War had

ended up on opposite sides. Turan's rebuke would be damning. She wished she could afford Daniyar the courtesy of privacy—he deserved that from her. But time was slipping past them, the time to make choices that could be costly to her Audacy, and even costlier to Hira. There had been a thin strand of connection between herself and the Talisman captain—the feeling too strong to ignore as coincidence. She needed to unravel it.

Sensing her determination, Daniyar didn't argue further. Altan took them to the yurt where Turan was guarded by two of Zerafshan's men. One of the men searched Daniyar for weapons.

"I would not betray your Aybek's trust by freeing his prisoner without his consent."

Altan snorted. "You are both Shin War. What trust can be reposed in a man who doesn't stand with his tribe?"

Daniyar gave the only answer he could.

"There are higher values than kinship."

Arian intervened before Altan could say more. "Captain Turan is my prisoner. You heard your brother gift me with his life."

Altan knew the truth of it. He sought a way to save face.

"There will be no secret consultation, I will stand at the entrance."

Winter light flooded the yurt, splaying against the harsh angles of Turan's face. The Shin War captain was seated on a thick pile of blankets that covered a plain wool carpet. His back rested against a rounded wall. His hands were bound in front of him with a leather tie that Daniyar released.

With a wary glance at his kinsman, Turan rubbed his wrists.

"Why did you bring me here?" he asked, speaking in the dialect of Candour to defeat Altan's design.

"I thought it best. I couldn't leave you to die."

Arian's gentle words drew Turan's attention to her face, then to her circlets. He nodded to himself as if he'd confirmed something.

"You recited the Claim for me. I wished for nothing more."

"Do you know me, Captain? For I do not think we have met before."

His was not a face Arian had seen during her campaign against the caravans. And the Shin War would not waste a leader of his talents as a common slave handler.

Instead of answering, Turan focused on Daniyar.

"You betrayed us. The Immolan didn't send you. You brought the Companion to the Sorrowsong for a purpose. What did you want?"

"The blue stone."

"And you risked the chastity of the Companion for that?"

His words chilled Arian. Why did this man of the Shin War recognize the Claim? And how could he know so much about her?

She knelt beside him. His color was better than it had been the previous night, less tinged with gray. His eyes were clear and grave, those of a man used to living at altitude. In the cold light of morning, he was much older than she'd first guessed, his hair and beard threaded through with silver. She had thought him striking before, wearing his command with dignity. With a closer look, she saw that authority was something intrinsic to him.

"*Do* you know me?" she asked him. She could sense something between them.

"Do you not know me?" He could see that she didn't. "You were too young to remember, but I would have known you anywhere, as I knew your father."

Sickness rose in her throat, horror flooding her mind.

Had he been there that night?

Was this the connection she'd imagined? The recognition that passed between a killer and his victim?

She had recited the Claim for him.

"Are you the man who killed my father?"

The Claim was buzzing in her throat, ready to spill forth, to rage.

Turan looked surprised.

"Your father was my friend, your mother also." He showed her his hands. His index and middle fingers were callused. "There was a time when tribal bonds were not everything in Candour. People of goodwill could form other relationships. Your parents were my friends," he repeated. "I worked in their scriptorium."

"By the pen and what they inscribe."

Arian's breath was raw in her chest.

His gray eyes quizzed her.

"Yes," he said. "You were the one chosen to be a linguist."

"You are Shin War," she mumbled. "You couldn't have been a friend."

The captain leaned forward to whisper a word in her ear, a word formed of a single letter.

Nun.

A word symbolized by a curved open bowl with a diacritical mark above it.

It meant "Inkwell."

The name of her parents' scriptorium.

He nodded at Daniyar.

"There is such a thing as divided loyalty. Ask the Silver Mage. He received the utmost honors of the Shin War only to refuse them all. What did he say to our guard? There are higher values than kinship."

The two men weighed each other. The Shin War recognized no higher value; the tribal bond was everything. Without it, the entire

252

tribal structure would fail. Yet both men had sought a way to reconcile the demands of identity with justice.

"When you offered the Companion to me at the Sorrowsong—" Daniyar broke off.

"I knew you as the Silver Mage. I knew you would protect her."

"You gave me the Immolan's lajward."

"My men spotted you on the ridge five days before you struggled into our camp. I sent the ghost cat to help you. There are times when a thing is destined, and so it comes to pass."

His revelations stunned them.

"What do you mean?" she whispered. "Why would you help me?"

"You truly do not know?"

Turan waited but she said nothing else.

"The night your family was killed, you were hidden by your parents at Nun. I didn't know the Talisman's plan—it was not of the Shin War's contriving." He motioned to Daniyar's crest. "You know it for the truth. You know what the Shin War are, what they are not."

In Arian's mind, memory unfurled. Hands that gripped her childhood self with urgency. The smell of a man's cloak, the rough scrape of his beard. And the patient voice, speaking to her of her parents' murder. The act that had brought down her house.

What had she seen? What had she not seen?

"It was you?" she asked like a child.

And from the look in his eyes, she knew Daniyar had realized, as well.

"Yes," said Turan. "I found you at Nun. I was the one who delivered you to Hira."

He'd held her fast in the saddle, murmuring words of consolation in her ear, cradling her against the chest that wore the Shin War armor.

Making her a promise.

Whenever you need my aid, you will find me.

She had never needed it more than when they had stumbled their way to the Sorrowsong.

"How did you know me again after so long?"

"Your face, your eyes—they are your mother's."

A new discovery was upon her. She could hear the emotion that colored Turan's voice.

"You loved her."

"She wasn't Shin War, we couldn't marry. In time, she met your father." Arian pondered the implications of this.

"But you stayed at Nun."

"I loved them both, I couldn't leave."

Suddenly clear-eyed, Arian asked him, "And what would you have done in your encampment at the Sorrowsong, if your men had wanted me?"

His jaw hardened in response. "Whatever I had to. But I thought the Claim would protect you, if you were as gifted as your mother."

There was something else. Something Arian hadn't fathomed yet.

"If this is true, why do you work for the Talisman? What were you doing at the Sorrowsong?"

"Do you still not know? Did you not follow the falcon of Hira?"

Turan looked from one face to the other, puzzled. And saw that the Silver Mage understood the truth of things.

"The Talisman didn't send me to the Sorrowsong—I was placed there by Ilea. The High Companion told me to wait for you."

Turan was not the Talisman's man, he belonged to the Council of Hira.

"You've betrayed the Shin War." Her lips were numb as she spoke.

He had carried her in his arms. He had taken her to safety. He guarded her still.

Turan echoed Daniyar's words again.

"There are higher values than kinship." He cleared his throat. "I haven't seen you since the day I left you at Hira, but I followed your progress. I knew we would meet again."

She shook her head in disbelief. "How could you know that?"

"On the day I delivered you to Hira, I was pledged in your service. I have never been released."

"Have you been at the Sorrowsong all this time?"

"I have been wherever Ilea needed me to be. There was something at the Sorrowsong I was sent to find and keep safe."

Daniyar glanced at the door where Altan had stopped listening, bored by a language he didn't understand.

"The Immolan's lajward," he guessed. "The pieces are significant—why? So that we might trade our way through the Cloud Door?"

"For the same reason the Immolan was told to retrieve those pieces for the Preacher." Turan's words were slow and deliberate, his hand pressed against the wound at his throat. "The Preacher doesn't concern himself with the Cloud Door. The pieces are clues to the Bloodprint."

Arian tried to conceal her shock and failed. Turan knew of her Audacy. She had taken the road west without knowing where she was going, or how to achieve passage beyond the Wall. Yet the Sorrowsong had been prepared for her by Ilea, confirming her suspicions.

Ilea knew far more of the Bloodprint than she had revealed

during Arian's submission at the All Ways. Yet she hadn't spoken of it.

Because she needed to keep her knowledge secret from the Black Khan?

Did Ilea trust the Black Khan no more than Arian did?

Having traversed the rough places of the world, Arian could understand this. She welcomed it as a sign that she and Ilea might finally have found common ground.

You seek to deny the Talisman legitimacy. I seek to do the same.

Perhaps it was true.

"Do you have the pieces still?" Turan asked her.

Daniyar removed them from his pack to Altan's great interest.

"We intended to barter them for passage through the Cloud Door."

Turan shook his head. "It would not serve you. The Cloud Door is sealed until the thaws set in. The High Companion sent no message of the Cloud Door."

"What message did she send? What news did Saqar bring you?"

Turan reached for the Shin War crest at his neck. A small opening had been worked behind it. From its interior, he produced a thin scroll.

They studied it together, conscious of the long-forbidden nature of the act of reading the written word.

The message was stark, unrevealing.

Use the box to find the tomb.

33

Zerafshan came to stand beside Arian as horses thundered through the camp. The Buzkashi had gathered to celebrate their victory. Fires that were lit from sweet-scented yak dung were dotted about the valley. Women came to the field dressed in bright garments. The married women wore white headdresses, the girls a brilliant crimson. Jewelry flickered over their clothing.

The Aybek had called his men together for the deafening game of buzkashi, the sport from which his warriors had taken their name. Forty men competed on swift, sleek horses for the prize of a goat's carcass, slung low across the plain. The carcass had been soaked in water to harden it before the match. The goat's head and limbs had been cut from the carcass, its body stuffed with sand to increase its heft.

Half the men took the field at a time, forming temporary alliances, with each man playing for himself. To win at the game, a rider had to seize the carcass, drag it around the black banner posted at one end of the field, then cross the field again to throw the carcass into a circle marked by chalk at the opposite end of the valley. This form of buzkashi was called qarajai, demanding of the men exceptional horsemanship, and no small measure of brutality.

The riders wore robes over their trousers and booted feet. Karakul hats covered their heads. Many of them clenched whips between their teeth as they rode hard and fast, out of their saddles. At any particularly daring move, the women would gasp and cheer.

Altan led his side, scooping the carcass from the plain, beating off other riders with his crop. Standing beside Arian, Wafa flinched.

"This boy serves you?" Zerafshan asked.

"He is under my care," she answered.

"Then he shall be under mine."

"We must speak with you, my lord, about the Cloud Door. The time for my Audacy runs short. And my need is urgent."

Zerafshan allowed his hand to brush across Arian's hair. She stiffened in response.

"My men play qarajai for your amusement."

"And I am grateful, my lord." She said this though she could scarcely bear to look at the headless carcass. "But we have matters to discuss. You held your council without us."

He pulled her back several steps as the pack of riders drew too close. A broad smile brightened his face.

"Outsiders are not permitted to attend the khuriltai. There were matters of the Yassa that were delayed because of our venture to the Sorrowsong. As Aybek, I must deliver the law."

"The Yassa is your law?"

"Yes. Whoever thwarts it must face the penalty. My people would be ashamed to be punished in the presence of the Companions of Hira. We did not discuss your Audacy."

"Have you decided if you will aid us in our endeavor?"

His hand was still on her shoulder. Now he withdrew it.

"What will you barter in exchange?"

She knew what he was asking. Across from her, on the other side of the field, she caught the flash of Sinnia's eyes.

"I thought I'd explained my duty, my lord."

Zerafshan stroked his chin. At his side, Storay had taken an interest in Wafa. Earlier in the day, she had shown him how to wash and given him clean clothing. The Hazara boy held as a slave by the Talisman was now dressed as a miniature Buzkashi.

"Yes, your duty." Zerafshan returned his attention to the field. "You spent years of your life breaking Talisman slave-chains?"

"Yes."

"What a waste of your youth and beauty."

"I do not count it so. Just as your mother and sister were delivered by your raid upon the Sorrowsong, it is my hope that many families among my people saw their women again."

He nodded, perhaps seeing the wisdom of her words.

"I will give you the assistance you require on the road to the Wall if you give me your bond you'll return to my side." A wide arc of his hand encompassed the Ice Kill. "My people need a teacher. Not one among them is literate. It would be a worthwhile cause if the man alone does not impress you."

He took Arian's hand and brushed his lips against it.

This was the moment she had sought to avoid. An intimacy that would indicate she was ready to barter herself because she did not refuse it. She could not afford to give offence.

A flush arose in her cheeks. She looked away and found Daniyar watching her, his face shuttered. Quickly, she drew away from the Aybek.

"My lord—"

"Zerafshan."

"My lord Zerafshan," she tried again, "any woman would be honored to share your name, but I have taken oaths at Hira that I cannot forswear. And time is against me now."

His eyes never left her face. "And afterward?"

Sadness filled Arian's voice. In all this time, she had never considered an afterward. But she answered him honestly, her pale eyes direct.

"You would not want a woman whose heart is given to another."

"Perhaps I could make you forget him."

But he saw that wherever the Silver Mage went in the camp, the Companion's soft eyes tracked him. Arian's words confirmed this.

"I have no wish to forget him."

Zerafshan's response was swift.

"Then it would seem you have nothing to barter. Unless what Altan tells me is true."

He meant the lajward Turan had given them.

Arian was at an impasse. She needed the Aybek's knowledge of the route that lay ahead. But she couldn't afford to give up any clue that would aid in her search for the Bloodprint. What could she offer the Aybek instead? The blue stone was precious to these people of the mountains. It was a mark of honor and respect among them, believed to endow strength and good fortune; she need only look at the stone mounted in Zerafshan's collar.

Neeli inscribed with the tongue of the Cloud Door. A tongue she spoke but did not read.

"My lord, your medallion. What does it say?"

He touched a hand to his throat, tracing over the letters.

"There are no scribes among my people. The ancestors of our valley were raiders, people of the northern steppes. They raided Inklings from the lands of Shin Jang, who formed our language for us. The medallion comes from the Shin Jang court. It once adorned the crown of a taihe princess. Our Inklings inscribed it to read 'Aybek Who Upholds the Yassa.'"

"The commander who delivers the law. Will it pass to your son in time?"

"If he proves himself worthy. Aybek is not a hereditary title. It must be earned by a vote of the khuriltai. The man who demonstrates the greatest ability will be chosen as the next Aybek."

A system based on merit. Or so it seemed.

"I see your brothers hold ranks of high honor."

She guessed this from the blue stones set into the neckbands that Zelgai and Altan wore. It was a gentle reminder that it was Altan who led one side of the men engaged in buzkashi, while Zelgai challenged him from the other.

Both brothers looked to the Aybek for his approval. Their mother waited to declare a champion. The Yeke Khatun had donned a splendid ceremonial dress in red silk. She appeared as a scarlet gash against the backdrop of the mountains. Her delicate jade headdress shone like crystallized moonlight.

"Altan is the son of my mother," Zerafshan agreed. "As the youngest, he is Prince of the Hearth. His responsibility is to protect the family. But Zelgai is my andas."

"Andas?"

"Blood brother. We share no bond of heredity, the andas is a bond freely chosen. He has demonstrated a loyalty beyond any of my men."

Sinnia joined them. She'd been given an embroidered red dress that she wore over her riding clothes.

"You see my veil is red, Aybek."

Zerafshan's bold glance approved her, a smile teasing his lips.

"I hear you, woman. Your companion has refused me. She offers nothing else in exchange for my assistance. What would you give in her place?"

Sinnia bowed her head. Her close-cropped curls were hidden by the fine red veil.

"What would you have of me, Aybek?"

When he didn't answer, she swept the veil from her head with a brisk gesture.

"It wouldn't matter what you asked," she said, ignoring his silence. "What we have need of is fresh horses, supplies, and whatever intelligence you can give us of the Wall. You say the Cloud Door is closed." Her eyes searched the pass to the north, where the cloud cover was impenetrable. "Then share your secret. Is there another way?"

"There is a way," he said. "A most dangerous path north. And I would send a party of my men to show you the road, to the place where the Wall may be breached. Despite what they say of the Wall, we continue to trade with the northmen."

Here was a thing unheard of—that the Wall could be breached, or that there was regular congress with the men of the north.

Arian's eyes scanned the Aybek's people. The men and women were distinctly of his own kind.

"And what do you trade with the northmen, my lord?"

He heard the wariness in Arian's words and understood it. He grasped her arm just beneath her circlet, turning it this way and that to ponder its inscription.

"Not women, as you are thinking." He spat upon the snow. "We follow the laws of our ancestors."

He'd said this to her before. She'd failed to understand its significance.

"You do not engage the Talisman. You haven't spared any slave-chains."

He jerked her closer, staring down at her from his great height, his eyes narrowed against her accusations.

"Understand me, Companion. When my people go to war, it is not as others go to war, not even your Talisman. It is not a thing we undertake lightly." His eyes pinned hers. "War is the unmitigated effort of one people against another."

He released his grip on her arm, taking note of Daniyar's approach.

"As for women—they are not khubi to be allotted among ourselves. You see that no man among us has clamored for you or your dutiful companion. I ask for your hand, but I do not force it."

He gave Arian a moment to think over his words.

Around them, the sounds of the qarajai had quieted. The valley had stilled to hear the Aybek.

He lowered his voice. Its dark growl sent a shiver through Arian.

"We follow the law of our ancestors. We do not mimic the ways of wild dogs."

She took a step back, relieved to find Daniyar at her side. She had been misled by Zerafshan's bonhomie, underestimating his ferocity, his clarity of purpose.

"Forgive me, Aybek," she managed. "I meant no insult to the people of the Cloud Door. It has been long since women have been honored in any land, and I am unlearned in the Yassa."

Zerafshan bent his head. The women around him copied the gesture at once.

"A Companion of Hira need make no apology. Wherever she goes, the Claim is enough, all must accede to her power. Yet you humble yourself for me." His eyes marked Daniyar. "You would be a fool to forfeit a woman like this."

Daniyar's response was terse.

"I am no fool."

The Aybek threw back his head and laughed. His lion's roar filled the valley. A whistle sounded. Zelgai had succeeded in hoisting the goat's carcass into the chalk circle.

Zerafshan signaled his mother. "It's time. Begin the celebrations."

34

THE PEOPLE OF THE CLOUD DOOR THRONGED THE PITCH, SHOUTS OF laughter and congratulation filling the air. Zelgai and Altan clapped each other across the shoulders, celebrating their mastery. Storay darted forth into the frenzy and was lost to sight, Wafa following at her heels.

"What did you barter?" Arian asked Zerafshan, hoping to learn how to persuade him.

"Furs for the winter, wool from our sheep. We gained food stores in exchange because the northern lands are fertile. The men we trade with are members of the Ahdath, but they act outside the Authoritan's knowledge. He believes the Wall is secure, that all congress with the south is closed off."

"Except for the slave-chains."

"Their point of entry is further west. Ours lies to the north."

"How were you able to persuade the Ahdath to trade with you? How did they know you had anything worth bartering?"

The Aybek gave his sister an absentminded wave. She had gathered the carcass and carried it to the bonfire the Yeke Khatun tended.

"Do you remember the year of the Zud, a decade past? Most of Khorasan was affected."

The animal famine. Much of the south had starved that year.

"Yes," Arian replied. "I remember it well."

"My people were desperate, I couldn't let them starve. We took a force to besiege the Wall, in hopes of scavenging food for ourselves. The Ahdath have vast reserves of grain."

"They are hardly known for their charity. Did you breach the Wall?"

The Aybek's smile was grim with memory.

"There was no need. It was the worst winter of a decade. Unlike those who dwell in the Cloud Door, their people are not immune to the cold. They were willing to trade grain for furs. It was a good bargain. On both sides, we consider it a relationship worth preserving. No one can say when the Zud may fall again."

At Arian's side, Daniyar counted the men in the valley. "Aybek. You said you took a force to besiege the Wall. What hope did these few hundred have against the Ahdath?"

Zerafshan drew himself to his full height.

"Do you count yourselves as friends of the Buzkashi? Would you swear your loyalty?"

The Silver Mage reached forward and gripped Zerafshan's hand.

"I would, I do."

Zerafshan nodded at the Cloud Door.

"These are the best-trained among my men, the first to battle. The regiment of the One known as the Mangudah. Many more train for war in the Cloud Door, the Army of the Left. The Army of the Right trains in the lowlands to the north, on the path to the Wall."

"My lord, why?"

But even as she asked the question, Arian was remembering the discipline Zerafshan's men had shown in their raid of the Sorrowsong.

He echoed where her thoughts had led. "The Talisman may push east at any time, the Ahdath south. The people of the mountains are more than rumors to them now. They may seek our land, our resources, or our women. We have lived peacefully until now, but our ancestors were men of war."

The history of the people of the steppes was recorded in a manuscript at Hira.

They came, they uprooted, they burned, they slew, they despoiled, they departed.

"You will not find us seized of bloodlust," Zerafshan told them. "But we are ready to answer blood."

"You fear a war."

Zerafshan skirted Arian's conclusion, perhaps because he was a man who feared nothing.

"Your powers will be needed. Yours also," he said to Sinnia. "And those of your Companions who still reign at Hira. The Talisman conquest was slow and steady. The next phase will be otherwise."

Arian considered his words, considered the possibility of an alliance with Hira that would help them fend off the Talisman. Or perhaps the bargain had already been struck. If the Ahdath were not allies of the Buzkashi, a space of hope for her Audacy might have opened up.

"If you believe that war is coming, why have you continued your trade with the Ahdath?"

"I think I know," Daniyar interjected. But he waited for the Aybek's permission to speak further. Zerafshan gave it with a quick nod.

"If truly you follow the laws of your ancestors, you prepare for war in their manner. You train your armies for battle while gaining knowledge of your enemies—reconnaissance and preparation. What remains then, are tactics and propaganda."

Daniyar's gaze was drawn to the bonfire lit in the center of the playing field. A fire stoked not by wood and branches on this treeless plateau, but rather by smoldering heaps of dung. The goat carcass had been dismembered. A severed shoulder blade was heating above the dung, presided over by the Yeke Khatun.

"You continue your trade at the Wall not for material benefit, for yours are a hardy and self-sufficient people, but rather to sow fear about your army's might."

Zerafshan led them to the bonfire, the Buzkashi moving to one side to let him pass.

"I do not travel with the traders. My Mangudah spread fierce tales of my prowess, my legend grows in my absence. When war comes to the Cloud Door, my people will be at an advantage."

It was a wise maneuver, a far-seeing one. But would it be enough if the war were to be fought on two fronts at once?

"The Ahdath are suicide warriors," Arian cautioned the Aybek. He shrugged.

"The Mangudah are a death squad. And now, no more talk of war. We must consult the Yeke Khatun, then I will decide. What does the Great Empress say?"

Arian reflected on this title. He spoke of an empress of wind, of a kingdom of snow and martagon lilies. Though it was unlike the honors of other lands, it was clearly a title of eminence.

Tochtor used a pair of iron tongs to scrape the cracked bones of the goat from the flames.

Storay brought forth a metalwork bowl. The smoke-singed white bones were dropped into the bowl. The Buzkashi fell back with a frightened murmur. Only Storay held her place at her mother's side.

"What happens here?" Sinnia muttered to Arian.

"Scapulimancy," she answered. "The Yeke Khatun will divine the future from cracks in the heated blade."

It was a ritual she had seen in other places, but it was one at odds with the traditions of Hira. This was what the Aybek had called a different finger of the hand.

Tochtor held up the bowl. She began to recite in a monotone.

"The world was created by the One. The heavens in forty-five days, water in sixty days, the earth and its people in seventy-five. The sky is made of silver, the stars are cut like glass. There is a star for each one of us. When an inhabitant of the Cloud Door dies, a shooting star is seen. What is the uppermost sky?"

"The uppermost sky is asmaan," Storay intoned.

"The One dwells in the uppermost sky, we dwell upon the earth, the place between worlds, where male and female dwell together."

Tochtor peered into the bowl. She reached a hand inside to trace the cracks in the bones with her fingers. She whispered to herself. The Buzkashi watched in silence.

Wafa had squeezed himself between Arian and Sinnia. He clutched a fistful of Sinnia's dress in his hand.

This would have been blasphemy to the Talisman, Arian knew, but her own calculations of the paths to the One were not as unbending, even as she believed the future and the past were known only to the One. Tochtor's ritual wasn't the dark magic the One-Eyed Preacher practiced, or the stark execrations of the rites of the Nineteen who ruled the Empty Quarter.

The Yeke Khatun tipped back her head, showing them the whites of her eyes. They echoed the flash of the yurungkash jade of her headdress.

"The wind from the east has blown into this valley bringing four heralds with it."

Her finger pointed to each member of their company of four.

"One is missing. One will fall."

Her pointing finger traced an intricate gesture in the air. A cold conviction rang through her voice. A spear of worry prodded Arian's spine.

"They wake the people of the Cloud Door, the Cloud Door opens."

To the east, the clouds began to roil. Silver plumes filled the horizon.

"The Cloud Door will open to the world."

Tochtor's arm formed an arrow pointing north.

"The War of the Wall will come. The north wind brings it, one will fall."

The urgency left her voice. She lowered the bowl into Storay's waiting palms. Then she reached for her son's hand.

"Blessed be the Lord of the Buzkashi."

Her strident voice sounded through the valley.

It was echoed back to her by her people.

"Blessed be the Lord of the Buzkashi."

She lowered her head, her gaze clear and candid.

"What do the bones say of the Companion's request of me?" Zerafshan asked. "Should I aid her when she has nothing to barter in exchange?"

His mother's answer was sharp. "We are people of Hira— we submit to the One. We must give the Companion what she seeks."

Zerafshan motioned to Daniyar's pack.

"Will you yield your lajward in exchange?"

Standing before his people, it was important that the Buzkashi's traditions be upheld. But what could Arian say? She had long since learned that her choices would satisfy no one.

"My lord, had you asked anything else of me, I would yield it. The lajward means nothing to me, except as an end to my quest."

"You wouldn't give me your hand," he said, a hint of mischief in his eyes. "You claim your heart is forsworn."

Arian's face warmed with color. These were things she hadn't said to Daniyar, things she couldn't be sure she would ever have the chance to say. She loved one man, admired another, and still her dreams tasted like smoke.

Tochtor's declaration troubled her.

Four heralds.

One missing, one to fall.

Tochtor placed her hand on Wafa's shoulder.

"Something must be given in exchange," she agreed. "You must honor the customs of the Cloud Door." She nodded at her son. "If you've nothing else to give us, we will keep the boy."

Four heralds. One missing.

What if Wafa was the one to fall? Many times on the dangerous journey Arian had thought to leave Wafa behind—his life had been full of hardships, but beyond the Wall was a reckoning unknown. No one she loved should pay such a price.

She nodded her agreement.

"No!" the boy cried out. "You mustn't leave me here!" His throat working, he searched for the right words. "I'm not an object to be sold! I am Wafa, the loyal." Tears stained his face. "You swore you wouldn't leave me, now you trade me like the Talisman."

"The Wall is too dangerous a place for you," Arian said. "The Aybek will protect you, and Storay will be here to care for you."

Storay held out her hand, a smile on her face.

Wafa's tears came faster.

"I was dead before you found me, and now I'm alive. Don't take that from me!"

The words were agonizing to hear.

Sinnia tried to distract them.

"Well, I've offered myself and been refused."

What if Sinnia was the one to fall? Who would Arian risk on the road at her side?

With an effort, Arian kept her thoughts from the Silver Mage.

Wafa glowered at Storay.

"I don't belong with you. I am for the Companions."

He clutched Sinnia's dress, afraid he would be ripped away.

"We're at an impasse, it seems," Zerafshan said, his voice calm. "What is your will, Companion?"

Arian pressed a hand to her forehead.

She didn't know. Either the way forward or the way back. Too many outcomes rested upon her choices.

"Let me." Daniyar stepped in front of Wafa, urging him back into Sinnia's arms. He unbuckled his pack, reaching into its depths.

The puzzle box, the ewer, the key.

The lajward Zerafshan had wanted from the outset.

No matter the breach of honor, they couldn't afford to yield it.

"Daniyar—"

His glance at her was warm with reassurance, his eyes like weightless silver coins.

Shaken, she took a slow breath.

"We would honor your customs," Daniyar said to Zerafshan. "But the boy isn't ours to trade. Whatever the bones reveal, he has the right to choose his own course."

"Then what do you offer in his place?"

Daniyar removed a leather parcel from his pack. He raised it to his lips and kissed the two letters embossed on its cover before touching the book to his forehead. He held it high so the Buzkashi could see. Then he placed it in Zerafshan's hands.

"Will you take the Candour in place of the boy?"

He was greeted by a silence thick as snowfall. The sobs dried up in Wafa's throat. He stood paralyzed by uncertainty in Sinnia's embrace.

A tear slid down Arian's cheek.

If she'd ever questioned what she meant to Daniyar, she knew it now.

Just as she knew she wasn't worthy of his love.

Now beyond thought or personal calculation, she reached for her tahweez, her right hand working to unlace the circlet on her left arm.

She would sunder the unbreakable bond before she would permit the surrender of the Candour. To be barred from Hira was no greater a loss than to take from Daniyar his birthright. The Candour was a trust. It was everything to Daniyar.

Wafa couldn't understand this but Arian did.

She was everything now.

Her fingers slid under the circlet.

She felt a wrenching inside.

She was giving up her sisterhood, her safety.

She would lose her status as Companion of Hira.

She would no longer be First Oralist of the Claim.

And she found it didn't matter.

Some things were greater, truer, dearer.

The tahweez came loose.

She offered it to Zerafshan.

Tochtor fell to her knees with a groan. She pressed her forehead to the snow-covered ground. Moans sounded from the Buzkashi. The lamentation of women echoed through the Ice Kill.

Too much was happening here. Too much had happened.

Zerafshan raised the Candour to his lips and kissed it. Then he placed it back in the hands of the Silver Mage. He went to Arian and freed the tahweez from her grip. His fingers traced its markings. With careful hands, he bound it about her arm.

"*Mllaya moya.*" His voice tender with restraint, he spoke in a language none in the Cloud Door knew, a language of the Transcasp. "*How will I learn to content myself again, once you have left my valley?*"

Arian stared at his collarbone, unable to meet the emotion in his eyes.

"I do not understand, lord."

He raised her chin with his hand.

"It was I who did not understand. You told me," he said, with a half-smile. "But I didn't listen. Yeke Khatun."

He let Arian go, calling for his mother.

Zelgai and Altan raised Tochtor to her feet. They brought the old woman forward.

She reached into the bowl Storay carried and snapped the bones with her hands, casting the shattered fragments wide into the snow.

"Forgive us, Companion, we have treated you like common traders. It was a blasphemy to have done so. My son will grant whatever you ask."

Her face was shrunken beneath the weight of her headdress, bereft of its power. Behind her, columns of clouds scudded down the mountains.

There was a change in the wind.

Something was coming.

The wings of a falcon glittered against a backdrop of sky, diving at the frozen lake.

Ilea's falcon. Arian remembered Turan.

"Would you come with me, Wafa? Though I wished to leave you behind?"

The boy knuckled his eyes. He hung his head as he nodded.

"The gift was sincere," Arian said to Zerafshan, whose eyes still held a tenderness that rocked her.

"You carry a great weight," he returned. "I would not add to it. As I cannot take this road with you."

He relayed a series of instructions to Zelgai and Storay. They hurried away to do his bidding. His voice boomed out to address the Buzkashi.

"People of the Cloud Door. The Companions of Hira and the Silver Mage of Candour have graced your valley with the blessings of the Claim. For the sake of your traditions, they offered you the Candour, the tahweez. Do you dare demand more?"

Altan made a token protest.

"What of the lajward, brother? Why do they withhold it?"

Zerafshan thumped him with the back of his hand.

"The Prince of the Hearth has raided little, thus his mind is occupied with treasure. Yet you couldn't win the carcass of a goat on your own merits."

Catcalls and jeers rose from the Buzkashi. Altan flushed in response.

"Do you think the sahabiya cares for treasure? That she hoards riches to gratify her desires?"

"You didn't see the lajward," Altan said. "But I meant no disrespect, sahabiya."

Whatever Arian did, she caused harm. She wouldn't see Altan shamed on her account.

"Says the One, were your sins to reach the clouds of the sky, and were you then to ask forgiveness of Me, I would forgive you."

Her voice rang through the valley, a reflection of the Claim.

Altan shivered at the words, his mouth going slack with relief. He hastened to help Zelgai with the horses.

Zerafshan shrugged off Arian's thanks, a smile playing at the corners of his lips as he watched Sinnia detach Wafa's grip from her dress.

"Red suits you," he said to Sinnia.

Sinnia turned her smile upon him to worthwhile effect.

"White would suit me better, Lord Zerafshan. Forget what is not for you—consider the woman before your eyes."

Though Sinnia didn't know its meaning, the tender endearment Zerafshan had offered Arian stung her pride. Or was it her heart?

He gave Sinnia a lazy grin.

"You will feast with us before you leave our valley. Perhaps your arguments may persuade me."

Sinnia tossed her head like a mare of the khamsa.

"Perhaps if you accompany us, *you* will have the chance to persuade *me* of your merits."

"Would that I could, Lady Sinnia. But the Army of the Left descends from the Cloud Door within the week. I must be here to receive them."

Sinnia would have kept up her raillery, except that Arian stopped her with a look.

"My lord, your kindnesses have been many already. I fear to ask for anything more."

Sinnia forgotten, he turned to Arian.

"Ask, *mllaya moya*. Whatever you wish shall be granted."

"My lord, I require another horse. Captain Turan must ride to the Wall."

Four heralds from the east.

One missing, and one to fall.

276

35

THE SHARP BLACK PEAKS OF THE DEATH RUN FORMED A GLITTERING tumult against the vacant sky of the Cloud Door. If they had been able to see past the accumulation of clouds at the mouth of the valley, they would have seen light drift over the Fire Mirrors like a glossy red rain. As it was, the women's dresses danced like poppies in the wind, the Ice Kill left behind.

The air was sweet and cold, the bodies of the kuluk horses warm beneath the weight of wool blankets. Arian's small company had been fêted in the aftermath of the game of qarajai. The Yeke Khatun had blessed them with handfuls of snow from the field of victory.

The Aybek had bowed over her hands with a last wicked glance at Daniyar.

The Lord of the Buzkashi had taken nothing from them. Instead, he'd sent a party of six men to take them as far as the encampment of the Army of the Right. To Arian alone he had confided his stories of the Wall, as a sign of trust.

Zelgai led their company. He issued orders, gathered men, prepared supplies without drawing notice to himself. In coloring he was nothing like his blood brother, the leader of the Buzkashi. The cast of his features spoke more of the people of the steppes, indicating a long history of the commingling of the races in this last outpost of Khorasan. In temperament, he was mild, his glances self-contained. He issued no directives to the Companions, addressing them with respect.

Zelgai and four of his guards rode ahead, scouting the path. Again, Arian noticed the precision of their movements, the skill with which they negotiated the terrain, anticipating Zelgai's commands. They were armed as if for war in leather armor, with small horns at their hips. They had taken leave of their women without levity or regret.

Strong and fierce, these outriders of the Mangudah.

A death squad.

Did they prepare to meet upheaval or deliver it?

Daniyar rode with Sinnia and the boy. Arian knew he was angered by the Aybek's gallantries, jealous of her attention. Yet she had discouraged the Aybek at every turn, and done nothing that required her to account for herself. She would focus on Captain Turan, who rode at her side instead, an opening she was glad of, for there was much she needed to ask him.

"Are you well, Captain? Have you recovered?"

He slowed the pace of his horse to hers. There was an improvement in his color and in the steadiness of his hands.

"The injury was not as severe as either of us thought, sahabiya. What of you? I feared the leader of the Buzkashi would insist on taking you to wife. They are known as traders. They do not barter lightly."

Arian felt color warm her skin. She strove to change the subject.

"So you've heard of these mountain people."

"Rumors, no more. It was chance that we stumbled upon their caravan. From the report of my men, their numbers are small."

The truth would surprise him, then.

"May we speak of the High Companion? And how you came to be at the Sorrowsong? Or would that be intrusive?"

"I am at the Companion's service. Whatever you would know, I would share."

"Will you not call me Arian? As you must have done when I was a child."

A fleeting expression crossed the captain's face, so fleeting she couldn't put a name to it.

"What would the lady Arian know?"

"Why did Ilea send you to the Sorrowsong? And when?"

"It has been some months. The previous commander fell out of favor when he failed to discover the lajward the Preacher sought from the mines."

"How did the Preacher know these pieces could be found in the quarries? Did he not expect the Sorrowsong to yield raw stone mined from the veins?"

"There is a palimpsest in the Preacher's possession that is a catalogue of manuscripts. It was stolen from the northland, from the House of Wisdom at Black Aura. You can imagine the prize it foretold."

"The Bloodprint."

"Yes. He knows it was held by the Authoritan, but also that it was stolen and taken west. And now he knows it has been returned."

Without naming him, Turan was describing the efforts of the Black Khan.

"Ilea told you this?"

"Part of this story comes from the High Companion, part from my spies among the Shin War."

"Then the Shin War are not united on this question."

Turan glanced at her briefly. "It was a mistake, I think, to spare some of the conservators of Candour's scriptoria to work the Preacher's ends." His voice was dry. "The Preacher thought his mastery of the Claim could control them, but there are many among the literate who survived the Talisman purges. They bide their time in the Preacher's service until a killing blow can be struck."

Arian's face paled.

"You mean to the Shin War."

"I mean to all the tribes of Candour. Immolans rise and fall, the Preacher is rarely seen, and this ill wind will blow over our land and vanish into the desert. There are many who resist the Talisman creed."

"It has been decades." Arian's voice was bleak.

"It has been centuries, Lady Arian, but you must not despair. The High Companion anticipates the Preacher's stratagems. She will triumph in the end because we serve her cause."

Arian couldn't be as sure. There was another player to consider. And she feared the Black Khan's motives, the strike of shahmat that could checkmate her Audacy. But she kept such thoughts to herself; she needed to learn what she could of Turan.

"So you come from the ranks of those who resist, while disguised as a Talisman loyalist. The kind of double game that pleases the High Companion. And yet I think the cost to you must have been great, Captain."

She was remembering his stoicism at the Sorrowsong. None of these hardships showed in his face. She admired him for it, even as she felt the pain of it.

"Neither has your path been easy," he replied. "We cannot afford regret, Lady Arian. I told the High Companion of the manuscript, she directed me to the Sorrowsong to await you."

For the little Ilea shared, there were a hundred things she held in reserve. As Arian mulled this over, Turan directed her attention back to the importance of the palimpsest.

"The scribe who prepared the catalogue added a coda in his own words in the High Tongue."

"You're an Affluent, Captain Turan?"

"It was your mother who taught me." His voice caught on the words. He turned his face away. And as much as Arian wanted to know, she suppressed her longing. There would be another time to ask after her mother, to ask why Turan, of all men, had been chosen to deliver Arian to Hira. She let her silence act as encouragement, until Turan picked up his story.

"The coda described three pieces of lajward that serve as clues to the Bloodprint's location—its safehold."

Arian frowned. A piece of the story was missing.

"The catalogue in the Preacher's keeping must be a manuscript of the old world."

"It is, yes."

"Then why would the lajward hold clues to the Bloodprint's safehold?"

Turan flashed her a sharp look.

"You met with the High Companion and the Black Khan, I believe."

She nodded, surprised. "You knew it was the Black Khan who brought word of the Bloodprint to Hira?"

Turan's lips thinned into a harsh line.

"I've dealt with the Black Khan before. It shouldn't surprise me that he withheld this from you. You knew the Bloodprint was removed from the Stone City at his request?"

At her nod, he continued, "But not perhaps that it was *originally* stolen from those sworn in the Bloodprint's service."

"You think the Bloodless have returned it to their safehold."

"That would be my guess. It's what the palimpsest suggests they would do. Just as it tells us that centuries ago, the clues to this safehold were spirited away into the depths of the Sorrowsong."

"The oldest continuously worked mines in Khorasan."

"Yes."

Arian was seeing another connection, one she wondered if either Ilea or the One-Eyed Preacher knew. The Bloodprint itself was a manuscript of plain ink on parchment. Its beauties rested in the eloquence of the Claim.

But subsequent copies, lost to ignorance and time, were said to be ornamented with gold leaf and an ink of the bluest indigo, the lajward stone ground into powder and liquefied.

Was there a connection between the stone of heaven and the men who guarded the Bloodprint? Could one or more of them have been scribes?

She was curious about their name, as well. What could the Bloodless signify?

When asked, Turan responded, "They are ascetics. They have no other calling except to protect the Bloodprint."

He hesitated, unwilling to continue.

"Tell me," Arian said, reading his face. "I would know it all."

"There was a time when the Bloodless held great renown as guardians of the Bloodprint. They were chosen from among the ranks of scholars who traveled the world to study at Black Aura. To serve as Bloodless was a position of the highest honor. It is not so with the Authoritan."

A despot steeped in blood and lawlessness, whose ancestors built the Wall that divided the northland from the south. He had instituted the slave trade, bartering a thing as precious as the Verse of the Throne.

"He holds the Bloodless to ransom in some manner?" she guessed. For the Authoritan would wish to secure his monopoly of the Claim.

Turan brought his horse to a halt. His hand covered Arian's where it rested on the pommel of her saddle.

"Some manner, indeed. It is said the Authoritan has cut out their tongues."

36

It took the rest of the day to complete their long descent through the mountain pass to the rough, uncharted terrain that lay ahead. The sun sloped down into the west, its rays thrown like arrows against a fruitless wind.

The air became rich, the snows giving way to a sinuous mud that slowed the steady pace of the kuluk. Arian felt her lungs expand to drink in the warmth of the lower altitudes.

"There is drier ground ahead," Zelgai assured them.

Although he had been appointed head of their party, he did not carry the horsehair banner. Arian asked him about this, curious.

Zelgai spoke to her without taking his gaze from the path ahead.

"The Sulde is our spirit banner. It signifies the strength endowed by wind, sky, and sun. It remains with the Aybek to be carried to war."

"To carry it must be a great honor, then."

"The greatest. A warrior of the Buzkashi may permit anything to fall except the Sulde."

"And who is the Aybek's right hand, should he fall?"

Zelgai didn't answer. He rode ahead, silencing a rustle of displeasure from his men.

Arian turned to find the Silver Mage at her side.

"The people of the mountain have their own traditions," he cautioned her. "Their warriors do not speak of death because to acknowledge it may cause it to occur. By law, they assume their warriors are immortal."

"You speak of a martial philosophy," Arian mused. "And the Aybek spoke of preparing his armies for war as if that war is imminent. But Ilea didn't speak of this at Hira. She spoke only of the danger to the Citadel."

It was a reasonable point for Arian to raise, but it earned her an unwarranted response.

"If we had tarried longer, we could have learned more about the forces at the Wall. But I saw no benefit to keeping you under Zerafshan's eye."

Arian twisted in her saddle. She had not mistaken Daniyar's anger.

"It was a matter of fortune that we found our way to the Ice Kill."

"It was a matter of fortune you were not wed to him before our departure. If Zerafshan had then seen fit to let you go."

The contempt in his eyes was scathing.

Arian lowered her voice.

"It was you who asked me to prevail upon him. I sought no contact with him."

Daniyar struck out with his riding crop. It fell harmlessly against his saddle bag.

"You were not loath to hear his compliments, nor to suffer his attentions."

"You grasped his hand in the bond of trust."

"To gain us safe passage."

"I did no less, as should be clear to you."

"You did more. For a Companion who took a vow of chastity at Hira, your ease with strangers discredits you."

The vicious words hit at her, the rancor behind them palpable. She set her jaw and looked away.

"You were prepared to relinquish the Candour for me—"

"For Wafa. Another admirer you so carelessly accrued."

Now Arian's temper flared. She would not accept injustice, even from Daniyar.

"Have a care how you speak to me," she warned him. "I am not blind to your jealousy—it leads you to accuse me without cause. Look deeper. Read me, if you must, though you should have no need."

He had the grace to look ashamed though he couldn't manage an apology.

Perhaps it was no longer possible for Daniyar to trust her. His first taste of betrayal had come from the hands of the woman he loved—her hands. She hadn't wanted to leave him in Candour. He wasn't a man to be given up lightly, nor the kind of man whose equal she'd ever found.

She had filled the loneliness of the years without him with an implacable hatred of the Talisman.

The world she had seen was black and white, men against women, Talisman against herself. A perspective that failed to account for Daniyar and Turan, leaders among the Talisman. Or Zerafshan and his Buzkashi.

She understood the Silver Mage now with a clarity she hadn't possessed in Candour.

The women of the Shin War lived lives of grueling, painful seclusion. But they were safe from the Talisman slave-chains, an end Daniyar had effected by staying in Candour, doing what he believed to be right.

Arian had tried to do the same.

Except for that moment in Zerafshan's camp, when setting everything else aside, she had put Daniyar first.

"I surrendered my tahweez to spare you such a sacrifice. How can you not read the truth of this?"

Her voice breaking, she rode ahead, leaving their caravan behind.

"Arian—"

He called after her in vain. Sinnia's horse cantered to his side.

"Leave her, my lord. Her Audacy troubles her, making her spirit restless."

"I misspoke earlier," he said grimly. "I *am* a fool."

Sinnia studied him, curious. "Do you not want her then, my lord? Did I misunderstand your purpose in coming on this journey?"

A caustic smile settled on his lips.

"Have you come to take the measure of my conscience?" His eyes followed Arian's progress down the slope. "Because I've never wanted anyone else."

A wide expanse of blue met them upon the plains, the first blush of spring sweeping across the lowlands. Green blades of grass sprang from the cellar of mud-brown hills. Clusters of cyclamen and gentian dotted the fertile plain. Fruit trees stirred under the heavy hand of winter, their branches sprightly with budding life, while stands of wild poplar bordered the lake.

A low gold light brushed the sky.

"Lop Nur," Zelgai said.

Daniyar spurred his kuluk to Arian's side. Unable to think of a suitable gesture of contrition, he settled for stroking a hand across the kuluk's mane, catching his fingers in the coarseness of its hair.

"Lop Nur," he explained, "is the name of the wandering lake. It was once a lake of the Tarim Basin, fed by rivers that sprang from glaciers. In times of drought, the lake was swallowed by the desert. When it reappeared, a new civilization would flourish on its banks."

But it was not the lake that captured Arian's attention.

It was the Army of the Right camped upon its banks.

And the thousands of horses pastured behind them.

37

A HERALD RODE UP TO MEET ZELGAI. HE WAS DRESSED IN BLACK AR-
mor. In his right hand he carried the standard of the Army of the
Right, a flame-coated horse stamped on a field of gold.

"Aybek of the Right!" he called.

From the camp behind him, a volley of horns sounded.

He met Zelgai on the plains; they embraced like brothers. They
sniffed at each other's hands and necks, laughing.

Soon they were joined by others from the camp, an escort of
dozens, all in black armor with a gold crest embossed at their
throats. It astonished Arian that as each man joined their group,
he made an obeisance before Zelgai, who nodded at each soldier,
taking stock of the state of his uniform, and the time to praise or
correct his bearing.

Zelgai made rapid introductions, beginning with the Silver Mage.

"My lord Daniyar, this is Shiremun of the Army of the Right."

More men joined them.

The soldiers wore fur-lined coats secured by leather belts that
held swords, daggers, or double-headed axes. Silk undershirts
with long, flaring sleeves were worn beneath the coats. The crest at
the neck of these shirts was the insignia of the flame-coated horse,

red upon gold. Beneath the shirts, baggy trousers were tucked into boots made of leather and felt.

Arian could see heavier armor—iron breastplates and corselets, cone-shaped helmets with leather neck guards stacked in rows against the walls of an armory. In the distance, the clang of steel rang out as soldiers tested their speed and strength against each other. Small yurts darkened the plain, busy with preparation for battle.

To the east of the camp, the sound of a doleful singing arose. A group of commanders, distinguished by the quality of their armor, was gathered about a small fire, echoing a series of low-pitched phrases to each other.

Arian and Sinnia exchanged a look. The Lord of the Buzkashi had left much unsaid in his discussion of his people's philosophy. His army wasn't preparing its defence of the Cloud Door. It was readying itself for full-scale war.

We have intelligence of the north, Zerafshan had said.

What intelligence did he have? Were the Talisman and the Ahdath in league? Did Arian need to send an exigent warning to Hira? Or did Ilea already know, and was the urgency of Arian's Audacy based on Ilea's foreknowledge of the war?

She would ask Zelgai what he knew of the Ahdath's plans when they found a moment alone. Shiremun, his deputy, escorted them to a small yurt established by the lake, close to the command tent. As their horses were pastured, she caught more than one suspicious glance flung in Turan's direction, taking note of the Shin War crest he still wore at his throat.

The presence of the women at the camp aroused little interest, the Army of the Right continuing its training exercises with unrivaled focus and discipline. Arian found herself unnerved by this without knowing why.

Zelgai spread the news of the success of the Mangudah raid upon the Sorrowsong, and as he did, Arian observed something else. She had scarcely noticed Zelgai in his brother's presence. Altan had made more of an impression, whereas Zelgai had remained in the background, attentive to the Lord of the Buzkashi. Even his victory with the goat's carcass had been achieved more by stealth than flourishes of fanfare.

But it was Zelgai who commanded the vast army at the banks of Lop Nur, his men greeting him with a mixture of warmth and respect.

Zelgai excused himself from their company, making for the command tent. He left six guards behind. To bring them food and water? Or to stand watch over the party from the Sorrowsong?

Daniyar addressed her in the dialect of Candour.

"Come inside," he said, gesturing to one of the yurts. He nodded at Turan. "You also."

Inside the yurt, the Silver Mage wasted no time.

"Zerafshan's army prepares for war."

Turan agreed. "A fearsome force, waiting for the spring thaw."

"Did you know of this?"

"You think this war comes to us?" Turan massaged the still-healing wound at his throat.

"It was Talisman who offended the Buzkashi, transgressing against their women. Perhaps the raid of the Mangudah was the preliminary event."

"Kill. Don't mourn," Arian said. "Their philosophy of war. Zerafshan said his people do not seek war, they ready themselves to answer it."

"A war through the mountains doesn't sound like something the Buzkashi would risk. To take this army through the Death Run?" Turan shook his head. "They would lose too many."

"Look at the way they've laid out this camp, consider their formations. They prepare to ride north, not west. They're fortified against the north, not the west. What does this suggest to you?" As Arian spoke, the answer became clear. "Their war is with the Authoritan. They're riding to the Wall."

But would Zerafshan promise an escort to Marakand if his men were going to war with the north? She turned to Daniyar.

"You're the Authenticate. Was he sincere?"

Daniyar stared at her, studying her shadowed face.

She found herself looking back at him, mesmerized.

He was reading *her*.

Her uncertainty, her self-doubt, the susceptibility of her feelings. His thoughts moved swift and sure, like a vulturine blade through the softness of flesh.

She held herself still, forgetting Turan's presence in the tent. Daniyar's eyes dropped to her mouth.

A stinging color flooded her face.

"He didn't mislead us," Daniyar said after a moment. "His war will wait upon our task if he sends his brother as our guide. What troubles me is how to find the Bloodprint once we're beyond the Wall. Can you speak to this, Turan?"

"The puzzle box will aid us."

"How do you know this?"

Turan spoke simply. "The High Companion told me as much. I have never doubted her."

Daniyar produced the box from his traveling pack. It was six-sided, the lajward etched with geometric motifs, a repetition of stars and rectangles that represented the infinite span of the heavens, but that suggested to Arian a kind of cloistering, trapped and closed off, like the alleyways of a maze.

It had no hinges or lid that Arian could see.

"Have you worked this?" she asked Turan. "Can it be opened?"

"For many nights, over many months. It did not yield its secrets to me."

"And Ilea tells us nothing beyond the fact that the box can be used to find a tomb. *What* tomb? Why does it matter? How is it connected to the Bloodprint? Unless—" Arian reached out to take the box from Daniyar, studying the fine lines etched upon its surface. Something about the markings was familiar to her. "You said the Bloodless take the Bloodprint to its resting place. Could this tomb be the resting place?"

"Perhaps at one time." Turan's tone was doubtful. "But I do not think a manuscript would endure in such an environment. I would expect the Authoritan to keep the Bloodprint close at hand after losing it once. I know only that the tomb lies in Marakand."

Arian pondered this. "But Ilea did not tell you how to open it."

"She did not know," Turan said, quick to defend the High Companion.

Or Ilea had reasons for keeping her knowledge secret, reasons she wasn't prepared to share with Turan, any more than Ilea and Rukh had told Arian anything about the Cast Iron, the Bloodprint's binding. Arian said nothing to the others of the secret the Alamdar had confided. She thought of the blue key, the third piece buried deep in the tunnels of the Sorrowsong.

Would it unlock the Cast Iron? Was that its purpose? And if it did, what of the secret to the Cast Iron the Alamdar had entrusted her with?

Daniyar took the box back from her hands, his fingers shaping its sides.

"The lines are interlocked. They remind me of something I've seen before." He traced a finger over the white lines, picking out a single image. "Do you see it? It's a chair."

Buried within the pattern, the white lines resembled a chair, a series of stars crowning its back like a fan.

"It's not a chair," Arian whispered. "It's the Black Throne." She stared at Turan, amazed. "It explains how Ilea could have learned about the One-Eyed Preacher's palimpsest. The Black Khan must have told her. There must be something in the histories at Ashfall."

"I don't think this is meant to represent the Black Throne. Look." There was a note of wonder in Daniyar's voice. He held up the box so all could see. "Six sides. And above the throne, six stars. I've seen this before. In a manuscript I found in a market stall in Maze Aura, describing the Verse of the Throne."

A throne to comprise the heavens and the earth.

Six stars, six sides, the significance of six, the symmetry of the Verse of the Throne, the only verse of the Claim to describe the virtues of the One.

There is no one but the One. And so the One commands.

"Do you know the six virtues? Did your manuscript name them?"

But the Silver Mage was uncertain, recounting what he could from memory.

"Life, knowledge, dominion, power, and will. But there is one that escapes me." His voice had slowed, and Arian could see that he was searching through his memories, grasping at something just out of reach. His fingers pressed against the sides of the box, counting to himself. He stopped again at five.

"Arian," he said urgently. "Tell me what you know of the Empty Quarter."

He set the box down in their midst.

"What you know also, I suspect. The Empty Quarter was burned during the wars of the Far Range. The holy cities were destroyed. Now it is a place made desolate by time."

"But not unpopulated, despite its name." The note of excitement in Daniyar's voice caught at Arian. "It was the land of the One-Eyed Preacher once."

"Yes. The Rising Nineteen lay claim to it now."

"Do you know anything of their philosophy?"

Arian frowned. "They call themselves numerologists. To them, the Bloodprint is a formula."

"But not just a formula." Daniyar tapped the box. "The verses of the Bloodprint are numbered. We know the Claim from memory alone, from the recitation of an oral tradition." He smiled at Arian. "And so you are called Oralists. But the Bloodprint arranges the verses of the Claim in numerical order. It *numbers* them. Here, let me show you."

He pressed his index finger down hard over the second star that appeared above the throne on the surface of the puzzle box. A pressure inside the box gave way, creating a small space between the upper half of the box and the lower. Daniyar rotated the upper half clockwise two full rotations. A series of clicks and whirrs could be heard from within the box. The white lines broke apart, the image of the throne vanishing as the pattern on the surface shifted, diminishing the throne to open up the stars.

One of the stars was missing. Five stars remained.

The Silver Mage sought out the fifth star. He pressed the star five times in succession. The jewel-green box shuddered under his touch. And then, as delicately as with the peeling of an egg, the surface surged upward and folded back upon itself, exposing the small, dark chasm within.

Nestled inside was a fragile scroll sealed with dark green wax.

None of them dared touch it.

The Silver Mage offered the box to Arian, his hands a little unsteady.

"There is much to discredit about the Nineteen, but they are correct in one thing: the numbering of the verses *matters*. Beside the description of the Verse of the Throne, a number was inked on the page. Two, two, five, five."

"The second chapter," Arian guessed. "The two hundred and fifty-fifth verse."

A throne to comprise the heavens and the earth.

With trembling fingers, she reached for the scroll. As soon as she lifted it from the puzzle box, the chasm sealed itself with a sigh.

With careful pressure, Arian applied the tip of her dagger to the seal. Hardly daring to breathe, she spread the scroll before them, using only her fingertips.

A curious sight met her eyes.

At the top of the scroll a single word appeared, followed by an unfamiliar symbol.

Самарканд.

Beside it, three small circles were stacked like a triangle inside a five-point star.

Beneath this, a pattern similar to the one on the surface of the puzzle box was sketched out in lines and rectangles. At irregular intervals, a flower, a leaf, or a star appeared beside one of the rectangles. At the very bottom of the scroll, a small dome had been inked in a vivid turquoise green.

Arian looked first at Daniyar, then at Turan. They couldn't read the word written on the scroll. She alone held the power of it, of a world she had not truly believed existed until this moment. The name of an ancient city from a time before the wars of the Far Range, the wars that had severed the old world from the new.

From legends we come to loss, from loss to wonder.

But wonder was a distraction they couldn't afford. She felt her thoughts turn bitter, as she recognized that her calculations were little different from Ilea's or the Black Khan's, both of whom had withheld the truth to further ambitions of their own.

"It's written in a language of the Transcasp." She turned to Turan. "A language I don't read fluently, but I know what the word represents. It points us to a city."

Even as she said it, Arian knew she was sharing with them the smallest part of the lore passed down by the women of her family.

"What city?" Turan asked, his voice hesitant, as if he didn't want to know.

A pang of conscience smote her. These were the bravest and most loyal of her friends. But the secrets kept by Hira had stolen the hopes of many.

"Marakand."

She didn't give them the city's ancient name.

"Marakand?" Daniyar echoed, his silver eyes grave.

Her voice was sad as she answered him.

"A place we were destined to find. A city behind the Wall."

"Why destined?"

"'Use the box to find the tomb,'" Arian quoted harshly. "Don't you see?"

But it was clear they didn't. They had spotted the throne on the surface of the puzzle box more easily than this. Arian held up the scroll. The light from a small stove flickered against its texture, causing the pattern to dance.

"This is the map of a graveyard. We were sent to Marakand to find it."

38

Morning brought about a quick and hurried departure. Daniyar and Turan, two members of the Shin War, spent the rest of the evening scouting the Aybek's army, seeking to understand the forces at play. Their verdict was chilling. If an army this size was about to descend from the Cloud Door, the combined might of the Army of the Right and the Army of the Left would bring to the Wall a catastrophic war.

War is the unmitigated effort of one people against another.

She had censured Zerafshan for refusing to disrupt the Talisman's slave-chains. How did she account for this, then? What did this mighty army prepare itself for? And why hadn't Zerafshan defended himself, if he was planning a full-scale assault on the Wall? He'd insisted that the Buzkashi's point of contact with the Wall was separate from the route traveled by the slave-chains, but surely any war against the forces protecting the Wall would spread to encompass the Talisman. And the women ransomed beyond the Wall.

What of their fate?

What of her sister's fate?

Lania had been beautiful. Had she spent her life languishing as the captive of a Talisman Commandhan, or had she been sold behind the Wall to service the soldiers of the Ahdath until, too broken to be of use, she was sent to die in the Plague Lands?

Another revelation of Zerafshan's that had robbed Arian of peace.

Had Lania ended her days in the Plague Lands? Or was she still alive somewhere behind the Wall? And why did the Authoritan send any woman to the Plague Lands, as Zerafshan had claimed? The Plague Lands were poisoned by the wars of the Far Range. Nothing could grow in those lands, the rampant spread of disease curbed by the building of the Wall.

Arian's thoughts circled back to her sister. To Lania, sweet-faced and kind, an Oralist of the Claim, perhaps not as gifted as Arian herself, but soon to be selected as a Companion of Hira. She had been ten years older than Arian when the slave handlers had taken her, a fate that would have been Arian's, as well, had her parents not hidden her in time.

A fate Turan had rescued her from, watching over her from afar.

She was riding beside him now, Wafa and Sinnia behind her, Daniyar scouting the path ahead with Zelgai and his men. Several more of the Mangudah followed at the rear.

Turan had ridden beside her in silence all morning, pondering the mysteries of the scroll.

"A map is nothing without a key," he'd said, without disputing her conclusions.

Arian pointed at the small dome, inked in the color of turquoise.

"This dome is the key."

He hadn't pressed her for more, but she could see his desire to speak further. She had no wish to speak of Marakand, Ilea, or the map. She found Turan's devotion to Ilea disturbing. No friend of the High Companion's had enjoyed the reward of constancy. Ilea saw members of the Council as tools to be used to further her furtive agenda.

Turan was a man Arian was learning to value. She wished him safe from Ilea's machinations.

"You are troubled, Companion," the captain said, breaking his silence. "Do you fear what lies ahead?"

Turan studied the road as he spoke. The temperature was warmer, the ground beginning to thaw beneath the hooves of the horses the Buzkashi had supplied.

Arian spoke softly, not wanting the others to hear.

"I think more of the past than the road ahead," she answered. "I was thinking of my sister, Lania. You must have known her, if you knew my parents."

Turan's head snapped around. The ligaments of his jaw and neck tightened, emotion coloring his face. But when he spoke, his voice was mild.

"You've been searching for her. It's why you hunt the slave-chains."

"If they were going to kill her, they would have done so that night, just like they killed my mother."

Turan flinched from the words. He took a moment to collect himself before addressing Arian again.

"The Talisman feared your mother's power. As curators of a scriptorium, your parents were at risk from the first. Sayah was too well-known. The Council should have protected her."

Sayah.

Arian mouthed her mother's name.

No one had spoken it in her presence since the day her mother had died.

To hear it now on the captain's lips, spoken with such sweetness and such grief, broke something inside Arian. Something she hadn't known she was struggling to keep intact. The stone wall erected against her memories, dividing her heart from itself.

"I miss her," she said, surprising herself.

"Then you remember her."

"I've tried to forget. But her voice is everywhere. It's in everything I know, everything I've learned."

"And in the things you refuse to share."

Arian looked at him, slowing the pace of her horse.

"What do you mean?"

"You know more about the map, but refuse to speak of it. You chase Lania behind the Wall, not the Bloodprint. And I think, though the Silver Mage loves you, you would risk the loss of his love to pursue Lania's ghost because you cannot let her go."

The hard shell of Arian's heart began to splinter, the captain's words slipping between the cracks. Tears edged out from the corners of her eyes.

"How?" The tears came thick and hot, streaking her cheeks. "How do I let her go?"

Turan placed a gentle hand over hers, driving their horses from the road. He used his cloak to wipe the tears from Arian's face. He held her hand to calm her.

Ahead of them on the road, the Silver Mage glanced back. And turned his horse around.

"Lania was beautiful and gifted, though not so gifted as you. She was meant to be a Companion of Hira. If you had not proven yourself more adept, she would have been First Oralist. Then you could have chosen what other Companions have chosen. You could have stayed at Hira under the Council's protection. But you chose the most dangerous course, chasing after the slave-chains, in pursuit of Lania. You think it should have been you. You whom the Talisman had taken, Lania safe at Hira. You think Lania is the one your parents should have saved, but you should know you are wrong."

"How can I be wrong?"

Turan's answer was simple.

"It wasn't a choice your parents made—you or Lania. They would have saved you both. There was no warning of the Talisman attack. You were closest to the safe room. I don't know what you witnessed, but try to think back. Try to remember what happened that night."

Had Arian ever forgotten?

The brutal sound of the knock on the door. Her mother's quick action, drawing her away, urging her to silence.

Lania and their brother at the door, her father behind them.

The fateful clamor of swords.

The blow to her brother, Lania's screams.

And the sound. The thudding sound she would recognize anywhere, accompanied by its full measure of dread.

Her father's head cleaved from his body, to roll across the blood-soaked floor. Her mother's body falling at the door to the safe room, shielding Arian even in death. Sayah's eyes finding her daughter, terrified and mute behind the door.

The smell of burning.

A lifetime's learning set to the fire.

Rampaging boots, the acrid scent of parchment, the sickening stench of blood.

Then silence and smoke.

When Arian came out of her reverie, she was in Daniyar's arms. He was murmuring a verse of the Claim in her ear, so no one else could hear.

Be patient in adversity, for the One will not permit your reward to be lost.

She felt the words seep into her, calming the confusion of her thoughts.

Turan was watching her, waiting.

"Did you remember enough?" he asked.

A memory escaped from the turmoil, the memory Turan had wanted her to see. Her mother calling out to Lania, warning her away from the door, pleading with Lania to hurry to the safe room.

It was a memory Arian had lost.

Lania was blameless, for how could she have foreseen the ruinous intent of the Talisman?

But Arian was blameless, too.

"Lania opened the door," she said, after a long silence. "How did you know?"

"It's the first thing you said when I rescued you from the fire."

Small arms clinging, face and hair singed by smoke.

Frightened at first by the sight of Turan's armor. Until he'd smiled at her and held her against his heart, as Daniyar was doing now. Shading her eyes to step around the bodies.

With a last look at her mother, Turan had taken Arian to safety.

"I think that's enough."

Turan spread his hands in a conciliatory gesture. The Silver Mage was not an enemy he cared to make, but this was not a memory he dredged up lightly.

"It's important the Companion knows what it is she seeks behind the Wall."

Arian turned her face into Daniyar's neck. She murmured her request against his throat.

When they took up the path to the Wall, Daniyar rode at her side, as Turan recounted stories of her mother. His recollections were colored with love. As Arian listened, she thought how blessed her mother had been to have known Turan's love. He had stayed with her mother even after she'd married his friend, he had risked his life to deliver her child to Hira.

Arian would count herself blessed to know a loyalty like his.

Then the troubling thought occurred that she herself had never been as constant.

39

THEY CROSSED THE AMDAR RIVER UNDER COVER OF DARKNESS, muf-
fling the hooves of their horses with padded cloth to traverse the
iron bridge.

Buzkashi sentries stood watch at the bridge, two on either side
of the river. The bridge was wide enough to support a regiment
on horseback. The Silver Mage observed in silence as the Aybek
of the Right engaged in a consultation with his men, in the form
of the same dolorous singing they'd heard upon the banks of the
Lop Nur.

"We have intelligence of the north."

And they communicated it by this method of throat-singing.

When they had cleared the bridge, Daniyar rode up to join
Zelgai.

"Who built this bridge?"

Zelgai glanced over at the Silver Mage, his eyes alert.

"My brother, the Aybek."

"Why do you leave only four men to guard a bridge you need?"

Zelgai glanced back at his men, straight-backed and calm in
his saddle.

"They are Mangudah. Four are enough." His eyes made a slow count of Daniyar's party. "You are only five, one of whom is a child. And yet you dare the Wall."

Daniyar made note of the fact that Zelgai didn't discount the authority of the women who rode with them.

"As you trust in the strength of your men, so I trust in the power of the Claim. Had the Aybek not offered us your escort, the Claim would have been all that we had."

"Will it be enough behind the Wall?"

The Silver Mage frowned.

"I cannot say. What can you tell me of these Ahdath? Are they as fierce as their reputation?"

A quick smile crossed Zelgai's face.

"They are killers who live and die at the Wall, but we do not fear them. They are settled and soft, they do not scout beyond the Wall. They ready themselves for war without expectation of a battle."

Daniyar thought of the Army of the Right. He considered the expert raid the Mangudah had carried out on the Sorrowsong, and the fortified iron bridge, guarded by four riders.

"You seem confident of success, should it come to war."

A spark brightened Zelgai's eyes.

"Let us say we have no expectation of defeat. Not when Zerafshan rides as Aybek."

"Zerafshan has established trade with the Ahdath. Why would he seek war?"

But now Daniyar had said too much, for Zelgai's eyes turned wintry.

"War comes to us. And when it does, we must be ready."

He spurred his mount forward, leaving the Silver Mage behind.

As they rode, the path turned west and a freshness filled the air. Behind them, Wafa's raised head registered the scent. The wind carried the first ripening of apricot and plum trees west from the Damson Vale.

Now the mountains were behind them, a snow-capped edging against the sky, stars striking against their jagged peaks, the Damson Vale to the east.

Its beauty was etched in Daniyar's memory, a place he'd hoped to take Arian, far removed from the dangers and toils of their present journey. Lush and green, unlike the arid plains of Candour and Hira, a gold-strewn river darting through its meadows.

He'd wanted to see the blossoms of the fruit trees tumble down onto Arian's dark hair. He'd wanted Arian to feel the sweetness of the wind against her skin. And he'd wanted to take her as his own, giving and receiving the love he'd long been denied.

He no longer belonged with the Shin War. But neither could he abandon the orphaned boys of Candour, the lost children of Khorasan. He was the Keeper of the Candour, a trust he couldn't set aside. Were he the kind of man to have done so, Arian would not have wanted him.

If she wanted him now, his jealousy was a mark against him.

He tightened his grip on the reins of his horse, the lines of his mouth turned down in reflection.

Perhaps the ghost of Lania would always stand between them.

And perhaps these were excuses, and Arian had never loved him at all.

She concerned herself with the Wall, choosing not to resume their closeness. Was she truly so stoic? Did she never think of him with the same longing and regret that were all he'd known since the day she had left him in Candour? Did her willingness to yield her tahweez signal anything other than a momentary softening?

He could determine the answer for himself—but the act of reading her would be a violation of her trust. It would also expose his weakness.

He studied Arian with troubled eyes.

She was engaged in a discussion of strategy with Sinnia and Turan.

She hadn't thanked Daniyar for unraveling the mystery of the puzzle box, nor for his continued presence at her side.

His thoughts turned dark.

It wasn't her thanks he needed, nor her soft words of praise.

His needs were fierce and unrelenting.

He wanted all of her, everything, every last bit of sweetness.

And he wanted her to want him the same way.

40

THE BLACK KHAN READ THE SCROLL DELIVERED BY HIS PEREGRINE with a frown. Matters were urgent in Ashfall. The Talisman were pressing west; he had tarried at Hira too long. The High Companion was a bewitching creature, but it was not her enchantments that kept him at the Citadel.

He waited for word from his spies, spies in the north, spies to the east, spies in the occupied south. When his picture of events was complete, he would determine his course. Or so he'd planned, discerning more from the whispers of the Council than any of the Companions could have guessed. It had been reckless of him to count on Hira as an ally when Hira could barely defend its own keep.

He'd lingered in the scriptorium hoping to discover the source of Ilea's certainty. The High Companion stayed aloof when there was every indication the Citadel would fall. If not this day, then the next.

The theft of the Sacred Cloak had strengthened the Talisman's resolve. They would bring their war to Hira soon. He couldn't wait for the return of the First Oralist, though he hoped to see her again.

He would have to make a choice.

Hira, Ashfall, or the Wall.

It was just a matter of time.

41

THE LION'S GATE WAS A FORMIDABLE DOUBLE-DOOR STRUCTURE BUILT of iron, marking the eastern approach to Marakand. The Wall dominated the horizon, solid blocks of rectangular stone piled upon each other until they achieved a pinnacle, piercing the sky. A crenellated wall topped by a sturdy measure of coping stone, teeming with turrets, battlements, and flanking towers, its parapets thronged by regiments of Ahdath.

Two lions' heads, their mouths agape, were emblazoned on the doors of the Lion's Gate, a crimson splash against the metalwork. Centered above these was the same symbol Arian had found on the map concealed within the puzzle box.

Three small circles stacked in a triangle inside a five-point star.

On either side of the symbol, two words were etched in bright crimson.

RASTI, RUSTI.

Truth is safety. Safety is in right.

Or as the Authoritan had corrupted the motto to mean, *strength is justice.*

Justice is strength, Arian reminded herself. A dictum that had been Marakand's legacy to the world, long before the rise of the Authoritan in the north or the Talisman in the south.

Their plan was simple. Daniyar and Turan would accompany Zelgai to the Lion's Gate. The sentries that guarded the gate changed shifts on the hour, so that fresh eyes patrolled the surround. At twilight, the soldiers who'd reached a secret arrangement with the Buzkashi would be on duty. They would recognize men of the Shin War tribe as leaders among the Talisman, allowing the Silver Mage to attempt a familiar ruse—the bartering of the Companions, this time in exchange for safe passage into the city. The Buzkashi would remain behind after engaging in their usual trade, so as not to alert suspicion among the Ahdath.

Now, though, looking at the Lion's Gate with its crosshatching of iron beams that barred entry, Arian found her courage failed her. Her eyes beseeched Daniyar.

How can we possibly win through?

He answered her with a verse of the Claim that was almost a growl in his throat.

"If the One is with you, who then can stand against you?"

She tried to smile at him, shivering as his eyes lingered on her lips.

"We won't be able to aid you beyond this point," Zelgai warned, interrupting her thoughts. He took in the collars and slave bracelets that Arian and Sinnia had donned. "Are you certain you wish to proceed?"

Arian's answer was indirect.

"Where are the slave quarters that serve the Ahdath?"

Lania, she thought. *Lania is on the other side of the Wall.*

"In the Gold House at the center of the Registan," Zelgai answered. He was the commander of a powerful army, second in command to the Aybek of the Cloud Door, but he would not gain-say a Companion of Hira.

The Registan was the public square, once a great center of learning, with fountains leaping between its three titanic portals. The faithful had once gathered in the house of worship, astrono-mers had flocked to a conservatory of the stars, while scholars had traveled from every corner of Khorasan to study the Shir Dar's far-ranging treasury of manuscripts.

But the portals were subverted now.

Despite his confiscation of the Bloodprint, the Authoritan had no need of a gathering place for the faithful, or for the Shir Dar House of Wisdom, now known as the Shadow Mausoleum. It was said to be littered with skeletons of the dead, those who had dared to stand against his rule in defiance of his despotism. Under the Authoritan's direction, the Registan was a square where executions were carried out, blood splashing against a superfluity of tile.

Arian shuddered at the thought. If she waited any longer, she would lose her courage entirely. Sinnia, too, was nervous and drawn.

"Please," Arian said. "Summon the Ahdath."

She and Sinnia and Wafa remained a small distance behind, hemmed in by Zelgai's men. The light in the sky began to fail, a muted gold that gilded the Wall, softening its harsh edges, imbuing the city with a quality that rendered it outside of time and place.

She was reminded of a saying of the northland.

In all other places, light descends. In holy Black Aura, it as-cends.

Surely Marakand was the city of light, a golden dust scattered about the hills that dipped and swelled behind the ominous but-tresses of the Wall.

A Wall built to hold back the plague, dividing the people of

Khorasan from each other, while unnamed depravities took place behind its shelter.

Lania, are you there? Will I find you in the Gold House?

Her eyes slipped to the Silver Mage.

And if I don't find her and will not give up the search, will I lose Daniyar's love, as Captain Turan warned me? Will the Silver Mage turn from me if I dare to refuse him again?

She couldn't bear the thought of continuing without him, any more than she could abandon her search for Lania.

As two soldiers of the Ahdath approached, fear leapt into her throat. What if they saw through the ruse? What if she'd sent Daniyar to his death?

The soldiers of the Ahdath were men of the Transcasp, tall and well formed, with ash-fair hair and pale blue eyes. They wore crimson armor, and on the black crest at their throats, the Authoritan's motto was stitched in crimson thread. Which meant the Talisman's hatred of the written word had not extended this far.

Perhaps there was reason to hope.

And now she observed the differences between the Ahdath and Zelgai's men. There was a military precision about everything the Buzkashi did. The Ahdath had grown their fair hair long and wild, a darker stubble on their jaws. The belts that carried their weapons were cinched loosely about their waists. There was an attitude of disregard about them, whereas Zelgai stood attentive to their banter, his hand on the pommel of his sword, his posture stiff and straight, while his men stayed in formation, their eyes trained on the Ahdath. Two of the Buzkashi observed the Wall, the rest attended Zelgai.

Zelgai motioned the women forward. They were brought before the Ahdath, bareheaded and tremulous, Wafa following behind, a riding crop in his hand.

One of the Ahdath whistled at the sight of Sinnia. He pulled her closer, both hands on her shoulders. He spoke to the other in the language of the Transcasp.

"What a beauty! We've not seen her like in the Gold House before. This one I will take for my own."

He brushed his lips against Sinnia's cheek, letting out a bellow of laughter when she jerked away. The laughter faded, as Arian stepped forward.

The two men studied her face in silence.

A startled glance passed between them.

"Isn't she—"

"Leave it," the other guard said sharply. "What is your business in Marakand?"

"I've told you. We thought to enjoy the pleasures of Marakand while we transact the business of our master." Daniyar injected a note of steel into his voice. "The One-Eyed Preacher."

The soldier named Semyon considered the answer. He conferred for a moment with his comrade, a man called Alik.

And then, with a slight relaxation of his shoulders, he gave the signal for the Lion's Gate to be opened. The crosshatched beams grated against each other, before lifting and separating in an elaborate sequence that reminded Arian of the puzzle box. A full minute later, one of the doors of the Lion's Gate swung outward, allowing space for their party to pass.

Two guards approached from behind the gate to offload the Buzkashi's goods.

Semyon signaled his permission to proceed. The company of five parted from Zelgai without another word.

Wafa was the last to pass through, the crop rigid in his hands.

As his eyes fell on the boy, Semyon asked, "Why do you need him? Can you not manage two women on your own?"

The question was not perfunctory. It was asked as a test.

Turan responded in the languid tones he had often heard from Sartor.

"The boy has his uses."

"Does he, indeed?"

Semyon murmured something to his confederate before returning his attention to Sinnia, whom he kept close by his side.

Something was amiss. And Arian was not the only one to sense it. Daniyar and Turan tightened their grips on the weapons they hadn't been asked to yield. Under his blithe façade, Semyon remained alert as the head of their escort into the city.

Intimations of Marakand's beauty appeared in the gold light that brushed the city's soft hills and groves, a tower here, a flash of blue there, ribbons of green and gold bouncing against the eye, just at the edge of discovery. A city equally of minarets and gardens, peach blossoms scenting the air, plane trees unfurling the first buds of spring against the luminous brush of the wind.

Marakand.

As blue and gold as a miracle.

But it wasn't the fabled city that held Arian silent in wonder.

It was the army preparing for war in the valley that lay below.

42

As they moved across the plain, the boisterous roar of the Authoritan's battalions filled the air. Much as they had witnessed on the banks of Lop Nur, men were arranged in regiments, engaged in practice drills, or were busy stockpiling armor. Giant carts transported stacks of arms to the interior doors of the towers. There they were lifted by a series of pulleys to the parapets. Men were stationed at brattices along the Wall, a concentrated force deployed above the Lion's Gate.

Again Arian noted the differences between the Buzkashi and the Ahdath.

The crimson-clad soldiers were rowdy and unkempt, purposeful in their display of combat skills, yet with the underlying ease of arrogance. As Arian's party progressed past the Ahdath's encampment, men whistled and jeered at the women. More than a few called out to Semyon. Turan and Daniyar were ignored.

"War *is* coming," Sinnia muttered to Arian.

Semyon caught the words. "You need not concern yourself with war. Your fate has been decided."

Arian kept her head bent. Whatever had sharpened Semyon's attention was not something she cared to risk again.

"We can find our way to the Gold House," Daniyar said. "You need not accompany us."

Daniyar's words seemed to confirm something to the men of the Ahdath. But still they did not ask to search the party, or demand they yield their weapons. Their progress continued until the army was left behind them. Swirling rays of dust-filled light gilded the city with a patina of gold, the loess that gave the oasis its fertility.

As their party crested the hill, the city's plan declared itself. Six thoroughfares lined with mulberry trees radiated from the public square at the heart of the city to each of the gates. Along each route, marketplaces heaved with small round domes and canvas roofs, crowded with the custom of daily life. Noise fell away as the thoroughfares reached the Registan.

There were granaries and spices down one lane, metalworkers and armories down a second, carpet-weavers down a third, a bustling trade in livestock, skilled artisans who fashioned ceramics, or jewelers who worked precious metals and turquoise, and a single artery that stretched into the distance, going dark at the eastern gate.

Black Aura Gate, taking its name from the road that led to the capital. And the entire bazaar remarkable for chattering teahouses . . . and for the absence of women.

"Why has that market been covered over?" Daniyar asked, pointing to the artery that led to Black Aura Gate.

Suspicion flared in Semyon's eyes.

"Did your master not tell you? It was done at his request, as part of his agreement with His Excellency, the Authoritan. It was the kaghez market."

When Daniyar made no reply, Semyon interpreted the word for them.

"Paper milled from mulberry trees." He gestured at the empty bazaar. "The calligraphers' market." An unpleasant smirk crossed his face. "Scribes, calligraphers, Inklings—all burned in the square at the Preacher's request."

An unparalleled loss that couldn't be recovered. Something a lieutenant of the Preacher should have known.

Arian risked a glance at the Silver Mage.

His jaw was set, his face otherwise expressionless.

"That is not what I asked. The Preacher requested the market be burned to the ground. Perhaps your men were not thorough enough. The market still stands. It may provide cover to the scribes."

Semyon spat at the ground, just missing his own boots.

"My men hunt that market every day in search of Basmachi. You can assure the Preacher that not a single soul survives there."

This time the Silver Mage was careful not to reveal that he had no knowledge of the Basmachi, even as he read the falseness in Semyon's voice, giving the man away.

The city around them was quiet. Isolated from the street life of the teeming bazaars, they had reached the Registan, an enormous square on the scale of theater, its turquoise domes throbbing softly with light.

The portals formed three sides of the square.

In the center was the Tilla Kari or Gold House, the last of the structures to have been erected upon the square. Its retaining wall was decorated with mosaic insets and underglazed painted tile. From its spiral columns sprang a motif of stars and flowers worked in gold and lapis lazuli blue, the stone of heaven for a heavenly structure.

As they approached its resplendent façade, a wondrous discovery thrilled through Arian's thoughts.

The blue-and-gold columns were inscribed with notations in the language of the Claim, the written word reaching as high as the stars.

GLORY TO THE ONE. PRAISED BE THE ONE.

And a phrase she prayed would see them through the night.

MAY THE END BE WELL.

She could feel the weight of dozens of pairs of eyes pressing down from the double arcade that flanked either side of the entry to the Gold House. But from within its interior, not a single soul could be spied, nor the faintest murmur heard.

To the left of the Gold House stood the splendid structure that had once been a conservatory, where generations of students had studied the heavens' sciences.

Arian caught her breath. The flanking pylons of the conservatory's central pishtaq were worked in the script of the Claim, just as the sides of the building were covered in the Claim's calligraphy. The labor of generations, the accumulation of innumerable lifetimes.

There was so much to read, her eyes could scarcely take in the words.

Sinnia's braceleted hands reached out to squeeze Arian's, the gesture swift and stealthy.

If they had more time, the Companions would lose themselves in the Claim—a longing they had to be careful not to betray.

And there were other things to consider, a realization that couldn't have escaped the Silver Mage or Turan, the Shin War captain.

The paper market had been destroyed to satisfy the Preacher, yet the monuments of Marakand had escaped unscathed. Even a depiction of gold lions chasing after a pair of gazelles—a depiction prohibited under the Talisman—shone freshly against the Shir Dar's façade, an indication that the objectives of the Preacher and the Authoritan were not as aligned as Arian had feared.

The Talisman had taken the south; the Authoritan claimed the north.

And an army was preparing for war, while somewhere between a deserted House of Wisdom and a crypt that housed the shattered bones of the Authoritan's enemies, the women of Khorasan were trafficked through the Gold House.

As the square was claimed by the shadows of night, nothing could be seen of the portals' interiors. Facing the Tilla Kari, an ominous black structure with a bloodred door menaced the horizon. A five-point star was etched upon the door, a duplicate of the emblem stamped upon the Lion's Gate.

Semyon knocked at the Tilla Kari, a smile playing about his lips, his eyelids heavy with contemplation of the night ahead.

"You may take your ease here," he said to Daniyar.

It was a lie so little disguised it didn't need the gifts of an Authenticate to read it.

"What of the women?" Daniyar asked, his voice cool, weighing.

Semyon snaked an arm around Sinnia's waist.

"This one is mine," he purred into her ear. "The Khanum will want to meet the other. What you do with the boy is up to you."

Another lie. Two guards stepped into the courtyard. At a nod from Semyon, they sprang upon Daniyar and Turan, giving them no chance to react. Both men were disarmed and bound.

"Zelgai must take us for fools." Semyon seized Arian by the

arm, gripping her chin. "You are no emissary from the Preacher, not when you bring this one with you. Search them."

Their packs were stripped from them, the contents scattered at their feet. Semyon and Alik pushed aside the cloaks the Companions wore. As soon as they saw the circlets on their arms, the Ahdath went still. Then with ruthless efficiency, Arian and Sinnia were gagged.

It was too late for Arian to reconsider her decision to withhold her use of the Claim until they had reached the cover of the Gold House. It would have been her first time attempting the Claim on such a scale—she had thought better not to risk it. Now she no longer had the option.

The bracelets at their wrists were tested. A snort escaped Semyon as he found the shackles unlocked. He removed them, binding their wrists with rope. Alik confiscated their weapons.

The guard who'd searched Daniyar's pack held up the Candour.

Semyon took a step back, his face pale. The sight of the black book seemed to shake him.

"Quickly. Gag him also. It's the Guardian of Candour, the Silver Mage. Take him to the Mausoleum for questioning. Lock the Talisman and the boy in the Blood Shed." He spared a cruel smile for the women. "There is never enough blood for the Authoritan."

Wafa struck out at Semyon with his crop. Semyon dodged the blow by pivoting on his heel. He broke the boy's grip on the crop with a single hand, sending him sprawling with a blow from the other. Wafa fell to the ground, unmoving.

"Take them to the Blood Shed," Semyon repeated. "Bring the lajward and the book of the Silver Mage. They brought these things into Marakand for a purpose. The Khanum will wish to see them." His lip curled in contempt, he approached Daniyar. "I did not think you would yield so easily, Guardian of Candour. The Immolan usurps your authority, so perhaps this has left you weak." He rolled back on his heels, his hands easy at his sides. "Nor have you encountered Ahdath before—no wonder you were taken. Still, I would not have risked two as beautiful as these in a city full of soldiers." He nodded at the Tilla Kari. "You will have plenty of time to consider their fate before Commander Araxcin arrives."

Daniyar strained against his bonds, his silver eyes ablaze. Semyon chuckled.

"Which one concerns you most, I wonder?" He trailed a hand down Arian's bare arm. "This one's fate will be decided by the Khanum. Take her to the Gold House. The other—" He switched his attention to Sinnia. "The other I will not share. As captain, that is my right."

Arian's muffled cry drew Daniyar's attention to her. She gestured at Wafa, motionless at Semyon's feet. Turan answered Arian before he could be gagged.

"I will protect him, Companion. You need not worry."

Semyon's fist struck Turan across the face, raising a welt on Turan's jaw.

"Worry for yourself, Talisman. No one survives the Blood Shed."

43

Arian wasn't worried for Daniyar. He was more adept at survival than the Ahdath could predict. He'd spent ten years living a double life under the Talisman. If he'd allowed himself to be captured, it must have been for a reason, much as she now waited to be admitted to the Gold House, Alik as her guard. She could escape, but the Gold House was where she had wished to be taken.

It was the Blood Shed that worried her. How would Turan rescue Wafa? Her hopes rested on her observations of the Ahdath as soldiers. They were careless in their assurance of martial strength. They'd been bred to indolence by the Authoritan's absolute rule.

Or perhaps there was something more sinister about their power.

No one survives the Blood Shed.

Was that why the Registan was so quiet, empty of signs of human habitation?

A mirrored door beneath the Tilla Kari's portal gave way. The mirrored inlay of the door was patterned in six-point stars.

From six to five, Arian thought, remembering the puzzle box. For Daniyar had forgotten the sixth attribute described in the Verse of the Throne. Something significant, something that mattered—

something that would serve them because there was always more to Ilea's plotting than was first apparent. She wished Ilea had chosen to share her secrets. And Arian asked herself if the Black Khan was privy to those secrets now.

Alik nudged her forward, into a palace of wonder.

The Tilla Kari's interior was stuccoed with spectacular artistry in gold leaf and periwinkle blue, its ravishing motifs climbing skyward, until they were lost to the heavens themselves.

Corner squinches ascended to a glorious cupola whose extravagance dazzled the eye. The transition from walls to dome was achieved by a sight that for a spell of unbroken time robbed Arian of thought or calculation, wonderstruck into silence.

A band of inscription, its gold calligraphy shimmering against a blue so pure that it put the sky of Marakand to shame, and above this, a second band to crown the first, stenciled in immaculate white.

The Claim.

The Claim she had been taught to memorize as a child.

She read fluently, recognizing verses and benedictions that her mother had promised her were a gift, a gift that would serve all of Khorasan one day.

And here the Talisman hand had been stayed. No violence had come to this beauty.

She was lost in contemplation of a ceiling constructed entirely of stars.

A sob caught in her throat.

As it registered, she became aware of her surroundings. As she had been led to the dome by her captor, she had passed an assembly of women.

Hundreds of women, the most beautiful she'd ever seen, painted and decorated, with long, lustrous hair, their full lips pouting, their eyes large and bright and vivid with interest, marking Arian's progress through the hall. They murmured to each other as she passed.

They were dressed in gleaming silks in shades of blue and rose and peach so lovely they resembled a garden of flowers. Their costumes were elaborate, yards of fabric wound about their figures, intricate pieces of gold and silver shining from their hair, their wrists, their throats. Their fingers sparkled as they motioned to each other. The thrum of their laughter filled the hall.

Around them, jeweled plates of sweetmeats were arranged. Silver platters garnished with lilacs were piled with apricots, peaches, and plums. Figs, dates, almonds, and pistachios spilled from crystal bowls. Rose petals were scattered on the carpets, imbuing the air with sweetness. Samovars of lemon-scented tea perched on small gold stands.

The sight of Arian, bound and gagged, guarded by Alik—whose attention was fixed on the women who surrounded him—was unremarkable to them. There was curiosity in the delicate faces, not fear.

Arian's heart thundered in her chest.

From a contemplation of the sublime, she was brought to this moment, this endpoint of the slave-chains. This place where Lania at last might be found.

But the women gathered in the great hall were young, too young to be Arian's sister. In the first bloom of youth, they were younger than Arian herself.

Most were of Arian's bloodline. Some were of the mixed races of the east, others from the Transcasp. They did not appear under threat, though a languor about their eyes dimmed their radiance.

It seemed to echo the indifference of the Ahdath.

There were no soldiers in the hall.

If these women had been trafficked by the Talisman, they should have borne signs of ill-use and hopelessness. Instead, their flesh was pampered and rounded, not tautened like hers and Sinnia's from the famine in the south.

And here behind these walls, while the people of the south starved, was abundance. Of food, of comfort, of luxury. Of beautiful girls chattering together like doves in a royal dovecote.

Where were the women of the slave-chains?

Two women approached Alik from one of the hall's alcoves. He shoved Arian at them with an ungentle hand, turning over Daniyar's pack.

"This one is for transport," he said. "She's to be taken to the Khanum. She doesn't look like much, but she's dangerous—keep her gagged."

He focused on them for no more than a moment, his attention skittering away.

"Understood," said the taller of the two women, securing the pack. "You should return to your post."

With a grimace, Alik ambled back to the portal. He made no mention of Sinnia.

Arian turned to the women who had taken her into their custody. One was a dark-haired beauty whom Arian recognized at once as a woman of the south, a woman of one of Candour's tribes. She wore a bright gold dress with an overlay of coral silk, gathered at the waist. Gold bracelets chimed from her wrists to her elbows. Her hair was dressed in a coronet of curls. She made a moue of distaste as she reached out to take Arian's hand.

The other woman was nothing like her companion. Taller, thinner, older, with pale, lank hair and watery, suspicious eyes, she wore an ill-fitting dress in an unflattering shade of pink. Her jewelry was limited to a set of jade bracelets on her arm. Her left arm was tucked out of view, but not before Arian had glimpsed the line of pinpricks that stippled her blue-veined skin. There was a strange round mark on the side of her neck.

Before she could consider what the woman's appearance meant, the two women shepherded Arian down a long corridor that led from the dome into darkness.

The woman with the scarred arm reached out with a jagged, abrupt gesture to remove the gag from Arian's mouth.

"At least let her breathe while we move her, Gul."

Her voice was gruff, and though she spoke to the other woman in the Common Tongue, the clipped accents of her speech marked her as a woman of the Transcasp.

"Who are you?" Arian asked as she worked her jaw loose. "Where do you take me? Who is the Khanum?"

They ignored her, jostling her down the corridor. They had almost reached the wooden doors at its end, where there was a dimness that failed to echo the magnificence of the Tilla Kari's portal and starry door, when the pale-haired woman drew them off to one side.

"What are you doing?" the woman named Gul demanded.

Her companion answered her with another of her sudden gestures—a quick blow to the temple. The woman in the gold dress sank to the floor. Her assailant dragged her into the shadows. Then she freed Arian's hands.

"Quick," she whispered. "Take off your clothes, we don't have much time."

She bent over Gul's body, stripping it of its clothes.

"Hurry," she insisted, when she saw that Arian hadn't moved. "You have to change places with her. If we don't supply someone to the Khanum, they'll tear down the Tilla Kari searching for you. We need to buy time." She nodded at Arian's arms. "Keep your circlets, Companion. Take off the rest."

As she spoke, she worked the bangles free from Gul's arms, adding them to the pile of silks. Slippers followed, then her hands were in Gul's hair, pulling it free of its coronet, leaving it long and loose.

"Put on her dress. Do as I say," she said impatiently. "My name is Elena, I'm here to help you."

The fear in Elena's voice caught at Arian. She began to undress, shrugging off her cloak, peeling the armor from her body. Elena dressed the dark-haired woman in Arian's clothes.

She tied the woman's hands with the same rope that had bound Arian, forcing the gag into her mouth. As Arian dressed in Gul's costume and bangles, Elena joined her. She arranged Arian's hair as the other woman had worn it. She passed Arian a small blunt stick.

"Line your eyes. Bite your lips and pinch your cheeks. It's the most we can do to make you look like one of them."

Elena knelt down to Gul, applying a rag to the other woman's face, smudging her kohl to create an impression of shadows. Gul came to consciousness with a gasp. Elena shouldered her to her feet and covered her with Arian's cloak. She scooped grit from the soles of Arian's boots, and rubbed the dirt over Gul's hands before forcing the boots onto Gul's feet.

Gul's struggles intensified. Elena whipped out a silver dagger from her belt, pointing it at Gul's throat.

"I don't need you," she said. "I could kill you and leave you here. If you'd rather take your chances with the Khanum, you'll have to stay quiet, understood?"

She nicked Gul's eyebrow with her knife.

Terrified, Gul nodded.

"Good? Are you ready?" Elena studied Arian's transformation. "You look—too military somehow. Try to seem subservient. When we get to the doors, don't talk. Whatever you do, don't raise your head. They'll see what they expect to see. If they ask you to talk, use the Common Tongue and say your name is Gul. Leave the rest to me."

She slung Daniyar's pack onto her shoulder.

A heavy knock sounded against the doors.

Elena hurried to answer it, dragging Arian and Gul with her.

"Support her from the other side," she said to Arian.

They moved through the door into a space that opened onto a warren of alleys, lit by the sputtering torches of soldiers. A covered cart was waiting with an escort of a dozen Ahdath.

Elena shoved Gul at the soldiers.

"Take her." The words were a command. "The Khanum doesn't like to be kept waiting."

Gul muttered against the gag.

The commander of the squad was a sharp-eyed man with long, fair hair, and a high-planed face in the manner of the Ahdath.

"Who sends her?"

"Semyon." Elena spoke with a truculent confidence. "And Alik, too, if you must know."

Gul continued to struggle.

"She doesn't look like much. Why does the Khanum want her?"

"Why don't you ask her, Illarion? If you feel so inclined."

Illarion's men laughed. "A spitfire, this one," one of them said. "Bold enough to know you by name."

"You have the advantage of me," Illarion said, intrigued.

"Anya," she answered. "Now will you take her or will you continue to dally here pointlessly? There are girls awaiting instruction in the hall."

Illarion looked at Arian.

"And this one, what does she say?"

"She answers to me, not to you. If you intend to delay further, make sure the Khanum knows it is your choice to do so, not mine."

She thrust Gul's struggling body at him so that he had no choice but to take hold of her. He issued a curt instruction to his men. Gul was locked inside the cart.

"Good night, Captain."

Elena turned on her heel, carrying Arian along.

"Not so fast, Anya." Illarion caught her by the arm. "Aren't you forgetting something?" He tugged at the strap on her shoulder. "The pack. I was told to send the pack, as well."

"By whom?" Elena shrugged off his hand. "Because *I* was told to deliver it to your Commander. Before the Khanum sees it."

It was a gambit. A desperate one. But Elena's face was smooth and disdainful, giving nothing away.

Illarion studied her cold expression.

"You aren't beautiful and pampered like the others. What purpose do you serve in the Gold House?"

Elena raised her eyebrows. "I train the pampered ones, the ones you and your soldiers dare not dream of. But thank you for the reminder, Illarion. Should the Commander grant you the privilege of access, I will remember your words."

Illarion's mouth twisted in a wry smile.

"I'm certain that you will." He reached for the pack again. "How is it you've received an order from Araxcin that I am not privy to? You're a woman of the Tilla Kari. I'm his second in command."

His voice was not quite bland enough to conceal his skepticism. Elena didn't hesitate.

"Then as second in command, *Captain* Illarion, Commander Araxcin must have told you where he spent his afternoon—and with whom." She indicated Arian. "But I beg you, please do question him further. I am told he is a great one for sharing stories about his conquests."

Arian could see from Illarion's face that nothing could be further from the truth.

"Perhaps you would care to ask him now?" she said sweetly. "You could join us inside."

Illarion shook his head, knowing when he'd been bested.

"Keep your prize, Anya. Whether the Commander and the Khanum have a new object to battle over is no concern of mine." His eyes raked over her. "But I will remember your face. And soon, perhaps, my turn will come."

Elena shrugged, an exaggerated gesture of unconcern, before she turned her back on him.

"I will count the hours, Captain."

Her own smile was bitter, as she heard his laughter recede into the distance.

"Come," she said to Arian. "We'll wait until their caravan is gone."

When they had found safety inside an alcove close to the doors, Arian pressed the other woman for answers. She felt vulnerable without her armor and riding clothes.

"Who are you? How did you know to look for me here? Why are you helping me?"

The other woman kept an eye out for the presence of others, prodding the door open with her shoe. The sounds of the cart began to fade.

"I told you, my name is Elena. My sister, Larisa, will answer your questions."

"How did you know about Araxcin? The captain might have caught you in a lie."

"I know their rotations. Araxcin and Illarion are never on the same patrol. Illarion was at the eastern gate today. He'd have no way of knowing Araxcin's movements." She shrugged again. "I took a chance." She aimed a quick look through the narrow opening of the door. "It's clear. We should go."

Arian shook her head. "I don't know where you're taking me, but I need to find the Blood Shed. My friends are there, they need my help."

"If they were taken to the Blood Shed, they're already dead."

The matter-of-fact words stabbed Arian.

"And even if they haven't been killed, there's a full patrol mounted outside the Blood Shed. Araxcin comes to interrogate the man they took to the Shadow Mausoleum. We have to hurry," she insisted. "Illarion's not quite as stupid as the others. The switch may not fool him."

"I thank you for your help, but I must take my own path."

Suddenly, the silver dagger was at Arian's side. In her borrowed silks, Arian could feel its point against her ribs.

"You're coming with me. Larisa needs to see you. She promised the Black Khan."

Arian froze in place. She remembered the silky voice with its cryptic promise.

I have men in Marakand who will help you find the Blood-print.

Reading her face, Elena said, "If you want answers, you'll have to come with me."

44

UNDER THE COVER OF NIGHT, ARIAN WAS LED DOWN COBBLED PATH-
ways that twisted in on themselves, sometimes sloping, sometimes
climbing, dank and covered in darkness despite the ambiguous
sliver of moon and the fugitive wind that chased them.

Night catches us, Arian thought. *What of Daniyar and the
others?*

The alleyways grew narrower, dwellings on either side crowding together, their rooftops meeting, their haphazard awnings listing in the wind.

Elena moved through the streets, marking a rising path through
mud-bricked domes and towers aslant from their foundations,
rare and surprising blue-green tiles flashing from the darkness. A
city of the missing, forlorn, and forsaken.

They came to a halt before a dwelling buried between two
storefronts. Its awning dipped over the door. Elena rapped against
the door, four quick hard knocks.

A small wooden panel at eye level slid open. Elena held up her
bracelets. The door gave way, admitting them into burgeoning
darkness. The room they passed through was small and cramped.

Arian could sense the presence of a motionless crowd, pressed up against each other, though no one spoke.

Elena tugged Arian along with scant regard for the flimsy nature of the slippers on Arian's feet.

"Hurry."

They climbed the set of uneven risers that passed for a flight of stairs to the roof. The house was on a hill. On the side that fronted the street, it faced a turquoise dome. The city lay sprawled before them, the Wall glowing with countless fires.

As Elena had warned, the Registan was filled with soldiers, the Ahdath Arian had dismissed as disorderly now a disciplined force between the Shir Dar and the Blood Shed.

An agonized cry rent the night.

Arian recognized the voice as Wafa's.

"*Please.*" She turned to Elena. "My friend is alive, I must reach the Blood Shed."

"There is nothing you can do for your friend," another voice said. "No one escapes the Blood Shed."

Arian looked around. Two figures materialized against the darkness, their hoods outlined by the wan light of the moon, a man and a woman. The woman took Arian's hand.

She was of the same slight build as Elena, with a thin, lined face and hypnotic blue eyes. She was dressed in hunting clothes, a leather vest and close-fitting breeches covered by a dark cloak. Both she and the man beside her wore the same bracelets as Elena. And like Elena, the woman's arms were pitted with scars. The same dark circle, outlined in white, was pressed into her neck.

"You found her then."

"Ruslan was right." Elena's voice filled with a sudden warmth. "They were sending her to the Khanum."

The woman in the shadows studied Arian's face.

"I can see why. Semyon is not quite the imbecile I took him for."
She let go of Arian's hand. "You are safe, Companion. I am Larisa
Salikh. The Black Khan sent us to find you."

Arian examined the man who stood beside Larisa—tall, thin,
with a pockmarked face and tilted eyes that burned. A ragged scar
ran from the corner of his left eye to his jaw.

A note of surprise in her voice, Arian asked, "You are the Black
Khan's 'men'?"

"Surely a Companion of Hira does not believe that men alone
are capable of command, though I'm not surprised you were misled. Rukh takes pleasure in twisting the truth."

There was a grim acceptance of reality in the other woman's
voice that was familiar to Arian through her own experience. Larisa Salikh had been at war. And not just on this day, but for many
months or years. There was suffering in her face, and a poised
calculation that came from having to wait out a course.

"We have an arrangement with the Black Khan, just as we have
an arrangement with the Buzkashi. But we serve only our own
ends, as we see them."

Questions filled Arian's mind, questions she suspected Larisa
Salikh could answer. She would have to use the Claim. She had no
time for prolonged discussion.

She opened her mouth to speak, arranging phrases in her mind,
phrases that would search out vulnerabilities and elicit truth,
words forming within her throat.

The man named Ruslan stepped closer, a dagger in his hand.
Elena shadowed the movement at once, her eyes hungry on his face.

Larisa Salikh smiled a bitter smile.

"The Claim doesn't work on us, so don't bother. I'm not your
enemy. I'm here to help you find whatever you're seeking. Then I'll
be about my business."

"What is your business?"

"The same as yours. Protecting the women of my city. Doing what I can to undermine the Authoritan, fighting a war."

"Don't say anything else," Elena warned her sister. "We don't know this woman."

Larisa removed a roll from the belt at her waist. At first, Arian thought it was a scroll, a written message, some unexpected communication from the Black Khan. But the other woman struck a match against her leather boot and touched it to the roll. It was a leaf-crop called timbaku, commonly smoked among soldiers. Larisa drew on it, expelling smoke from her lungs.

"You must not doubt everyone, Elena. Some strangers can be friends." She drew on the timbaku again. "A Companion of Hira, particularly this one, shares our work and our vision. She's the one who hunts the slave-chains." Larisa tapped the ash from the roll. Its gray residue vanished into the wind. "You must forgive my sister—she worries for me too much."

"With good reason," Ruslan said. Elena flashed him a grateful look. He missed it, his attention fixed on Larisa.

As Larisa raised the timbaku to her mouth, her bangles clinked together. A stray bit of memory came to Arian. There was a rumor she'd heard of the northland and dismissed as a kind of fable. But Elena, Larisa, and Ruslan wore the bracelets. Their faces and bodies were pitted with scars. And they moved with the speed and agility of those who'd learned to anticipate an ambush.

In the history of the northland, there was a man who'd given his life to facing down the Authoritan. The man's name was Salikh.

"Your bracelets," Arian whispered. "Do you follow the Usul Jade?"

Ruslan placed a protective hand on Larisa Salikh's shoulder.

Larisa dropped her leaf roll to the ground, extinguishing it with her boot.

"You've heard of us, then."

Arian shook her head. "Rumors, nothing more, from slave handlers whose caravans I tracked. They spoke of a teaching practiced beyond the Wall, known as the Usul Jade—a corruption of the High Tongue. And the Ahdath spoke of Basmachi. Did they mean you?"

"Yes, it's what we call our fighters. Whereas, Usul Jade means the 'New Method,' a philosophy taught by my father, a scribe of the Shir Dar." Larisa's sense of loss was evident as she spoke. "The Usul Jade challenged the status of women in the northland. My father tried to end the slave trade. He was put to death for his pains."

"Larisa inherited the struggle," Ruslan said. "She's fulfilled her father's vision."

Larisa's mouth turned down at the words. Ruslan squeezed her shoulder, a wordless gesture that brought a scowl to Elena's face.

"I was ambushed by the Ahdath—it was Elena who kept the resistance alive. Without Elena, there would *be* no resistance."

"Yes," Ruslan said softly. "And Elena pioneered your rescue from Jaslyk."

"Jaslyk?"

"Jaslyk Prison." Larisa gave Arian a crooked smile, revealing a mouth full of broken teeth. "Where the Ahdath held me and drugged me for more than a year." She held up her arms for Arian to see. "Given a choice, I would have preferred the Blood Shed."

45

In hushed voices, Larisa and Ruslan recounted the history of the Usul Jade. Salikh had used his knowledge of the Claim to try to force the Authoritan's hand. His disappearance and murder had been held up as a warning to others who thought to emulate his ways.

"The prisons were full," Elena muttered. "There were many who died defending our father's beliefs."

Salikh's death had acquired the status of martyrdom. The Basmachi grew in numbers, new fighters recruited each day. Broken families sought each other out, learning the teachings of the Usul Jade, ready to accept the risks.

And they had paid the price. The Blood Shed had broken hundreds of bodies. The Shir Dar was piled high with corpses of Basmachi. And many more had suffered in Jaslyk.

Larisa and Elena had taken up the fight, as well, but not without consequences. A Basmachi fighter broken at Jaslyk gave up what he knew of Larisa and Elena. Larisa was captured and taken to Jaslyk. Elena and Ruslan had organized her rescue.

"Elena is adept at disguise. She infiltrated Jaslyk." Larisa fingered the mark on her neck. "They place a mask over your head, and then they gas you."

Arian learned that each of the three had spent time in the Authoritan's prisons. In Larisa's case, the Authoritan had been afraid to martyr her. Instead, he'd had her drugged with strange and mysterious opiates.

It had taken weeks to revive Larisa from her dependency—the timbaku was its last remnant.

Arian passed no judgment. Without the comfort of the Claim, who knew what form of oblivion she might have sought? What struck her was that she and Sinnia had felt themselves alone in their struggle, while behind the Wall, others had been battling the same cruelty, the same despair, seeking a chance at freedom.

In the end, she judged herself. Her struggle had been too narrow. She could have served as a friend to the resistance.

Now she listened as Elena described their work freeing women from the slave-chains and hiding them away in the necropolis of the Hazing. The living sheltered among the dead when the Ahdath came to call.

Arian asked after the women of Marakand, wondering why so few were at the Tilla Kari.

"The women in the Gold House are safe from the soldiers at the Wall, by decree of the Authoritan's consort. The Khanum sees they are trained in music and dance before they are summoned to Black Aura to serve at the Authoritan's court. Araxcin is a member of that court. He comes and goes from the Gold House as he pleases."

"And the rest? How does the Authoritan sate the men who guard the Wall?"

"There are pleasure houses throughout the city where women from the slave-chains are taken and drugged. When they're broken, they're sent to the Plague Lands. We rescue as many as we can. Ruslan leads the Basmachi in their raids. We've taken many of the Ahdath down, though not enough. It's why they hunt us through the Hazing, the Tomb of the Living King."

"I am looking for a tomb," Arian said slowly.

Could she have stumbled upon it? Here in this dark warren, along these blind alleys?

Larisa's nod was decisive. "Yes. Rukh told us to help you find whatever you seek." She considered for a moment. "It will take time—there are hundreds of tombs in this city."

Larisa hadn't asked the Black Khan more, to forestall the questions he might think to ask in exchange. He supplied the Basmachi with arms, contributed soldiers to their cause, without asking about Larisa's plans for the Ahdath. She preferred it that way. Her congress with the Black Khan was the most frugal exchange of needs.

Arian reached for the tahweez on her left arm. She had tucked the map from the puzzle box behind it, a last refuge from defilement or disgrace.

As much as it instilled reverence, the Claim also instilled fear.

Larisa and Elena took a step back, their eyes wide with disbelief.

Though they'd known she was a Companion of Hira, the circlets gave them pause.

"It's a map," Arian told them. "A map to the tomb."

Larisa and Elena examined it, their heads close together. A finger capped by a dirty fingernail pointed to the dome inked on the map. It was Ruslan's.

Arian shook her head. "There are domes everywhere I look in Marakand. Blue-green domes." She stretched out her hand. "Could this be it?"

The dome that faced their sheltered roof was crumbled half away.

"Its dome would have been unique had it not been for the heavens," Larisa murmured. And when Arian looked at her, "It was something my father used to say. If this is the dome on the map, it doesn't bode well for us. The architect who built it insisted on a kiss from the queen as payment for his services. The kiss left a mark on the queen's face that she tried to hide by veiling herself. When the king learned of the architect's kiss, he had the queen burned alive."

"And the architect?"

"He developed wings and flew to safety from the top of the dome." Larisa's tone was harsh. "A woman's fate is always worse."

Ruslan interrupted her. "This isn't the same dome. Look at the drawing."

Four pairs of eyes contemplated the tiny figure on the map. The dome's circumference was gently fluted, ribbed in a brilliant blue.

Ruslan's eyes met Larisa's in perfect understanding.

"It's the Dome of the Gur-e-Amir. And it's under guard."

46

THE NIGHT WAS SILENT, THE AHDATH PATROL IN THE SQUARE OF THE Registan watchful.

"They're waiting for Araxcin, the commander. Once he arrives, the blood sport will begin."

"Then I have time," Arian said. "I can still rescue them."

Larisa shook her head. "You don't understand. There is only one door to the Blood Shed. Three hundred men stand between you and your friends. How will you fight them? With the Claim?" Her tone was doubtful.

Arian paused.

"You say the Claim doesn't affect you. Your father was a scribe, a learned man. Did he not teach you of the Claim?"

"For all the good it did him or any of us. But it wasn't that." She lowered her hood and turned her head to the side, uncovering ears that were tattered shells, crisscrossed with curved scars. "This is how they mark followers of the Usul Jade. It's a special torture of the Authoritan's that prevents the Claim from falling on our ears. He thinks us skilled in its use, so he reserves its power to himself."

A savage inheritance for the daughters of Salikh.

But Arian knew the others didn't understand the power of the Claim as she did. Its words, its essence entwined with her own, waking a majesty she'd barely tapped.

Though she had spent her life learning its secrets, the Claim was still unpredictable.

And if Larisa and Elena were the daughters of Salikh, the Claim might still lie dormant within them, despite the Authoritan's tortures. But this wasn't the moment to instruct them in the mysteries of the Claim—she had to think of Wafa and Turan.

"How much time before the commander arrives?"

"It won't be long." For the first time, Larisa appeared uncertain. "The Gur-e-Amir isn't far from here. Marakand is a city that wraps around itself. I'll send Basmachi to scout the road. If we do not tarry, there's a chance you could still reach your friends in time. If you truly believe you can save them."

If Daniyar or Sinnia were here, she could have sent them to the Blood Shed. As it was, she would have to make a choice.

"I'll need more practical clothing."

If she didn't find the tomb now, storming the Blood Shed would leave her little chance to do so. If the Ahdath discovered Gul, the city would be swarming with soldiers.

She didn't know why their ruse at the Wall had failed, but it had robbed her of the chance to search for Lania. There was nothing she could do for her sister now.

But for Wafa, Turan, the women of Khorasan—there was still the Bloodprint.

Elena equipped her with clothing and weaponry. She handed over Daniyar's pack.

"Do you come with us?" Arian asked her.

"I go wherever Larisa commands me." But Elena's eyes were on Ruslan, and Arian guessed she was bound as much to Ruslan.

She turned her attention to the scouts of the Basmachi, the silent, waiting men who'd filled the cramped room below the stairs. After a moment's consultation, Ruslan sent them ahead. As the streets dipped down to meet the horizon, Arian lost sight of the Registan and the Blood Shed.

She didn't hear Wafa's voice again.

She prayed he wasn't already dead.

As she trailed Larisa through Marakand's empty streets, she heard thuds, bodies falling to the ground—the Basmachi's quiet skirmishes with Ahdath who emerged from the darkness at intervals.

There were no lanterns in the city's quiet streets. Occasionally, the pitiable sound of weeping could be heard from torchlit balconies or the desolate interiors of safeguarded dwellings. She saw that Elena and Ruslan marked each of these as they passed for later reconnaissance.

And she wondered again where Daniyar was and why the Blood Shed was silent.

She whispered the question to Elena, whose sullen face provided no answer.

Nonetheless, Arian was grateful for the Black Khan's intercession with the followers of the Usul Jade. Marakand was a labyrinth. Beyond the ordered square of the Registan, the city sprawled in a dozen different directions, crammed with tunnels and blind corners. She couldn't have found the route from the Registan to the Gur-e-Amir on her own. And she was heartened to learn of the Basmachi, to know that she and Sinnia were not alone in their bitter, unending struggle.

And if I find the Bloodprint—

But that was thinking too far ahead.

For now, she needed to focus on finding the tomb in the complex of the Gur-e-Amir, a maze of graves within graves.

Then she would rescue Wafa and the others.

And Daniyar, if he hadn't turned up by then.

Two torches in iron brackets illuminated the entrance to the mausoleum. Most of its exquisite façade was chiseled away. What was left was the faintest blue-green murmuring against brick. Guards strolled the perimeter of the mausoleum in pairs.

Between the massive entrance and the Dome of the Gur-e-Amir, the complex was empty, a sprawl of broken arches overrun by a creeping system of leaves and vines, crooked trees leaning against tiers of moldering brick. The night air was filled with the sickly sweet stench of decay. The feeble light of the torches flickered against the melon-shaped dome, now green, now blue, as the light danced over its surface.

Beyond the dome, the graveyard waited, silent against the gloom.

"Don't use the Claim unless you have to," Elena muttered. "We must delay Illarion's discovery of Gul for as long as we can."

As yet, Arian had seen no need for its use—the Basmachi were effective at dispatching Ahdath patrols, dragging their crimson-clad bodies into the shadows. But she understood the caution.

They passed through the rotted vegetation into the octagonal complex. A complement of four guards was stationed before the soaring cupola of the dome, a faint light playing against their crimson armor. Elena and Ruslan moved swiftly. The Ahdath had no sooner looked askance at the intruders than knives were drawn against their throats, their scrabbling movements smothered into stillness.

"Hurry. Take out the map."

No stranger to death herself, Arian found herself disturbed by the gleam in Elena's eyes.

Answering her thoughts, Elena said, "You have no idea what these men are capable of in Jaslyk."

Arian nodded. Sometimes killing was a necessity, not a choice. She took no pleasure from it, but her record with the Talisman was no different from Elena's with the Ahdath. She had rarely discovered a moral compass to war. Saying nothing, she passed the map to Ruslan who scanned it with a miniature eyeglass, mumbling to himself.

Arian studied the room. The people of the Claim had labored over these monuments, slaves of a distant era. But this one was a commemoration of the dead, built for the glory of man. The lavender-and-gold ceiling shone like the eye of a fulgent sun. Blue and white tiles lined the terracotta walls, assembled into patterns of astonishing expressiveness. The interior of the chamber echoed the loveliness of the dome. Slabs of yellow-gold onyx paneled the lower walls. Marble cornices hung above the paneling like stalactites. Gilded cartouches in high relief sprung from the chamber's arches. Letters of an ancient script were chipped away from the walls, scattering tiles at their feet. A single lantern kindled the darkness.

The air inside the chamber was musty, a strange sweetness rising from the earth. Ruslan rotated the map in his hands. He pointed ahead into the gloom.

"It's not a graveyard," he told Arian. "It's a map of the complex itself."

Arian unhooked the lantern from its brace, throwing light upon the chamber ahead. Nine tombs were arranged beneath the dome in a geometric configuration. A stone barricade separated one tomb from the others.

Ruslan traced the lines on the map with his finger.

"This way."

They moved forward with caution, Elena standing guard.

Two steps descended to the floor of the mausoleum. A profusion of six-point stars shone from the gilded walls. The tombs' headstones had been destroyed, the names of the dead lost to time. The inscriptions that had once marked the onyx were broken off, leaving the tombs bare.

They turned right and then left, following the lines on the map.

"It doesn't lead anywhere," Arian said. "It just turns back on itself."

She searched each tomb for a sign or a marker that would give a clue to the Bloodprint. Perhaps there had once been flowers and stars that served as echoes of the map, but these had been chipped away. The tombs were too much alike.

Ruslan traced a solitary path between the tombs, counting aloud.

He came to a stop in front of the tomb that lay at the center of the complex. It was covered by a crosspiece of nephrite, a block of jade so dark it looked black.

It was a green mirror of the dome above.

And she realized, the Dome of the Gur-e-Amir was the Dome of the Green Mirror.

There was no name on the tomb, nor was it raised higher than the others, reclining upon a set of modestly carved tiers.

Ruslan beckoned Arian forward.

The dark green jade was cracked down the middle.

"No matter how you move through the complex, the lines return to this tomb."

Arian knelt before the crosspiece. She found a battered verse in the script of the Claim.

WERE I TO RISE, THE WHOLE WORLD WOULD TREMBLE.

Beside it, the now-familiar symbol was stamped. Three small circles collected inside a five-point star.

"*Rasti, rusti,*" Larisa whispered. She viewed it with horror. "The king's grave." She shuddered. "We must not disturb the king's grave, not for anything. His tomb is cursed."

Arian shivered at the words, at the sense of something unseen, unknown.

The five-point star in a room bursting with six-point stars. The green mirror, an echo of the symbol from the map. This was the tomb she sought, the tomb with the clue to the Bloodprint.

"You speak of superstition," she said.

"You don't understand. This is the grave of the Amir, a tyrant who ruled the greatest Khorasan empire of the age. He built pyramids from his enemies' skulls. Marakand was his capital." She looked around. "What do you need from here, Companion?"

Arian gazed at the tomb helplessly.

"I don't know."

But there had to be something. Ilea had sent Turan to the Sorrowsong to procure the puzzle box. The Black Khan had directed the leaders of the Basmachi to await Arian's arrival in Marakand to guide her to this spot.

The place on the map marked by the five-point star.

Besides the inscription, there was nothing to distinguish this tomb, nothing to suggest it as the hiding place of the Bloodprint.

"What lies beneath the tombs?"

"The crypt," Larisa answered. "The tombs are for show. They distinguish the Amir and his family, but their bodies molder in the crypt below."

Could that be it? Could a clue to the Bloodprint lie beneath the cenotaph? Or perhaps the Bloodprint itself, secreted away by the Bloodless? Even as she thought it, Arian realized how improbable the idea was. Hadn't Turan told her the manuscript wouldn't survive in a crypt?

"You're taking too long," Elena warned. "There are soldiers at the gate."

A sense of urgency clamped down on Arian. She examined the slab of jade. Perhaps a message had been scratched into its surface, a single word that would point her to a safehold.

But apart from the crack down the middle, the block of jade was unmarked.

The sound of voices was growing louder. Ruslan and Larisa joined Elena at the entrance to the chamber.

Six-point stars. Everywhere Arian looked there were six-point stars.

And etched at the foot of the grave beside the tyrant's motto, a five-point star.

There had been six stars on the surface of the puzzle box, six stars that shifted into five.

Arian scrutinized the tiers that supported the tyrant's tomb. It rested upon a slab of pale green marble that was buttressed in turn by a block of yellow onyx, a stone surround serving as the base. Her attention was caught by the tier of yellow onyx, wider than the others, the only one to be carved with a motif.

A pattern of diamonds rather than stars appeared at staged intervals, five to each side, one at the head and foot of the tomb.

Five to each side.

Six into five.

The voices were coming closer. Elena and Larisa moved away from the threshold of the chamber, crossing beneath the dome.

Arian must have missed something.

She looked again and realized not all of the tomb's markings were diamond-shaped.

Beneath the inscription at the foot of the tomb, a round medallion was set into the base. Arian had seen the medallion before. She had carried it here from the Sorrowsong.

An inconceivable idea flashed through her mind.

Daniyar had remembered five attributes of the One from the manuscript from Maze Aura.

Life, knowledge, dominion, power, and will.

Out of a snatched fragment of memory, Arian discovered the sixth.

Oneness.

The Oneness of the One.

The sixth and final virtue.

"They're coming," Ruslan warned, moving away to the portal.

Arian wrenched Daniyar's pack from her shoulders. She rummaged through it, discarding the puzzle box and the key, taking the ewer in her hands.

Intercalated into its surface was the round medallion carved of the form of lapis lazuli known as asmani.

The sky-blue stone marked with drifts of white.

"*Oneness,*" Arian said to herself.

With a twist, she broke the medallion free of the pitcher.

Breathing harshly, she inserted the medallion into its counterpart at the foot of the grave, pushing down hard.

Nothing happened.

And then she heard a click. It reminded her of the mechanisms of the puzzle box, with its grinding and whirring of gears.

The medallion rotated clockwise twice, lajward scraping against stone. Then back again twice. Then clockwise five turns. Then back again five times.

Two, two, five, five.

Its movement ceased just as the sounds of battle reached Arian.

Ahdath were in the antechamber. Six men, maybe eight.

One of the Basmachi scouts engaged with them, Elena at his side.

Larisa called to Arian. The Ahdath tried to break past her.

Arian pressed the medallion again, fear blocking the words in her throat.

With a groan, the medallion popped out of its groove. Behind it, a dark space had opened beneath the crosspiece.

With a hurried prayer, Arian reached inside.

Her fingers touched parchment.

She recognized the texture of deerskin.

The Bloodprint was said to be written on deerskin.

The noise from the antechamber faded, the strike of steel, Ruslan's grunt, Elena's cry.

All of it dwindled away. Arian read the scroll in her hands.

And read it again, shaken by her discovery.

She was holding a page of the Bloodprint in her hands.

She was reading a verse of the Claim.

A verse of dazzling symmetry.

Four lines above, four lines below its central axis, the verse arranged as a chiastic structure inked in green, a mirror of itself.

A green mirror.

The verse she had never believed she would find, its power and glory blazing through her mind, suffusing her body with light.

The unknown verse.

The Verse of the Throne.

She gaped at Larisa who stood panting at the threshold to the room.

"Hurry," Larisa gasped. "More are coming."

In the antechamber, Ruslan was slumped on the ground, Elena at his side, the bodies of Ahdath littered around them. Elena kissed the craggy scar on Ruslan's cheek. His tired eyes focused on Arian.

"Did you find it?" he asked. "Will it help?"

He was dying. She nodded quickly, kneeling at his side. Larisa's face was tight with the knowledge of loss to come.

"It means everything." Arian touched a hand to her tahweez. "It will change our fortunes in this war." She whispered into his ear. "It's the Verse of the Throne, Ruslan. You've led us to the Verse of the Throne."

For a moment, his eyes were touched by wonder.

Then he was gone.

"No—Ruslan, no!" Elena's wail was buried in Ruslan's chest.

Larisa nudged her sister with a gentle hand. "We have to go."

Elena clung to Ruslan's body.

"Please, Larisa," she begged. "Do something." And then, to Arian, "Bring him back." Ruslan's blood colored her face and chest. "Use the Claim. The Claim will work, it *has* to."

The agony of her desperation tore at Arian.

"Elena," she said, using the Claim as a balm. It had no effect. "You know what the Authoritan did to him. The Claim cannot recall him."

Elena's bloodstained face was acrid with recognition.

"Of course," she said. "When has the Claim ever been of use to us? It took our father's life, now it has taken Ruslan." She faced her sister, defiant. "I won't leave his body for the Blood Shed, help me move him." She pointed to the tomb of the king. "He deserves a king's grave, help me move him there."

Larisa stood firm, her face as pale as her sister's was bloody.

"We can't afford the time." And when Elena's face darkened

with rage, she added, "Forgive me, but you know it's true. The Ahdath will have signaled others."

Elena turned on Arian, fiercely. "You bring calamity with you, Companion. Was your prize worth it?" Her voice was filled with venom.

Justice is strength, Arian thought, a familiar weariness seeping into her bones.

She couldn't deny the truth of Elena's accusation. She had brought ruin to the man who had given his life for hers.

"Yes," Arian said.

"Then calamity will find you also." Elena turned to her sister. "She was meant to bring us hope, not death. Do what you want, Larisa. Just don't expect me to help you again." She found the gate to the garden, melting away into the shadows before Larisa could say another word.

"Forgive me," Arian said. She murmured a prayer over Ruslan's body. "I know he loved you."

Larisa nodded, her eyes bleak.

"I wish he'd loved Elena, it's what she always wanted." She caught Arian's hand again, seeking a nameless comfort. "They drugged me at Jaslyk, but they used their worst tortures on Elena. It was Ruslan who rescued her." She brushed a weary hand against her eyes. "He was the best of men. To die serving a cause he loved is more than most of us can hope for. Too many of our men have been murdered at the Blood Shed."

Fear struck at Arian. She had let herself forget Wafa and Turan.

"Please." She squeezed Larisa's hand. "Take me to the Blood Shed. I must do what I can for my friends."

"How can we fight a battalion of Ahdath? You overestimate my skills."

"Just take me there. I don't ask you to fight, but I won't be able to find the way alone."

Larisa hesitated. "Companion," she said. "If ever you loved your friends, you shouldn't witness what happens at the Blood Shed."

"I can't just leave them." Arian held out the scroll to Larisa. "I trust its power to aid me."

"It didn't serve my father."

"Your father was not a Companion of Hira." Arian tried a smile. Just as he'd withheld so much from Arian, there was something the Black Khan hadn't told Larisa. "My name is Arian, but perhaps you know me as First Oralist of the Claim."

47

THREE HUNDRED SOLDIERS OCCUPIED THE REGISTAN, THE SQUARE MADE bright by the glow of torches. Striding between their rows was a fair-haired man of unusual height with an eagle's profile and close-set eyes, his weathered face mottled with rage. He carried a whip in one hand, striking his men at random.

Silver bosses at his shoulders, a crimson cape down his back, this was the man who commanded the Wall, the Authoritan's right hand.

Araxcin of the Ahdath. Larisa whispered to Arian of his reputation for savagery. His actions in the square confirmed it.

As his lash fell, his men betrayed no sign of pain. They accepted the blows until the commander moved on.

Araxcin shouted at them in the language of the Transcasp, his words clipped with fury. Had she not known the language, Arian still would have understood.

"How did he escape?"

Semyon and Alik waited at the forefront of the battalion, their heads bowed for the whip. Illarion stood to Araxcin's side, his sword in hand, his eyes searching the square.

"I don't know what tricks aided the Silver Mage. Perhaps the Companion freed him."

It was the wrong thing for Semyon to say. Araxcin's whip struck him again.

"You let the Companion escape, as well! A woman alone bested all my men save Illarion, the only one who can think for himself."

Arian frowned from her vantage point behind the pylons of the Shir Dar. Illarion had discovered the ruse, but had clearly left Elena's role—and his own mistakes—out of his report to Araxcin. Arian could only speculate as to why.

"What will you do?" Larisa murmured. "What *can* you do?"

"How do I enter the Blood Shed?"

"You won't need to. Look."

The massive crimson door to the Blood Shed gave way.

The whip was stayed in Araxcin's hand.

"Ahdath," he shouted.

The two halves of the battalion stationed between the Blood Shed and the Shir Dar snapped to attention.

"You will search this city. You will find the Silver Mage. You will kill him where he stands. The Companion you will bring to me. Is that understood?"

With one voice, the men thundered, "As the one commands."

Arian bit back a gasp. It was a terrible distortion of the Claim.

"But first a punishment. It has been weeks since the last execution, but tonight we are gifted with fresh blood."

The Ahdath battalion thumped their fists against their chests. A lurid chant filled the air.

"Blood will be shed. Blood will be shed."

Araxcin responded by rote.

"Lawful for you are carrion and blood."

"That's a lie," Larisa whispered. "My father taught the opposite. *Un*lawful are carrion and blood."

Arian signaled her recognition of the verse.

The crimson door of the Blood Shed gaped wide. An enormous wooden structure was propelled through the door on crimson wheels.

A bloodred gallows for a public execution.

Wafa and Turan were hanging from the gallows by their ankles, their bodies stripped to the waist, their torsos a welter of bloodmarks.

Arian choked back a scream.

"*Lawful is blood*," the Ahdath chanted. "*Lawful is blood.*"

"Bring them," Araxcin said, the bloodlust in his voice.

What could she do? How could she stop them all?

The gallows were wheeled to the center of the square. Araxcin prodded Semyon and Alik with his whip. They stepped forward to take two curved metal basins from the men who wheeled out the gallows. The basins were placed beneath the bodies of Wafa and Turan, their bound hands dangling above their heads.

Wafa and Turan were unconscious.

Arian stared at Larisa in horror.

"First they will drain the bodies of blood. Then the bones will be crushed and deposited in the crypt." A gesture of Larisa's hand indicated the Shadow Mausoleum.

Araxcin's whip whistled through the air, rousing Turan to consciousness. His quiet groan tore at Arian's heart. The lash fell again, propelling her into action.

She grabbed Larisa's hand.

"Whatever you do, stay hidden."

The chant echoed again.

"*Lawful is blood, lawful is blood.*"

Araxcin signaled to Semyon. The Ahdath soldier vaulted onto the platform, a silver dagger in his hands. Methodically, he slashed at Turan's ankles, before severing the rope that bound Turan's wrists together. Blood began to drip into the basin.

"Lawful is blood, lawful is blood."

Arian sprinted through the square.

"Stop!" she called out. Soldiers began to turn. "It's me you want, let them go!"

She threw off her cloak as she ran, dark hair tumbling free, her circlets shining in the torchlight.

No one moved except Arian. She held the attention of every man in the square.

Turan's hand snaked up to remove the knife he had hidden in his breeches. With a final determined effort, he swung his battered torso up and across. His sudden, swift lunge slashed the rope that bound Wafa at the heels. The boy crashed to the platform, unmoving.

"Run!" Turan roared, the last breath of a lion.

Wafa lay still.

"Run, Wafa!"

The sound of Arian's voice broke the spell over the square.

A venomous smile on his face, Araxcin strode to the platform. Before Arian could reach him, he slashed his knife across Turan's throat.

"No!" Arian screamed. Her agonized cry rent the night.

Turan's blood spurted across the platform, draining the last bit of color from his face.

His gray eyes found Arian. With his hand, he motioned at Wafa.

"I promised you," he managed, his mouth filled with blood. "And I am glad to give my life in your service."

"No!" she cried. "Turan, no! I haven't released you, *please. Don't leave me, please—*"

"Sayah," he whispered. "I come to you, at last."

The grave, gray eyes went dark.

Araxcin moved to Wafa.

The anguish of a decade surged up through Arian's skin, a volcanic rage swelling through her veins, commanding her very lifeblood, until it erupted through her voice like the cleaving of an enormous, mercurial sword.

Turan was dead. He would never ride at her side again.

Her protector, her guide, her friend—the one who'd loved her all her life, for her mother's sake, for her own, holding her in his hands, urging her to keep faith—with the past, with the future, giving her reason to believe—making her feel less alone only to leave her again, another piece of her heart claimed by the Talisman's war, by a cycle of endless darkness.

Taking everything.

It was still taking everything.

T he captain's whisper echoed through her grief.

I am glad to give my life in your service.

No, no, no, no, no!

A n incandescent violence exploded from her throat.

"There is no one but the One, the Living, the Everlasting. Neither slumber overtakes the One, nor sleep. To the One belongs all that is in the heavens and the earth. Who is there that can intercede with the One, except as the One allows? The One knows what lies before you, what lies after you. You comprehend nothing of the One's knowledge, except as the One wills. The throne of the One comprises the heavens and the earth. The upholding of them does not weary the All-High, All-Glorious One."

The words scalded her larynx, seared her tongue, overpowered her thoughts with their majesty and might, until all that was left was the dagger of light raging against her skull from inside, and the worn and ravaged cry on her lips.

"*A throne to comprise the heavens and the earth.*"

An encompassing silence fell on the square.

Wafa raised his head.

Arian's hand faltered toward his.

"Lady Arian," he said, as he'd heard Turan address her so many times. It was the first time Wafa had spoken her name. "Look."

She turned around.

The Blood Shed was crushed into dust, its crimson door dismantled. The Shir Dar had crumbled to ash, alongside its massive pylons. The Tilla Kari's mirrored door was shattered into glass fragments.

And every man in the square lay dead, blood leaking from his ears and eyes.

Larisa limped across the square, slinging her arm around Arian's shoulders.

Arian shook her head hopelessly.

"I killed them with the Verse of the Throne."

"It wasn't the Verse," Larisa said. "It was something inside you."

"My friend," Arian croaked. "I have to cut him down."

The ugliness of Turan's wound brought her to despair. She had thought him dead once before, but she hadn't loved him then.

She captured his head in her hands, mingling her tears with his blood, kissing his forehead, his cheeks.

She wanted to hold him, keep him close, keep him part of her forever.

It didn't matter that her arms were slippery with his blood. She couldn't bring herself to let go.

I let go.

Why did I let go?

How could I make such a choice?

What have I gained?

How do I count what I've lost?

"Turan, please," she whimpered. She thought now of Elena's plea that she use the Claim to bring back the dead.

She could kill, but she couldn't give life.

How damning her legacy as Companion of Hira.

"Turan."

She fastened her arms around his neck, tasting the copper tang of his blood.

"Let me help you."

A man stumbled his way across the square, his crimson uniform shredded, traces of blood trailing from his ears to his jaw. It was Illarion, sole survivor among the Ahdath. And even in the depths of her grief, Arian guessed at the truth. Illarion must be an adherent of the Claim, for only the Claim could have spared him.

Still, she pushed him away. "No! This task is for me. He was mine, mine alone."

"Would you keep him like this, as the sport of carrion birds?" he asked gently. "Will you not bury him with honor? Let me cut him down."

"No," Arian said again, this time with less conviction. "This task is for me."

"You hold him," Illarion said. "So he doesn't fall from the gallows. It will take a strong arm to release him."

He held up his hands in a gesture of peace as Larisa drew her short, sharp sword.

Illarion's gaze flitted between the women.

"Where's the other one?" he asked Larisa. "Did Anya survive this?"

"I wouldn't seek her out, if I were you. Tonight the Ahdath killed the man she loved. I can't begin to know why you are still alive."

He stared at Larisa, abashed. Then he turned to the gallows, where Turan's body swung in the wind, his blood draining into the basin. When they had cut him down, Arian sank to her knees, burying her face in his chest.

Wafa clung to her side, listening to her cry, his face worked in lines of distress.

He didn't know how to comfort her.

He only knew that the Shin War captain had shielded him in the Blood Shed, just as he'd freed Wafa from the gallows.

Wafa had never known kindness from the Talisman.

What could he make of Turan?

A friend, a guardian, a man of moral purpose such as Wafa had never known.

And then a hopeful flicker picked at the corner of his mouth as another man strode forth from the dust of the Shir Dar. A man whose face was bruised and bloodied but unbroken and very much alive.

Daniyar, the Silver Mage.

He took Arian into his arms without a word.

"Where were you?" she murmured brokenly. "How could you have left me? They killed my captain. They killed him before my eyes."

She clung to him with a fierceness that surprised him, her face marred by tears and blood. A wave of tenderness broke over his heart.

"Forgive me, my love. My use of the Claim is not as yours. I couldn't breach the Blood Shed. I knew Sinnia to be your heart, so I went after her."

Arian stirred in his arms.

Apart from their company, the square was deserted.

"Where is she?" And at his grim expression, "Please tell me."

"I found a man who was willing to tell me," he said. He said nothing of how he'd obtained his knowledge. "I don't know why and you won't have heard of it. They've taken Sinnia to a place called Jaslyk."

Arian gasped. Elena's malediction floated through her thoughts.

You bring calamity with you, Companion.

At this moment, she was saturated with Elena's pain.

She was the bringer of prophecy.

To Khorasan and all those she loved.

Turan dead and Sinnia taken.

One missing and one to fall.

They buried Turan in the garden behind the conservatory of sciences, a solemn garden of moon and stars, an invocation of grace for the man who had cherished the Claim.

Illarion took the measure of the Silver Mage in the silence that fell in the aftermath.

"What do you need?" he asked, not bothering with preliminaries.

Daniyar answered in kind.

"We need passage through Black Aura Gate."

48

LONG-LEGGED STORKS NESTLED IN WHITE-FEATHERED MUSTERS HAD taken up occupancy in the minarets of Black Aura Scaresafe. The Wall lay to the south. A second rampart of clay ruins circled the Authoritan's capital.

The river that gave Zerafshan his name—the gold-strewer—faltered alongside their path. Closer to the city, it extinguished itself with a final, parched gasp. Unlike the soil of Marakand, no golden loess from the mountains dusted the streets of Black Aura. The soil was an alkaline gray made arid by accretions of salt. A stunted forest formed the other side of their path.

Behind the broken ramparts, the old city descended, a convolution of windowless, fortified tenements whose wooden beams projected from rooftops. The labyrinth of turtle-domes that marked the city's bazaar shrunk under the weight of a disturbing soundlessness. No customers or shopkeepers beetled between its alleys.

Where Marakand was a city of turquoise and gold, Black Aura was a battlement of unrelenting dullness, mud-brick and clay.

A tenuous light heralded the dawn in the eastern sky, a stark tower jutting against the horizon like a solitary finger.

The tower was known as the Clay Minar. A testament to the skill of brickwork masons, its dun-colored monotony was lit only by a band of turquoise, its gallery of fenestrated arches topped by cornices that served as pigeon roosts.

The rest of the city had sunk under the heavy hand of time, the tower alone soaring against a sky of Black Aura blue. Its conical design was proof against the shifting of the earth and the frequent shocks that tumbled ill-supported domes and improvised dwellings.

A legend held that coins were buried inside each of the tower's bricks. After the bricks were sun-baked, they were laid end to end to be trampled by a horse. If the bricks cracked, the entire lot was recast and pounded again. Earthquakes had shaken the city over the centuries, but the Clay Minar stood firm.

They were only three now: herself, Daniyar, and Wafa.

Arian had begged Daniyar to take her to Jaslyk. Sinnia *was* her heart. If Sinnia were to suffer the damage that marked Larisa and Elena, nothing Arian had ever done would matter. Even Lania's fate was something she could set aside.

"I can fight them now," she promised Daniyar. "I can use the Verse of the Throne as a shield." But her voice faltered a little, and she wasn't entirely sure that she could.

He marveled over the parchment she had shown him, memorized it quickly, then asked her to hide it away. She pressed it between the pages of the Candour.

"We can bring war to the Wall," he agreed. "Beginning with Jaslyk. Or we can find the Bloodprint. As you decide."

The last choice Arian had made had cost Turan his life, a parallel that made her think of the significance of the green mirror.

She shivered at the thought of it.

The Dome, the tomb, the Verse.

She had won the Verse and lost Turan.

This time, the choice was simple. She chose Sinnia and the route to Jaslyk.

It was Larisa who persuaded her otherwise.

"I know Jaslyk as you do not. Elena and I will find your friend before further harm can come to her. We'll have Basmachi to aid us—Avazov and Alimov, two of our best." She scanned the battalion of Ahdath dead with something like bitterness. "They won't be so quick now I think, to hunt us in the calligrapher's market, or throughout the Hazing." She scowled at Illarion. "You'll need time to count your dead."

"I'll go with you," he offered. "My presence will distract them."

Larisa rejected his offer out of hand. "Why would I trust you? You're one of the Ahdath."

Daniyar studied the other man, using his gifts as Authenticate.

"No," he said. "I don't know who he is, but he isn't just Ahdath."

"It doesn't matter," Larisa said. "Elena would kill you the moment she laid eyes on you."

Illarion canvassed the fallen bodies of his comrades in the square.

"I think you'll find I'm not so easy to kill."

The Silver Mage decided the matter, his articulacy so compelling that only Arian realized he was using the Claim. Both she and Illarion could feel its effects. Larisa and Illarion were commissioned to set about the rescue of Sinnia, after Illarion secured them safe passage, serving as their escort to Black Aura Gate.

He'd taken a moment to warn Arian in farewell.

"Black Aura is the city of death. As much as you've learned to be wary of the Authoritan, you must guard against his consort."

He hesitated. "No matter what you've heard, the Khanum is twice as dangerous."

Arian learned nothing further of Illarion, nothing of his motives in not giving away Elena, nothing of the reasons Illarion had survived the havoc she had wreaked in the Registan. And nothing of why he now wished to come to Sinnia's aid. But the Claim was an arbiter she could not doubt, and Daniyar had confirmed its judgment on Illarion. Beyond that, her mind was too crowded with thoughts of the danger ahead to wonder at his motives, the loss of Turan a black stone pressing against her heart.

And now, all she felt was the menace of the Clay Minar.

As they approached the old city by stealth, she heard a frightful cry. A body fell from the heights of the tower, followed by another. She heard the bones shatter in the courtyard.

A third man screamed as he waited his turn to die. His cries for mercy went unheeded, his body crashing to the ground. Others followed, thrown from the tower by members of the Ahdath.

She was close enough to stand as witness, close enough to make use of the Claim.

But something disturbed her. Something about the way her throat and tongue and mind had felt after she had used the Verse of the Throne. Something she had shared with no one.

She hadn't meant to use the Verse of the Throne to kill.

Men had died in the past when she had used the Claim, but only as she had defended herself or others from their violence, and not because she'd used the Claim as an instrument of destruction.

Nor had she tried to do so in the square, when her voice had brought down the Registan.

Then, the Verse of the Throne had spilled from her throat as the purest expression of grief.

At what point the grief had melded with her loneliness and

rage to express the losses of a decade, her futile counterpoint to the Talisman ascent, she didn't know.

She had grieved the death of a good and just man, who'd been her friend unknown through so much darkness. And now he was gone, and she was different.

The Claim *felt* different in her mind.

She wasn't certain she could trust it.

Daniyar was waiting for her to act. She shook her head, a hand to her throat.

"The Verse of the Throne did something to my voice."

His glance at her was sharp. For the briefest instant, she'd forgotten he was the Authenticate. There was nothing she could hide from him.

"I'm sorry," she said at once. "I don't want to kill, not like this."

He didn't argue with Arian about shadings of morality. His beautiful face showed only concern.

"I would not urge you against your judgment, but did you not intend to rescue Sinnia by making use of the Verse?"

Arian hesitated. "I'd hoped the Verse would aid us in subterfuge. You must know I didn't intend what happened at the Registan."

This wasn't a lie. It was as much of the truth as Arian knew herself.

"It's changing me," she whispered. "And I don't know how."

If there was more to be said, she didn't know how to say it.

Daniyar took her hand and squeezed it. They would have need of the Claim again, and soon, but his thought was always for Arian. He would use his own skills in lieu of hers, even if they were lesser in scope.

"Leave combat to me, then. Use the Claim only as far as you are able." His eyes scanned the tower again. "We'll be visible to the Ahdath soon. Where do we go from here? Did the king's grave yield anything other than the parchment?"

Besides the parchment, Arian had found nothing at the tomb of the king. The hiding place of the Bloodprint was still a mystery.

"I don't know," she admitted. "I can't think of anything I overlooked."

Daniyar considered this for long moments.

"There must be something more to the parchment. Something we haven't understood."

Wafa asked for water. He was weak from his session in the Blood Shed.

As Arian passed him the ewer from Daniyar's pack, her thoughts dwelt on the notion of Oneness. She had fitted the medallion back into its groove on the side of the ewer. And she wondered for the first time why the second clue to the Bloodprint hadn't been the medallion itself. A pitcher was a cumbersome thing to carry around.

Wafa drank from the pitcher.

He'd learned manners from Sinnia, using a cloth to wipe his mouth. The cloth came away discolored.

Arian dismounted.

Of all the attributes described in the Verse of the Throne, Oneness was the most significant.

She dampened the cloth in the river. It came back wet, its color intact. She reached for the ewer and poured water over the cloth. It discolored the cloth again. She sniffed the ewer. The faintest trace of apple wafted from it.

"What is it?" Daniyar asked, joining her.

The guardians of the Bloodprint would not have poured water over the Verse of the Throne. The parchment was too fragile to risk. But the scent of apple that rose from the pitcher was noteworthy.

"I think there's something more written on the parchment, invisible to our eyes."

She removed the parchment from the Candour. She sniffed it, then passed it to Daniyar.

"Apple," he said. He took the parchment from her fingers, holding it up to the sun. At first, nothing happened. Then, warmed by the sunlight, a word appeared in the right-hand corner.

Written in the High Tongue, the word was *Call*.

Amazed, Arian and Daniyar stared at each other.

Call.

It had no meaning that Arian could think of, no connection to the Verse of the Throne. Perhaps it had been rendered invisible to protect the sanctity of the Bloodprint. She was at a loss.

"What does it say?" Wafa asked, hopping from one foot to the other, his thirst forgotten.

"Call."

"Call what? Call who?"

And just like that, Daniyar knew. She could see the realization in his face. He urged them away from the river into the shelter of the forest. He pointed to the looming tower, to the gallery of arches at its peak.

"It means the Call to the people of the Claim. A call given to summon the faithful."

Arian was doubtful. "But why this tower out of so many others? The Bloodless wouldn't choose such a place as the safehold of the Bloodprint. It's an execution site."

Silver eyes settled on Arian's face.

"This was the tower."

"The city is crowded with minarets. How can you be certain this is the one?"

"The Clay Minar." He ran the words together. "The Claim Minar. The Tower of the Claim."

49

THERE WAS A MOMENT WHEN THE SILVER MAGE CONSIDERED NOT breaching the ramparts of Black Aura to skirt the defences of the Clay Minar, where soldiers patrolled the perimeter, their movements brisk with purpose.

The city that should have been soft with apricot and fig trees stank of nothing but death, the scent of blood intermingled with the wretchedness of decay. Shards of smashed jade were scattered through the courtyard. If Black Aura was home to a populace other than those who'd been thrown from the tower, Daniyar saw no sign of it.

He could take Arian and Wafa and insist they flee to the Damson Vale, setting aside the quest for the Bloodprint. And ask that Sinnia join them.

He knew that death was waiting in the tower, calling to him, stretching out its fingers.

He was the Authenticate, not an Augur, yet he felt the pull of fate, the brittle conclusion of destiny. One step in the wrong direction . . .

One missing, one to fall.

He knew he should not take Arian to the tower.

She'd risked outcomes so abhorrent it terrified him to contemplate them. How often could the Claim protect them? The fetid air, rank with an inhuman odor, the blood-baked brick, the sun casting its baleful eye upon them—these were portents of the doom that awaited them.

Arian was stunning in her resolution, priceless to him beyond anything the Bloodprint could offer. He wished he could think in those terms—the salvation of Khorasan—but all he could see was the woman before him, the woman he'd always loved.

"Arian," he said. He wondered if there was any way to persuade her against her Audacy. If he spoke plainly to her now, would it change anything?

Her use of the Claim was more muted now, small sounds, a low hum casting a pall upon the courtyard, a stifling of sight and hearing. It gave them the cover they needed to creep across the courtyard.

Relief gladdened Arian's face as they escaped detection, sheltering behind the shell of a storehouse.

It pained him to see it.

She was hastening them to ruin.

"Don't worry," she assured them. "If this is the Tower of the Claim, we will find a way."

Daniyar touched her hair. He made up his mind to try.

"Arian," he said again. "I would ask you to relinquish this quest. We have the Verse of the Throne, let us take it and be free of this. There's a place I would take you, a valley of peace."

Her pale eyes widened, the same shade of green as the leaves of persimmon trees. She fought back a surge of joy.

"You would take me to the Damson Vale." Daniyar had described it as a paradise on earth. "And I would love you there." He caught his breath at the words, words she hadn't offered him before. "For a time, there would be peace. But what of Candour? And Hira? War comes to Khorasan, what would you have me do?"

He took her in his arms.

"I would have you love me," he said, his voice rough. "As you wouldn't before."

The words struck her, caught her, made her weak.

"I have my Audacy," she whispered. But she knew it was no longer enough, just as she knew she couldn't confess as much to Daniyar.

Not now, not yet.

Disheartened, he let her go, silver eyes scanning the door that led to the top of the tower.

"Ready yourself, then. There will be guards."

I choose you, she should have said. *I will take the Bloodprint to Hira, then I will come to you in the Damson Vale, or anywhere else you ask of me.*

She kept the Claim muffled in her throat, as low and raw as the pain of denying him.

When she had left him in Candour, stealing away in the night, she couldn't have guessed she'd be given another chance at his love. Their paths should have crossed many times, but he'd never come to Hira, the betrayal too bitter, coloring his memories of her love for him.

She wasn't to be trusted. A Companion of Hira would always choose Hira.

Except that she hadn't.

In the valley of the Cloud Door, she had forgotten Hira, forgotten Lania, forgotten the Audacy. Her heart had cracked open, scorched by an urgent, immaculate heat. The white fire of Daniyar's love, the indivisible peace of giving herself over.

She should have fled with him through the Cloud Door, her

heart locked in his, the world of the Talisman abandoned, to the Damson Vale, the last green harbor of her hopes.

In the Damson Vale, the night would be covered with stars. She would know joy and a love out of time.

There will be a time, she promised herself.

Won't there?

She couldn't look at Daniyar. To look at the beautiful face or the passion that blazed from his eyes was to see everything she most wanted turned against herself in wretched disavowal. She knew what it was to be hungry and in pain.

She couldn't hurt Daniyar without suffering the damage herself.

"Wait," he said. "There's a new patrol coming in."

A troop of Ahdath swept the square around the tower, the bones in the courtyard snapping beneath their boots.

Twenty men, strong, disciplined, focused, their crimson armor flashing against the tower, a harbinger of blood to be spilled.

They waited for the patrol to sweep by.

Half the Ahdath took up the collection of bodies in the courtyard.

Six more took over from the guards at the perimeter.

Straggling at the back, four men guarded a young man in chains, his face wearied by pain, his body desperately thin. Tracks of tears marked a path through the bruises on his face. He shook with fear as the door to the tower was wrenched open.

"Take him up," the commander told the others, holding the door.

"Please," the young man begged. "Please, not this. Send me to Jaslyk instead."

An Ahdath soldier spat in his face.

"Basmachi scum. You'll die where you're meant to."

The commander was kinder, if kindness could be found here.

He touched the prisoner's shoulder with a hand, their eyes meeting briefly.

"You won't believe it now, but this is better than Jaslyk."

The door shut behind them, the young man's sobs echoing through the tower.

Daniyar motioned to Arian.

"Will you risk the Claim to gain the tower? You could save him."

"What about you?" she whispered. "I can't leave you to fight a patrol on your own. There are too many men."

"Use the Claim to shield me, allow me to draw close. Then head for the door."

She tried to stop him, her hand grasping his arm, her fingers flexing against its strength.

He shook it off, reaching for the knives he carried on his back.

"Daniyar—" She wanted to plead with him, make him believe in her. He jerked away.

"Don't," he said. "We came for the Bloodprint. Nothing else matters."

Arian couldn't bear it. She had suffered this torment too long.

"You'd be a fool to think you don't matter more than anyone." Her pale eyes blazed with the truth. "And I believe you told Zerafshan you are not a fool."

And when he still didn't speak, she said the words unreservedly at last.

"I love you, Daniyar. I can't remember a time when I didn't."

He stared at her, stunned.

All noise ceased in the courtyard.

Then he seized her in unyielding arms, while his mouth sought hers with the fervor of a man rekindled to life. His lips burned her skin everywhere they touched. Possessive, hungry, unrelenting, the kiss was everything she wanted. A thousand pricks of light flaring under her skin, she kissed him the same way.

They stood locked together as if there was only this, the desire for a long-withheld consummation, the world falling away at their feet.

He kissed her until she could no longer stand, and when he drew away, her mouth followed his, blindly seeking his lips.

"My love," he murmured, his breathing ragged in his chest. "Would you still pursue the Bloodprint?"

The sounds of the Ahdath patrol returned. They broke apart, suddenly conscious of Wafa, who had bashfully retreated to the shadows.

Arian pressed her hand to her swollen lips.

My love, he had called her.

The sweetest words of any language.

Her eyes searched his.

"Only if you are with me."

"Then use the Claim."

He kissed her once more, then with a last look, he broke cover.

50

THE CLAIM WAS CLUMSY IN HER THROAT, COATING HER VOCAL CHORDS with misery. Wafa covered his ears, thinking of Turan, of the men lying dead in the Registan.

It didn't happen.

Instead, a ribbon of mist welled up from the ground, snaking around the ankles of the men collecting the bodies in the court-yard. Then it faltered, vanishing as swiftly as it had come.

There is no one but the One. And so the One commands.

Arian took a deep breath, invoking the calm the Claim had always brought her, seeking to cleanse the words of the Ahdath's corruption. Looking across to the tower, she murmured the words again, this time with more force.

Mist descended on the courtyard. Daniyar raced across it.

She couldn't see but she could hear the sound of Daniyar's knives. She grabbed Wafa's hand and followed, staying low to the ground, inching closer to the tower.

The calm she had found wavered and the Claim wedged in her throat. She was murmuring intonations from feel as much as sound, trying to push past the barrier.

Cries of surprise rang through the courtyard just as the mist turned blue, thinning out in patches.

The Ahdath had recognized an enemy in their midst.

A knife sprang toward Daniyar's back, propelled by a crimson arm. He sensed the danger in time, whirling about to confront his attacker. The silver knives flashed, the guard sagged to the ground.

The mist blanketed the courtyard again.

Arian was at the door, her throat working furiously.

How many generations were brought to ruin . . .

How many . . .

It wasn't working.

A knot of Ahdath surrounded Daniyar. They called to the men on the perimeter.

Arian watched helplessly as the crimson band tightened around Daniyar.

Wafa escaped her grasp, darting to the aid of the Silver Mage, a small, sharp dagger in his hand.

She had to think of something.

She had to act now.

There is no one but the One. And so the One commands.

Please.

The grip on her throat eased. Knives flashed at Daniyar, at Wafa. The boy fell back, his arm bloodied. Slashes penetrated the cloak of the Silver Mage. A line of blood ran from his jaw to his collarbone.

He put up an arm to block the onslaught.

A knife slashed across it, blood spraying across the courtyard.

I seek refuge in the One! I seek refuge in the Claim!

She could not allow Daniyar to fall.

She reached the group of soldiers, the mist tumbling from her shoulders like the robes of a wraithlike empress.

"Arian!" Daniyar shouted.

His voice was muffled by the mist.

She drew no weapons, her eyes marking the face of each soldier.

She chanted the words at a measured pace, at odds with the urgency of their position.

"Consider the night as it veils the earth in darkness, and the day as it rises bright."

The knot of soldiers fell back a pace.

Daniyar gathered Arian under his wounded arm, his face aghast.

"You should have headed for the tower."

She kissed his cheek, then turned to face the Ahdath again.

"Consider the creation of male and female. Verily, you aim at most divergent ends."

The Claim had never sounded quite like this in her mouth. She felt a thrill of power at the fear reflected in the Ahdath's faces. No man lunged at her with his sword.

"Thus, as for him who gives to others and is conscious of the One and believes in the truth of the ultimate good—for him, the One shall make easy the path toward ultimate ease."

The men's arms began to move, bringing up their swords.

Daniyar brandished his knife, pushing Arian and Wafa behind him.

But the swords were moving away from him, pushing up to the crimson breastplates.

Arian's voice hardened.

"But as for he who is miserly and thinks he is self-sufficient, and calls the ultimate good a lie, for him shall the One make easy

the path to hardship. What will his wealth avail him when he goes down to his grave?"

The swords of the Ahdath plunged through their own armor. The men fell to their knees in ranks, the mist swirling up around them.

Daniyar wrenched Arian around.

"What are you doing? What are you doing with the Claim? Answer me, Arian!"

"I warn you of the raging fire," she whispered. *"The fire which none shall have to endure but the most wretched who gives the lie to the truth and turns away from it."*

The men fell dead.

Arian's voice seized up.

She shook her head blindly.

Daniyar pulled her close, wrapping her in his arms.

"Wafa, my knives."

The boy took them, urging them away from the square to the tower. Footsteps sounded behind them.

Arian stared at the dead in horror.

"It wasn't me," she gasped. "The Claim is overtaking me."

She saw the same distress in Daniyar's eyes.

The Claim was a force for good.

Wasn't it?

"We have to talk of this but this isn't the time."

Do you believe in the truth of an ultimate good?

She was no longer certain.

There was no time to contemplate the question. They scrambled for the tower door, chased by Ahdath arrows.

Wafa sealed them inside, sliding the crossbeam home.

There were shouts of alarm in the courtyard.

The Ahdath had found their comrades in the square, each with a sword buried in his breast. The mist had dissipated when Arian had ceased her use of the Claim. Soldiers called to the guards inside the tower. Others battered the door.

"Climb," Daniyar said. "Hurry."

They sprinted up the steps, no longer hearing the sobs of the young man who'd been taken to the top of the tower. The Ahdath guards were quiet, waiting for them at the top.

Daniyar went first.

"Don't use the Claim unless you have to," he told her. "Give it time."

There was a recognition in his face that she had used it at his urging, after sharing with him her fears.

He was angry at what the quest for the Bloodprint had cost them. The Silver Mage, the Keeper of the Candour, the Authenticate who read the truth—he'd never once doubted the rightness of the Claim. To doubt now, when they drew ever closer to it, was a dagger that sliced at his heart. Had he risked Arian for this, renouncing the Damson Vale?

If the Claim could compel men to take their own lives, what would it be in the hands of the One-Eyed Preacher? What destruction would it wreak on Khorasan? What use would be made of the Verse of the Throne?

Daniyar didn't recognize the verses Arian had used to slay the Ahdath.

He knew he'd never heard them.

And he realized with a shiver that he didn't want to know where Arian had learned them.

51

DANIYAR VAULTED ONTO THE PLATFORM, A KNIFE IN EACH HAND.

Two of the Ahdath met him at the head of the stairs.

"Take cover!" he shouted to Arian, his silver knives slicing quick and deep into unprotected flesh. His arm was stinging from the earlier blow; his reflexes were slower.

"Watch out!"

The cry came from the Ahdaths' captive. Daniyar ducked low just in time, dodging the blow aimed at his back. The third Ahdath blundered into Daniyar's path, carried forward by his own momentum.

Daniyar's knives slashed at the guard's heels, bringing him down. He took a blow to the chest from a heavy fist, another to his right shoulder. Daniyar shifted, dropping to one knee, bringing his blade up with his left hand, driving it into his assailant's ribs. It caught in the man's armor as he reeled away.

One man was left. He faced Daniyar, sword in hand.

Wafa tried to climb up to help, but throughout the attack Daniyar had shielded the stairs from the Ahdath. It left his back unprotected and his footing unsteady, but the tactic had kept Arian and

Wafa safe. Now he challenged the last guard with a solitary blade in his hand.

The Ahdath didn't speak, waiting for his chance.

He circled Daniyar, probing for a weakness. And then he caught sight of Arian.

He lunged forward, knocking Daniyar back.

The Silver Mage fell hard, his head striking stone. The Ahdath leapt at him, his sword raised in a killing stroke.

Arian's dagger caught him in the throat. He gurgled once, then collapsed.

Daniyar kicked at the Ahdath's body with his boot, dislodging it from the tower.

He blinked. A shadow moved in the corner of his vision.

The commander of the Ahdath stood poised beneath one of the arches, the prisoner's chains gripped tight in his hands.

"You're too late to save him," the commander said. "You're too late to save yourselves."

Below them, bodies threw themselves against the door.

"Watch them," Arian said to Wafa. The boy shadowed her, his eyes on the commander. She knelt at Daniyar's side, taking him into her arms.

"You're hurt," she said, ignoring the commander.

"It's nothing. My head will clear in a moment. Do what you can for the captive."

She traded places with Wafa, summoning him to Daniyar.

"Who is he?" she asked the Ahdath.

The commander held the young man at the brink. If he released his grip on the chains, the prisoner would plummet over the edge.

"When you've come to rescue him, why dissemble? You know who he is as well as I do. You know why he's here."

She had a moment of quiet discovery.

The Ahdath didn't know who she was. The news hadn't reached him from Marakand.

"Please," the young man whimpered, his gaze fixed on Arian. "Help me."

He was a few years older than Wafa.

Something had changed inside Arian, grown hard with the death of Turan. Too many innocents had pleaded for their lives, their lives discounted by Talisman and Ahdath.

She waved a hand at the Ahdath, a rumble in her chest, its power surging forth before she could recite. This was new. And it felt glorious.

The chains fell from his hand. She caught them in her own, yanking the prisoner to safety. The Ahdath commander froze in place, his eyes squinting in the glare of the sun.

She pulled the boy to her, dismantled the chains, rubbed his wrists.

"Who are you?"

"Alisher," he said. "Who are you?"

She whisked aside her cloak, her golden circlets catching at the light.

His mouth hung open. He sank to his knees.

"Sahabiya," he gasped.

The Ahdath commander tried to move.

Arian held him with a growl, her hand raised again.

"Why do you murder children?" she demanded. "This one is but a boy, what threat could he pose to you?"

The commander's hands grappled at his throat.

"Mistress," he muttered, catching sight of Arian's face in the light. "I cannot breathe."

"Answer me."

The Claim was tight and urgent in her chest.

"He's a scribe," the man panted. "A scribe and a poet. Both have been outlawed."

The Ahdath's eyes began to leak blood.

Horrified, Arian dropped her hand. What was she doing? What was happening to her?

She hadn't spoken a word of the Claim.

The Ahdath commander stumbled back, falling to his knees.

"There's no other way out of this tower. My men are coming."

Daniyar lurched to his feet, his face leached of color. Had he seen what she'd done to the commander? If so, he said nothing other than, "He's right, we must hurry."

Freed from restraint, the Ahdath launched himself at Arian, a short sword in his hand. He was tripped by the prisoner, who flung himself at his captor's knees. They grappled for a moment, then it was over.

The Ahdath went sailing from the heights of the tower.

Arian closed her eyes.

Death. Everywhere death, and she the cause of it.

Daniyar's soft voice called to her.

"Arian, hurry."

He pointed her to the center of the rotunda. An enormous marble stand was positioned at the hub, equidistant from the arches. Its giant marble halves rested on a base supported by stone columns, weighty and immovable.

Why had the Ahdath brought this stand to the top of the Clay Minar?

It had to mean something. It had to bring them closer to the Bloodprint.

She brushed the sun-warmed stone with her hand, looking up.

Light splashed across Wafa's anxious face. Dapples of light, patterns of light. She looked at the stand again, at the smooth, wide space between its wedge-shaped halves. It was a space large enough to accommodate a manuscript.

And its Cast Iron case.

This had to be the repository of the Bloodprint, brought to Black Aura from Task End—hallowed, revered, and utterly precious.

She thought of the objects they had carried on their journey from the Sorrowsong.

Instead of the stone key, she took the single page of parchment from Daniyar's pack. She placed it on the stand.

"Come see," she said to the others. They came to stand at her side in the shade.

From half the arches, the rising light that splashed Wafa's face fell upon the stand, warming the Verse of the Throne.

There were sounds from the base of the tower, an angry ramming against the door bolted from the inside, the striking of swords from their scabbards. Their time for discovery was short. Yet Arian counted the danger as nothing.

The scent of apples was the first hint of sweetness to penetrate the pungence of the room.

At the top of the parchment, the ink that had formed the word *call* darkened to brown. Beneath it, a pale notation blushed against the page. Two numbers and a word.

4:40. Hazarbaf.

Daniyar frowned at the words. They stirred something in his memory of the Candour, something that made him better appreciate Arian's growing sense of uneasiness with the Claim.

He thought of what they had seen and done in the courtyard, and of the actions of the woman he loved, the woman for whom the Claim was a calling. It gave her a power that transformed her into something other than herself.

Something other than the woman who had met him like a flame.

And he understood that neither he as Silver Mage, nor Arian as First Oralist, had begun to plumb the depths of that power.

The Ahdath's prisoner tugged at his elbow.

"We must defend ourselves. The door won't hold them for long."

Wafa rebuked the young man.

"The Silver Mage is the Keeper of the Candour. He knows how best to save us."

Arian smiled at Daniyar, her smile a brief and beautiful thing.

He was shaken to his soul by its tenderness.

He needed time, but there was no time.

He was Keeper of the Candour, and it was the Candour he needed now.

"Arian, pass me the pack."

When he had it in his hands, he withdrew the Candour as the others watched. He lifted it to his lips and kissed the interwoven letters on its cover.

He signaled to Arian to remove the Verse of the Throne, setting the Candour in its place. He leafed through its pages, passing over passages that listed the duties of the Keeper of the Candour, cartographs that depicted a world before the wars of the Far Range, the script of ancient tongues that had blended together with time, the incantations of the Silver Mage—these were the treasures of the Candour. As he turned the pages, Arian's head rested against his shoulder. He inhaled the scent of jasmine in her hair. And tried to focus on the task at hand.

He came to the last page, to the verse inscribed beneath an enigmatic coda.

4:40.

The verse had no name.

There was only the inscription. *Verily, the One does not wrong anyone by so much as an atom's weight. If there is good, the One will multiply it. From the One's presence will be bestowed an infinite reward.*

"This is the only part of the Claim to be recorded in the Candour."

Arian's lips brushed his shoulder, an unconscious caress. "I didn't know."

He turned to her, his silver eyes molten. "I didn't remember, until this moment. I thought it a call to righteous action."

"Isn't it?"

Daniyar addressed Alisher, the scribe.

"If I speak of this before you, you must give your word it will go no further."

Instead of a promise, Alisher flapped his hands at the Candour. "You carry a book upon your person, and such a book as this one—how?" His voice trembled with the words.

Wafa scowled at the scribe. "I told you. You speak to the Silver Mage. It's the book of the Silver Mage."

"Do you give your word?" Daniyar insisted.

Alisher's eyes widened at the question.

"Would you trust my word? Here in Black Aura, where no one trusts anything?"

Arian looked pained. "This was a holy city once."

Daniyar's answer was frank.

"A man's word is his bond. I judge men on little else."

The younger man's face flooded with painful color. He looked away from the brightness of the Silver Mage's eyes—seeing into him, seeing *him*.

"I won't betray your trust," he said at last. He bowed his head to Arian. "If I can serve the sahabiya in any way, you have only to ask."

Daniyar's eyes met Arian's.

The legend of Hira had passed beyond the Wall.

How secretive and powerful were the Council's machinations. And how well they served Arian's purposes now.

Daniyar read the verse aloud.

"The verse speaks of an infinite reward. We have the Verse of the Throne in our hands."

Alisher reeled away from the stand. He gaped at the parchment in Arian's hands, reading it for himself.

"The Verse of the Throne?"

Arian's response was gentle. "You are literate, then. 'Tis a rare thing to meet a scribe."

A grinding noise was heard from the base of the tower.

"They've brought a battering ram," the Silver Mage said. "Arian, listen to me. What else embodies an infinite reward?"

It took her a moment to understand.

"You think it means the Bloodprint," she breathed. "The Claim as an infinite reward."

A great reward, a mighty reward, a moment of spiritual reckoning. She was alive to the significance of the words—to the links in the chain that had led them to this place, so close to the Bloodprint, the end of all they sought.

Wafa cleared his throat. The Bloodprint mattered to him because it mattered to the Companions, otherwise it was nothing.

Sinnia was gone. He couldn't bear the thought that Arian would be wrenched from him, as well. He tugged at her arm.

"They're coming."

Daniyar canvassed the arches again.

"We were directed to this tower. The notations on the parchment appeared because we placed the parchment on this stand. Wherever we're meant to seek the Bloodprint, it's connected to this tower."

"What of the word written on the parchment? Hazarbaf? What does it mean?"

Alisher answered Arian.

"It's a style of ornamentation, the style used to embellish the exterior of the Minar. The word translates as 'a thousand interweavings.'"

Daniyar thought of the letters interwoven on the cover of the Candour.

"Look for another building in this style," he said. "A tower, a dwelling, anything. It will be simple, brick-colored. Discount anything that's still covered with faience. You and Alisher search. Wafa, stay with me."

A groan shuddered through the tower. Arian and the scribe ignored it, scanning the city, its buildings in sharp relief against the brilliance of the sun. If Arian had wondered why the Authoritan would choose this mud-brown city as his capital instead of the glory that was Marakand, the forty-foot escarpment was her answer.

Behind the escarpment, a bulwark enclosed the Authoritan himself, the Ark, his unbreachable fortress, its ramparts crowned by bloodied skulls, its gates strewn with mangled bones. A strong stench rose from the direction of the Ark, a construction of bulging towers and pulverized brick, mortared with blood and flesh.

Beyond it to the west, a forest of overgrown brambles choked off the thoroughfare between the Ark and the outer Wall. Alisher spotted it first. A modest square covered by trees, capped by a wickerwork dome. He pointed to it.

Heavy boots pounded on the stairs.

"They're inside," Daniyar said to Arian. "You'll go down first."

While they'd been searching the city, he'd knotted the sturdy length of rope from his pack through the base of the marble stand. He peered down at the courtyard.

"It's empty, go quickly. You first, then Alisher. I'll bring Wafa."

Arian gathered up the pack, slinging it over her shoulder. She tested the rope.

"It will hold." Daniyar raised her chin with his fingers and kissed her hard on the mouth. "I will hold it. Hurry."

The press of death was in the room. Arian felt it licking at her skin. Grabbing the rope, she swung herself from the window, rappelling down the side, dust rising where her boots skidded against the tower.

Then she was down with her sword in hand, waiting for Alisher. She looked around the courtyard for a means of blocking the half-hewn door. She found it in the heavy stones littering the courtyard. With Alisher's help, she piled the stones into place, waiting for Daniyar.

The sound of clanging steel echoed from the tower. Low grunts, a thud. And then boots tramping down the stairs. At the sound, Alisher flinched. Stricken, he turned to Arian.

"I cannot face this fate again. Forgive me, sahabiya, I must flee while I can."

"Alisher, I need your help!"

Men's voices sounded on the steps.

The rope went taut. As soon as she looked up, Alisher vanished. She braced herself against the door. Daniyar had Wafa in his arms, one arm fastened about the boy's neck. There was a cry as they were discovered. More men in the gallery, others on the stairs. A flash of crimson against brick. Arrows rained down the side of the tower. Arian sheltered against the door. An Ahdath grabbed hold of the rope from the top, his long sword in his hand.

"Bring the axe," he bellowed, beginning to saw.

Daniyar's body bounced against the tower, shielding Wafa from the force of the blow. The rope sagged. He bounced again, arrows flying through the courtyard. The man at the top slashed at the rope. Wafa reached over Daniyar's back, scooping up the last of the silver knives. Coiling his strength, he launched the knife at the soldier with the sword. It caught him in the neck. As the rope went slack, Daniyar and Wafa slammed into the tower again.

A soldier with an axe appeared at the top.

"Jump!" Arian cried.

Fifteen feet from the ground, they did.

An arrow winged through Arian's cloak, striking a circlet and falling away.

"Use it," Wafa said, motioning to his throat.

Arian grabbed his hand. "I can't. I'm sorry."

They fled across the courtyard, followed by the sound of boots kicking against the door, the barricade giving way.

"Where's the scribe?" Daniyar asked, pushing Wafa and Arian through the square.

Arian shook her head. "It was a question of survival for him."

"He would have been better off with us. This way."

They found a deserted alley off the square.

It looked like a blind but as they raced down the lane, they saw openings into smaller, darker warrens. They couldn't outrun the

Ahdath pursuit, so Arian drew them into the shelter of a dwelling. They crouched beneath the window.

Wafa motioned to his throat. "Will you use it?"

Arian squeezed his hand. "I'll try."

Ahdath moved past them and doubled back. They began a door-to-door search.

Daniyar shook his head. "There's no verse you can recite, when you cannot know the consequences."

She knew he was right. Perhaps he feared her power now, just as she distrusted the pleasure she had taken in the Ahdath's fear before driving them to their death. Somehow her actions had tainted the Claim. It was more comforting to believe this rather than the reverse.

That the Claim had tainted *her*.

She had to purify her intentions.

She was First Oralist of the Claim.

She and the Claim were inseparable.

She gave Daniyar an encouraging smile, taking a deep breath.

"It is the One who makes the night a garment for you and your sleep a rest."

The footsteps in the warren went silent. They heard a series of thuds outside their door.

Arian recited the verse again.

Daniyar risked a glance from the window.

One finger to his lips, he motioned the others from their hiding place. When they made their way to the alley, Ahdath were slumped all around them.

"Dead?" Wafa asked.

"Asleep," Arian said. She could see the rise and fall of the Ahdath's breastplates. And she thought of the men she had killed since breaching the Wall.

The power of the Claim was dormant. The harshness she had felt before had softened.

Had she imagined it?

No, she hadn't imagined the dead, the men in the Registan, the men at the Clay Minar, or Turan—lost to her forever.

As her grief rose up, a ruthlessness stirred within.

She felt the touch of darkness.

The Ahdath slept.

She hummed another verse.

"Let each new day be a resurrection."

They crossed the square, the tower silent. It pulsed with an indefinable energy.

Frightened, Wafa took Arian's hand. He placed his other hand in Daniyar's.

"Where now?" Daniyar asked her.

Arian considered her companions. They were battered, bloodied, and bruised. They had yet to take stock of their injuries. But there was no help for it.

"We must make for the bramble wood."

52

THE MAUSOLEUM WAS SMALL BENEATH A CENTRAL DOME. BRICK BEAD-
ing framed its doorways, a dogtooth pattern worked in the span-
drels above its porticos. It stood on a distended base, the columns
at its corners narrowing at the top, each topped by a small domed
finial. Beneath the cornice, rows of miniature arches formed a
four-sided arcade. A honeycomb weaving, imprinted with circles,
adorned the building's façade.

Hazarbaf.

Brick that breathed in a play of gossamer light.

There was a staleness in the air, a dim and watery quality to
the light that recoiled from the bramble wood. Despite the sun,
the day was cool.

Arian thought she understood the message on the parchment
now. Apart from the Clay Minar, the modestly scaled mausoleum
was the one building camouflaged with wickerwork.

The structure itself was a geometric miracle. Four-sided, four-
columned, with four arched doorways, an arcade of arches running along each side, forty in total. Under the architrave, a metal
grill served as a door, the grill conspicuous with six-point stars,
four across the top, ten down the side, forty in number.

4:40.

The mathematical quintessence of the crypt, the building a verse unto itself.

As they pulled the brambles away, Arian found what she had expected to see.

A keyhole was buried in the brick.

"This is the place," she said, taking the key they had found in the Sorrowsong from Daniyar.

The key fit the lock, the lajward finding the grooves in the brick. Tumblers fell, scraping the stone. The iron grill swung neither forward nor back. It slid into an insert in the wall.

A cool wind escaped from the chamber, freshening the deadness of the air.

Daniyar stepped in front of Arian, shielding her as they entered.

An ethereal light trickled through the arcade. It illuminated four men in the corners of the chamber. White-haired, white-skinned, their eyes without pigment, each man carried in his hand a white staff inscribed in the High Tongue. On one staff, a word was painted green. It entwined upon itself as an echo.

Submission or peace.

The word meant both.

Or at a more transcendent level, submission *as* peace.

The doctrine of the Bloodless, the silent men dressed in white robes, the apocryphal custodians of the Bloodprint.

In their midst was a tomb sheathed in white marble, the same marble as the stand in the Clay Minar, the Tower of the Claim. Small holes perforated the ends of the tomb, the holes crammed with pieces of parchment.

Arian offered the key to the man who carried the engraved staff.

"Peace be with you, Bloodless," she said. "I have come for the Bloodprint."

The four men took up stations around the tomb, barring further transgression.

The man with the engraved staff mimed a series of gestures. He pointed to himself and held up the stub of a finger. Then he opened his mouth to show her the ragged absence of a tongue. Wafa let out a scream. The Bloodless turned as one, their colorless eyes calm on the boy's face. He shrank from them, diving behind Daniyar.

"First Blood." Arian nodded, though whether it was a name or a title she couldn't tell. "Will you show me the Bloodprint?"

He held up his staff in answer.

Light glanced off the staff, setting its inscription aflame.

The writing danced on its surface, infinitely reflected, like ripples in a green mirror.

She heard Daniyar's swift intake of breath as he came to the same realization.

How cleverly the Bloodless had laid this trail. The clues to the location of the Bloodprint were reflections of each other. The tomb in Marakand, a mirror of the Dome above it. The Verse of the Throne, a perfect chiastic reflection of itself. The Clay Minar and this small mausoleum, mirrorworks of hazarbaf. The writing on the staff, etched in green.

Submission. Peace.

Mirrors of each other.

Submission to gain peace.

Peace to achieve submission.

The clues arranged with astonishing symmetry, astonishing eloquence.

As if they were meant to come here.

If she hadn't been twisted by the Claim in the Registan, or wrenched by its darkness in the courtyard, she would have doubted the simplicity of this moment.

Was this a thing foreordained?

Was this the pressure she felt inside her skull? And now, at her throat?

Daniyar whispered into her ear.

"Finish it," he said. "We've come this far."

And she saw in his face the same misgivings that had seized her thoughts.

Only the righteous could serve the good.

Was she still among the righteous?

Arian shook off her cloak. For a moment, there was silence in the tomb. No one moved. The air was still. Arian's circlets blazed in the light from the portal.

The Bloodless gaped at each other. A signal passed between them. It seemed to combine wonder and despair. The First Blood touched a hand to Arian's circlet.

Daniyar moved in front of her, gripping the other man's wrist. His eyes flashed silver in the gloom, his face hard with warning.

"Look. Don't touch."

The First Blood stepped back.

He studied the silver eyes, glanced at his companions. Another signal passed between them.

He pointed to Arian's tahweez, then to his lips.

She didn't understand.

Was this a rite of some kind? An exchange? Could she only win the Bloodprint if she was willing to relinquish her status as a Companion of Hira?

The First Blood touched his lips again.

"No!" Wafa cried. "Don't do it!"

Arian stared at the boy. He couldn't mean—did the First Blood expect her to maim herself, as he was maimed? Was she meant to cut out her tongue?

Was the Bloodprint so dangerous that those who sought to study it were silenced as a consequence?

Was this the price demanded for knowledge of the Claim?

She was an Oralist of the Claim, First Oralist of Hira. She couldn't possibly—she wouldn't—

"Daniyar," she said, her voice low. "The Bloodprint is won at a cost."

And she thought this was something the Black Khan must have known, something he had kept back by design. Perhaps it explained the disappearance of his spy.

She thought of Rukh's seductive voice, laced with its undertones of irony.

Had he sent her to pay the price instead?

Was this what the Bloodless meant by submission?

She wasn't given the chance to find out.

Daniyar touched his sword to the lips of the First Blood, his eyes black with anger.

"She's given too much already. The First Oralist owes you nothing else."

The Silver Mage was slow to anger, dispassionate in his judgments, unhurried in his undertakings—but now he'd witnessed enough.

"We are not thieves," he said with contempt. "Nor is the First Oralist a beggar. If you cannot recognize the Companion for who she is, you have failed as the Bloodprint's custodians. When will you ever meet her like?"

He took Arian by the arm, nodding at Wafa to retreat.

Arian's eyes flashed to his. She needed more time with the Bloodless. But Daniyar's expression persuaded her to follow.

When they were at the portal, they heard a new sound. The Bloodless were striking their staffs against the tomb. Daniyar turned.

A faint tide of pink stained the First Blood's face. He lowered his gaze. Humbly, he pointed to Arian's tahweez, then to his lips again.

He couldn't speak. And he didn't move to touch her.

Daniyar waited.

The First Blood gestured at the tahweez. He made a tracing movement with the stubs of his fingers. Then he opened his mouth.

Daniyar shook his head, impatient.

"They waste our time, time we do not have."

The First Blood's eyes burned into Arian's.

His lips mouthed a word.

Once, twice, three times, beseeching Arian to understand.

The pressure inside her skull blazed white-hot.

Could he have said—

Had he said—

"*Iqra?*"

She spoke the word aloud.

As soon as she said it, the tension inside her skull vanished.

Iqra bismi rabbi kalladhi khalaq.

"Read."

Read in the name of the One who created all there is in existence.

Arian felt her knees give way.

Daniyar caught her and held her fast.

This *was* a thing foreordained.

"What is it?" he asked her. "What does he want you to read?"

Arian pressed one of her circlets.

"The tahweez," she said. "They are the key to the tomb."

The First Blood nodded, something akin to relief on his face. He bowed at Arian this time, his fingers slipping on his staff.

Their eyes met and held.

First Oralist.

First Blood.

An unparalleled communication.

Arian recited the words engraved on the circlets, her voice pitched low and sweet.

The Claim split open inside her mind.

And in the mausoleum, a hollow sound rose within the tomb.

The Bloodless waited at the foot of the tomb.

A light came into the First Blood's eyes. He responded to Arian's words with a sigh, lowering his staff as if relinquishing a burden. He gestured at the tomb. He waved to her, sniffing at the air. Arian mimicked him. The air above the tomb was cool and odorless, signifying the absence of a crypt. But if this was the hiding place of the Bloodprint, the tomb was sealed, and she didn't see a way to open it.

"Help me," she said to the First Blood.

He waited without moving, his bleached eyes imploring her.

Again, she felt that stroke of warning.

The pressure inside her skull returned.

"Arian." Daniyar pointed to the holes that stippled the tomb. He extracted a scroll from one of the notches. "It's a prayer," he told her. He read several of the others. They were all the same. Prayers for deliverance from the Authoritan.

She sensed the First Blood was suddenly alert.

402

Prayer, she thought. *The green mirror. The clue within the clue.*

She withdrew the Verse of the Throne from Daniyar's pack. There was an empty notch at the head of the tomb. With careful precision, she rolled up the parchment and inserted it into the groove.

The Bloodless joined hands, interlocking the stumps of their fingers. The sight of their hands jolted Arian.

These men could recite the Bloodprint from memory; it was why the Authoritan had severed their tongues. He'd taken their fingers to thwart a secondary record, just as he'd burned the kaghez market, hanging scribes and calligraphers in the Registan.

He was an enemy of the Claim.

The Bloodless were his antagonists.

But still she was harrowed by forewarning.

She waited with Daniyar, not daring to breathe.

A second scroll whistled through a notch at the foot of the tomb.

The leader of the Bloodless nodded at her. She took the scroll in her hand. When she smoothed it out, she found a single word on the parchment, a word in the High Tongue, a word she'd long known:

Kalaam.

The word that meant *Word.*

The name of the Claim, one name among many.

Shaken, she stepped back. The parchment she had inserted at the head of the tomb sprang free. The tomb split open like the halves of the Bloodprint's stand. The sides grated against each other, opening into the air, then folded back like the walls of the puzzle box.

In the cool, dark chasm within, sunlight flickered on gold.

With a steady, gradual progression, a pedestal rose from the tomb.

A massive golden case glittered upon the pedestal, the emeralds on its surface agleam. Diamonds, rubies, and sapphires danced in an intricate pattern. The mortise lock on the side of the case was formed of a single large stone.

The emerald that shimmered like a mirror.

The Cast Iron.

The cover of the Bloodprint.

And within the encasement, the Bloodprint itself.

Without the Alamdar, without her fateful discovery of Firuzkoh, without Sinnia, without the disruption of the slave-chains— she would never have come to this moment: Wafa, the Sorrowsong, Larisa, *Turan*.

The black stone of grief shifted against her heart.

Daniyar held her close.

Arian blinked back tears. The pattern on the Cast Iron danced before her eyes.

Wafa clung to her waist, his blue eyes wide with amazement. The golden encasement was priceless, a treasure beyond reckoning.

And one that didn't matter in the least.

Arian moved her fingers over the pattern of flowers and leaves with agonizing care.

The Alamdar's secret now echoed in her mind.

The seventh diamond, the eighth ruby, the sixth sapphire.

Up, down, across, she pressed each one in turn.

Seven. Eight. Six.

The words inscribed on her circlets.

The opening words of the Claim.

She shifted the emerald stone, springing the latch that locked it. The stone slid upward and out, dividing the case at its seam.

Shivering profoundly, she opened the case.
The Bloodless sank to their knees as one.
Arian read the elegant script.
Seven. Eight. Six.
Tears formed in her eyes.
She pressed her lips to the bloodstained page.

53

"DO NOT CRY, MY LOVE."

Tears were in his eyes also.

More than a decade ago, Daniyar had stumbled upon a manuscript in Maze Aura. It had described the virtues of the Verse of the Throne. Without having seen the Verse, he'd drawn comfort from the proof of its existence, comfort he'd needed during the Talisman ascent.

And now he, the most unworthy of men, stood humbled—nay, *awestruck*—in the presence of the Bloodprint, this oldest known record of the Claim, its strong, square script blocked out on vellum in word after glorious, palpable word.

The Word.

With its words of equity, beauty.

Words that would return sanity to the Talisman, peace to all of Khorasan.

He kissed the bloodstained page. And now he held the hand of the woman who had risked her life for its purchase, urging her to gather herself, though he was far from doing the same.

"We must leave, Arian. The Ahdath will soon be upon us."

The trail of bodies they had left in their wake was the first indication of their presence. Word from Marakand, the second.

Their horses were tethered behind the mausoleum.

"My love, please."

"May the end be well," she murmured, smiling through her tears. To believe in a thing was not the same as knowing it.

Rumors, promises, hints of legend.

Deception, betrayal, loss—suffering.

And now she felt strengthened, reclaimed, cleansed by her tears—pure in a way she hadn't believed possible.

The Bloodprint was real.

And the Bloodless had released it into her care.

She thought of the man whose life had been taken inside a place of worship, the man who'd assembled the verses of the Claim, the modest man murdered at prayer.

His blood had given the manuscript its name.

His reverence for the written word would make their deliverance possible.

I cannot express the debt that I owe you, most selfless servant of the One.

She closed the Cast Iron without locking it. It took Daniyar's strength to heave it from the tomb.

The Bloodless watched without protest.

"It would be as well to leave the case behind. We have no need of it. Nor will it travel lightly," she said.

The First Blood discouraged her by placing his hands upon the binding. Daniyar nodded his agreement. It was a burden, but one that would keep the Bloodprint safe and dry. There was rope left in his pack. He would strap the case to his back. When he tired under its heft, it could be transferred to Wafa's horse.

Arian thanked the Bloodless. They had guided her to this moment.

The moment of revelation.

She pressed a hand to her tahweez.

"I swear to preserve it as you have done. If ever you should seek it again, you will find it safe at the Citadel." Somehow it wasn't enough. She nodded at Daniyar. "We pledge to you as First Oralist of Hira and Silver Mage of Candour that we shall never use it amiss."

A fleeting look passed through the First Blood's eyes—was she wrong to read it as despair? Did it pain him to relinquish his charge?

Or did he somehow sense she'd been damaged by the Claim?

She couldn't know.

She bid him farewell, disturbed by his silence.

She'd wanted his blessing, one guardian to another.

But the Bloodless had seemed only to pity her.

"Find the horses, Wafa."

But Wafa could not obey.

Because the Ahdath were waiting on the other side of the gate.

In moments they had seized the Bloodprint, bound and gagged the three of them, and driven them on their horses through the orchard.

A man with a heavy red blemish on his face was in charge of the company of soldiers. He rode beside Arian, scanning the ramparts of the city as they rode, watchful for signs of rescue. His men addressed him as Captain Nevus.

They moved through the bramble wood, making quick work of the ground between the mausoleum and the escarpment. As they approached the Ark, a monstrous stench congested the air, accompanied by a gruesome shriek.

On either side of the gate, giant black cauldrons were stationed.

Oil bubbled in the cauldrons, thick plumes of smoke streaking the horizon.

The screams came from within.

"Who burns today?" one of the Ahdath asked.

"Avazov and Alimov, Basmachi commanders." The Ahdath captain met Arian's gaze, taking note of the horror in her face. "We boil the rebels alive," he explained.

As the gates to the formidable fortress spread wide, he added without emphasis, "Welcome to Black Aura, the capital of the Authoritan."

54

WAFA KNEW THAT MEN COULD BE CRUEL. HE KNEW WHAT IT WAS TO BE starved, cold, beaten, abused, to spend his life in suffering and want. And now he knew other things were possible. There were those who would shelter him, risking themselves to save him from pain. Feeding him, trusting him, choosing even to name him.

Sinnia had kept him close by her side. The Silver Mage had shielded his body from arrows, taking the brunt of their fall from the tower. And Captain Turan—one of *them*, one of the Talisman—freeing not himself from the gallows when given the chance, but rescuing Wafa at the cost of his own life.

The beating in the Blood Shed had been brutal.

And Wafa saw that death could come in many forms beyond the Wall, just as the Companion of Hira had warned him.

The lady Arian had been telling him the truth.

The Ark was a terrible place. He was choking on the smell of charred human flesh, his ears filled with screams so abominable they made him forget the Blood Shed. The screams were all he could think of; they made him acknowledge the Blood Shed as a mercy. He should have died there. But he no longer believed that suffering was a punishment he had earned, or that he was power-less against his fate.

If he was venturing into the Ark, he was doing so at Arian's side.

The courtyard of the Ark dwarfed the Registan in Mara-kand, bristling with battalions of soldiers. Battle-hardened, weary-eyed, they watched the prisoners proceed up the ramp to the Ark. Two watchtowers framed a portal, the parapet that linked them manned by a unit of hawk-eyed archers. Heads were impaled upon spikes that extended beyond the ramparts, blood leaking from the skulls.

Arian searched for Alisher's face among the dead.

The gate was lowered behind them.

They proceeded through the courtyard, past massive store-rooms where food stores were stacked and an armory so extensive it seemed measureless.

Arian's shoulders sagged at the sight.

The war would come to them soon, but they weren't given time to linger.

They were taken to a magnificent hall deep inside the interior of the Ark. Its painted ceiling was supported by columns topped with muqarnas. The color blue was everywhere. Dripping from the capitals, springing from the fountains, sprouting in bursts of tur-quoise. The hall was filled with low divans and banquettes, cush-ioned in a fanfare of blues—turquoise, azure, indigo. Crowded among the cushions, lingering under the arches, trailing their silken hands through the playful cascades of the fountains, were women trained at the Gold House.

Young, fresh-faced, well-fed, they were as lovely as those Arian had seen at the Tilla Kari. Some were playing stringed instruments or beating upon small drums. In one corner, a cluster of girls in peach and gold silks moved through the steps of a dance, their movements mimicking the rise and fall of the fountains. Elsewhere, there was singing and the flirtatious recitation of poetry. Senior commanders of the Ahdath lolled among the women. Junior ranks patrolled the perimeter with a strict attention to duty.

Everywhere Arian looked, there were women of stunning loveliness engaged at their ease with the Ahdath. She couldn't fathom the women as prisoners, their glances were much too artful. There was a deliberation about their movements that suggested a sphere of influence. She was reminded of Gul at that moment, and briefly wondered what had happened to the girl.

In the center of the hall, a mother-of-pearl sideboard held a vast array of delicacies. Beside it, the arms of a sculpted gold tree extended over the banquettes. Silver fruit descended from the branches. Four serpents were interwoven into the trunk of the gold tree, their raised heads branching away from the base. Drink poured from the serpents' mouths to be captured in three gold basins. The heady scent of wine mingled with honey and milk. Women scooped up the wine with golden cups and offered it to the Ahdath.

A fourth basin was filled with blood.

It was a scene of unparalleled luxury, more decadent for its contrast with the ruin beyond the gates.

Arian was not an ascetic, but she shuddered at the sight of it.

Nevus ignored her, directing his captives through the hall with purposeful strides. Silence fell in his wake, laughter stifled, instruments stilled. Some of the Ahdath commanders relinquished the arms of their companions to follow their small procession.

Nevus brought them to a halt before a dais carved from lapis lazuli, streaks of white in the blue stone shining in the light. A six-tailed whip was chained to the canopy that projected above the dais. On either side of the whip, the Authoritan's emblem was etched in stone. Below the whip, iron manacles were fastened to the wall.

Set a little apart from the dais was a solid stone plinth carved of lajward.

Two of the Ahdath placed the Bloodprint on the plinth.

"You found your prize, after all. How clever of you, Companion."

Her heart beating rapidly, Arian raised her head.

Dread was upon her. She had brought them to this—Wafa, Daniyar, herself. Perhaps Jaslyk was a mercy for Sinnia, as there could be no escape from the Ark. She felt despair sink into her stomach. How brief had been her taste of Daniyar's love.

A pair of thrones occupied the dais. One was golden, its arms and back embellished with gemstones, the Authoritan's motto picked out in rubies at its head.

Rasti, rusti.

Strength is justice.

And straight-backed on the throne was the man who had spoken, his voice thinly insinuative, odiously compelling—a voice that sounded inside her skull.

At her side, Wafa whimpered.

The Silver Mage held himself still, his thoughts self-contained, his bright eyes wary.

The Authoritan rose from his throne, a man as tall and well-built as Zerafshan, but without the Aybek's golden warmth.

He was dressed in white silk, a white cape streaming from his shoulders, his head crowned by white hair under a doppilar cap.

Arian choked behind her gag.

His pale skin ghostly, his eyes tinged red, the Authoritan was an albino.

A member of the Bloodless.

He nodded at Captain Nevus.

"Remove her gag. And that of the Silver Mage." He flicked a warning glance at Arian. "Should you attempt to use the Claim in my palace, I will sever the tongue of the Silver Mage." He nodded at the golden tree behind her. "You see my bloodbasin."

Arian closed her eyes in horror.

Nevus took hold of Daniyar by the jaw, his dagger at the ready. "You will look at me."

The Authoritan was using the Claim. She could feel it inside her mind, narrowing her veins, slowing her heartbeat—but how was he doing it?

Constrained, she opened her eyes.

Was it as with Ilea? Did he use the Claim in the same manner as the High Companion, as a form of compulsion?

There is no compulsion in the Claim.

She could feel herself fighting back, resisting. And shielding her resistance from the Authoritan's knowledge.

He was sneering at her openly, his eyes narrowed in cruel folds.

"Did you think you could take my treasure with so little effort, robbing my people of their birthright? Did you think I would permit the theft of the Khost-e-Imom?"

I burned its sanctuary, he seemed to be saying. *The Khost-e-Imom crumbled to dust.*

The words keened inside her skull, battering her secret resistance.

I wasn't seeking the Cast Iron. The Bloodprint is the treasure.

He was one of the Bloodless. Didn't he know the worth of the manuscript?

But Zerafshan had told her.

He sells the Verse of the Throne, a letter at a time.

How? The Bloodless had hidden the Verse in the tomb of the Gur-e-Amir.

And then she realized. As one of the Bloodless, the Authoritan would know the Verse by heart.

Just as he knew the safehold of the Bloodprint.

She glanced at Daniyar, whose face betrayed no sign of fear.

The Authoritan's voice lashed out against her skull.

"Do not look at him, look at me! Or I will kill him where he stands and drain his blood into the bloodbasin."

The memory of Turan's body, slashed at the throat and the ankles, flashed through Arian's mind, a coruscation of horror. She had no wish to learn the meaning behind the ritual.

With an effort, she kept her eyes from Daniyar.

She was alone here. And she could not make use of the Claim.

"That's better, Companion. You begin to acknowledge your reality. For this meeting was fated, as my Augur foretold." He motioned to his side, to a throne less grand and glittering than his own, bedecked with diamonds and pearls. With a sense of relief, Arian turned away from his eyes, to the woman enthroned at his side. The Authoritan's consort, the Khanum.

She hadn't known the Khanum was an Augur.

Upright and slender, the Augur was dressed in crimson, the color of the Ahdath, the color of the blood spilled at the Citadel's gates, the color of the damask woven in Marakand's fabled bazaars. She wore a crimson cape, embroidered in gold, a thin, white veil drawn over the lower half of her face. Her face was daubed with white lead to resemble a paper mask. Above the mask, her eyes glittered out at the assembly, missing nothing that passed between the women of the Gold House and the commanders of the Ahdath.

Her head was crowned with a helmet framed by loose-hanging silks. A white plume danced above the helmet. The helmet was set with turquoise cabochons, encircled by a gem-studded wreath. A triune of rubies blazed from the wreath, inscribed with a Khorasani script.

The Khanum gripped the Authoritan's scepter, a staff blotched with blood, the vow of the Bloodless offset in white.

Submission, not peace.

Another corruption of the Claim.

Do not sow corruption in the land.

The fleeting verse gave Arian comfort.

Do not sow corruption in the land, came the echo.

The Claim began to hum, the same verse that had filtered through her thoughts, powerful and dark, its meaning twisted.

It wasn't Arian who whispered it.

It was the Augur who snatched it from her thoughts.

The Authoritan was speaking, oblivious to the knowledge staggering through Arian.

"The Augur foretold you would come here, Companion. She led you to me. Whereas I might have killed you when you first transgressed the Wall, the Augur wished you brought here alive. She knew the Bloodprint would tempt you." He nodded at his consort. "Khanum. Have what you will of this creature."

The Augur gathered her robes in one hand. Her green eyes glistened above the veil.

Believe in that which is beyond the reach of human perception.

Words from the Bloodprint—words stained by virtuous blood.

They rose in Arian's mind without her calling them forth, the Augur once more speaking the words in the silence of Arian's mind.

She descended from the dais.

A flick of the Augur's hand subdued Daniyar's sudden surge toward her. The same hand loosened the veil from her helmet, dropping it to the floor.

Arian gasped.

"You've been a long time coming."

The face looking back at Arian was her own.

55

LANIA.

The same green eyes, the same chiseled face older by a decade, with fine cracks at the eyes and mouth of the mask, a weariness of loss shrouded by a shimmering seduction.

It could not be.

Lania was laboring in the cotton fields or had been sent to the Plague Lands to die or had been broken in Marakand long ago.

When Turan had died at the Blood Shed, Arian had told herself to accept Lania as lost.

How could Lania be here, the Authoritan's consort—the Khanum Illarion had warned her against?

Twice as dangerous as the Authoritan himself, the Ahdath captain had said.

She heard the echo of Turan's voice in her mind.

Your sister would have been a Companion of Hira, First Oralist before you. Perhaps not so gifted as you.

A linguist like herself, trained as an Oralist of the Claim.

Why did she serve the Authoritan? *How* did she serve the Authoritan?

He called her his Augur, a seer who prophesied the future.

A dark art denied to the people of the Claim.

But surely the man who murdered scribes and calligraphers, who presided over arcane blood rites—who'd crippled the guardians of the Bloodprint—was no longer one of the people of the Claim.

Augury would seem as nothing to him.

And with the powers of an Oralist at his side—

First Oralist. Perhaps not so gifted as you.

"Lania," she said.

Daniyar's head came up.

"Lania, *why?*"

Her sister's face was almost feline in its cruelty.

"You were not summoned here to question me, *sister.*" She hissed the last word at Arian.

Had she been summoned? Was the quest for the Bloodprint nothing more than a conspiracy, with the Black Khan and Ilea as participants in the deception?

The Claim surged forth in Arian's throat.

Believe in that which is beyond the reach of human perception.

The words of the Bloodprint found their way to her thoughts again, a private communication between Lania and herself. She didn't understand it.

If Lania was an Augur in the service of the Authoritan—

The Bloodless would have known.

Now she understood the First Blood's despair.

To have guarded the Bloodprint so well and be powerless—

They had known.

And hadn't been able to warn her.

Speak to me, sister.

Lania's voice spoke inside her head, distracting her from the Bloodless, from the Authoritan who had maimed them.

"I thought you dead or lost to the Plague Lands."

"And so you pursued your futile path, which seems to me a pity. There is much you could have achieved as an Augur of Black Aura. Much you could still achieve."

"*Lania.*" Arian's voice broke on her sister's name. "*I am an Oralist of the Claim.* I cannot act as an Augur."

"Then you're of no use at my court," said the Authoritan. "She is not what you promised me, Khanum. Return to my side at once."

The Authoritan's consort took up her throne on the dais.

"You venerate the written word, do you not, Companion?" he said. "You reek of its superiority." The Authoritan gestured at the Bloodprint. "A lesson then, in disobeying my wishes. Nevus."

The Ahdath captain moved swiftly. A soldier took hold of the Silver Mage, while Nevus sorted through Daniyar's pack. Item by item, he extracted its contents.

"As the one commands," he said.

"As the one commands," Lania murmured from the dais.

Arian recoiled in horror.

There is no one but the One.

She held the thought fast in her mind.

The puzzle box, the ewer, the key, each was dropped to the floor and smashed.

The Candour was next.

The Verse of the Throne thrummed through Arian's body. But with the knife at Daniyar's throat, she was powerless.

"Set it at my feet," the Authoritan commanded, his hair a glowing nimbus about his head.

"No!" Arian cried. "Please! *It is the Candour!*"

The letters on its cover gleamed silver in the light.

The Authoritan snaked out a hand toward it. A ripple of fear whispered through the gathering.

"Burn," he said.

The single word set the Candour aflame.

"No!" Daniyar shouted.

The Ahdath's knife grazed his cheek.

"Kill him so she can watch. Then kill the Oralist next."

Before the Ahdath could obey, another voice spoke.

"A moment, my friend."

The voice was smooth and darkly familiar. A voice that vanquished the hope in Arian's heart. It made her believe that everything she'd endured up to this moment—her family lost, the Talisman ascendant, a decade of fighting the slave-chains—all of it was for nothing.

The Ahdath made room for the speaker to approach.

"I cannot delay for these trifles. Matters in Ashfall require my attention."

The Black Khan.

Here in Black Aura Scaresafe.

At his ease before the Authoritan.

The Ahdath followed his progress up the hall, waiting to see what the Authoritan would do. The soldier with the knife to Daniyar's throat paused for confirmation.

A smile passed over the Authoritan's bloodless lips. He signaled a moment of respite, dipping his head at Rukh.

"Excellency," he said. "What would you have of me?"

The Claim trembled in Arian's throat. She needed something, anything.

You shall not know fear. Her eyes communicated with Daniyar. *Neither shall you grieve.*

But the words were not enough.

Events were moving out of time.

The Black Khan was here, in the Authoritan's stronghold. He stood between Arian and Daniyar, bowing before the dais.

"Khagan," he said. "Khanum."

"Rukh—"

The Black Khan's name was a plea on Arian's lips.

His answer was cold. "You will address me as Excellency or not at all."

She flinched from him.

How had he so utterly deceived her?

She tried to reason through it. In the chamber of the Council of Hira, he had taken the Sacred Cloak upon his shoulders, swearing to the truth of the Bloodprint. He'd promised his help, and in the labyrinth of Marakand, Larisa and Elena had made good that promise.

And then she remembered. Before he'd told her the Bloodprint belonged with her, he'd removed the Cloak from his shoulders.

Call me Rukh, he'd said. *Your presence would enhance my court.*

Even that had been a lie.

Now he spoke to the Authoritan, responding to his question.

"I would have what was agreed upon between us. I delivered the Companion in exchange for the Bloodprint. Give me the manuscript and I'll be on my way."

He didn't need to add that out of all the men gathered in the Ark, he would be the most dangerous to cross.

His betrayal of Arian was complete.

How foolish she had been, how blind.

She'd never had any hope of holding on to the Bloodprint, but *why?* Why had the Black Khan needed her, when he'd held the Bloodprint in his hands?

The Authoritan waved a hand at the plinth. His cruel eyes were vigilant.

His velvet cape swinging behind him, the Black Khan reached the plinth in three strides.

An icy smile on his lips, he mocked Arian. "You alone held the key, First Oralist. The Cast Iron was impregnable. I do not know how you solved its mystery, but the High Companion assured me that you would."

A yawning white chasm opened in Arian's mind. Canyons of snow. Fields of white cotton. An all-encompassing nothingness.

She had long suspected the Black Khan's motives. But she hadn't guessed him capable of *this* treachery.

He had used her.

With the Cast Iron in his hands, he'd never laid eyes on the Bloodprint. He'd needed her skill to unlock its secrets, each step leading to the next, each a trial of her worth and sincerity.

And like a fool, she had yielded to the enemy his prize.

The Claim was a roiling nightmare in her mind.

"The Cast Iron wasn't part of the bargain."

The Black Khan nodded. "I do not seek the Cast Iron, Khagan," he said. "It doesn't matter to the men who wage war upon my capital. The Bloodprint alone will hold them back."

Careful not to betray his feeling for the manuscript, he parted it from its binding. At a signal, two of his men came forward to secure the Bloodprint in folds of cloth before bearing it away. His gaze fell upon Wafa, bound and gagged by the Ahdath. "And if I might have the boy. My enemies despise his kind—he may prove to be useful."

His bow to the Authoritan was unhurried. He stroked the onyx rook at his collar.

"You may do as you please with your captives, of course." The Prince of West Khorasan shrugged. "But as I learned at Hira, the First Oralist is the most gifted of the Companions—I would not squander her gifts. As to the Silver Mage—" He shrugged again. "Were it my decision, I would make his execution a public display to my enemies. I believe you have a tower."

Lania lent support to the words.

"Kill him, bleed him, my love, I do not care." Her tone was cavalier but her eyes dwelt on Daniyar's face at length, a fact the Authoritan noted. "Just know my sister will be useful, should you grant me time to reclaim her." Lania's voice became sulky. Arian wondered if she alone sensed the undertone of the Claim. "You gave up the Bloodprint to lure her. The Black Khan should not gain the better part of the bargain."

The Authoritan reflected upon this.

"The Claim is powerful within her," he told his consort. "Perhaps her knowledge is greater than yours."

The Khanum raised a painted black eyebrow.

"She is foreordained to submit. For the sake of the Silver Mage, she will serve as a slave at your court." A thin smile settled on her lips. "And if not, you will find the blood of the Silver Mage potent."

Arian broke free of her captor. She spat at the Black Khan's feet.

"How unworthy you are of the Bloodprint."

His answer was cool, his dark eyes enigmatic.

"You mistake me, First Oralist. I am unworthy of anything less."

Then he was gone, taking Wafa with him, giving Arian no opportunity to touch the boy, to offer a word of comfort. But what comfort could she give him? Wafa might survive in Ashfall, whereas death awaited them all at the Ark. He had already cheated the blood rites once.

The guard reached for Arian again.

She feinted past his grip, pressing her lips to Daniyar's, her tears searing his skin.

"Forgive me, beloved. I should have let you take me to the Damson Vale. Instead I brought you to this."

Daniyar kissed her fiercely. There would be no other chance to tell her.

"You are everything, Arian. You have always been everything."

Lania's smile froze on her face as the Authoritan crushed her hand. He snapped his fingers at Nevus.

"You will have your wish, Khanum. Your sister will serve as an object at my court. And the Silver Mage will be taken to the tower."

Nevus proffered the six-tailed whip. The Authoritan stroked it with loving fingers. "But first a demonstration is required. Strength is justice. *Rasti, rusti.*"

Daniyar was stripped to the waist. Two guards chained him to the wall by the dais.

The Authoritan raised the whip.

The Claim fell silent in Arian's throat.

The Bloodprint had gone beyond the Wall.

But she had not gone with it.

HERE ENDS BOOK ONE OF THE KHORASAN ARCHIVES

Acknowledgments

How blessed and grateful I am to be able to tell a story like *The Bloodprint*, inspired by history and legends I was taught from earliest childhood. To my mother, with gratitude for the wonderful stories she told me, and my father, who never let an occasion pass without giving me a book. To my siblings with whom I have shared everything worth sharing: endless hours of *Star Trek*, hundreds of SFF novels, far too many conversations about which realities are possible and which are only imaginary, and umpteen trips to the comic books store, each for our own nefarious reasons.

To my friends and family who haven't seen me much in two years, but who still supply copious amounts of love and reassurance, my grateful love in return—especially to Hema (Bobo) Nagar for arguing your way through each successive draft. Thank you for believing so much in this book, and for being willing to read the roughest of rough drafts.

Thank you to Nader, as always, for listening to my doubts and soothing them away.

My deepest gratitude to David Pomerico and Natasha Bardon at Harper Voyager for your invaluable guidance in shaping this book into what it is and for seeing a place for its history and future. Thank you especially for raising the voices of women. And thank you to Priyanka Krishnan and everyone at Harper Voyager who works on my books.

And finally to Danielle Burby—I've loved discussing every aspect of this series with you. Thank you for everything you do for me, but especially for believing in my stories even more than I do. For answering every text, every email, every call, and every question. That's how we ended up here.

Cast of Characters

THE COUNCIL OF HIRA

Ilea: the High Companion
   Other titles: the Golden Mage, the Exalted, the Qari, Ilea the
   Friend, Ilea the Seal of the Companions
Arian: First Oralist, a Companion of Hira
Sinnia: a Companion from the lands of the Negus
Ash: the Jurist
Psalm: the General of the Citadel
Other Companions of Hira, the Affluent: Half-Seen, Mask,
   Moon, Rain, Saw, Ware, Zeb
The Citadel Guard: Captain Azmaray, others

CANDOUR

Daniyar: the Guardian of Candour
   Other titles: the Silver Mage, the Authenticate, the Keeper of the
   Candour
The Akhundzada: the Guardian of the Sacred Cloak
Wafa: a Hazara boy of Candour

THE TALISMAN

The One-Eyed Preacher
The Immolans
The Talisman Tribes: the Shin War, the Zai Guild
Commandhan Hask
Commandhan Sartor
Captain Turan

ASHFALL

The Black Khan: Rukhzad, Rukh
Other titles: Commander of the Faithful, Prince of West Khorasan, Khan of Khorasan, Sovereign of the House of Ashfall, the Black Rook, the Dark Mage

FIRUZKOH, THE TURQUOSE CITY

The Hazara
The Alamdar: Mir of the Hazara

THE WANDERING CLOUD DOOR

Tochtor: the Yeke Khatun
Other titles: Great Empress, Mother of the Aybek of the Cloud Door
Zerafshan: Aybek of the Wandering Cloud Door
Other titles: Lord of the Wandering Cloud Door, Lord of the Buzkashi, Aybek of the Army of the Left
The Buzkashi: Army of the Right, Army of the Left
The Mangudah: Buzkashi Death Squad
Zelgai: Aybek of the Army of the Right, andas (blood brother) to Zerafshan

Altan: Otchigen, Prince of the Hearth, brother to Zerafshan
Storay, Annar: sisters to Zerafshan, daughters of the Yeke Khatun

THE WALL

The Authoritan
  Other titles: Khagan, Khan of Khans
The Khanum
  Other titles: Consort of the Authoritan, the Augur
The Ahdath: Suicide Warriors, Guardians of the Wall
Araxcin: Commander of the Wall
Captain Illarion: second in command at the Wall
Semyon, Alik: soldiers at the Wall in Marakand
Captain Nevus: commander in Black Aura Scaresafe

THE USUL JADE

Salikh: founder of the Usul Jade
The Basmachi Resistance
Larisa Salikh: leader of the Basmachi Resistance
Elena Salikh/Anya: second in command
Ruslan: Basmachi captain

THE BLOODLESS

Guardians of the Bloodprint
First Blood

OTHER

Alisher: a poet of Black Aura Scaresafe

Glossary

ab-e-rawan. A type of silk known as running water.

Adhraa. The most highly venerated woman mentioned by name in the Claim.

Affluent. Those who are fluent in the Claim.

Ahdath. Suicide warriors who guard the Wall.

Akhundzada. A member of the family of the Ancient Dead, guardians of the Sacred Cloak.

alam. A flag.

All Ways. The fountains of the Citadel of Hira, imbued with special powers, and a foundation of the rites of the Council of Hira.

Amdar. A river of North Khorasan that flows on both sides of the Wall.

andas. Blood brother.

Ark. The stronghold of the Authoritan in Black Aura Scaresafe.

Aryaward. A territory of South Khorasan.

Ashfall. The capital of West Khorasan, seat of the Black Khan.

asmaan. Sky.

asmani. Sky-blue lapis lazuli.

Assimilate. The proclaimed law of the Talisman.

Audacy. A mission assigned to any of the Companions of Hira, a sacred trust.

Augur. One who foretells the future, a rank in the Authoritan's court.

Authenticate. A title given to one who can verify the truth. See also Silver Mage.

Authoritan. The ruler of North Khorasan, the land beyond the Wall.

Avalaunche. A Talisman warning horn used to defend the Sorrowsong.

Aybek. Commander of the Buzkashi, leader of the people of the Wandering Cloud Door.

aylaq. Summer camp of the Buzkashi.

Basmachi. A resistance force north of the Wall who follow the teachings of the Usul Jade.

Black Aura Scaresafe. The Authoritan's capital beyond the Wall.

Black Khan. The prince of West Khorasan, the Khan of Khorasan.

Bloodless. The guardians of the Bloodprint.

Bloodprint, The. The oldest known written compilation of the Claim.

Buzkashi. The name of the people of the Wandering Cloud Door.

buzkashi. A game of sport involving the carcass of a goat chased by horsemen.

Candour. A city in the south of Khorasan captured by the Talisman, home of the Silver Mage.

Candour, The. The book of the Silver Mage, instructing him in the history, traditions, and powers of the Claim, as well as his responsibilities as Silver Mage and Guardian of Candour.

chador. Shawl.

Citadel. The stronghold of the Council of Hira.

Citadel Guard. Warriors who guard the Citadel of Hira, assigned to the protection of the Companions.

Claim, The. The sacred scripture of Khorasan, also a powerful magic.

Clay Minar. A tower in the city of Black Aura Scaresafe.

Common Tongue. A language common to all parts of Khorasan and beyond.

Companions of Hira. Council of Hira, Oralists, the Affluent, sahabiya in the feminine singular, sahabah in the plural. A group of women charged with the guardianship of Khorasan and the sacred heritage of the Claim.

Council of Hira. See Companions of Hira.

dakhu. Bandit, disreputable person.

Death Run. A chain of mountains that forms one of the boundaries of the Wandering Cloud Door, east of the Valley of Five Lions.

East Wind. A people of a sister-scripture to the Claim. See also Esayin.

Empty Quarter. The lands of southwest Khorasan, destroyed by the wars of the Far Range.

Esayin. A people of a sister-scripture to the Claim. See also East Wind.

Everword. A people of a sister-scripture to the Claim.

Far Range. The uninhabitable country beyond Khorasan.

Fire Mirrors. A mountain chain that forms the northern boundary of the Wandering Cloud Door, just south of the Wall.

First Oralist. A rank of highest distinction among the Companions of Hira, reserved for the Companion with the greatest knowledge of and fluency in the Claim.

Firuzkoh. The Turquoise City, lost to time.

Five Lakes. A territory of Khorasan, north of Hazarajat.

ger. Home, tent, yurt.

geshlaq. Winter camp of the Buzkashi.

Gold House. A palace in the Registan where women are trained in the arts. See also Tilla Kari.

Golden Finger. A minaret at the meeting place of two rivers.

Gur-e-Amir. The Green Mirror. A tomb complex in Marakand.

Hallow. A hall in the valley of Firuzkoh.

haq. Truth, right, justice.

haramzadah. An epithet that means "bastard."

Hazara. A people of central and east Khorasan, persecuted by the Talisman.

Hazarajat. A territory of central and east Khorasan, home of the Hazara people.

Hazing. A district of Marakand that is home to the Basmachi resistance. See also Tomb of the Living King.

High Companion. Leader of the Council of Hira.

High Road. A river of central Khorasan, also called the Arius, the Tarius, the Horaya, and the Tejen.

High Tongue. The language of the Claim.

hijra. Migration.

Hira. The sanctuary of the Companions.

Ice Kill. A valley at the entrance to the Wandering Cloud Door, home to the Buzkashi.

Immolans. Deputies of the One-Eyed Preacher, tasked with book-burning.

Inklings. Scribes from the Lands of the Shin Jang.

iqra. Read.

Irb. The language spoken by the people of the Wandering Cloud Door.

Jahiliya. The Age of Ignorance.

jorgo. Fast mountain horses.

kaghez. Paper manufactured from mulberry trees.

Kalaam. Word, one of the names of the Claim.

Kamish. A type of calligraphy pen.

karakash. Black jade.

Khagan. Khan of Khans or King of Kings.

khamsa. One of five mythical mares.

khamsin. A desert wind.

Khanum. A consort of the Khan, the Authoritan's consort.

Khorasan. The lands of the people of the Claim, north, south, east, and west.

Khost-e-Imom. A protective cover or place for the Bloodprint.

khubi. Bounty, spoils of war.

khuriltai. Council.

kohl. Black eyeliner.

Kufa. A style of calligraphy taken from a city of the same name.

kuluk. Load-bearing horses with stamina.

lajward. Lapis lazuli.

likka. Raw silk fibers used in the practice of calligraphy.

Mangudah. A death squad of the

Buzkashi, a regiment of the Army of the One.

Marakand. A city of North Khorasan beyond the Wall.

Maze Aura. A city of central Khorasan.

Mir. Any leader of the Hazara people.

mllaya moya. My sweet, my love.

morin khuur. Horsehead fiddle.

neeli. Dark blue lapis lazuli.

Negus. Ruler of the lands south of the Empty Quarter, also the name given to these lands; the leader of Sinnia's people.

nurm. Soft.

One-Eyed Preacher. A tyrant from the Empty Quarter whose teachings have engulfed all of Khorasan.

Oralist. A Companion of Hira who recites the Claim.

Otchigen. The Prince of the Hearth, a title given to the youngest male member of the family of the Lord of the Buzkashi.

pagri. A thick wool cap worn by the Talisman.

Plague Lands. A northern territory of Khorasan destroyed by the wars of the Far Range.

Plaintive. A warning horn sounded by the Buzkashi.

qarajai. A dangerous form of the sport buzkashi.

Qari. One who recites the Claim.

qiyamah. Resurrection, rising.

rasti, rusti. Originally "safety is in right"; the Authoritan's motto, "Strength is justice."

Registan. A public square in the heart of the city of Marakand, literally translated as "sandy place."

Rising Nineteen. A cult that has come to power in the Empty Quarter.

Russe. A name given to the people of the Transcasp.

sabz. Green lapis lazuli.

Sacred Cloak. A holy relic worn by the messenger of the Claim.

Safanad. One of the five mares of the khamsa, Arian's horse.

Sahabah. A title given to the Companions of Hira in the plural; sahabiyah, feminine singular.

Sailing Pass. A mountain pass en route to the Sorrowsong Mountain.

Sar-e-Sang. Sorrowsong, the Blue Mountain. Location of the oldest continuously worked lapis lazuli mines in Khorasan.

Sea of Reeds. A sea that divides the Empty Quarter from the Lands of the Negus.

Sea of the Transcasp. A body of water that divides West Khorasan from the Transcasp.

Shadow Mausoleum. A crypt used for storing the bones of the Authoritan's enemies. See also Shir Dar.

shahadah. The bearing of witness.

shah-mat. Checkmate.

shahtaranj. A chess board.

Shin Jang. A northeastern territory of Khorasan.

Shin War. One of the tribes of Khorasan, allegiant to the Talisman.

Shir Dar. A former House of Wisdom in the Registan. See also Shadow Mausoleum.

Shrine of the Sacred Cloak. A holy shrine where the Cloak has been stored for centuries and guarded by the Ancient Dead.

shura. A council or consultation.

Silver Mage. The Guardian of Candour, Keeper of the Candour.

Sorrowsong. See Sar-e-Sang.

suhuf. A sheaf of paper.

Sulde. The spirit banner of the Buzkashi.

tahweez. A gold circlet or circlets, worn on the upper arms by the Companions of Hira, inscribed with the names of the One and the opening words of the Claim.

taihe. A princess of Shin Jang.

Talisman. Followers of the One-Eyed Preacher, militias that rule most of the tribes of Khorasan.

Task End. A city of North Khorasan beyond the Wall, the original home of the Bloodprint.

Tilla Kari. A former site of worship in the Registan. See also Gold House.

Tomb of the Living King. A lost tomb in a district of Marakand known as the Hazing.

Tradition. The accompanying rites and beliefs of the Claim.

Transcasp. The lands of northwest Khorasan.

Valley of Five Lions. A territory in central Khorasan, fought over by the Shin War and the Zai Guild.

Valley of the Awakened Prince. A territory in central Khorasan.

Wall. A fortification built by the ancestors of the Authoritan to ward off the plague, dividing North Khorasan from South.

Wandering Cloud Door. The lands of the Buzkashi in northeast Khorasan.

Yassa. The law of the people of the Wandering Cloud Door.

Yeke Khatun. Great Empress of the people of the Wandering Cloud Door.

Yurungkash. White jade.

Zai Guild. One of the tribes of Khorasan, allegiant to the Talisman.

Zerafshan. A river of North Khorasan, beyond the Wall.

ziyara. A religious pilgrimage.

Zud. Animal famine.